The Eternal Footman

ALSO BY JAMES MORROW

Blameless in Abaddon

Towing Jehovah

Bible Stories for Adults

City of Truth

Only Begotten Daughter

This Is the Way the World Ends

The Continent of Lies

The Wine of Violence

The Eternal Footman

JAMES MORROW

HARCOURT BRACE & COMPANY

New York San Diego London

For my son, Christopher Morrow, who presides over the temple of decency

 The excerpts from *The Divine Comedy* in this novel represent the author's amalgamation and reworking of several translations, including those of Thomas Bergin, H. R. Huse, and Dorothy Sayers.

Library of Congress Cataloging-in-Publication Data
Morrow, James, 1947–
The eternal footman/James Morrow.
p. cm.
ISBN 0-15-129325-2
I. Title.
PS3563.0876E87 1999
813'.54—dc21 99-25684

Designed by Ivan Holmes
Text set in Electra
Printed in the United States of America
First edition
C E F D B

ACKNOWLEDGMENTS

ALTHOUGH I CONCEIVED *The Eternal Footman* as a self-contained story, its heritage stretches back through my two previous novels about the Corpus Dei. *Towing Jehovah* concerns an attempt to dispose of this scandalous artifact, whereas *Blameless in Abaddon* recounts an effort to put the Corpus Dei on trial for crimes against humanity. While these three books can be negotiated in any order, some readers may prefer to experience it as an epic, sequentially.

I want to acknowledge the particular editorial debt I owe to Michael Kandel. The manuscript also benefited from intense readings by my beloved wife, Kathryn Morrow; my bodhisattva cousin Glenn Morrow; and my talented colleague Elisabeth Rose. Several other dear friends invested time and energy in marking up the early drafts: Joe Adamson, Shira Daemon, David Edwards, Daniel Dubner, Margaret Duda, James Stevens-Arce. Thank you, my critics. I shall never impose God on you in quite this fashion again.

Finally, I must express my gratitude to Merrilee Heifetz for encouragement above and beyond the call of agenthood, to Alessandra Paloschi for the Italian translations, and to Fiona Kelleghan for the death jokes.

CONTENTS

I have seen the moment of my greatness flicker,
And I have seen the eternal Footman hold my coat,
and snicker,
And in short, I was afraid.

—T. S. ELIOT, "The Love Song of J. Alfred Prufrock"

PART ONE

Kevin's Fetch

The Flower Woman

WHEN GOD'S SKULL WENT INTO geosynchronous orbit above the Western hemisphere, reflecting the sun by day and rivaling the moon each night, Nora Burkhart tried not to take it personally. But in recent years she'd known so much bereavement—a father lost to throat cancer, a mother to Alzheimer's, a husband to coronary thrombosis—that the omnipresent death's-head seemed to be monitoring her life alone, beaming down a grin of dark mockery and sadistic glee.

Nora Shafron and Eric Burkhart had fallen in love under conditions simultaneously public and private. The event occurred before six hundred pairs of eyes, but only Nora and Eric knew what was happening. He'd brought his magic act to Cary Hall in Lexington (a low point in his career) and needed a volunteer from the audience. Nora raised her hand. She thought him Byronic. Seconds later she ran onto the stage, and by the time she'd plucked the outsized Jack of Spades from the pack, displaying it for everyone except Eric to see, the two of them had achieved mutual infatuation: so said their incandescent stares. When Nora knocked on his dressing-room door that night, Eric the Uncanny was already pouring the champagne.

Even by the standards of newlyweds, Nora and Eric were an unusually self-absorbed and hermetic couple. On their best days they functioned as each other's closest friend, cleverest therapist, wisest mentor, and wildest obsession. On their worst days they argued bitterly, words coated with gall and saliva, but even these distressing exchanges boasted an energy that made Nora and Eric loath to waste their uncommitted hours on gossiping with neighbors or prattling at dinner parties. Better the ordeal of honesty, they felt, than the narcotic of chitchat.

Eric died on the job, two weeks after his thirty-eighth birthday and seven days before their fourth anniversary. Having just imprisoned his marginally clothed female assistant in a plywood sarcophagus, he was merrily skewering it with a scimitar when his heart suddenly ceased to function. With a guttural groan he clutched his chest, stumbled forward ten paces, and, as the audience's murmurs filled the Cabot Theater in downtown Boston, fell into the orchestra pit. He was a corpse before he hit the floor, bequeathing to Nora but three sustaining circumstances: a $75-a-month pension from the North American Conjurers' Guild, a steamer trunk full of magic props, and a male embryo developing in her womb.

Eric's mother rose to the occasion, changing half of the first two hundred diapers and feeding the baby from bottles of expressed milk, but it was little Kevin himself who really rescued Nora, soothing her grief with his chirpy laugh and talent for buffoonery. Although her child could not claim Eric's comeliness (he looked, in a word, goofy), he had clearly inherited his father's theatricality. One hot August afternoon in 1998, when Kevin was nine, he rounded up the neighborhood kids and made them watch a vaudeville show featuring Kevin the Incredible telling jokes, juggling tennis balls, and performing magic tricks. He charged each child twenty-five cents; the take, $3.75, went into the family till. As an eleven-year-old Webelos Scout, Kevin routinely enthralled his peers around the campfire by spinning out versions of Edgar Allan Poe stories more lurid than the originals. For "The Pit and the Pendulum," he astutely increased the number of tortures from two to five. For "The Tell-Tale Heart," he exploited the possibilities in other organs, adding a tell-tale sneezing nose and a tell-tale farting colon.

With an amalgam of pride and wistfulness, acceptance and melancholy, Nora watched her son grow older, turn inward, move beyond her. Santa Claus had long since vacated Kevin's pantheon. The boy hadn't gone trick-or-treating since 2001. He still did magic, but his act had recently grown morbid, the standard disappearing goldfish and transmigrating rabbits supplanted by routines such as "The Gourmet Ghoul," "The Giggling Mortician," and "The Brainless Brain Surgeon"—not to mention "The Roman Oracle," in which Kevin, posing as a soothsayer, would seemingly sacrifice a live cat on stage, open its abdomen, and pull from its innards a dozen plastic Easter eggs filled with predictions about upcoming Red Sox games and presidential elections.

What endured was his generosity. Some months he donated as much as twenty dollars to their communal cause, though usually more like ten. They needed it. On Kevin's sixth birthday, the Lexington School Committee had informed Nora that her English-teaching position at Paul Revere Junior High School no longer existed—dwindling enrollments, atrophied ideals—and after that the only job she could get was clerking and driving for Ray Feldstein's Tower of Flowers in Copley Square, her salary barely sufficient to buy the groceries, pay the phone bill, and appease the landlord of their East Cambridge apartment. Thanks to Kevin's magic act, their life together included many small amenities, from pet turtles to cable television, compact discs to take-out pizza.

Working for Ray Feldstein had its perks—pleasant scents suffused Nora's day, stray cuttings beautified her kitchen, and Ray let her use the delivery truck after hours—but she yearned to get back in the classroom. An English teacher was a person. An English teacher possessed a name. In the mouths of admiring ninth graders, "Mrs. Burkhart" had sounded almost like a military rank or a hereditary title: Mrs. Burkhart, English teacher, captivating Lexington's adolescents with Greek myths and Norse legends. But now she was just the chick at the cash register, the lady behind the steering wheel, the girl with the gladiolas.

She resolved to make the best of it. The Tower of Flowers appealed to Nora's philosophical side. A human life was measured out in bouquets, was it not? New mothers received them. So did graduating seniors, young lovers, blushing brides, and the dead. A flower woman was time's avatar, colorizing the hours, perfuming fleeting instants. Aided by the shop's battered copy of *The Language of Flowers,* Nora took satisfaction in pointing customers toward blossoms to which tradition had attached particular sentiments. Chinese chrysanthemums meant "cheerfulness under adversity." Jonquils said, "I desire a return of affection." Red carnations cried, "Alas for my poor heart." Yellow tulips stood for coquetry, geraniums for anxiety, ferns for sincerity, dame violets for watchfulness.

Flowers, Nora noticed, were rarely given lightly, and never received so. The beneficiaries reacted with gratitude, amusement, happy surprise, a sentimental tear, a gasp of ecstasy—though sometimes the gift caused pain. In such cases the recipient often sought Nora's advice, knowing intuitively that a sympathetic and intelligent listener stood on the doorstep.

"He loves me," averred Wendy the Somerville waitress—purple eye, puffy lip, bruised brow—as she carried the dozen fresh-cut roses into her kitchen and hunted around for a vase.

"You think?" said Nora, following.

"He sent me these flowers," Wendy argued.

"They aren't about you. They're about him."

"You don't understand. Mickey *hates* what he did."

"And if you go gushing over these roses, he won't hesitate to do it again."

"We have a complicated relationship," said Wendy.

"Tell me about it," said Nora.

"*Everything's* about him."

"Exactly."

For the next twenty minutes the waitress recited the assorted indignities, psychological and physical, to which Mickey Morgan had subjected her. Whatever decadent echelon the orbiting skull occupied, Mickey's moral plane was evidently even lower. As Nora set off for home, she was gratified to see Wendy start the therapeutic process of ripping the petals off every last rose.

Nora's metaphysical difficulties began on the first Friday in September. Kevin had just started seventh grade, an event that by all appearances had further strengthened his resolve to put childhood behind him. That particular morning, however, he forsook sophistication and smiled joyfully when he saw an unopened package of breakfast cereal on the kitchen table. A magic trick lay concealed in every box of Wizard of Oats. Collect all six, kids. To Nora's delight, Kevin suggested that they upend the box then and there, dumping out the cereal until the treasure showed itself. His enthusiasm did not surprise her. The universe of illusion was so important to Kevin that even its most degraded emanations thrilled him.

As Nora pulled a stainless-steel mixing bowl off the shelf, her son scanned the back of the cereal box. "I hope I get the Chinese rings," he said. "The rubber thumb would be good too."

She set the mixing bowl on the table, reading the box over his shoulder. "I like the Indian rope trick."

Kevin inverted the box. The auburn nuggets tumbled over each other as they avalanched into the bowl. Myths were embedded everywhere, Nora thought, even in the hyperindustrialized West. Cereal, from Ceres, Roman goddess of grain.

He said, "Maybe it'll be the vanishing coin."

Excavating cereal boxes had been for Kevin a singularly pleasurable activity ever since, six months earlier, he'd hit the jackpot. Attack Force Flakes was among the many products spun off from a popular TV cartoon series about a United Nations commando unit battling its way across the oil fields of an unnamed Middle Eastern country. Nora hated the cereal's politics, but Kevin loved its taste. Each box came with a trading card portraying either an Attack Force hero or a member of the fanatical opposition, but every ten-thousandth box also concealed a coupon good for one Swiss Army knife. Despite the odds, Nora's third purchase of Attack Force Flakes yielded this very bonanza, the precious paper fluttering out of the box like an origami bird and landing on the kitchen floor.

Within a month the amazing Swiss Army knife arrived. Nora and Kevin marveled at its versatility, prying up each tool and testing it (scissors, bottle opener, corkscrew, magnifier, insulation stripper, wood saw), and soon afterward they began mythologizing the great knife's prowess. If they got a flat tire, Kevin would say, "We'll have to use the lug wrench on my Swiss Army knife." If he seemed to be running a fever, she would say, "Time to use the digital thermometer on your Swiss Army knife." And so it went: time to use the snow shovel on the Swiss Army knife, the hedge clippers, the welding torch, the posthole digger, the chain saw, the jack hammer—a running gag that never ran out.

The Wizard of Oats box was nearly empty before something other than a nugget appeared atop the mound. Curiously, it wasn't a magic trick but a simple magnifying glass, no larger than the lid of an olive jar, distinguished only by an odd inscription on the plastic handle:

LENS * LOBO * LIGHT OF GOD

"They made a mistake," said Kevin, twisting the handle of the magnifying glass, hoping to unscrew it. The prize remained intact. "Lens, lobo, light of God . . . what does *that* mean?"

With a measuring cup Nora transferred some oats into his cereal bowl. "Beats me. *Lobo* is Spanish for 'wolf.'"

Kevin slapped the magnifying glass onto the table. "I was hoping for the Chinese rings."

"I'm sorry, honey." Surreptitiously she surveyed his face: his ill-proportioned features had lately acquired a certain offbeat charm—stark china-blue eyes, thin mischievous lips, large upturned nose, sandy hair that curled every which way like wheat in a storm. "Maybe if I mail it to the company, they'll send us a real trick."

"You think so?"

"Not really, no." She glanced at the clock. The school bus would be at the corner in nine minutes. "Shit, we're running late."

"Can we get another box next week?"

"Sure. Better eat."

Her gaze drifted toward the kitchen window. Jehovah's gigantic headbone—the Cranium Dei, as the classically inclined called it—flashed her a smile. What a strange and frightening phenomenon was upon them. God dead, His corpse decayed, His skull in orbit. Nobody in the present age, no theologian, philosopher, psychologist, poet, or English teacher, could discuss it coherently.

She closed her eyes and said, "Come on, Kevin. Eat."

"Do you think it was meant just for us?" He stared through the magnifying glass while simultaneously inundating his Wizard of Oats with milk.

"No, I don't. Eat, darling. Have you got your key? Is your homework in your backpack?"

"I think it was meant just for us." He put a spoonful of cereal in his mouth and chewed. "Somebody's trying to get our attention."

"Could be."

"He sure got mine."

"Good. Eat."

The enigmatic magnifying glass not only seized Kevin's attention, it ultimately claimed Nora's consciousness as well. Instead of sending the prize to General Mills and demanding a magic trick in its place, she kept it near her at all times, removing it from her handbag during free moments—coffee breaks, lunch hours, railroad crossings—and running a finger along the etched handle. *Lens, lobo, light of God.* The words sounded oracular, incantatory, like Dante's forbidding "All hope abandon, ye who enter here," or the prophet asking Ishmael and Queequeg, "Shipmates, have ye shipped in that ship?"

Nine weeks after the magnifying glass arrived, Nora was assigned to deliver a thousand orchids to Brookline's Arborway Cemetery in advance of a 4:00 P.M. interment—her last stop of the day. Striding toward lot 49A, she watched as three grimy workers used cranes and winches to lower an intact 1999 Cadillac Catera into the hole. A battered backhoe rose from a nearby knoll like a mutant steam shovel. Having just scooped out the oversized grave, the backhoe operator, a rangy man with a gold tooth and a bad shave, was enjoying a cigarette.

She approached the Catera and looked through the windshield. Behind the wheel sat the embalmed remains of an elderly gentleman dressed in Bermuda shorts and a splashy Hawaiian shirt. His teeth were bared in a grin of astonished joy, as if he'd just won the car in a raffle. Nora wasn't surprised. She'd expected some such burial since noticing that the crib sheet specified a scion of the fabulously wealthy and extravagantly nutty Gansevoort family. In April of 1993, Estella Gansevoort had roared into Heaven astride her beloved Harley Davidson. Two years later, Horace Gansevoort had gone to glory in his speedboat. The previous summer, Roger Gansevoort had piloted a Cessna through the Pearly Gates.

Climbing out of the backhoe cab, the operator volunteered to help Nora unload the panel truck. He looked her in the eye, flirtatiously. What her face had going for it, she felt, was not beauty but rather a certain drama: black irises, full lips, ambitious cheekbones—features that had proved particularly useful in staring down unruly students.

"Offer accepted," she said. There were times, such as today, when she missed sex so much that doing it with a semiskilled laborer in the cab of a backhoe would seem, on balance, more earthy than degrading.

"First time I heard about these wackos and their crazy coffins, I thought it was pretty funny," said the operator, wrapping his long arms around a cluster of orchids. "Now I think, what a waste."

"It's always a thin line between panache and decadence," said Nora, wondering whether the man knew how blatantly he was staring at her breasts.

"Whatever. Personally, I don't get why people bother with funerals anymore." Approaching the hole, he set down the flowers and nodded toward the celestial skull. God shone brightly in the clear autumn sky. "If you want my opinion, Heaven's been locked up tight for a long time now. These days, even a billionaire can't get in."

Later, leaving the scene of the impending funeral, Nora steered the panel truck along the labyrinthine roads of Arborway Cemetery. A colossal granite vault loomed before her, more lavish than any residence she was likely to occupy in either life or death. Whoever these aristocrats might be, their mausoleum could easily accommodate a dozen generations.

The Cranium Dei's rays poured down, streaming through a stand of poplar trees and throwing patches of divine light on the tomb portal. Above the greenish black steel door, chiseled deep into the lintel, the name LOBO glinted amid the shifting shadows.

Pulse pounding, Nora pulled over. She grabbed her handbag, quit the truck, and rushed toward the mausoleum. Framed by leaf shadows, a brilliant spot of skullshine danced atop the first O in LOBO. Tiny printing, inaccessible to the unaided eye, filled the oval like an engraved motto on a gold watch.

She took out the magnifying glass and positioned it over the minuscule words, easing them into focus. Three distinct inscriptions hovered before her gaze. She blinked. The top quotation, deadly serious, was the most commendable sentiment she'd ever seen attributed to the central figure of the English Civil War.

> I BESEECH YOU, IN THE BOWELS OF CHRIST,
> THINK IT POSSIBLE YOU MAY BE MISTAKEN.
> —OLIVER CROMWELL

The bottom quotation, more playful than its counterpart, was ascribed to a Manhattan sculptor whose work Nora had grown to admire over the years.

> THE ABSENCE OF GOD IS GOD ENOUGH.
> —SAINT CLAIR CEMIN

The central quotation seemed to Nora little more than a joke.

> I AM INDEED IMPRISONED IN A CHINESE FORTUNE-COOKIE FACTORY, BUT HAVE YOU PONDERED THE SUBTLE COGNITIVE SNARES IN WHICH YOU YOURSELF MAY BE TRAPPED?
>
> —LING PO FAT

Driving home that evening, palms locked tightly around the steering wheel, Nora experienced a profound and relentless unease. Whatever fulfillment she'd felt in solving the magnifying-glass mystery, it was evaporating before her fear that she'd been appointed a kind of messenger. In the days ahead, she sensed, the Cranium Dei would be expecting her to function as a postmillennial Moses, revealing to the world the arcane connections among Cromwell's skepticism, God's absence, and the fate of Ling Po Fat.

She intended to turn the job down. The universe had kicked her around enough of late. She'd assumed her fair share of obligations. Having endured the death of a husband, the loss of a career, the ordeal of single motherhood, and the banalities of driving a delivery truck, Nora Burkhart was not about to become, under any circumstances, God's little errand girl.

On Saturday afternoon she returned to Arborway Cemetery and, magnifying glass in hand, approached the Lobo mausoleum. Much to her relief, the three inscriptions still lay etched inside the first O. She hadn't imagined them. She wasn't losing her mind.

For half an hour she studied the arcane graffiti, seeking a common theme. According to her research, Oliver Cromwell had indeed once made a plea on behalf of self-doubt, Saint Clair Cemin's remark was recorded accurately, and Ling Po Fat was probably fictitious. But what, exactly, were these specific quotations doing on this particular tomb? Did they tell a kind of story? A man named Ling Po Fat finds himself trapped in a fortune-cookie factory, but then he considers, in Christ's bowels, the possibility that he isn't, after which he decides that those bowels, though absent, might help him learn the truth of his situation?

Not likely.

She abandoned the tomb and drove across the cemetery.

Blanketed with orchids, Dexter Gansevoort's mound disclosed no hint that an entire luxury sedan lay only ten feet down. The monument was surprisingly tasteful, an exquisite Pietà featuring a frail Jesus and a Korty Madonna. Nora had always liked Korty Madonnas. Here was an intercessor you could respect, as far from the insipid Blessed Virgins who graced working-class Catholic lawns as Malcolm X was from Uncle Remus. The Korty Madonna was at once loving and wise, sensual and virtuous: Jesus' mentor, not his incubator.

With God dead, of course, both Christ and his mother had suffered severe blows to their prestige. Still, it was bracing to imagine that, somewhere beyond the damaged and skullridden planet called Earth, a better world obtained, a place where cereal boxes always delivered the right prizes, teachers got to keep their jobs, and every decent husband lived to see grandchildren.

As rain spattered out of the grimacing sky, supplementing the Korty Madonna's tears, the flower woman climbed back into her truck, started the engine, and headed homeward.

A Crisis in the West

On nights like this, when gin and self-pity coursed through his veins in equal measure, Gerard Korty would walk out of the jungle and, crossing the beach, stagger barefoot along the foamy shore as he lifted his eyes toward the star-flecked Indonesian sky.

A full moon was the only incitement he required. Dropping to his knees, he would feverishly mold the moist silver sand, never knowing for sure what image might emerge. Sometimes a Gospel event took shape: Lazarus's rude awakening, Judas's fatal kiss. Often he would sculpt a scene from the Pentateuch: Noah supervising his lions, Moses wielding his laws. And occasionally, with a nod to his former benefactors in the Vatican, Gerard would fashion a nonbiblical moment: a martyr writhing in agony or a saint experiencing spasms of rapture.

He stood back to behold what he had wrought. A life-size, buxom woman, a kind of bas-relief centerfold. Eve herself, perhaps, poised for a postlapsarian debauch. A fine job, he decided as his eyes traced her gritty hips and grainy thighs. A triumph of his art, in fact, pornography fit for a chancel niche.

Eagerly he disrobed and embraced his creature, kneading her crumbling breasts as he pushed himself deeper and deeper into the mounded sand. She disintegrated beneath him. He continued his ancient dance, grinding her down, erasing all evidence of his sin, until at last he climaxed, consumingly, vigorously, as if he'd drilled through the island's bedrock to tap some subterranean fountain of youth.

Rising, he strode into the waves and massaged away the sand. His testicles sought the warmth of his groin. Bobbing gently, he cast his gaze across the Andaman Sea and fixed on the impenetrable horizon.

A vital world lay beyond the tiny, deserted, geographically insignificant mass known as Viatikara Island. Three hundred kilometers to the west, Great Nicobar pointed toward the Bay of Bengal and the Indian subcontinent. One hundred kilometers to the southeast, the Strait of Malacca broke against the upper shores of Sumatra. But tonight, as on most nights, the isle on which Gerard Korty pursued his monkish existence seemed the loneliest place in the universe: a disowned planet, abandoned by its parent sun.

Technically, of course, Gerard was not a monk, for he and Fiona inhabited the same cottage and occasionally even the same bed. But in recent years his wife had gone native: beyond native, actually, straight to Viatikara's wild core, turning herself into a kind of female John the Baptist, a connoisseur of salted ants and raw fish, someone who related only to Komodo dragons and God. The irony was not lost on Gerard. Fiona had joined him on the island under protest, and yet it was she who'd ultimately taken the place to heart, transforming her affection into an ever-expanding mass of autobiographical fiction about an art student who travels to Indonesia, befriends the local deities, and founds a new religion back home in Manhattan.

Gerard's spare and spartan life on Viatikara had in fact given him the inspiration he'd required. His retreat had roused his dormant muse. After ten excruciatingly unproductive years, he'd started working again, and even though the resulting sculptures—his epic *Paradiso* marbles—had failed to find buyers, he nevertheless ranked them among his greatest achievements. But now the siren call of civilization beckoned. Gerard craved indoor plumbing. The artist required air-conditioning and Pop Tarts.

For twenty soothing minutes he lay on his back, rode the waves, and listened to the sea soughing against the beach.

"Don't do it!" cried a familiar but wholly unexpected voice. "Don't! No! Don't!"

Gerard lifted his head and surveyed the gloomy beach.

"No!" screamed Victor Shamberg. "Don't! No!"

"Don't *what*?" called Gerard, crashing through the surf toward his apoplectic manager, his ambassador to reality.

"Don't!"

Gerard waded onto the shore. A slight man by any criterion, Victor Shamberg looked especially tenuous in the moonlight: a phantom agent, specializing in posthumous careers.

They clasped hands. "No surprise visits, Victor," said Gerard testily. "You're breaking the rules."

"So are you. 'Thou shalt not kill thyself.'"

"The jungle was hot, that's all—I needed to cool off."

"Jesus, Gerard, you *terrified* me."

As a man who styled himself a "practicing lapsed Catholic," a man who no longer believed in God yet remained in awe of Holy Mother Church, Gerard had never considered suicide a serious personal option. Indeed, when he got around to sculpting the *Inferno*, he hoped to render with particular passion the Christian self-slaughterers, whom Dante had envisioned as transmuted into trees and tormented by Harpies.

"What brings you to Asia?" asked Gerard. "Scouting for new clients? There's a spider monkey on Mount Camorta who does marvelous things with driftwood and bananas."

"I believe I've landed you a commission," said Victor.

"I won't sign for less than fifty thousand." Gerard climbed into his pants.

"You won't believe what I'm about to say, but I brought along plenty of evidence—newspapers, magazines, even a videotape, though Fiona says you don't have a VCR." Victor extracted a crisp white handkerchief from his windbreaker and mopped his sweaty brow. "There's a crisis in the West."

"The rise of soulless technocracy. Ask Fiona about it."

"No—something else, utterly dismaying."

"Nuclear war? Ecological collapse?"

"You can't imagine."

"Agents are supposed to bring *good* news."

"This *is* good news, after a fashion. Of all the world's artists, you topped the Vatican's list. Tullio Di Luca himself phoned me. 'We must have Gerard Korty,' he said. 'Only Korty can design the ultimate reliquary.'"

Indulging in an immodesty that embarrassed him only slightly, the sculptor thought: They made the right choice. He was Gerard Korty, after all, the man who'd given Christendom a wholly new image of the Blessed Virgin, a Korty Madonna admired by feminists, adored by priests, and celebrated by art critics. "Ultimate reliquary? I don't get it. What're they putting in there, the bones of God?"

"The bones of God."

"What?"

"God's bones."

"What?"

"He's dead."

"I know. Nietzsche told me."

"This isn't philosophy, Gerard. It's life. God died. Only the bones remain."

Gerard slid into his John Lennon T-shirt, the highlight of the most recent crate from Calcutta, then guided his agent across the beach and into the jungle beyond. "You flew halfway around the world to tell me a *joke*?"

"I'm not joking."

"To begin with, God isn't mortal."

"Mortality has become an ambiguous concept of late. Our deepest thinkers are stumped. I realize this all sounds crazy."

Ever alert for predators, Gerard stared at the moon-glazed path ahead. Tigers inhabited Viatikara—one tiger, at least, a solitary male who'd probably swum over from Great Nicobar in search of crippled macaques. Fiona sometimes spotted the animal during her daily ablutions in the Minangkabau Lagoon, prowling the shore, but it never took any interest in her.

"Oh, *now* I understand, early sixties death-of-God theology, of course," said Gerard. "I hardly imagined Holy Mother Church embracing it—but, hey, if she wants a reliquary, I'll give her one. You discussed a figure?"

"Two million dollars for a scale model plus supplementary watercolors."

Owing to either his imminent wealth or the gin residues in his brain, a profound well-being spread through Gerard. "Now tell me whose bones the cardinals are planning to entomb."

"God's."

"No, I mean *really*."

"Ten years ago, a gigantic, male, comatose form, two miles long and humanoid, appeared off the coast of Africa. The Vatican hired a supertanker to haul God's body north and preserve it in an iceberg. Six years went by, and then an earthquake knocked the body loose, and so the Pope was forced to go public, after which the American Baptist Confederation bought the Corpus Dei for eighty million dollars and made it the centerpiece of their Orlando theme park."

"So how have the Yankees been doing lately?"

"Once it became clear that God wasn't brain-dead, a Pennsylvania judge named Martin Candle convinced the World Court to impound the body and try it for crimes against humanity."

"I don't suppose you packed along any Hershey bars?"

"Candle lost his case, went berserk, and destroyed the body's life-support system. So now God was *completely* dead, but the Baptists wanted Him back anyway—He would probably still draw crowds—which meant another towing operation, west across the North Sea, through the English Channel, and over the Atlantic."

"Or maybe you brought some beer? The Calcutta packet won't be here for a week."

"The mission ended abruptly. No sooner had the flotilla passed through the Strait of Dover than something extraordinary occurred."

Gerard cocked an ear toward the rain forest. The regular nightly concerto had begun: screeching apes, squawking cockatoos, fiddling cicadas. "Something extraordinary? You mean, as opposed to God getting buried by a supertanker crew and murdered by a judge?"

"Define *extraordinary* any way you wish. Nothing like it has ever happened before."

Captain Anthony Van Horne took a hearty swallow of coffee, popped a constellation of migraine pills—two Zomigs, three Maxalts—and stepped onto the starboard bridge wing of the SS *Exxon Galveston*, flagship of the fleet charged with taking the Corpus Dei on its fifth and, God willing, final voyage. Straining under the weight of their cargo, the *Galveston*'s sister ships, the SS *Arco Fairbanks* and the SS *Chevron Valdez*, barely managed to maintain their positions along the Corpus Dei's flanks. If they continued this sluggish and disreputable performance, Anthony decided, he would have to radio the engine room and order Bateson to drop the *Galveston*'s speed two full knots.

To his left the entire population of Brighton, England (or so it seemed), thronged the docks, observing the aquatic procession with sad eyes and long faces. Many onlookers wept. Several dozen knelt in prayer. Through his binoculars Anthony saw two little girls, sisters probably, giggling in private delight, their merriment merely intensifying the poignancy of the moment. In a decade or so, their parents would tell them, "You were there when the Corpse of Corpses steamed past our town," but that would be a lie, for the girls occupied this occasion only in the literal, physical sense, just as God occupied it only in the literal, physical sense—or so Anthony hoped. Surely a dimension or two of his Creator had survived. The Pythagorean theorem, the Heisenberg relation, the Golden Rule—something.

Inhaling, he caught a nascent strangeness in the air. Expectancy hummed through his exhausted flesh. He raised the binoculars and pivoted aft, fixing on the towlines leading from the stern windlasses to the waterborne bier—an amazing construction, as ponderous and impressive as Noah's ark. Gulls circled above the Corpus Dei, periodically landing atop the glass coffin and pecking on its panes.

At first the rumblings were low and rhythmic, like the passage of some Brobdingnagian subway train. Soon they grew louder and more random, thunderclaps announcing an imminent storm, then louder still. Anthony's pulse quickened. His mouth grew dry. And then, in a single astounding instant, the coffin disintegrated, its steel girders toppling into the strait and sending up plumes of foam, its panes shattering like china plates encountering a psychotic ox.

Leland Appleblatt, Anthony's first mate, rushed out of the wheelhouse shouting, "What the hell was *that*?"

"Did we hit something?" yelled Cherry Baldwin, the radio officer, following right behind.

"No," Anthony replied evenly. "If I'm not mistaken, something hit our cargo."

"What?" said Cherry.

"A barge?" said Leland.

"Mortality," said Anthony.

Instinctively the captain focused the binoculars on God's bosom. A bloodless fissure opened, then another, then a third, until His torso came to resemble the fractured face of a salt flat. The crevassed chest began to move, and soon a full-blown fleshquake had seized the pectoral muscles. With a stupefying roar the tissues parted, exposing the bones below.

"Christ Almighty!" cried Leland, his habitual flippancy deserting him as—*crack, crack, crack*—the ribs detached themselves from His sternum. "He's coming apart!"

Never before, Anthony thought, had death throes been so violent or dramatic. God's last gasps were characteristically off the scales and beyond the charts.

First the sacred heart appeared, pulsing and booming as it rose from the cavity, its moist, gluey nakedness suggesting the birth of some raging mythological beast. Reaching an elevation of two hundred feet, the heart suddenly shot away, arcing across the frightened sky like a comet. Within seconds of attaining the stratosphere the organ exploded, releasing fifty million gallons. The air thickened with the iron odor of blood. A shiny crimson rain fell on the bewildered Brighton mourners, who, ever prepared for nasty weather, instinctively opened their umbrellas.

"What the Red Cross could've done with that stuff," moaned Leland.

Next the holy lungs emerged, flapping and fluttering as they climbed heavenward like a stupendous black butterfly. Anthony thought of his son's favorite Japanese sci-fi movie, *Mothra.* The lungs passed smoothly over Brighton, hauling their shadow behind them, and then they too exploded, scattering their cells up and down the beach.

"They're so dark," observed Cherry.

"Every once in a while," said Leland, "when nobody was looking, He would smoke a volcano."

Word of the bizarre phenomenon spread quickly throughout the ship. The afterdeck swarmed with food handlers, engine wipers, and able-bodied seamen gesticulating wildly as they described for one another the divine dissolution.

Next to exit was the bladder, manifesting itself like an immense plum pudding created to feed every actor who'd ever played Bob Cratchit in *A Christmas Carol.* As the huge balloon burst, the Brightonians again took refuge beneath their umbrellas.

And now came the intestines' moment of fame, all eleven and a half miles of them. Laden with blessed excrement, the vast and massive coils emerged from His broken abdomen, snaked across His legs, and slithered into the dark, oily waters of the Channel. Before sounding, the bowel beast swam for over a hundred meters toward the Isle of Wight, sinuating through the currents while gulls tore bits of tissue from its sides.

Thus it went, organ after organ, muscle upon muscle, sinew following sinew. Before vaporizing, the divine kidneys hovered briefly above the English coast, as tall and ominous as mushroom clouds. Prior to its deconstruction, the divine stomach darkened the morning sky like some preternatural dirigible. When the divine eyes finally surrendered to entropy, they were zooming toward London in an image suggesting two croquet balls launched by an elephantine Queen of Hearts.

For Anthony Van Horne, this lurid catastrophe was both depressing and gratifying. To all appearances the Supreme Being was truly dead this time—a sad situation, but never again would Anthony be assigned the enervating task of dragging His carcass across the sea. At last he could go home, kiss his wife, stroke his cat, and spend Saturday afternoons shooting hoops with his son.

"He blew up?" said Gerard, baffled by the fact that, while he did not believe his agent's tale, he did not completely disbelieve it either.

God had died. Died and come apart. Jesus Christ.

"After all His organs and muscles vanished," said Victor, nodding, "the remaining flesh disintegrated as well, and Van Horne's fleet ended up towing nothing but a load of bones."

"You're not making this up, are you?"

Victor stopped walking long enough to light a Galoise. "The next morning, the Baptists radioed Captain Van Horne that they'd arranged to sell God's remains, damaged goods, back to Rome. They feared the bones alone wouldn't lure many customers. Van Horne was to tow the bier through the Strait of Gibraltar and across the Mediterranean, then dock it at the mouth of the Tiber."

Gerard couldn't decide which event intrigued him more: his agent's news flash, or the catastrophe's failure to crush him. For the first time ever, he saw the loss of his faith as an asset, a protection against the desolation he might otherwise be feeling.

They continued through the jungle in silence, moving past velvet hibiscus and helical vines. A clearing appeared, the vast open-air studio where Gerard practiced his art. His magnum opus shone in the moonlight, Dante's *Paradiso*, each epiphany accorded its own fifteen-foot sculpture. Considered collectively, these mammoth pieces transformed Viatikara from a little chip of Indonesia into the Christian equivalent of Rapa Nui: Easter Island with its huge, droop-eared, vaguely comical heads carved from volcanic ash.

Gerard had never faulted his agent for the *Paradiso*'s unsaleability. Victor had questioned the project from the start. But Gerard was on fire in those days. Saleability be damned. For six whole years he'd inhabited Dante's rhapsodic vision of Heaven, translating epic poetry into carved marble. The College of Cardinals will love my *Paradiso*, he told himself each time he brought his hammer down, driving his chisel into the block. They'll hock the Vatican jewels to acquire these pieces.

The College of Cardinals had hated Gerard's *Paradiso*. Christendom's greatest poem, they asserted, must remain on the printed page. It was blasphemous to convert *The Divine Comedy* into graven images. And besides, in Canto XXVII Dante had Adam calling the medieval popes "rapacious wolves in shepherd's clothes" who'd turned their dominion into "a sewer of blood and filth," and wasn't that a bit much?

"I'm worried about Fiona," said Victor.

"So am I," said Gerard.

"I think she's losing her grip."

"That's one way to put it. Last month she discovered how in a past life Viatikara was her home—her *habitat*, actually, since she was a tigress then, so it's cosmically correct we ended up here. I need this job, Victor. I want Fiona and me back in America before we go insane."

Four statues dominated the atelier, each representing a hundred days of toil. As with all his sculptural endeavors since the move to Viatikara, the raw stone had come from the quarries at Makrana in Rajputana—source, it was said, of the very marble that constituted the Taj Mahal. Straight ahead lay *The Cross of Mars*, complete with a dozen crusaders kneeling at Christ's bleeding feet. Behind it towered *Jacob's Ladder*, its twenty tiers swarming with the luminous elect. To

Gerard's left, *The Eagle of Jupiter,* his feathers formed of interwoven souls. To his right, *The Mystic Rose,* a maelstrom of the blessed dead.

Victor took a meditative drag on his Galoise. The ember glowed red in the Indonesian night. "I'll tell Di Luca you said yes."

"You don't sound enthusiastic."

"Fiona says you haven't touched a chisel in five years."

"I've been working in sand lately."

Victor rubbed the eagle's claw and sighed. "She says you aren't a believer anymore."

"Nobody's a believer anymore. God is dead, remember?"

"Have you really lost your faith?"

"I can fake it."

"You must understand—in Rome's view, He's as *spiritually* alive as ever. This Corpus Dei business is simply number two in a theoretically endless series of incarnations. The Holy Father envisions the reliquary as a place of pilgrimage. It will breathe new life into the Church."

"But won't it also be a *sad* place? Gethsemane is sad. The Via Dolorosa is sad. Let me take my grief over losing my faith and transform it into—how can I say this?—into a marble lament for the physical death of the eternal Creator."

"A marble lament—I like that," said Victor. "And if you ever find your sadness fading, just return to the West, and it will be renewed. There's a fact I haven't told you yet. It's about God's skull."

"His skull, Captain!" cried Cherry.

"Look at His goddamn skull!" screamed Leland.

Anthony faced the bier and once again focused his binoculars. While the majority of the bones lay still, spread across the raft like an elaborate collection of dinosaur fossils—ribs, femurs, vertebrae—the skull itself was disquiet. Slowly, inexorably, with the sound of a ten-ton gate pivoting on rusty hinges, the mandibles began to move. The divine mouth grew wider, then wider still, until with a roaring fit the jaw flew open and, in a scene Anthony instantly ranked as the most disturbing he'd ever beheld, the Creator of the universe vomited out His own brain.

A collective shout of dismay arose from the sailors gathered on the afterdeck. Throbbing with ideas, pulsing with perspicacity, the cerebral mound ascended more than a hundred meters and then paused, hovering, above the Channel.

"Oh, please, God, don't let Your brain explode," wailed Cherry. "Everything we need to know is in there!"

"A cure for cancer!" moaned Leland.

Jackknifing, the brain now flew southwest toward Cherbourg, gliding over the *Galveston* like a gargantuan sea sponge capable of soaking up Lake Champlain or wiping away the world's worst oil spill. The organ did not prosper. Even this most central of God's anatomical possessions could not survive His death throes. No sooner had the brain cleared the tanker's bows than it decomposed into its constituent cells, each sailing a hundred yards into the air before falling toward France like a flaming meteorite.

"Damn, it almost hit us," gasped Cherry.

"I thought we'd be chipping neurons off the fo'c'sle from now till Christmas," said Leland.

The air behind Anthony vibrated with a short, sharp, cracking noise. He turned in time to behold God's grinning, slack-jawed skull break free of His uppermost cervical vertebra. The great white mass ascended, expanding all the while like a gigantic Mylar balloon sucking on a million-liter bottle of helium.

"Any minute now, it'll explode," predicted Leland.

But the skull merely continued to rise and grow, smiling malevolently on Europe as it vanished behind a puff of cumulus cloud.

As Gerard and Victor drew within view of the cottage, dawn broke over Viatikara, silencing the tree frogs and cueing the cockatoos to begin their daily squabbles.

"The skull came back the moment the millennium turned—on the night of December 31, 2000," said Victor. "In the interim it had grown as big as Delaware. The thing went into geosynchronous orbit directly above Times Square."

"A New Year's Eve to remember," said Gerard.

"Its movement meshes with the Earth's. Night or day, whatever the season, anybody in the Western world can walk out on his lawn and see it. The Vatican leases the forehead for laser ads."

Fiona lay on the porch hammock, eyes closed, her lips curled in a dream-induced smile. She was absurdly thin; an unobservant intruder might have taken her for a corpse. Gerard tiptoed past his unconscious wife, his gaze locked on the front door. He disliked even looking at her these days, so troubling did he find her draconian diet . . . her draconian diet, her nonnegotiable primitivism, her gimcrack vision quests. Perhaps it was this passion for purity, perhaps she no longer found him attractive, perhaps something else: whatever the reason, their erotic life had dried up. Over three years had passed since she'd remarked on his resemblance to Yul Brynner—a comparison she always intended as flattering, though Gerard perceived himself as being neither quite that handsome nor quite that stolid.

How far they'd fallen since their days of bohemian bliss in SoHo. At first the relationship had been strictly professional: the famous sculptor, trying to become more famous, and his young model, working her way through NYU. She would pose in the nude for hours at a time, shifting her weight sensuously from foot to foot as he translated her oval face and supple contours into a clay study for a forthcoming bronze, *Lilith Embracing the Tree of Life.* One steamy August night she looked at him intently, smiled, and said, "There's a much simpler way, you know. Sympathetic magic. Mold me directly, and—presto—your mound of clay over there will turn into Lilith." After catching his breath, he confessed to a fondness for unorthodox techniques, and soon they were up in his loft, the nice Catholic boy and the nicer Catholic girl, experimenting with sympathetic magic. They were married within a month, so profoundly had they scandalized their consciences and jeopardized their souls.

Gerard guided Victor through the front door and into the kitchen, the cottage's only substantial room.

"Want some breakfast?" asked Gerard.

"Just coffee," said Victor, removing his backpack from the table.

"Help yourself."

Victor lit the left burner of the propane stove, warmed the pot, and poured coffee into a blue-glazed ceramic mug, the latest artifact to issue from Gerard's backyard kiln.

"So our planet now has a second sun?" said Gerard.

"Second sun, second moon."

Rooting through the pantry, Gerard retrieved a box of generic corn flakes. He filled a bowl, added milk powder and a cup of water, and sat down to consume the insipid mixture.

"I brought you a book," said Victor. From his backpack he obtained a fat, doorstop-caliber volume called *Parables for a Post-Theistic Age.* "The author was the Vatican's liaison during the Corpus Dei's first voyage. Thomas Ockham, a real Renaissance man—cosmologist, physicist, writer, priest. He might give you some useful ideas. He might even convince you that I haven't been lying."

"If you don't want to read it, Gerry"—Fiona drifted ethereally into the kitchen—"pass it on to me."

"Ah, the Maid of the Mangos awakens." Gerard swallowed a spoonful of cereal. "I hope you slept peacefully, dear. Did you dream of your past life as a vestal virgin?"

Fiona tapped the cover of *Parables for a Post-Theistic Age.* "Every book contains a piece of the truth."

"You can't have a profound insight like that unless you travel all the way to Indonesia," said Gerard to Victor.

"So—are we going to design God's reliquary?" Fiona poured coffee into a Korty original: a ceramic ape head with an empty brainpan.

"We could use the money," said Gerard.

"Take the job," said Fiona. "Take it with my blessing. But be honest with yourself. Don't pretend it's for the money, and don't pretend it's for the creative satisfaction either."

"So why am I taking it?"

She pressed the mug to her lips and sipped. "Because you've got an *ego,* dearest husband. You've got the disease of the West, and I believe your case is terminal."

As the morning sun ascended, the sculptor stumbled out of the cottage, settled into the hammock, and began browsing through *Parables for a Post-Theistic Age,* fully expecting Ockham's ruminations to convert his present prostration into deep sleep.

Five hours later, he read the last sentence and snapped the volume shut, forcefully, as if to crush a beetle between adjacent pages. He pressed the *Parables* to his heart.

God, what a book.

A terrible choice lay before Gerard Korty, as awesome and intimidating as Dante's glimpses of the afterlife. He could create the reliquary the Vatican wanted, or he could create the reliquary God wanted. For if Thomas Wickliff Ockham, S.J., was even partly right, the same design could never serve both masters.

Memento Mori

THREE MONTHS AFTER Nora Burkhart discovered the triad of peculiar inscriptions adorning the Lobo mausoleum, her son awoke shivering, his lips and fingertips as blue as the oceans on his Rand McNally globe. Oddly, his temperature was normal—slightly below normal, in fact, 97.8° Fahrenheit. Was it possible to be battling an infection without running a fever? Nora didn't know.

"I don't like leaving you home alone," she told him.

"If a robber breaks in," said Kevin, "I'll shoot him with the derringer on my Swiss Army knife."

"It's probably one of those twenty-four-hour viruses. If you're feeling better, you can study for your algebra test."

"Bad idea, Mother. Algebra causes relapses. This is a known fact."

"Don't spend the day watching MTV. Television causes brain cancer. This is a known fact."

Descending to street level, she approached the delivery truck—Phaëthon, she called it, after the reckless young demigod who'd nearly incinerated the Earth while joyriding in the sun's chariot—its panels emblazoned with the motto RAY FELDSTEIN'S TOWER OF FLOWERS: WHATEVER THE DAY, WE HAVE THE BOUQUET. She pulled out her Lucite scraper and shaved the frost off the windshield, then climbed behind the wheel and checked her smile in the side-view mirror. Although Eric had never appreciated street makeup ("Illusions belong on the stage"), she liked the artistic challenge—Nora the portraitist, painting her fleshly canvas—and this morning, as always, she took pleasure in her subtly underscored features.

She backed out of the Meadowbrook Manor parking lot and rattled through her scruffy East Cambridge neighborhood past stale heaps of February snow, each mound topped with oil and grime, a polluted sundae. Reaching the Longfellow Bridge, she piloted Phaëthon over the half-frozen Charles River. The Arlington Street traffic knot was less tangled than usual, and she attained the Newbury intersection five minutes ahead of schedule. She parked at a meter, inserted a quarter, and glanced skyward. Cirrus clouds rimmed God's skull. He appeared to be wearing a white toupee. At least there weren't any ads today. Why the Vatican permitted the multinationals to aim their lasers at His brow was a mystery she couldn't fathom. Contemplating the Cranium Dei was depressing enough. You shouldn't have to read COKE IS IT in the bargain.

Eight years in Ray Feldstein's employ... and still Nora loved entering the Tower of Flowers on a winter's day: that wondrous jump from biting wind to tropical warmth. She slammed the door behind her and paused, inhaling the layered fragrances. Her favorite coworker, Ruthie Dart, a moody Lesley College dropout who sprayed her hair so liberally that the results suggested a crash helmet, greeted her with an affectionate grunt.

On the counter lay Nora's clipboard. She perused the crib sheet. Four deliveries by 11:00 A.M. Busy morning.

She loaded the bouquets into Phaëthon and sped off toward the first stop, a funeral home in South Boston. Swathed in black, Cynthia Beckwith took the basket of lilies in her arms. *With deepest condolences*, ran the greeting card. *Yours truly, Louis Thorpe*. "I'm so sorry," said Nora. "To tell you the truth, Bill and I didn't get along," the widow replied. "I'm marrying Louis next month." Nora's second destination was the Fairview Nursing Home in Brighton: a pot of ivy for a birdlike Irishwoman with trembling hands. Kathleen O'Leary was celebrating her eighty-fourth birthday. The ivy was from her estranged sister in Belfast. "You don't know what this means to me," said Kathleen, squeezing Nora's shoulder. Recipient number three was Nick Ambrose, a used-car dealer in Medford whose wife sought to make amends for the morning's altercation. "Some guys are so insecure, they can't stand getting flowers, but I think it's terrific," he said, taking the hyacinths from Nora. "You're a credit to your gender," she replied, tossing him a grin. Next came the Fresh Pond Leisure Club, site of an impending luncheon. As Nora entered the banquet hall, the organization's president, a stout woman with excessively rouged cheeks, seized the vase of roses and set them on the speaker's table. "A retired psychologist is addressing us today. 'Celestial Skull Anxiety: Nine Surefire Coping Strategies.' I can't wait."

At 11:15 A.M. Nora returned to Phaëthon and studied the crib sheet. The afternoon's duties were light—a private home in Everett, a hospice in Chelsea, a church in Revere, period. She had plenty of time to call Kevin before grabbing a sandwich and reloading the truck.

A telephone booth stood on the corner of Western Avenue and Harvard Street. Kevin answered on the third ring.

"Hello?"

"It's me," she said. "How're you feeling?"

"Mom, could you come home?"

Nora shuddered. He never called her Mom, only Mother. "What's the matter?"

"I'm frightened."

"Frightened?" She tightened her grip on the segmented cable. "Your cold's worse?"

"A boy came to see me today. I'm scared."

"I'll be right there."

When Nora reached the apartment, Kevin was in the bathroom, hunched over the toilet bowl, clutching the slick porcelain. He gasped and shivered. She knelt beside him and cupped her hand around his forehead. His brow was a block of ice. At last a foul blackness came up, shooting from his throat in a stringy mass. It was heavy and viscous, like liquid mercury, and redolent of turpentine.

She flushed the toilet. The vomitus became a thick, stinking whirlpool, spiraling clockwise as it descended beneath the streets of East Cambridge.

"Can you talk?"

Instead of answering, Kevin heaved once more, spewing a quart of black fluid into the bowl.

"There, there, darling. There, there."

At last he spoke, wheezingly, raggedly, the words splitting along their syllabic joints. "A boy visited . . ."

"Visited you, yes."

"Came into . . . my room . . . stood over . . . my bed." He leaned back on his heels, wiping his lips. "Here's the . . . weird part. The boy was . . . he was *me*."

"You had a nightmare."

"He wore my face . . . his skin was white . . . glossy . . . like this toilet."

"We've got to stop these chills. I'll call Dr. Furtado."

"He kept on saying, 'I'm going to climb inside you,' and the fourth time he said it—"

"'I'm going to climb inside you'?"

"—he dragged me out of bed, pushed hard against me . . . and then he . . . did it, he climbed inside me . . . and I'm scared he'll never leave."

"O! for a Muse of fire," cried the Chorus in *Henry V*, but Gerard would have settled for any sort of muse that month. A muse of marble would do nicely—or bronze, or limestone, or even volcanic ash. Day in, day out, sacrificing sleep and food—no more Bombay gin, no more mistresses of sand—he sat at the kitchen table, drinking cold coffee as he chased after a premise worthy of his Creator's bones. He scribbled down notions, tossed off sketches, realized raw ideas with bits of cardboard and balsa wood. Nothing. Zero. Drainpipe. For all his aesthetic huffing and puffing, a unified vision for the reliquary of reliquaries eluded his imagination.

"I've read Ockham's book three times now," he told Fiona, "and I still can't get an angle on it."

"Empty yourself of intent, and let the cosmos take over."

"What's that supposed to mean?"

"Shed the self. Drop the ego."

"I just need to push a little harder."

Though subtle in its allusions and poetic in its language, *Parables for a Post-Theistic Age* had a straightforward thesis. Despite the understandable protests of His angels and the justifiable fears of certain archbishops, God had *wanted* His corpse to be discovered. After fully apprehending His death, humankind would move beyond its traditional dependence on Him. Homo sapiens would achieve maturity.

"I shall not presume to imagine the exact words of His suicide note," Ockham wrote in chapter two, "but I am confident of its gist. To wit: although His first experiment with embodiment failed ('The Kingdom of God is within you,' Jesus had insisted, but his audience went and founded a Church instead), eventually He decided to give it a second shot. Perhaps the world would take Him seriously this time."

Before leaving on the Calcutta packet, Victor had carefully explained the parameters within which Gerard's genius could operate. The Curia Romana had been explicit. The reliquary must cost no more than 530 billion lire, about 300 million dollars, and must take less than a year to complete. A longer schedule would smack of irreverence. For a building site the Vatican had selected an abandoned movie set, the great Antioch Circus constructed for the chariot race in the 1959 *Ben-Hur,* its eighteen acres hewn from a rock quarry bordering Cinecittà Studios on the outskirts of Rome. The Curia Romana had commissioned legions of stone cutters, mural painters, mosaic workers, bronze casters, carpenters, electricians, and gardeners, all prepared to commence their efforts the instant the blueprints arrived.

Gerard tried everything. Prayer, fasting, even self-flagellation with a jungle vine. Locked in solitude, he walked Viatikara's deserted shores, screaming to the skies, demanding that the heavens provide him with a concept.

And then one sultry morning, the heavens obliged him. Staring upward, he saw looming over the island a bulbous cloud in the shape of a human brain. Each particular was in place: stem, cerebellum, pituitary gland, cortical hemispheres. It took but a minute for the cumulus brain to evoke a memorable passage from *Parables for a Post-Theistic Age:*

> As the new millennium dawns, may we finally rid ourselves of those grand absolutes, those terrible transcendent truths, in whose name human beings have routinely menaced one another. If the coming era must have a religion, then let it be a religion of everyday miracles and quotidian epiphanies, of short eternities and little myths. In the post-theistic age, let Christianity become merely kindness, salvation transmute into art, truth defer to knowledge, and faith embrace a vibrant doubt.

Knowledge, not truth . . . knowledge, mere knowledge, a church streaming not from the sky but from the mind: a church of the human brain! Gerard saw a great plaza spreading across the *Ben-Hur* arena. Along each edge rose a building devoted to one of Ockham's little myths: the Temple of Knowledge, featuring busts of Galileo, Newton, and their brethren . . . the Temple of Kindness, a gallery of history's most conspicuous saints, from the Good Samaritan to Mother Teresa . . . the Temple of Creativity, a museum bursting not only with art treasures but also with exhibits commemorating the spiritual insights of which Homo sapiens was occasionally capable (a Sermon on the Mount diorama, an audio-animatronic Koran, a tableau depicting Siddhartha's collision with infinity) . . . and, finally, the Temple of Doubt—doubt, "the miraculous faculty," as Ockham put it, that constituted "the West's great gift to the world"—hung with portraits of

Hume, Voltaire, Ingersoll, and other master skeptics encircling a ten-foot-high statue of Desiderius Erasmus, the admirable Catholic humanist who, in Ockham's words, "emerged as one of the few dissenting voices in an age when the keepers of both the Roman Church and the new Protestantism were out for blood."

In the center of the plaza lay an immense bronze brain, thirty meters high, its hemispheres cast separately and welded together on the Cinecittà site. As the visiting pilgrim approached, he would subliminally perceive that the *Ben-Hur* quarry shielded this convoluted mass of metal the way a cranium protects an organic brain. Entering through a portal in the pituitary gland, the pilgrim would face a choice. He could proceed to the left hemisphere—the reliquary proper, filled with fifty representative bone fragments, each accorded its own glass-walled niche—or he could tour the right hemisphere, its rotating exhibits celebrating whatever scientific, artistic, or religious breakthroughs had recently enthralled the species.

As Gerard charged into the kitchen and snatched up his drawing pad, Fiona said, "You've solved it."

"I've hooked Behemoth," he replied, sketching furiously.

His muse possessed him, a goddess of boiling bronze and flying sparks, of molten steel and burning marble. He labored around the clock, succumbing (but never acquiescing) to sleep as he gradually brought forth five preliminary 24″ × 36″ watercolors plus a 1:43-scale model fashioned from hardened wax, fired clay, painted plaster, and carved wood. At noon on Tuesday a blood vessel burst in his right eye, but he kept on working; on Wednesday morning his hands cramped up, and he had to sit still for an hour, his fingers immersed in warm water; on Thursday evening he gulped down his eightieth successive cup of coffee and began experiencing accelerated heartbeats. And yet somehow by week's end the paintings and the model existed. Gerard was especially pleased with the central brain, which he'd created by sculpting a sea sponge with garden shears and nail scissors.

"It's all there," he told Fiona, sweeping his hand across the diorama like a god conjuring a breeze. "Temple of Knowledge, Temple of Kindness"—he pointed to the hub—"and *this* is a human brain."

"I can tell."

"So . . . what do you think?"

Somewhat to his surprise, Fiona did not respond with oblique sarcasm, faint praise, or neopagan cant. She gave him a firm hug and a lingering kiss on the lips.

"Utterly marvelous."

"Really?"

"Victor will be ecstatic." Her face glowed with the same admiration she'd displayed when the first Korty Madonna materialized in Gerard's studio. "Father Ockham will shout hallelujah. Emily, if she were still around, would be enchanted."

"Emily?"

She smiled, cleared her throat, and recited:

The brain is wider than the sky,
For, put them side by side,
The one the other will contain
With ease, and you beside.

"I like that," he said.

"There's more. It's no accident you made the brain from a sponge."

The brain is deeper than the sea,
For, hold them blue to blue,
The one the other will absorb
As sponges, buckets do.

"I'm shipping the model to Rome on the next packet," he said.

"I'll help you crate it up," she said.

The brain is just the weight of God,
For, heft them pound for pound,
And they will differ, if they do,
As syllable from sound.

"She got it exactly right," he said, removing the roof from the Temple of Doubt. He reached inside, grasped Erasmus, and lifted the humanist into the light. "You really like my concept?"

"Dear, you've created a *world.*" She caressed the sponge as she might a lover's thigh. "It will confuse the hell out of the cardinals, but it's terrific."

"I didn't design it for *them.*"

"They'll probably toss it in the Vatican Dumpster," she said.

"Too prosaic," he said. "They'll crush it in the Vatican winepress."

"Feed it to the Vatican alligator."

"Hoist it by the Vatican petard."

Fiona laughed and said, "Jeez, Gerry, what if they think it's totally wonderful and send us the two million dollars?"

"We'll cope," he said, smiling.

"Except..."

"Except?"

"Except I don't *want* two million dollars," she said.

"Yes you do," he said.

"I want jungle nights and Indonesian gods and the Minangkabau Lagoon."

"The Bethesda Fountain is just as wet."

"But it doesn't have a tiger."

Nothing worked. No matter what antinausea drugs Dr. Furtado prescribed—no matter how high the doses of vitamins or mood elevators—Kevin's symptoms persisted. By day he shivered. Each evening he ejected the same black muck from his stomach. He continued to insist that he'd absorbed "a boy," but whenever the pediatrician questioned him about it, Kevin grew hysterical, screaming, "He's inside me! He's inside me!"

His condition worsened. The mildest perturbation—an inaccurate weather forecast in the *Boston Globe,* the preemption of *Galaxy*

Squad by a presidential press conference—made him weep. His skin grew pale, his weight fell. On hearing that the school principal had granted him sick leave, Kevin promptly retired to his room, crawled under the blankets, and stayed there.

"Got any new tricks to show me?" asked Uncle Douglas.

"He doesn't like tricks," Kevin replied.

Douglas Shafron was a maddeningly uncomplicated man who professed the sort of hardball Lutheranism whereby only a small percentage of humankind could expect salvation, every individual being earmarked for either Heaven or Hell at the moment of conception. His beliefs outraged Nora, whose atheism had intensified during the Corpus Dei's trial (better a godless universe than one ruled by the inscrutable superthug the Job Society had unmasked in The Hague). Their father had been Jewish, their mother a lapsed Catholic, and for Nora her brother's embrace of predestination theology was a postmortem insult to both parents.

"I hear you're making a vampire bat pop back and forth between two birdcages," Douglas persisted.

"Leave me alone," rasped Kevin, muck seeping from the corner of his mouth.

"Tell you what," said his uncle. "After you're better, we'll fly to California and visit the Magic Castle."

"I've been there."

"I'll bet you'd like to go again."

"He says I'm not allowed out of bed."

Abandoning his initial diagnosis of viral pneumonia compounded by clinical depression, Dr. Furtado resorted to specialists—to hematologists, neurologists, and endocrinologists. They drew Kevin's blood. They tapped his spine. They cultured his saliva, scanned his brain, biopsied his bone marrow, analyzed his urine. Lacking comprehensive health insurance, Nora charged the crisis on her Visa card. The hardest part was the waiting, those cruelly protracted periods between the infliction of some costly new diagnostic procedure and a nurse calling to say, "All results negative." The first time Nora heard this phrase, relief surged through her. The seventh time, it made her furious. All results negative, and yet she was living with a thirteen-year-old invalid.

She hated abandoning him during the day, but she couldn't afford caregivers, and her job was essential to whatever dismal future lay before them. While keeping up the minimum Visa payments was easy, one more expensive test would rupture her $6,500 credit limit, and she'd be forced to borrow from a relative—Douglas's sister-in-law, most likely, who owned a chain of beauty salons.

Returning to her marooned son at day's end, she usually found him sicker than when she'd left. He continued to leak, his every orifice now an outlet for the muck. Words deserted him. His speech descended to a prelinguistic plane. Two successive snorts signaled that he was going to throw up. A prolonged moan meant that his diaper needed changing. From his tongue the paralysis spread to other muscles. As the school year ended, his feet became as inert as stones, his hands as useless as flippers. His ball-and-socket joints stopped working, frozen by some physiological equivalent of rust.

For several weeks Nora resisted getting him a wheelchair, as if the presence of such a device would augur permanent quadriplegia. But then one stifling August afternoon, browsing through a Somerville thrift shop, she spotted a wheelchair for only twenty dollars. The first time he saw his new conveyance, Kevin smiled, though she couldn't tell whether this reaction traced to the promise of greater mobility or to the memory of his routine called "Them Dry Bones," in which a wheelchair manufacturer evaluated his product using a crash-test skeleton that magically reconstituted itself after every wreck.

The worst part of each day, worse even than the diapering and the muck removal, was the feeding. The procedure went quickly enough—so far, at least, Kevin retained the use of his jaw muscles—but each time she placed the spoon in his mouth, she couldn't help looking at him. There was endless sadness in his eyes, and fear as well, a bone-deep fear of the sort that infected the cataleptics who populated his beloved Edgar Allan Poe movies (he'd collected every available Roger Corman video)—Monsieur Valdemar in *Tales of Terror*, Guy Carrell in *The Premature Burial*, Madelaine in *House of Usher*. At other times, Kevin seemed not so much a Poe protagonist as a shipwreck survivor, flung against a coral reef, trapped in the prison of his own broken bones, waiting for the sun to finish him off. But where was the reef? she wondered. What chart disclosed it?

Each night after dinner, Nora wrestled Kevin from his wheelchair, lugged him to his bed, and performed the prescribed physical therapy, scissoring his legs in a manner that mimicked walking, swinging his arms in the pattern of brachiation. Then she would tuck him in and sit beside him on the floor, holding his hand and telling him she loved him. Gradually his room, previously off-limits to Nora by virtue of a judicious mother-son treaty, became etched in her mind. He'd been in transition when the illness struck, the accoutrements of childhood—military models, Lego tableaux, Hollywood action figures—giving ground to CDs, rock-star posters, handheld computer games, and an alabaster diorama depicting Groucho, Harpo, Chico, and Zeppo. In recent weeks she'd embellished the place, filling it with potpourri jars and rejected cuttings from work. Unlike most boys, Kevin loved flowers. The nectars, as he put it, "took him to other planets," and bouquets routinely figured in Kevin the Incredible's magic act.

The night that Quincy Azrael first appeared began like any other. Nora put Kevin in bed, exercised his limbs, tucked him in, and lingered. His breathing soothed her. She kissed his cheek. She shuffled into the parlor, eased herself into the vinyl lounge chair, and, propping her feet on the ottoman, began reading *Threading the Labyrinth*, a novel that purported to retell the myth of the Minotaur in modern dress. Fixed in the cold November sky, the Cranium Dei shone through her lace curtains. It was the Chrysler Corporation's turn to lease His brow. PLYMOUTH INVICTUS: YOUR CHARIOT TO THE STARS.

Kevin walked into the parlor, milk white and completely unclothed, balancing his plastic model of the aircraft carrier *Enterprise* on his palm.

"Darling!" Nora, gasping, clutched *Threading the Labyrinth* to her breast and rose. "Oh, Kevin, sweetheart..."

"I'm not Kevin," said Kevin.

Legs working! Tongue healed! "Darling, you're all better!"

"Kevin's in his room." He sat on the ottoman. His chalky skin lay taut across his chest, all twenty-four ribs lumping outward. "I'm Kevin's fetch."

"What?"

"His fetch. His leveler. His pale priest. His death."

"You shouldn't say things like that."

"Mutual understanding will not come easily, Mrs. Burkhart, but you must grasp one truth at the outset. I cannot be bargained with."

"Stop talking crazy, sweetheart. It isn't healthy."

The boy lifted the aircraft carrier to his lips and blew, launching the little bombers, fighters, and torpedo planes toward the ceiling. "A plague has begun, and Kevin is its first victim." The planes fell to the floor, caught fire, and turned into kernels of charred plastic. "Your son is riddled with nihilism. He has contracted the abyss. He has caught death awareness, with attendant vulnerability to lethal malaise and malignant despair." The stench of burning polystyrene filled the room. "How far will the pestilence spread? No one can say. Millions of us stand waiting in the wings, and we shall flourish as long as God's skull hangs above. Call me Quincy Azrael."

Nora closed her eyes. *Threading the Labyrinth* slipped from her grasp and thudded onto the carpet. For the first time since its advent, she doubted that the manifestation was Kevin. "I find this . . . very difficult."

"We live in difficult times. Theism is fading from the West, and with it the lie of Heaven. Look out the window. Behold His hollow eyes, His gaping nostrils, His skinless grin. A bulwark has been thrown down, Mrs. Burkhart. Death can no longer be denied. My species is leaking into the world."

Nora stared at the black lumps that had once been plastic airplanes. Who was this terrible boy, this Quincy Azrael who so obscenely resembled her son? Kevin's fetch, his leveler, his . . . death. A wave of nausea rolled through her. She took a breath and pressed her sweating fingers against her stomach.

"We never abandon our hosts for long," said Quincy, rising. "It gives them delusions of remission."

He drifted into the hallway, Nora right behind. Not since she was a toddler had walking been for her such a conscious and deliberate act. Left foot forward. Now the right. The left. The fetch trailed his scent behind him, a blend of humus and rotting leaves.

"Three months ago somebody stuck a magnifying glass in Kevin's cereal," she said.

"'The absence of God is God enough.' Plus a caveat concerning cognitive snares and an appeal to the virtues of uncertainty."

"*You* did it."

"Not I, no."

"Of course it was you."

"Why should I communicate using granite tombs"—the fetch stepped into Kevin's room—"when you and I can have such stimulating conversations face to face?"

She crossed the threshold and saw her sleeping son. She glanced at Quincy, returned her gaze to Kevin. It was true. The boy had a private demon. Her throat constricted as if caught in a garrote. Tears blurred her vision, warming her cheeks as they fell.

"Our first meeting went well, don't you think?" said Quincy, crawling onto the bed. "I was afraid you'd start throwing things at me." He pointed to the black muck bubbling from Kevin's mouth. "Fear syrup," he explained. With his index finger he transferred a viscous blob to his tongue. "Sartre sauce. To a fetch, it tastes like honey."

Poised atop Kevin's chest, a crouching gargoyle, Quincy began his descent. The resulting image, unmatched in Nora's experience, suggested some everyday disgorgement (yolk falling from a cracked eggshell, seared bread shooting from a toaster) made bizarre through reverse-motion photography. A mere twenty seconds, and Kevin and his fetch were fused. The boy didn't wake up. He lay on the mattress, grimacing, trembling, his brain possessed by some primordial nightmare, his spasms turning the sheets into wild eddies of cloth.

Nora embraced her child. Gradually his dream dissolved. She released her grip and swallowed a mouthful of sooty East Cambridge air.

"You're mine, Kevin," she said. "Not his. Mine."

Charging into the parlor, she grabbed the telephone handset and called her closest relation.

Kind and loving brother that he was, Douglas overcame his initial Lutheran horror of Nora's story—his suspicion that she'd become Satan's pawn—and listened until 2:00 A.M. He was sympathetic and supportive, and his concluding remark enabled her to shed her supposition of insanity and get some sleep that night.

"I'm looking out my window, and I see God's skull telling me to buy a Plymouth Invictus, and I say to myself, anything's possible these days, absolutely anything, including an invasion of zombies."

I hate it when Quincy leaves. Every time he exits me, I can't help imagining he's gone forever. Then he comes back, and my hopes shatter like the seven mirrors in "The Devil's Speculum"—Dad's greatest trick, I think. At the climax, the pieces assemble themselves into a glass demon. A *Globe* reporter once asked him to reveal the secret, and Dad laughed and said, "It's done with mirrors."

Quincy tells me Mother had trouble comprehending who the fetches are and why they're here. When she finally got it, she cried. I feel sorry for her. Before I was born, she lost my father, and now she's losing me. I don't remember seeing any men around the apartment when I was little, though a few started appearing after I became a third-grader. Most of them were jerks, except for Ben Sawyer, who built me a plywood doghouse for my "Fangs of Cerberus" trick. He went back to Canada, I think, so maybe he was the biggest jerk of all.

I'm sealed inside myself—"a psychic King Tut," Quincy says, "entombed in static flesh." My heart still beats. My bowels move, eyes blink, tear ducts drip. My brain jumps from thought to thought. Like all magicians, I don't believe in magic (show me a ghost, and I'll show you smoke and misdirection), but I still like to imagine that this diary of mine is getting recorded, every word etched on the inside of my skull.

Mother tries to do right by me. She tucks me in each night and puts hyacinths in my room. I can smell them. When our eyes meet, she turns away. Quincy says I'm the plague's first casualty. He makes it sound like I've won a prize.

"Eventually you'll slip into oblivion," he says.

"Will I see Dad there?"

"It's not a place, Brother. Nobody lives in oblivion. Not your father, your grandfather—not even God. You simply stop thinking, and then the universe dissolves, forever."

The journeys that constituted his life, Thomas Wickliff Ockham now realized, had always entailed an uncommonly large gap between anticipation and actuality. His wrenching ordeal aboard the *Carpco Valparaíso* during the first towing of the Corpus Dei had proved nothing like the monotonous voyage he'd envisioned. His trip through the divine brain, which he'd thought would unravel a dozen scientific riddles, had instead taught him that the average cosmological conundrum paled beside the raw mystery of sheer existence. And now the process of dying was also foiling Thomas's expectations.

He'd always believed he would cross the bar unprotesting. That was the dignified method. Who among his friends was better prepared to meet the eternal Footman? How many men could check out saying they'd danced naked in God's navel with a Carmelite nun? Debated Manichaeism with God's Idea of Saint Augustine? Published a half dozen influential books, including *The Mechanics of Grace* and *Out of Many, One* and (his personal favorite) *Parables for a Post-Theistic Age*. And how many men—if the letter he'd received from Indonesia spoke the truth—could die knowing that their theological speculations had inspired the concept behind the ultimate reliquary?

But Thomas wasn't ready to go. The grave, he suspected, was a black hole, unfit for human habitation—nothing at all like the amazing planet he presently regarded from his sixteenth-story window overlooking the Hudson. Eleven years earlier, he'd set sail on that historic river, bound for zero degrees latitude, zero longitude, the Corpus

Dei's splashdown point. But tonight he was landlocked, bed-bound, awaiting the inevitable hour.

His pessimism had begun on the supertanker during the long hours of inhaling His spoiled flesh, and it had continued through the Trial of the Millennium with its catalogue of divine crimes. Although Martin Candle lost his case, he'd demonstrated to Thomas's satisfaction (if not the tribunal's) that the Creator in His day had been a duality, author of both butterflies and Black Plague, sunsets and skin cancer. And then, finally—a week after the verdict—the Cranium Dei had gone into its conspicuous orbit, and Thomas knew that no honest man anticipated bliss beyond the tomb.

The chest pains became relentless, a thousand microscopic jellyfish swimming through his blood, stinging his heart, invading his shoulders and arms. By one line of reasoning, he should call an ambulance now, but instead he swallowed two Aleves, removed Gerard Korty's letter from the nightstand, and read it for a third time.

While he admired the sculptor's passion, he shrank from the man's naïveté. Did Mr. Korty really believe that he could sell his patrons on knowledge, kindness, creativity, and doubt? Did he really imagine that the Church was about to cede the field to Galileo Galilei, Clara Barton, Pablo Picasso, and Desiderius Erasmus?

In his mind's eye Thomas saw the fabulous reliquary, its bronze brain gleaming and pulsing like the core of some embryonic planet. He sat up in bed, leaned forward, and groped toward the shining hemispheres. As he touched the pituitary gland, the entire brain exploded—*pop*, gone, a bubble meeting a thorn—and suddenly his pain was gone too, and he felt the light leaking from his soul like oil from a fractured chrism.

Nine months after Gerard shipped his scheme for a Cinecittà reliquary, the Calcutta packet steamed up to his private dock bearing two jars of instant coffee, a case of Hershey bars, a crate of Samuel Adams, and a manila envelope displaying the Mondrianesque logo of the

Shamberg Agency. With trembling fingers Gerard tore back the flap. A cashier's check and a one-page letter slid out and glided to the dock. Gerard retrieved them. The check bore his name. He hadn't seen so many zeros since pondering the speedometer on the brand-new Mercedes he'd bought with his Korty Madonna profits.

Dear Rich Man:

Once again, the Curia Romana has taken its own sweet time getting back to me—as I recall, they sat on your Paradiso *marbles seven months before rejecting them—but in this case their procrastination has a happy ending.*

Gerry, they love *it. "An astonishing idea,* magnìfico,*" Cardinal Di Luca told me over the phone. "Actualizing Father Ockham's theology—*bravo, *inspired."*

They imagine only "minor modifications" and "small amendments." By the time you read this, construction will be under way.

Alas, a cloud hangs over the project. I am sorry to inform you that, two weeks ago, Thomas Ockham died of a heart attack.

Love, Victor

Throat swelling, Gerard reread the last sentence. As far as he could remember, this was the first time he'd mourned the loss of someone he didn't know. He prayed that his letter to Ockham had arrived in time, the old priest slipping away fully aware that he'd seeded the reliquary of reliquaries.

"Fiona, they love it!" he shouted, rushing into the kitchen.

"Well, *that's* a surprise." She inhaled deeply, channeling the air along the back of her gullet as her yoga instructor had taught her to do. "Did they pay you yet?"

"Every penny," he said, handing Fiona the check.

"Good Lord, they swallowed the whole thing, didn't they, Erasmus and all."

"Erasmus and all."

Gerard set the teakettle on the propane stove and lit the burner. "We need to talk."

"Right."

"With two million dollars," he said, "a person could take in a Broadway show whenever she wanted."

"I know," she said.

"She could shop at Saks every day."

"That's true."

"Which of the following best describes your attitude toward returning to New York? A, infinite sadness. B, active hostility. C, intense indifference. D, fatalistic resignation."

She stood perfectly still, her brow knitted tightly. His wife was a statue, pensiveness in marble. "Intense indifference," she decided.

"I can work with that."

"Shading into fatalistic resignation."

"Let's grab the first plane home."

Only after they'd touched down at Kennedy International, lived for a month at the Waldorf, opened a joint checking account, and moved into their dream apartment on the Upper East Side—a studio and gallery for Gerard, a writer's loft and meditation space for Fiona—did he begin having doubts about the Holy See's intentions.

"What do they mean by minor modifications?" he asked Victor.

"Hard to say. I'll e-mail Di Luca."

"You'll do what to him?"

"E-mail him. You know. With my computer and modem."

Modems. And also, Gerard soon learned, laptops, compact discs, DVDs, and cellular phones. He and Fiona had been thrust into a revved-up, online, digitalized world. Mr. and Mrs. Rip Van Winkle. Consumer goods now came tattooed with "bar codes." Plastic cards had supplanted cash. A single handheld device could conjure ninety channels. Unctuous strangers called during dinner offering irresistible long-distance rates.

Maybe it was their newfound wealth, maybe the exhilaration of being back in Manhattan—or maybe they still loved each other.

Whatever the reason, they were giving it a second chance. If they both ended up preferring New York to Viatikara, they would toast their connubial bliss with Dom Perignon and set about spending their fortune. If Fiona decided she still needed Indonesia, they would let the marriage dissolve, no hard feelings, no questions asked. The experiment began auspiciously. Within a week of their return, Fiona stopped starving herself in the name of satori, abandoning her sugar-free, fat-free, food-free diet for conventional vegetarianism. As her flesh accumulated, so did the manuscript of her autobiographical novel, *Lost and Found,* the pages eventually coalescing into a complete first draft. Best of all, she once again had need of Gerard's libido: precious lust, pure concupiscence, unencumbered by any procreative designs. She would corner him in the shower, attack him in the parlor, and visit him in his studio, interrupting his *Purgatorio* sketching sessions with poetic and life-affirming seductions.

His agenda stretched gloriously before him, daunting as a triathlon, detailed as a Tokyo subway map. After the *Purgatorio* was finished, he would seize upon John Milton, carving a series of illustrations for *Paradise Lost.* Next he would sculpt an analogue to the Book of Job, delineating the sufferer's ordeal with a ferocity sufficient to remind people that, even though Martin Candle had lost his case, the man had certainly been within his rights to convene the trial. And then—if Gerard could summon the creative energy—he would in the twilight of his artistic life come back to Dante, struggling to give the *Inferno* the tableaux it deserved.

Once a week he telephoned the Shamberg Agency. The news was always the same. Tullio Cardinal Di Luca had not answered Victor's e-mail, replied to his faxes, or returned his phone calls. And yet the reliquary was evidently taking shape. Although all reporters and photojournalists had been barred from the site, the Office of Extraordinary Ecclesiastical Affairs periodically issued breezy press releases proclaiming that the most significant funerary project of all time, "the Cinecittà Reliquary, sparked by the theology of the late Thomas Ockham and designed by the reclusive sculptor Gerard Korty," was emerging on schedule and under budget.

Infuriated by the blackout, the American media refused to reprint Rome's puffery without comment. "Evidently God is getting a resting place worthy of a pope," *Newsweek* wryly editorialized. "Now that Soviet Communism is dead," opined *Time*, "the Vatican has overtaken the Kremlin in the arena of specious secrecy."

"Why don't they respond to Victor's messages?" Gerard asked Fiona with a groan.

"They're probably going crazy trying to meet the deadline."

"Do you suppose they're diddling with it? What if they've missed the *point*? What if they call it the Temple of Truth instead of the Temple of Knowledge?"

"It's out of your hands."

"And once you call it the Temple of Truth, then it's deuces wild—Father Ockham saw this—because truth is, quote, whatever the king wielding his scepter or the mountebank writing his self-help book wants it to be."

"Relax, Gerry. Forget about Rome and return to Dante."

There was wisdom in her words, he felt. And so, as a gray and gritty winter descended on Manhattan, he put God's bones behind him and threw himself into the *Purgatorio*, carving marble souls suspended between Heaven and Hell.

On the day he finished sculpting *The Gluttons*, the *New York Times* reported that "the Cinecittà Reliquary, conceptualized by the genius hermit Gerard Korty and executed by sixty-seven of the world's finest artisans," would be unveiled within three weeks. The Vatican had planned an elaborate opening ceremony, including speeches, choirs, and dignitaries.

"Can you believe this?" he wailed, waving the newspaper article in Fiona's face. "They're cutting the ribbon in less than a month, and we weren't even invited!"

"So? They paid you."

"What good is the money if they're warping my masterpiece?"

At noon he phoned his agent.

"Did you see today's *Times*?" he asked Victor.

"Most upsetting."

"Why wasn't I invited?"

"Maybe the cardinals forgot you'd returned to Manhattan," said Victor. "Maybe they think you're still on Viatikara, saying no to civilization, and an invitation would've only offended you."

"They're snubbing me."

"They're snubbing you, Gerard. It's outrageous. Naturally I'll fire off a new barrage. Phone calls, faxes, e-mail."

Gerard had a better idea. The plan that now gripped his imagination was as vivid and substantive as a block of Makrana marble. "I've reached a decision. Don't try talking me out of it."

"That sounds ominous."

"I'm going to Cinecittà," said Gerard.

"Unwise," said Victor.

"You're welcome to come along."

"I've got jury duty or something."

"I'm going, Victor, and if I don't like what I see, the world will soon know of my displeasure."

At 8:12 P.M. on Valentine's Eve, Nora locked up the Tower of Flowers. She climbed into Phaëthon, drove home, and, after feeding and exercising Kevin, took him to Jamaica Plain (she never left her son alone at night) and placed him in Uncle Douglas's care. Returning to the shop, she began to undo the damage.

By virtue of their sheer numbers, the day's customers—scores of perplexed but well-meaning males for whom the language of flowers was largely foreign—had practically destroyed the place. The displays were a jumble. Slushy footprints marred the floor. Somebody had shattered a grow-light bulb, littering the platform with glass fragments. The shoppers' children had festooned the checkout counter with depleted wads of bubble gum and partially dissolved lollipops.

"As you probably know," said Quincy Azrael, "Valentine's Day, like so many festivals on the Christian calendar, has pagan roots."

Nora looked up from her sweeping. Surrounded by red dahlias, the pale, terrible boy sat on the nearest display table, naked as before, exuding the odor of loam.

"Aztec lovers," Quincy continued, "used to exchange warm, dripping human hearts, recently torn from the chests of captive warriors. Such a romantic civilization."

"Kevin's getting worse."

"What did you expect? Do you think this is a game? Do you doubt my powers? With a snap of my fingers I could change these dahlias into a dung heap or your broom into a cobra. Dahlias, by the way, signify instability, but you know that."

Quincy snapped his fingers. Nora's broom changed, becoming not a cobra but a four-foot stalk of coagulated fear syrup.

"You want to strangle me, don't you?" said the fetch. "You want to spear me through the heart with that shepherd's crook. Impossible. Death is immortal. We are compacted ectoplasm, Jehovic Jell-O, the mattress that muted the princess's pea. Bullets only tickle us. Arsenic simply makes us sneeze."

She threw down the stick of fear. It hit the floor and shattered.

"Three messages," said Quincy. "A brief for humility, filed by Oliver Cromwell. I've always found politics tedious. An epigram concerning the absence of God. Theology bores me as well. A joke about being trapped in a fortune-cookie factory. Now *jokes* I can relate to. A woman phones a mortuary to arrange her husband's funeral. 'But you buried your husband two years ago!' the undertaker protests. 'I got married again—this is for my second husband,' she explains. 'Oh, I didn't know you'd remarried,' the undertaker replies. 'Congratulations!'" The fetch's lips parted in a smile as mocking as God's. "You're not laughing, Mrs. Burkhart."

"Is there any way you could—"

"Take you instead? No. Sorry. You can't die another person's death for him. The metaphysics gets too complicated." The leveler's smile collapsed. "In less than a year the streets will be crawling with my species, a fetch for every man, woman, and child in the Western world."

"You're planning to kill us all?"

"Death awareness doesn't kill people. Death kills people. Death awareness merely turns them into quivering blobs of ineffectuality. You're a Grecophile. You know about Prometheus. His transgression, you may recall, lay as much in blessing people with death amnesia as in telling them the recipe for combustion."

True enough, she thought. Death amnesia: a fitting term. According to Aeschylus, prior to Prometheus's intervention everyone on Earth knew the exact date and hour of his death, a situation inflicting chronic lethargy on the majority of humankind. When at last unburdened of this awful information, people gradually—inevitably—began acting as if they might live forever. They built cities, pursued sciences, practiced arts, and challenged the gods.

"So even if we weren't carrying a lethal disease in tow," Quincy continued, "the postindustrial world would still be doomed. Don't deny that death denial is central to the human enterprise. Take away the average person's obliviousness to oblivion, and he becomes as torpid as Hamlet on Prozac. Speaking personally, I shall be sorry to see Western civilization disappear. I think it was a hoot, especially the Stanley Cup and stud poker. Want to hear another joke?"

"No."

"A worried patient shares his misgivings with his doctor. 'I've heard of cases where the physician has treated someone for pneumonia, and he died of typhoid fever.' The doctor is offended. 'Ridiculous,' he says. 'When I treat a patient for pneumonia, he dies of pneumonia.'" The fetch rearranged the dahlias. "And still no smile from Mrs. Burkhart. Do you know your problem, lady? You refuse to look on the lighter side of bottomless pits. Not everybody takes your high-and-mighty attitude. Follow me."

"Don't tell me what to do."

"Your education is far from complete. Follow me."

She stomped on the syrup fragments, then allowed Quincy to guide her out of the showroom, through the back office, and into the vacant lot behind the shop. Bathed in moonlight, the abundant trash—discarded mattresses, castaway automobile tires, 55-gallon drums—seemed almost luminous. A thousand bits of broken glass sparkled like polished gems.

"Do you and Kevin talk?" she asked.

"Of course. I'm his only companion. *He,* at least, laughs at my jokes."

"Tell Kevin I—"

"You love him. A reasonable request. Happy to comply."

"Thank you."

"I might be irredeemably evil, but I'm not all bad."

Quincy gestured toward the far corner of the lot, where a brown Dumpster rose from the bare earth like a witch's crockpot. An emaciated, rheumy-eyed man approached the steel bin, pushing a corroded grocery cart, its cage containing a shoe, a boot, a raincoat, a flashlight, and a windup alarm clock. Reaching the Dumpster, he stood on tiptoes and peered inside.

"His name is Angus McPherson—a total nobody, just another old man without a home," said Quincy.

The derelict pulled out a tattered umbrella.

"Before the epidemic peaks, medical science will realize that fetches, like malignant tumors, come in many varieties. Some, such as your son's, act slowly. But others can fulfill their obligations in minutes."

As Angus McPherson dropped the umbrella in his grocery cart, his naked double limped toward him. The interloper was frailer even than McPherson himself, bony as the mannikin in Kevin's "Forgotten Prisoner of Otranto" trick.

"Hello, Angus," said McPherson's fetch.

"We have an appointment, don't we?" said McPherson.

"Yes."

"Why do you appear only in the West?" Nora asked Quincy.

"Even if the East had an orbiting Cranium Dei of its own, the thing's impact would be minimal," the leveler replied. "In Asia and the Muslim nations, death denial takes forms that render my species irrelevant. For a Hindu, death is merely the necessary antecedent to reincarnation, another turn of the wheel. A divine skull could haunt the Islamic world for generations without enjoying any power to depress, since Allah was never personlike. When it comes to Buddhism, of course, the whole game is an illusion. Death, life—same thing."

"Sorry about this," said McPherson's fetch.

"It's all right," said McPherson. "I've got no reason to go on living, except maybe..."

"I know all about it."

"You do?"

"Yes. The Red Sox will never win another pennant."

"Never?"

"Never."

"Take me."

The fetch extended his skinny arms, gates on the portal to oblivion. Smiling, McPherson stepped over the threshold. For a full minute the two stood pressed against each other, melding inch by inch into a single entity.

"The disease always follows the same course," said Quincy. "First comes the chill, engulfing the patient like an Arctic tide."

McPherson shivered.

"The patient attempts to expel the wraith but ejects only copious quantities of fear syrup."

The victim heaved, spewing out a familiar black fluid.

"Next comes a crippling of the voice box and paralysis in all four limbs."

The victim let out a choked cry and stumbled, falling to the ground like a marionette whose puppeteer had been shot through the head.

"Followed by the worst case of boils since Job."

Sprawled on his back, McPherson watched in mute terror as red lesions erupted all over his body. Exploding one by one, the sores released their cargos of pus, the viscid exudate dribbling down his face and chest. Sickened, Nora turned away. Kevin had already endured so much—did this torture too lie before him? Was there no mercy left, not a single mote of it, within the Cranium Dei?

Staggering across the lot, she slumped onto a tattered mattress and buried her face in her hands.

"The boils collapse and dry out, leaving a hundred black pocks. Look up, Mrs. Burkhart! You're missing the pocks!"

Nora wept.

"The flesh splits. The fissures spread among the dried lesions, connecting pock to pock, and then at last..."

Nora glanced toward McPherson's corpse. It swam in her tears. Rising, she picked up a half-empty beer bottle and hurled it against the Tower of Flowers, staining the wall with Guinness stout.

"Now let me tell *you* a joke," she said.

"Whatever his intellectual limitations," said Quincy, "McPherson knew better than to fight the inevitable."

"An old woman walks up a steep mountain path with a heavy load of wood balanced on her shoulders. Finally she can stand it no longer. She throws down her burden, raises her arms toward Heaven, and cries out, 'I want the Angel of Death to come!' Instantly the Angel appears before her, terrible in form and visage. 'You called?' says the Angel. 'Yes,' the old woman replies quickly. 'Will you help me get this load back on my shoulders?'"

"Not funny," said Quincy.

"Maybe you don't get it."

"Surrender to the Footman, Mrs. Burkhart. Kiss the pale priest. Embrace the abyss."

"Fuck you," said Nora to her son's death.

Oswald's Rock

BEFORE GERARD KORTY BECAME a hermit, surrounded by the Indonesian jungles and cloistered in the monastery of his mind, he had unfailingly availed himself of every opportunity to visit the fecund and boisterous nation of Italy. For a man of Gerard's enthusiasms, Florence was a kind of paradise, a continual intimation that his visual cortex, if not his other neural equipment, had attained a state of grace. Venice with its liquid streets and Turin with its sumptuous churches likewise enraptured him. But Rome rarely beckoned. Why settle for the prosaic Tiber when you could have the poetic Arno? The Eternal City, Gerard felt, far from being eternal, was imprisoned in the present, a city of industrial soot and acid rain, traffic jams and bureaucrats.

This time around, however, for reasons he couldn't name, Rome won him over. An hour after moving into the Abruzzi, a swank *pensione* beside the Pantheon on the Piazza della Rotonda, he went for a stroll on the site of the vanished Circo Massimo. The Mediterranean sun was warm and lulling. The fragrance of the ripe grass beat back the oily odors of the Maseratis and Vespas. If tourists had begun infiltrating the city, they were not yet conspicuous. Rome still belonged to the Romans—to the entwined lovers, seraphic joggers, chuffing cyclists, preadolescent soccer players, and married couples pushing baby strollers. In that hour the divine skull appeared oddly benign, its smile not so much a taunt as an exhortation. Savor life while you can, God seemed to declare, even as He explicitly urged His beholders to TREAT YOURSELF TO A TUBORG.

Gerard slept well that night, dreaming that he was back in the Circo Massimo, driving a winning chariot across the finish line.

In the morning he shouldered his rucksack, walked to Stazioni Termini, and, descending into the metro system, took the crushingly congested Anagnina train southeast to its penultimate stop, Cinecittà. He climbed back into the daylight and surveyed the lively crowds moving west along the Via Federico Fellini. Although the unveiling wouldn't occur for twenty-four hours, the *Ben-Hur* quarry was a focus of frenzied attention. Television minivans sporting microwave antennas nosed their way toward the site, along with police trucks bearing traffic cones and sawhorse barriers. Photojournalists on motor scooters joined the procession, their saddlebags stuffed with cameras and tripods. A diverse crowd of pedestrians—nuns, housewives, vagrants, truant teenagers—likewise sought the reliquary. On both sides of the street, enterprising vendors set up food racks, soft-drink dispensers, cappuccino makers, and displays of ceramic saints, making ready to meet whatever nutritional and spiritual needs might arise among the next day's mobs of red-carpet dignitaries and throw-rug hoi polloi.

Like an errant leaf settling onto the surface of a stream, Gerard joined the flow, allowing the collective mind to bear him west down the Via Federico Fellini and then south across a grassy field. To his left a grid of folding chairs awaited the posteriors of the invited guests. Beyond, a team of carpenters constructed a speaker's platform, its central dais supporting an oak lectern and a table draped in purple silk. According to the *New York Times*, over six hundred religious leaders from around the world would attend the grand opening—bishops, priests, pastors, ministers, rabbis, patriarchs, elders—along with two hundred elected heads of state plus scores of kings, queens, politicians, executives, and movie stars. Everybody who was anybody wanted to be seen paying his last respects to God.

A two-kilometer hike, and suddenly it appeared, the *Ben-Hur* quarry, cradling an edifice even more massive than its previous occupant, the Antioch Circus set. The reliquary itself was invisible, hidden behind a patchwork of tarpaulins. Slapped together from pine posts and barbed wire, a fence ringed the temple complex, giving it the ambience of a POW camp. Gerard studied the ocean of canvas, reading his various designs into the dips and swells: Temple of Knowledge... Kindness... Creativity... Doubt. It was all there, evidently, including the great bronze brain at the core. Maybe the College of Cardinals really *did* believe an invitation would have offended him. Maybe the portentous phrases "minor modifications" and "small amendments" portended nothing at all. If Gerard dropped by the Vatican that afternoon, Cardinal Di Luca might welcome him exuberantly and put him on the next day's program.

Minor modifications. What could it mean? What?

Setting down his rucksack, Gerard removed his B5 bushing chisel. Sunlight glinted off the tempered blade. It was a tool, of course, but to Gerard, a man for whom art constituted the only magical force in the universe, it was also a kind of sword, forged to battle the armies of insipidity and slay the dragons of kitsch. Weapon in hand, he marched around the perimeter of the complex, moving past makeshift portals of wood and wire, until the object of his search appeared, an isolated gate attended by a single pike-wielding sentry—a gaunt, weary man dressed in the garish Renaissance uniform of the Vatican Swiss Guard.

"Do you know who I am?" Gerard asked the sentry. "*Sa chi sono?*"

"I've never seen you before."

"I'm Gerard Korty, the master builder, and I've been looking for you my whole life."

"Signor Korty? Aren't you in Sri Lanka?"

"Indonesia, but now the West beckons, as does your amazing countenance."

"*Non capisco.*"

"Your face, sir, your *magnifica faccia.* I am presently laying plans to sculpt the *Inferno*, and I swear you are the Virgil I've been seeking all these years. I must have your face in my sketchbook. Can you come to my hotel this evening? I shall pay you two hundred thousand lire per hour."

"I'm busy tonight," said the sentry, cautious but interested.

"Tomorrow night?"

"This is *molto* flattering."

"So rarely does an artist find a model who perfectly matches the ideal in his imagination. What may I call you?"

"Stefano Degani."

"My dear Stefano," said Gerard, shaking the sentry's hand, "I am thrilled to be working with you." He flourished the bushing chisel. "Right now I must add a few wrinkles to Erasmus, but then we'll continue this discussion. A productive sitting always begins with a well-fed model. Have you a favorite *ristorante*?"

"I'm not supposed to let anyone inside."

Gerard placed his hand on the lintel and pushed. The gate pivoted soundlessly. "I understand, but Erasmus needs his wrinkles, a direct request from the Holy Father." He squeezed through the breach. "I won't be long. *Quindici minuti.*"

"I've never eaten at Grappolo d'Oro—do you know it? In the Piazza della Cancelleria?"

"Grappolo d'Oro! *Eccellente!*"

Gerard marched forward ten steps, stooped down, and ducked under the nearest tarpaulin like a child sneaking into a circus tent. A steamy, suffocating darkness enclosed him. His sinuses throbbed with the sickly sweet fragrance of the canvas. Slowly but reliably his rods and cones got to work, adjusting his eyes to the gloom. He was standing before the Temple of Doubt. His basic design, while hardly revolutionary (a circle of Ionian columns on the outside, a domed rotunda within), had been followed precisely. Here and there, a shaft of sunlight exploited the gap between adjacent tarpaulins, imparting a phosphorescent luster to the white marble. He entered.

There was no statue of Erasmus in the Temple of Doubt, no bust of Hume or Voltaire—not a single molecule of skepticism, in fact.

The building was actually a monument to Augustine of Hippo Regius, his enormous smile and poached-egg eyes beaming down from a pedestal.

"Shit."

He left the Augustine shrine and proceeded to the putative Temple of Kindness, where his dismay quickly crystallized into rage. Once again, the contractors had cleaved to Gerard's outward scheme—a rectilinear hall supported by caryatides of female saints—but inside, Ockham's little myth of kindness was nowhere to be found. It took Gerard only a minute to realize that the building celebrated not decency but Saint Thomas Aquinas.

The pattern continued with the gelded Temple of Creativity and the gutless Temple of Knowledge: stone paeans to Paul of Tarsus and Francis of Assisi, respectively. Gerard stormed toward the hub. He no longer expected a bronze brain, but he was wholly unprepared for the architectural monstrosity that now reared up before him. Twice the size of Chartres Cathedral, it could fairly claim to fuse, in a single building, all the worst features of the West's major architectural movements; it had the luridness of the Romanesque, the clutter of the Gothic, the turgidity of the Renaissance, the decadence of the Baroque, the chaos of the rococo, and the aridity of the modern. The materials were likewise a hodgepodge—metal, stone, glass, and wood thrown together with no thought to harmonizing their textures and tones. But the unkindest cut was the steel plaque set prominently in the south wall. RELIQUARY DESIGNED BY GERARD W. KORTY, "THE MODERN MICHELANGELO," A.D. 2003.

Retrieving his carving hammer from the rucksack, he placed the chisel against the raised K in KORTY. He struck the handle. The blade ricocheted, thwarted by the steel. Again he struck, and again—no effect. Hardly a surprise, but at least he'd tried.

He mounted the steps, passed through a pair of bas-relief bronze doors—Pentateuch episodes on the left, Gospel scenes on the right—and entered the vestibule. Hunting around, he spotted a cluster of switches behind a Korty Madonna, then activated them en masse. A blue-white glow flooded the reliquary, highlighting an immense corridor flanked by marble statues of dead popes. He held his breath and gaped.

An informative granite tablet lay embedded in the floor. Selected segments from 184 different bones were on view here, the inscription explained, the Creator's natural complement minus the twenty-two components of His skull, one bone entrusted to each of the 184 Holy Fathers who had ruled the temporal Church between A.D. 682 and A.D. 1963, beginning with Saint Leo II and ending with John Paul XXIII, excluding pretenders to the throne and otherwise illegitimate claimants. Gerard proceeded slowly, woozily, stunned by the epic vulgarity of it all. Boniface VI held a piece of God's sternum on his lap. Sergius III protected a shard of divine clavicle. Gregory IV guarded a fragment of holy scapula. Celestine II kept watch over a portion of sacred sacrum. And so it went, pope after pope, bone after bone. The overall impression was manifestly unintended. These 184 statues did not suggest vicars of Christ so much as members of some highly exclusive kennel club, each about to throw his dog a bone.

Gerard could take no more. Howling with dismay, he spun around and sprinted through the bronze doors. He quit the hideous building, circumvented Augustine's shrine, and crawled back under the canvas.

"Erasmus now has his wrinkles?" asked Stefano Degani as Gerard emerged into the sunlight.

"Erasmus isn't in there," moaned Gerard, clutching his chest. "It's nothing but a lot of popes!"

"That's not what you wanted?"

"One hundred and eighty-four popes, and there'd be twenty-two more if His skull hadn't gone into orbit!"

"What time shall I come to Grappolo d'Oro?"

"What're you talking about?!"

"Dinner tomorrow night at Grappolo d'Oro. After that you're going to sketch me."

"I've been betrayed, Stefano!" wailed Gerard, starting away. "My child has been tortured and killed"—he ran toward the Via Federico Fellini, screaming like a madman—"and Rome has not heard the last of it!"

When not telling stupid jokes or explaining how I'll soon be "covered with hideous boils," Quincy tries convincing me that death is a good thing. Without death, he says, there wouldn't be enough room on Earth for all the people. (I answer that maybe we could colonize the rest of the solar system.) Death gives life "its edge." (I tell him that magic tricks, Roger Corman videos, and the time I saw my cousin Cindy's tits give *my* life its edge.) Death allows each generation to "overthrow the dictatorship of tradition." (So why not just make it illegal for anybody over eighty to express an opinion?)

Only one of Quincy's points impresses me.

"For more than a billion years," he says, "life on this planet knew a kind of immortality. The bacteria, algae, amoebas, and primitive worms enjoyed ceaseless existence: a growing at one end, a sloughing off at the other, but nothing you would call death. Then, half a billion years ago, sexual reproduction came on the scene, along with its faithful handmaiden, death. The invention of death made possible the individual, in all his astonishing variety. Death broke life free of immortality's chains. Death said, 'Let there be sponges and coral, cockles and mussels, jawless fishes and duck-billed dinosaurs.' And there *were* sponges and coral, cockles and mussels, jawless fishes and duck-billed dinosaurs. Which shall it be, Kevin? Your individual identity, or the pre-Cambrian algae beds?"

I have no idea how to answer a question like that.

The instant Gerard realized that his watercolors would register vividly on television, he knew exactly how his counterattack would unfold. Hunched over his hotel bed, he arranged the five 24″ × 36″

images—products of his weeklong creative orgy on Viatikara—atop the blanket and gleefully pictured them entering the homes of every CNN viewer from Helsinki to Honolulu. In a mere fourteen hours the Western world would learn of the Holy See's knavery.

Sleep was out of the question. His blood boiled. His brain raced. He rode the elevator down to the lobby and strode out of the Abruzzi into the sultry Roman night. It was 11:45 P.M., but the city still rumbled, rattled, and honked as usual, hundreds of motorists zooming around the Colosseum and along the Via di San Gregorio.

Walking past the Arch of Constantine, Gerard noticed to his surprise that the eastern gate of the Forum Romanum lay open. The aberration beckoned. For the second time that day he entered a forbidden space, moving east along the Via Nova until he reached the House of the Vestals. It was his favorite place in the Forum. Nothing much remained—a few crumbling masonry walls facing a courtyard bordered by eight female statues in varying stages of dissolution—but the whole idea of vestal virgins fascinated him.

The Cranium Dei shone down, showering the elite maidens with a preternatural light. Gerard paused before the sole statue that had a head. What was it like, really, to be a vestal? The perks included good food, fine wine, immunity from sexual harassment, and the run of a comfortable palace. Still, the average Roman virgin experienced profound anxiety when the Pontifex Maximus tapped her for the honor. If a vestal allowed the hearth goddess's sacred fire to die, the palace guards would scourge her. If she lost her chastity, they would bury her alive.

A male voice said, "*Buona sera.*"

"*Buona sera,*" Gerard responded automatically. His intestines tightened. Rome after dark was a treacherous place. What pernicious imp had prompted him to wander so far from the Abruzzi? "*E una bella serata.*"

Gerard edged toward the Temple of Vesta, a rotund, columned building reminiscent of the Augustine shrine at Cinecittà. A tall man stood in the entrance, dressed in a white trench coat, his face cloaked in shadows, his teeth clenching an unlit clay pipe.

"Yes, Gerard, it's a beautiful night."

"How do you know my name?"

"Your name is the least significant thing I know about you. Ah, *bene*—I've aroused your curiosity. Return to the House of the Vestals. I shall join you momentarily. Do you see the seated maiden, the one who's nothing but a torso with legs? Look at her inscription. Tell me what you see."

Gerard was divided, as if a chisel had been driven through his sternum, splitting his heart. Half of him wanted to flee before this stranger pulled a gun, but his other half sensed that by continuing the encounter he would eventually learn what Fiona liked to call "a piece of the truth."

He did as instructed, approaching the marble torso and reading her pedestal.

"It says *9 June 364 A.D.*," Gerard reported.

"What else?"

"There's a letter C. The rest is gone."

"Deliberately erased. C for Claudia. An illuminating story. In the fourth century, a vestal named Claudia foreswore the sacred fire to enter the Convent of Lorenzo. Naturally the Catholic Church was pleased, but they hated the idea of Claudia's pagan past, so one night some bishops snuck into the Forum and rubbed out the last six letters on her monument. Cheer up, Gerard. Long before they got their hands on your reliquary, the Holy See was mutilating art in the name of piety. Don't take it personally."

"You've been to Cinecittà?"

"It's terrible what they did to your brainchild." The intruder climbed down from the Temple of Vesta. He struck a match and touched it to his pipe, sucking the bright orange flame into the bowl. "I know that nothing can keep you from appearing at the grand opening tomorrow, but I'll give you my advice anyway. Go back to New York."

"You're right," said Gerard, dumbfounded. "I was planning to crash the ceremony."

As the intruder drew nearer, the divine skull bathed him in a silvery radiance. A tremor passed through Gerard, head to toe. The man's features were the most disturbing he'd ever seen, shocking not in their strangeness but in their familiarity: this was *his* face—a white, withered facsimile of his face, rather, as if he'd carved his own portrait in marble and then submerged the bust in acid.

"You look like me," said Gerard, aghast.

"Who did you *expect* your death to look like, Winston Churchill?"

"My death?" sputtered Gerard. "What do you mean, my death? If you're advising me not to attend the opening, okay, fine, but please remove that ridiculous mask."

"It's no mask," said the doppelgänger, puffing on his pipe. "I am your personal wraith, Gerard, your reliable leveler, your devoted fetch, so naturally I wear your face. Call me Julius Azrael. You don't have to like me, but you *will* acknowledge me, much as an honest fornicator will acknowledge his bastard son." Nonchalantly he lifted a stiletto from the pocket of his trench coat. "The fetches are coming, millions of us, spawn of the holy skull. Fetches dancing in the Forum, swimming through the Tiber, hiding under your bed. We are the children of Nietzsche and the vectors of nihilism, and as surely as rats carry *Pasteurella pestis,* we bring a plague of death awareness and a contagion of malignant despair."

"What the hell are you talking about?"

"A perfectly rational response. Which I shall address with the following rational assault."

Before Gerard knew what was happening, Julius Azrael had rushed forward, stiletto in hand, and opened the sculptor's left cheek. The cut was shallow but long.

"Damn you."

"I didn't enjoy that. My species abhors violence."

As Gerard slapped a hand over the stinging wound, the doppelgänger turned and walked through the shadowy rubble that had once been the Domus Publica.

"Tomorrow, believe it or not, you'll be glad for that cut," Julius

Azrael called from the darkness cloaking the Via Sacra. "It will tell you that you haven't gone mad."

The boils have come, red and dripping, just as Quincy predicted. They aren't painful, but they're really ugly. Head to toe, my skin looks like a relief map of a volcanic island.

Whenever I ask Quincy how long this stage will last, he tells me a death joke instead of answering. He knows a million of them.

"Mr. Fitzpatrick is lying in bed, mortally ill, when the enticing fragrance of stew reaches his nostrils. He calls to his daughter. 'Katy, ask your mother if I could have a bowl of that tasty stew.' Katy goes to the kitchen and soon returns empty-handed. 'Mother says you can't have any,' she explains. 'We're saving it for the wake.'"

Not funny, but I laugh anyway. A boy in my condition needs all the chuckles he can get.

Riding the metro that morning, the rolled-up watercolors balanced on his knees, Gerard pondered the previous night's doppelgänger. A hallucination, quite possibly. Except the hallucination had slashed his cheek. A ghost, then? He didn't believe in ghosts. A psychotic episode? No, the sine qua non of insanity was the victim's inability to consider that he might be crazy.

When the Cinecittà stop arrived, Gerard tucked the watercolors under his arm, detrained, and climbed the stairs to street level. It was early, 8:45 P.M. by Gerard's watch, but thousands thronged the Via Federico Fellini, a raging torrent of citizens, tourists, clerics, laymen, pilgrims, and thrill seekers pushing toward the *Ben-Hur* quarry. He approached the nearest pavilion, its shelves overflowing with bumper stickers announcing *I've Seen the Bones,* T-shirts declaring *Citizen of the Third Millennium,* and a matched set of plaster apostles clustered like tenpins awaiting the arrival of a bowling ball. For 27,000 lire he obtained a cappuccino, a chocolate croissant, and a souvenir program book, its cover emblazoned with the Cranium Dei and the words *Cinecittà Reliquary Dedication Ceremony.*

The *polizia* were out in force, channeling the crowds away from the speaker's platform and into the quarry. Occasionally a person of consequence broke free and, flourishing a silver-foil ticket, demanded to be seated in the open-air theater. Although the program book specified an 11:00 A.M. commencement, half the chairs were already taken. The average, uncredentialed visitor was obliged to bypass the theater and walk down an avenue of sawhorse barriers toward the reliquary.

The temple complex was fully exposed, fence gone, grounds accessible, buildings bare. Flower gardens bloomed everywhere, an amenity Gerard had missed the day before, a crazy quilt of tulips, hyacinths, and lilies. Lit by the rising sun and its attendant skull, the reliquary proper looked more hideous than ever, an architectural enormity whose only value, he thought, might lie in persuading imperialist aliens that this wasn't a civilization worth conquering. The four shrines were locked up tight, as was the central abomination, but the visitors didn't mind. About half of them strolled around the reliquary, trying to decide whether this was postmodernism or merely idiocy, while the other half spread out picnic blankets and began devouring their caches of wine, cheese, and fruit. The sounds of the photojournalists' cameras filled the air, a cacophony of clicks and whirrs.

Gerard sat on the reliquary steps, thereby sparing himself a view of the goddamn thing, and leafed through his program book. The morning's schedule of events confirmed a rumor he'd heard back in Manhattan: the American Baptist Confederation had sold the bones to Rome on condition that Protestantism receive significant musical representation during the dedication ceremony.

11:00 A.M. *Highlights from "The Magnificat"*
by Johann Sebastian Bach
performed by the Vienna Boys Choir

11:15 A.M. *Benediction*
delivered by His Eminence, Tullio Cardinal Di Luca
Secretary of Extraordinary Ecclesiastical Affairs
Vatican City

11:30 A.M. *Opening Address: "Meeting the Millennium"*
delivered by His Holiness, Pope Innocent XIV
Bishop of Rome

11:45 A.M. *Medley of African-American Spirituals*
performed by the Jumpin' for Jesus Gospel Chorus
Nashville

12:00 NOON *Panel Discussion: "Designing and Building the Cinecittà Reliquary"*
led by His Grace, Archbishop Jacques Renault
Notre Dame Cathedral
Paris

12:45 P.M. "*A Mighty Fortress Is Our God*"
by Martin Luther
performed by the American Baptist Chorale
Orlando

1:00 P.M. *Closing Prayer*
delivered by David Bergmann
Rabbi, Beth Shalom Synagogue
Philadelphia

After lunch, guided tours of the shrines, gardens, and reliquary will convene every hour on the hour, beginning at 2:00 P.M.

With his Rapidograph Gerard circled the fifth event. High noon. Good. *That's* when he would make his move, exposing to the entire CNN-viewing public the betrayal of a learned priest's insights and a talented sculptor's epiphany. Which particular fools, he wondered, had the College of Cardinals recruited to grapple with the topic "Designing and Building the Cinecittà Reliquary"?

Gerard sipped his cappuccino and touched his wounded cheek. A contagion was coming, the so-called fetch had said. Universal death awareness. If that was true, would art then cease to matter?

The program book also featured photos of the popes holding their bones, plus an "Inspirational Message" from Innocent XIV, a wildly inaccurate précis of *Parables for a Post-Theistic Age*, and a biography of Gerard presumptuously titled "Portrait of the Artist as an Eccentric Recluse." Oddly enough, this last piece stayed largely within the domain of fact. They got his birthplace, early schooling, and advanced degrees right, as well as his various prizes. Most of the article concerned Gerard's Virgin Mary breakthrough, but there was also a long paragraph on his Dante project, "a series of brilliant *Paradiso* statues slated for acquisition by the Vatican." As for the reliquary, the anonymous author averred that "the Holy See could scarcely believe its good fortune in securing the services of this latter-day Michelangelo, who continues to seclude himself in the Indonesian rain forest, carving Makrana marble." The final sentence, while bullshit, had a certain plausibility: "He is rumored to be working on a series of sculptures derived from the Revelation to Saint John." Not a bad idea, actually.

The ceremony started promptly. Innocent XIV's address was a masterpiece of obfuscation, its keynote derived from Robert Browning: "God's in His Heaven, all's right with the world." Given the tepidness of the Pope's lament, a naive bystander never would have inferred that the Church had lost its principal Deity, but merely, say, its real estate holdings in Tuscany or its collection of high Baroque sugar bowls. The Holy Father finished up by requesting a moment of silence for "our dear departed brother, Father Thomas Ockham, whose speculations inform the theological heart of this beautiful reliquary."

The Jumpin' for Jesus Gospel Chorus performed its spirituals, the "Designing and Building" panel members assumed their places at the silk-swathed table... and Gerard sprang into action. Watercolors in hand, he scrambled under a dozen sawhorse barriers, sprinted down the aisle, and leaped onto the stage just as Archbishop Jacques Renault, a vigorous man with pink cheeks and snowy white hair, finished introducing his copanelists: an Italian architect, a Dutch landscape painter, a German philosopher, and—the sole woman—a Belgian art critic. Charging up to the lectern, Gerard located the CNN camera, faced the lens, and unfurled his watercolors.

"I am Gerard Korty," he screamed into the microphone, "and the thing behind you is a fraud!" His amplified words resounded across Cinecittà, all the way to the reliquary. The quarry walls replayed each syllable with a fearsome resonance. "I didn't design it!" Entering the mike, his shouts triggered a feedback loop; a metallic howl assailed the audience. He twisted the volume knob on the control panel. "Here's what Ockham wanted!" Like a matador antagonizing a bull, Gerard flourished the topmost watercolor. "A bronze brain!" Dropping the brain painting, he frantically displayed the next one. "A Temple of Creativity!"

Pikes in hand, two soldiers from the Vatican Swiss Guard lurched toward the lectern. The shorter one appropriated the control panel, throwing a toggle switch and killing the mike, then turned to Archbishop Renault and exclaimed his apologies in Italian.

"Temple of Knowledge!" screamed Gerard. Stripped of electronic augmentation, his voice sounded thin and pathetic, a barnyard squawk.

The second soldier, bearded and muscular, grabbed Gerard and wrestled him to the podium floor.

"Doubt!"

The Swiss Guard dragged him off the stage and hustled him toward the Via Federico Fellini.

He was about to scream "Kindness!" when the first guard struck him with the shaft of his pike. Darkness seeped through Gerard's neurons. His final thought, before blacking out, was that he would not sell the Vatican his *Paradiso* marbles even if they offered him all the kingdoms of this world.

As he came into consciousness, nausea beset him, rising up his esophagus and spreading downward through his bowels. Compounding his queasiness was the vibration of the metro car. He rubbed his eyes. To his right sat a weary businessman in a silk suit, to his left the burly soldier who'd tackled him. Before him stood the other soldier, leaning on the steel pike with which he'd whacked Gerard's skull. Between their outlandish helmets and their absurd pantaloons, the guards looked like two movie extras leaving Cinecittà after a hard day's shoot on a slapstick comedy lampooning the Renaissance.

"*Come si sente?*" asked the standing soldier.

"*Lo stomaco.*" Gerard pressed one hand against his belly, the other against his cranium. A bump the size of a walnut grew from his right temple.

"It's six o'clock," said the guard. "We've been riding under the city all afternoon."

"Where're my watercolors?"

"Monsignor Di Luca will return them upon receipt of your written pledge never again to criticize the Cinecittà shrines. Speaking personally, I think a bronze brain is a third-rate idea, and the cardinals were right to reject it. Which hotel?"

"The Abruzzi."

"We shall leave you at Termini, two stops away. When is your flight?"

"Tomorrow morning."

"Be on it."

The sickness lifted, replaced by a thundering headache and a creeping despair, as Gerard staggered across the Piazza della Rotonda and entered the hotel lobby. So the Vatican would get the reliquary it wanted—the reliquary it deserved. What had he expected, really? Justice? Hadn't Martin Candle's audacious presentation of God's rap sheet proved that justice happened only by accident in this world, if at all?

As he crossed the lobby, the thick Kurdistan carpet absorbing his footfalls, an imposing, bearish, but peculiarly graceful man dressed in a black caftan rose from a Barcelona chair and came forward. He held a brown leather attaché case to his chest, clutching it like a terrorist more worried about his bomb being stolen away than about a premature detonation.

"Excuse me," said the man. His eyes were a bright, luminous green, like polished jade, and his chin tapered to a goatee. "You are Mr. Gerard Korty?"

The sculptor nodded.

"Dr. Adrian Lucido, psychoanalyst, Freudian by training, Jungian by temperament. Like you, I live in New York City, and, like you, I came for the grand opening. Your performance on the platform today ranks among the most impressive displays of outrage I've ever seen."

"The cardinals weren't impressed."

"I beg to differ. They clearly felt threatened."

"My head hurts."

"Wine is not the worst analgesic. L'Antico Carbonaro is two blocks away. Their cellar is well stocked, and their pasta is the closest you'll ever get to ambrosia in this life. May I buy your dinner?"

Dr. Adrian Lucido had spoken the truth. The meal Gerard devoured at L'Antico Carbonaro that evening, fettucine with artichokes, was the second finest in his experience, outclassed only by the roast lamb he'd enjoyed at the Paris banquet honoring the debut of his Madonna. Even more memorable than the food was Lucido's capacity for wine. The psychoanalyst drank five brimming glasses of Brunello di Montalcino to Gerard's half-filled two, yet he showed no sign of inebriation.

The conversation, like the imbibing, was asymmetrical. While Gerard absently pried wax nuggets from the quartet of white candles decorating their table, his host related his life's story in long, looping, byzantine sentences. For the past two decades Lucido had been plying his trade on the Upper West Side, ministering to the neuroses of the Manhattan aristocracy. His recent celebrity derived from his unorthodox approach to "theothanatopsis syndrome," a disorder marked by a preoccupation with God's death. Lucido had enjoyed remarkable success in treating this illness, but it was his methods, not his results, that had earned him Vatican approbation. Believing that Freud had been disastrously misguided in ignoring religion's therapeutic value, Lucido encouraged theothanatopsis victims to cultivate their spirituality, a regimen that often involved converting (or reconverting) to Catholicism. His triumphs became the stuff of case studies and cover stories. When the Holy See began identifying potential invitees for the Cinecittà opening, Lucido had made the A-list.

Only after uncorking the third Brunello di Montalcino did the psychoanalyst reveal his purpose in tracking down Gerard.

"I require a sculptor. Not just any sculptor—an artist of unbridled passions and iron convictions."

"You picked the wrong man," said Gerard. "Since yesterday my convictions have been for sale to the highest bidder."

"This project, I promise you, will restore your idealism. It will reward you with something of incomparable value."

Gerard plucked a white bead from the south candle. "What would that be?"

"Professional satisfaction. The knowledge that your art helped conquer a transcendent evil." Lucido poured himself a sixth glass of dark red wine. "The divine skull has barely begun its reign. A satanic plague crouches at the gates of the West. The world is about to change, forever."

Rubbing the nascent scab on his cheek, Gerard said, "My fetch told me."

Lucido's lips assumed the contours of a crescent moon. "Ah, you've been visited, good. Then my motives will be clear to you." His bared teeth grew golden in the candlelight. "I've encountered my own death a dozen times so far. We have a complicated relationship. I listen to his troubles, and he permits me to keep on breathing. Therapy in exchange for ontological status—a fair trade, wouldn't you say?" He wet his fingertips and, reaching toward the east candle, pinched out the flame. "We live in extraordinary times, Gerard. The dawning millennium glitters with opportunity. Tell me something. Do you believe it's possible for a man to create a religion from scratch?"

"It sounds . . . presumptuous."

"My theothanatopsis patients have convinced me that religion, and only religion, can cure skull-induced despondency. Do you know what Jung said? 'Among my patients of middle age or older, there is not one whose cure did not involve finding a religious outlook on life.' Unfortunately, if my fetch speaks the truth, the coming pestilence will make theothanatopsis syndrome seem like the sniffles. What existing religion can stand against an all-consuming nihilism? Judaism? Catholicism? Not while those eyeless sockets stare at us twenty-four hours a day. If we want to heal the abyss, Gerard, we must fashion a faith unlike anything the West has ever known. The old outlook was monotheistic. *Our* religion will boast a pantheon. The priests of the passing order appealed to an invisible reality. *Our* religion will be corporeal: Somatocism, I call it, from the Greek *soma*, body. In short, I propose a Church of Earthly Affirmation—a joy religion, a sacramental shout, a hooray so reverberant, it will shake God's teeth right out of His jaw."

Gerard picked up a breadstick, dipped it in olive oil, and bit off the end. He chewed. What manner of man was this self-appointed prophet? He seemed some odd amalgam of mystic, egomaniac, genius, and nutcase. There was an otherworldly quality about him, the aura of one privy to secret communiqués in forgotten languages. If the universe was a machine, Lucido knew where to oil it. If it was a Chinese puzzle box, Lucido possessed the solution. If a joke, he got it.

"You've given this matter a lot of thought," said Gerard.

"The instant my fetch showed himself, I began plotting the downfall of his kind." Opening his attaché case, Lucido drew out a phial containing a translucent, icy-blue fluid and plunked it on the table like a grand master making a consummate chess move. "A scientist of my acquaintance has invented a drug, hyperion-15. At the moment there are only four ounces in the world, but by next winter we'll have buckets of the stuff."

"It cures the plague?"

"It affords a remission of several days' duration, long enough for the victim to discover the four affirming energies that lie deep within his psyche. Do these energies have names? Indeed—a simple matter of anagramming atheism's ancient father, Diagoras the Unbeliever, fifth century B.C., to bring forth Idorasag, Risogada, Orgasiad, and Soaragid. Thus do I restore Diagoras to the universe of faith." Lucido wet his fingers, tilted the west candle toward him, and exterminated the flame. "A human soul is thrown from the womb. What does it need? It needs, first of all, to imbibe nourishment from its mother." Puckering his lips, he drew wine into his mouth as if from a breast. "Ergo, our patients worship Idorasag, the world gland, goddess of suckling. Soon afterward, the soul seeks the pleasures of mirth. And so our patients serve Risogada, king of the risible, lord of the jest. Next, reaching sexual maturity, the soul requires erotic fulfillment." He kissed the bowl of his wineglass. "And so our patients make sacrifices to Orgasiad, queen of passion, avatar of copulation. Finally, the soul needs to celebrate itself." Rising from his chair, he broke into an amalgam of polka and jig—for a man of his proportions, he was quite athletic—a display that elicited approving smiles from some restaurant patrons and perplexed frowns from others. "And so our patients pledge their hearts to Soaragid, master of the revels, god of dancing."

Gerard, too, frowned, unable to decide whether Somatocism represented a breakthrough commensurate with the Sermon on the Mount, or a setback comparable to the Cranium Dei.

Caftan flying, Lucido circled the table, then dropped back into his chair. From his attaché case he took a fanfolded map, opening it panel by panel until the Mexican states of Veracruz, Tabasco, and Oaxaca lay before Gerard's eyes.

"Even as we speak, a temple complex is rising along the Bahía de Campeche," said Lucido. "The labyrinth of Idorasag, the hall of Risogada, the grove of Orgasiad, the cave of Soaragid. At the moment each deity lacks both form and visage, which is where *you* come in, Gerard. You must follow me to the Mexican jungle and give the new gods their faces."

Gerard finished his wine. "Wouldn't it be simpler to do all this in, say, the woods of Connecticut?"

"I knew from the outset that the Lucido Clinic must occupy sacred ground. Eventually I decided on the presumed locus of the imperially mysterious Olmec civilization." The psychoanalyst's extended finger glided through the Bahía de Campeche like an enormous sea serpent, then beached itself near the port city of Coatzacoalcos. "A thousand years before the birth of Christ, this forgotten empire flourished along the Gulf coast, ultimately spreading to the foothills of the Sierra Madre Oriental. But Coatzacoalcos attracted me for another reason as well. Do you know how the Cretaceous dinosaurs died?"

Absorbing this supreme non sequitur, Gerard scowled and said, "Something about a comet."

"An asteroid, actually. Sixty-five million years ago, a body the size of Mount Everest arrived from outer space and crashed into the Yucatán peninsula, kicking up so much debris that the Cretaceous climate was altered beyond the dinosaurs' capacity to survive the change. Now. Here's the exciting part. As the asteroid entered Earth's atmosphere, the trailing edge broke off and fell burning toward the hill country south of Coatzacoalcos. In 1999 a maverick geologist, Dr. Isabel Oswald of Penn State University, discovered the remainder of this gigantic fragment. The essence of Oswald's Rock is iridium compounded with a mineral unlike anything previously found on the planet. Dr. Oswald named the stuff reubenite, in honor of her late husband, Reuben Margolis. As it turns out, reubenite is an ideal medium for fashioning graven images, resilient as marble yet immune to fractures, supple under the chisel yet obdurate once the piece is finished."

"Sounds supernatural."

"Merely extraterrestrial." Lucido produced a half-dozen 5″ × 7″ photographs, laying them out like a fortune-teller dealing Tarot cards. Each shot showed an anomalous mass that, judging from the six humans standing on top, was the size of a football stadium. "The dinosaurs' tombstone, you might call it."

"On this rock you will build your church?"

"Precisely. There's enough reubenite here to furnish each temple with a hundred idols at least. Are you game, Gerard? Will you join me on the Isthmus of Tehuantepec and let the new gods reveal themselves to you?"

Gerard licked his left palm and, reaching out, quenched the remaining candle. "Isn't this scheme . . . well . . . a bit grand, Adrian?"

"Oh, it's *more* than grand—it's grandiose, it's arrogant, it's hubris beyond measure. But in willing Himself out of existence, did not God, too, engage in hubris? He has abandoned the field to His inferiors, and I, for one, stand prepared to fill the void."

"My wife won't like the idea of moving to a jungle again. She's grown rather fond of Manhattan."

"Explain to her that the Manhattan she knows and loves is about to be dismantled by demons."

Unsettling images paraded through Gerard's brain, visions of Lucido handing over the reubenite to another godmaker, and suddenly the sculptor wanted to seal the bargain. Even if this man was a thoroughgoing charlatan, he would probably prove a more reliable and respectful patron than the Curia Romana.

Gerard said, "I'll need two assistants."

"Done."

"State-of-the-art facilities."

"Naturally."

"Flexible deadlines."

"Of course."

"One further condition, Adrian. No matter what, I must have an audience. If the deities I create displease your priests or offend your sensibilities, you must exhibit them anyway."

In a devotion seemingly directed toward Orgasiad, Lucido touched thumb to forefinger and eased a breadstick into the orifice. Smiling subtly, he twisted the stick and spoke.

"You have my word."

Not by Bread Alone

As the malicious month of September ran its course, succeeded by an equally cruel October and a sadistic November, Nora took qualified comfort in the fact that Kevin now had company in his suffering. The existential pestilence had arrived in force, sweeping across the industrialized world like a thousand Mongol hordes, thrusting Western civilization into nihilism's icy grip.

It had a name now, plus a symptomatology, a prognosis, and a diagnostic procedure. Dr. Cyrus Armbruster of Johns Hopkins University, the first physician to describe the disease in the professional literature, coined the term "abulic plague"—from *abulia*, meaning "loss of will." The label prospered beyond its initial appearance in *Epidemiology Review*, entering common parlance in a matter of weeks. Dr. Gertrude Luckenbach of the Salk Institute discovered a heretofore unknown antigen in the bloodstreams of abulia-infected individuals, a protein she dubbed "Nietzsche-A" in the *Proceedings of the Mayo Clinic*. Thanks to Luckenbach's insight and a concomitant fluorescent antibody test, doctors could now identify "true abulics," as opposed to the terrified multitudes who merely *imagined* they'd seen their deaths. Dr. Nalin Chatterjee of the National Centers for Disease Control, writing in the *New England Journal of Medicine*, argued for distinguishing Nietzsche-positive patients from those who'd progressed to "thanocathexis," the phase during which a fetch periodically took up residence in its host. Thanocathexis itself comprised four stages, the initial chills and vomiting leading to a near-comatose state of aphasic quadriplegia, after which came abscesses, then a web of pocks and fistulas. The Nietzsche-positive, thanocathected abulia victim was regarded as terminal, though a small percentage of these patients, Kevin Burkhart among them, clung to life.

For those thousands of Americans and Europeans in the crepuscular condition of having met their fetches without experiencing thexis, such encounters across the death barrier became prime topics of conversation. This sociological phenomenon impressed itself on Nora during the dinner party that her bachelor employer, the endlessly amiable Ray Feldstein, threw for himself in honor of his decision to sell the Tower of Flowers and retire.

It was a swank affair, lit by candles and facilitated by caterers, though like many swank affairs of late, it occurred in the valley of the shadow of death. Released by the various wines—Spanish, French, German, and Italian vintages in vertiginous rotation—the fetch stories poured forth, increasing in length and complexity after Nora announced that none need sanitize their narratives for her sake.

"I met mine during the Superbowl," said Dick Aronson, the mechanic who kept Phaëthon on the road. "I'm watching the game—right?—and suddenly there's this shriveled old guy beside me on the sofa, wearing my face. The *Newsweek* story's just appeared, so I know who it is. I try acting calm. 'I'm rooting for Dallas,' I tell him. 'How about you?' Constantine, that's his name, he looks at me, and he says, 'Sometimes with a song, but always with a smile, the bottomless pit beckons.' I figure he's a Steelers fan. The game continues, and I keep hoping to start a conversation, like at halftime, when I say, 'Them cheerleaders sure are built,' but all I get back is 'The pit implodes, sucking us to oblivion's core.' Finally things get hot, twenty-one seconds left, fourth and goal from the six. Cowboys score, they win. The huddle breaks. I-formation with two split ends. Long count. The snap.

And suddenly my TV goes kablooey. I say, 'Hey, dammit, did *you* do that?' Constantine says, 'Taking football seriously is pathological.'"

"You think *you've* got a mean one," said Karen Whitcomb, Ray's thin and ethereal married sister. "Two months ago I'm in the Star Market, produce section, squeezing the cantaloupes. Suddenly there's a woman standing alongside me. Naturally I assume she's choosing a melon, but then I notice she's got no head on her shoulders. She's holding it in her hands, and it's *my* head, and the thing's *talking* to me. 'Kafka put it well,' says the head. 'The meaning of life is that it ends.' I got so scared, I bolted and kept on running and running. I had to send Lloyd back for the car."

"Mine's even worse," said Ruthie Dart, Nora's coworker. "It's late at night, and I'm at the automatic teller, making a withdrawal, four twenties and a ten. A voice behind me says, 'I'll take that,' so I turn around, holding the cash, and of course it's my Sophie. 'What do *you* want with money?' I ask. 'The abyss needs aluminum siding,' she says, and then the whole ninety bucks goes flying out of my hands and bursts into flames."

"They aren't always nasty," said Milton Stritch, the brawny director of the West Somerville Funeral Home and undeniably the shop's best customer. "Mine recommended a therapist to me, Lionel Ginsberg in Newton, and I couldn't be more pleased. I've been through a lot of personal growth lately."

"Mine told me where to get my hair done," said Joyce Chumly, Ray's next-door neighbor.

"Mine added a deck to the house," said Harold Feldstein, Ray's brother as well as Nora's gynecologist.

"You've got to be careful," said Avery Bloch, the FTD sales rep. "Last Thursday, mine offered to mow the lawn. He mowed it, all right—straight down to the dirt, and then he kept on going. My yard looks like Flanders field after World War I."

Nora, angry, took three quick swallows of Chardonnay. She liked her present companions, but she found their banter outrageous. It was obscene to be spinning after-dinner anecdotes from humankind's incipient extinction, as if the levelers were no more than a bunch of annoying relatives—dithery Aunt Agatha who knitted during your wedding, forgetful Uncle Willie who gave you a crystal punch bowl every Christmas.

"I have a confession," said Derrick Lane, the lantern-jawed, garrulous accountant who did Ray's taxes each year. An open homophile, Derrick had always impressed Nora as having assimilated his proclivities with a dignity far surpassing the average heterosexual's accommodation to conventional desire. "Last week, my boss told me to go fuck myself, and I thought, 'That's exactly what I'm doing.'"

"You're not the only one in that situation," said Ray's unmarried sister, Selena. All around the table, eyebrows lifted. Ray spat a Swedish meatball onto his plate. Selena asked Derrick, "What's it like for you?"

"Ambiguous," the accountant replied. "We understand each other's physical desires, but Roderick is cold to the touch, and he never wants to talk afterward."

"I've got the same problem with Veronica," said Selena.

"Selena—," muttered Ray.

"Later," said Selena.

"These stories are all fascinating, but I have a question," said Milton Stritch. "Are the fetches merely here to torment us, or do we have something they need?"

"What could a fetch possibly *need*?" asked Avery Todd.

"Acceptance, perhaps," said Hubert Whitcomb, Ray's diffident brother-in-law. "Have any of us really tried *befriending* our levelers?"

"Don't even *think* about it!" screamed Christine Onsa, a crisp woman in her early seventies who each spring grew day lilies and Siberian irises in her backyard for sale to the Tower of Flowers. "They're *not* our friends!" The source of Christine's distress was common knowledge. Her granddaughter, a beautiful young concert pianist of Carnegie Hall caliber, had lain in a state of stage-three thexis for nearly a year. "They'll never be our friends!"

"I'm sorry," said Hubert, chagrined.

Christine had it exactly right, Nora felt. But because the levelers were evil, did it follow that they were invincible? Like Thetis dipping Achilles into the Styx and neglecting to inoculate his heel, had the Angel of Death unintentionally cursed his minions with some secret vulnerability?

When she picked up Kevin later that night, she asked her brother, "Do you believe they're invincible?"

The boy lay slumped in his wheelchair, boils oozing.

She knew what Douglas's answer would be. In his view, abulia was simply the most recent visitation from the repertoire of plagues that God (the true, invisible God, not the Cinecittà bone pile or the skyborne death's-head) stood ready to inflict on sinners, a series that in biblical times had ranged from the hemorrhoids that punished the Philistines for appropriating the Ark, to the pestilence deployed against David for numbering the people, to the contagion that destroyed Sennacherib's army before it could capture Jerusalem.

"Fight them?" he said. "Bad idea. We must submit to the fetches or risk an even greater wrath. What about you, Nora? Do you think they're invincible?"

"My rational side says we're licked," she replied, wheeling Kevin toward Phaëthon. "And I beseech myself, in the bowels of Christ, to think it possible I may be mistaken."

It was inevitable, Nora realized in retrospect, that the United States government would attempt a technological solution to nihilism. For over half a century, Americans had reflexively deployed mechanical ingenuity against the fact of death. Better respirators. Superior pacemakers. If all else failed: cryonic suspension. As the appalling year 2005 unfolded, the Pentagon set its sights on a new enemy, abulia, and the Joint Chiefs wouldn't rest until they'd blown the Cranium Dei to bits.

Although Nora was doubtful that they could bring God down, she decided to watch the TV coverage anyway. Ruthie Dart came over for the broadcast, toting a bag of pretzels and a six-pack of Saranac. The women sat on the couch, feet on the coffee table, Kevin dozing beside them in his wheelchair. CNN, PBS, and the entertainment networks all carried the historic event live. The women ultimately chose ABC, reasoning that any organization so adept at presenting professional sports would also do right by Armageddon.

According to the commentator, the eternally chipper Ronald Glass, the strategists had never seriously considered atomic weapons. The thermonuclear option had prospered in the Pentagon for only two days. A sky clogged with radioactive waste, the particles sifting down to Earth and poisoning the biosphere, was not demonstrably preferable to a sky dominated by a Cranium Dei.

The attack would consist of a dozen guided missiles, each bearing ten independently targetable warheads, the salvos to occur at seven-minute intervals from a Polaris submarine cruising off Cape Cod. An uncommon patriotic thrill overcame Nora as the first missile arced heavenward, ejected its booster, shed its second stage, and spewed out its warheads. Forty-five seconds later, the bombs struck the sacred skull just below the WINDOWS 2005 advertisement (Microsoft being His present tenant) and exploded in perfect synchronization—a direct hit, according to ABC's array of orbiting cameras. A huge red fireball blossomed on God's bony brow like a physician's headband mirror catching the sun.

"Touchdown!" shouted Ronald Glass.

"Hooray!" screamed Ruthie.

"Way to go, Navy!" cried an elated Nora.

But God was a mighty fortress. Whatever the components of His forehead, they would not succumb to TNT. When the smoke cleared and the debris dissipated, the cameras disclosed, in Ronald's words, "not a scratch."

The rest of the strike proved equally impotent. Ten more payloads hit home; ten more ineffectual explosions filled Nora's TV screen. Skewed by a minor navigation error, the twelfth and final salvo made for the divine jaws. The warhead cluster struck His mouth squarely, lodging between His left canine and the corresponding bicuspid, as if the US Navy were currently running a dental practice, but the subsequent blasts failed to dislodge either tooth.

"Shit," said Nora.

"Let's have another beer," said Ruthie.

As it turned out, the Navy's unsuccessful assault marked the end of systematic human resistance to the plague. After that fateful April night, the levelers' toll increased logarithmically. Each day fifty thousand new victims tested Nietzsche-positive, while another fifty thousand suffered penetration by their fetches. Stunned by death awareness, paralyzed by stage-two thexis, Western civilization stopped functioning. Laborers, clerks, technicians, bureaucrats, politicians, executives—no level of society enjoyed a respite from the wraiths.

With Sophoclean inexorability, the American infrastructure unraveled. The first losses were subtle. Here and there, a radio station went off the air. Advertisements ceased appearing on God's brow. Supermarkets stopped offering frozen vegetables. Service stations no longer stocked spark plugs or motor oil. Drugstore inventories declined, with laxatives, tampons, suntan lotion, dandruff shampoo, and mouthwash vanishing altogether. Worse followed. Public transportation became a thing of the past, from the fanciest jetliner to the humblest crosstown bus. Shoes became as rare as four-leaf clovers, toilet paper as scarce as Mark McGwire's rookie card. Gasoline disappeared. Credit cards yielded to currency. The Internet died in gibberish, the Web in abstract expressionism. So many professional athletes had been thected that the NBA Championships and the World Series were both canceled. Power plants, telephone companies, and fuel-oil distributors suspended their services. Huddled amid flickering candles in naked kitchens, New Englanders cast a worried eye on the calendar, toward a winter bearing down on them like a Fifth Horseman of the Apocalypse, a rider with Freon in his arteries and an icicle hanging from each nostril.

Then the deaths began. Throughout the West, Homo sapiens staggered beneath the twin burdens of bereavement and interment.

Whenever Nora stepped outside, she saw that the Sanitation Department's newly formed Pallbearers Corps had resorted to yet another disposal method. Fresh Pond was now a mass grave, its macabre contents dissolving beneath a frosting of quicklime. Dead abulics clogged the Charles River like an immense beaver dam. Decaying corpses so totally obscured Cambridge Common that a film director in possession of a gantry, a 35mm camera, and Vivien Leigh would have had no difficulty replicating the famous railroad-yard crane shot from *Gone with the Wind.*

In every affected city, from Honolulu to Kiev, Saskatoon to Buenos Aires, mere animal survival became the rule. Neither time nor energy existed for burying the dead, reviling the fetches, or rebuilding the world. Starvation ruled like a psychotic king, its toll enhanced by the cruel fact that anyone foolish enough to devour an abulic's remains invariably succumbed to the plague in a matter of days. The needle of humanity's moral compass spun crazily and then fell off the dial. Altruism went the way of trilobites. Compassion imploded. On a bad day, you lay abed, vibrating with hunger and despair. On a good day, you looted your neighbor's vegetable patch, plundered his pantry, and shot his dog, consuming the feast that followed with an ambivalence unworthy to be called guilt.

Rumors buzzed about the dying civilization like the flies who stood to inherit it. Researchers in Paris had discovered a cure. No, the Paris team could merely forestall stage four, while the cure lay in Rotterdam. London held the antidote. San Diego. For whatever reasons, Portugal had proven immune to the plague. Let us flee to Lisbon. No, Portugal had an unusually high death rate, but Switzerland was exempt. Somehow we must get to Geneva. Throughout the Balkan peninsula, Dionysian anarchy had taken hold (eat, drink, and make merry, for tomorrow our levelers claim us). These tales of sybaritic rites were true, but the bacchanals were limited to Albania. Greece, actually.

For Nora Burkhart, one piece of hearsay towered above the others, a shining possibility into which she poured the shredded remnants of her faith. She wasn't sure why she'd elected to pin her hopes on this particular story. It was more complex than the competing rumors, but that hardly made it more plausible.

Somewhere in the jungles rimming the Gulf coast of Mexico, beyond the harbor town of Coatzacoalcos, a unique scientific-religious institution had arisen. At the Lucido Clinic, thected abulics learned a mental discipline called Somatocism, subsequently cleansing their psyches of death awareness. A plague family could get its stricken loved one into the Somatocist temples only if they arrived bearing a valuable donation, something that would please the clinic's medical director, Dr. Adrian Lucido. Diesel fuel almost always gained a victim admittance. So did vintage wines, exotic foods, precious gems, priceless art, and fancy clothes.

"I'm going to Mexico," she told Douglas, "and I'm taking Kevin with me."

"Coatzacoalcos is three thousand miles away," he said. "How will you get there? Skateboard?"

"Phaëthon."

"There's no gasoline."

"I'll steal some."

"What'll you eat?"

"I've been stockpiling groceries."

"You'll run out."

"Then I'll drive on an empty stomach."

"Brigands will attack you."

"I'll fight them off."

"You need to bring Lucido a gift."

"I'll find one along the way."

Nora realized that in her Lutheran brother's eyes, her obsession with the Lucido Clinic bordered on blasphemy. But wasn't blasphemy—raw, bleeding, irredeemable blasphemy—the precise attitude she owed her son?

"No argument I might make will convince you to change your mind," said Douglas.

"Quite true," she said.

"No amount of begging."

"None."

"Godspeed, Sister."

"God's speed is nine hundred miles per hour, same as the Earth's. Now help me score some gasoline, okay?"

If Gerard Korty had foreseen the psychic risks intrinsic to his new life in Mexico, the addictive and unholy rush of godmaking, he would have pledged himself to Lucido's service with far less alacrity. It was mind-bending and soul-warping, this business of providing Somatocism with a pantheon. It could make a sculptor oblivious to his mortality—make him forget that his veins flowed not with ichor but with simple blood.

While Gerard knew that he himself lacked divinity, he wondered whether his patron was likewise prepared to abjure godhood. Perched on the side of Mount Tapílula, Lucido's headquarters—a many-towered mansion from which the Veracruz governor, now dead of the plague, had once issued his fiats—placed the psychoanalyst in the same relation to Coatzacoalcos that the Cranium Dei enjoyed to planet Earth. Brooding in his private apartments day after day, the surrounding chambers jammed with sycophantic functionaries laying the groundwork of the new religion and dispossessed clerics seeking to administer it, Lucido courted solipsism at best and monomania at worst. He confined his interactions with Gerard to one hour on Sunday afternoons, each meeting typically consumed by Lucido taking up a loaded syringe, injecting himself with a "subtherapeutic" dose of hyperion-15, and then railing against the mechanistic monster that American psychiatrists, with their transfixion by science and unjustified hostility toward metaphysics, had allowed depth psychology to become.

At first Fiona had resisted the idea of moving to the Isthmus of Tehuantepec. She'd finally found a publisher for her novel, *Lost and*

Found, a small Arizona firm specializing in "cookbooks for incorporeal nourishment," and felt reluctant to leave the country when she could be doing readings at New Age emporia. While the advance was only $1,500, the company's president had argued persuasively that it was better to reign at Synergy Press than to serve at Random House. But then, three months after Gerard's return from Rome, while buying tofu at a bodega on 82nd Street, Fiona met her second self. In the leveler's informed opinion, Synergy Press was as doomed as the rest of Western civilization; *Lost and Found* would probably never see print. The longer her fetch prophesied, the more discouraged Fiona became, until eventually she saw that her best course lay in helping her husband launch the Church of Earthly Affirmation.

The privileges of Gerard's rank were many. His cup ran over with coffee from Chiapas, mescal from Oaxaca, and Carta Blanca beer from the town. True to his word, Lucido had secured ideal sculpting facilities, an outdoor studio surrounded by a stockade fence and equipped with scaffolding, derrick, winch, workbench, and grindstone, plus a convertible vinyl roof that Gerard and Fiona could roll into place at the first intimation of rain. The promised assistants also materialized, two sturdy brothers named Pelayo and Fulgencio Ruíz, baptized but nonbelieving Catholics into whose brains the nuns of Veracruz had poured European educations. Unspeakably honored to be serving the Korty Madonna's creator, Pelayo and Fulgencio pursued their duties (cleaning the studio, sharpening the chisels, preparing the blocks, chauffeuring Gerard in his pony cart) with a devotion bordering on adulation. They were artists in their own right—"post-surrealists" who gloried in the fact that their "spiritual mentor," the great Diego Rivera, had once lived on the Isthmus of Tehuantepec—and Gerard quickly realized that their powerful paintings of burning jaguars and psychedelic macaws, while freighted with superfluities and crude in technique, had forever blurred for him the distinction between the primitive and the primal.

Adjacent to the studio lay Gerard and Fiona's domicile, an abandoned trading post set on a bluff above the Rio Uspanapa, which flowed all the way from Presa Netzahualcóyotl, past the temple complex of Tamoanchan, and on through Coatzacoalcos before emptying into the Bahía de Campeche. The front yard offered a spectacular view of Mount Catemaco, an active but unambitious volcano marking the southern tip of the pine-covered Sierra Madre Oriental. Enchanted by the golden-fruited banana plants dotting the grounds, Fiona had named their home El Dorado, and it was a hacienda so spacious that they ended up dedicating half the rooms to impractical pursuits—to watching sunsets, making love, and reading Emily Dickinson.

A one-hour hike through the jungle west of El Dorado brought Gerard to the brick-red extraterrestrial mass called Oswald's Rock. Reubenite was everything Lucido had promised, the greatest medium since Makrana marble: sufficiently fine-grained to permit detailed modeling yet durable enough to withstand lashing rains and scouring winds. The mineral possessed another quality as well, a quality that he and Fiona unabashedly called *numinous.* Standing before a newborn reubenite god, they felt themselves in the presence of something that partook equally of stone and spirit, matter and magic. If he'd made his *Paradiso* statues from reubenite, Gerard decided, the Vatican would have bought them without debate, regardless of the price.

For the newly arrived Americans, the plague's impact was thus far minimal. The local shops no longer offered cigarettes, but Gerard and Fiona had both quit smoking years ago. Ballpoint pens and writing paper had disappeared, and so Fiona was obliged to compose her second novel in pencil on business envelopes. Condoms, razor blades, toothpaste, aspirin—all gone.

But the most crucial of the scarce commodities was fossil fuel. While a handful of the generators powering the temple complex ran on energy from the omnipresent Mexican sun, the majority consumed gasoline, a substance in fearsomely short supply now that abulia had stolen the wills of 780,490 refinery workers throughout the Western world. Unless the expected waves of pilgrims arrived bearing large quantities of diesel oil, Lucido would have to start rationing electricity, that precious force by which he and his staff enjoyed refrigerated food, incandescent lighting, and home video.

One could hardly imagine a more impressive field on which to fight eschatological battles than Tamoanchan. Through systematic research Lucido had determined that the ancient Aztecs had borrowed the strange word from an archaic form of the Maya language. For the Aztecs, *Tamoanchan* evidently indicated a fabulous, golden, vanished civilization to the east—quite possibly the mysterious Olmec empire. And yet, despite their beauty and grandeur, the labyrinth of Idorasag, the palace of Risogada, the grove of Orgasiad, and the cave of Soaragid had all failed to provide Gerard with the inspiration he required. Not since the terrible years of artistic impotence that drove him finally to Indonesia had he found himself so completely blocked.

He was on the point of declaring himself the wrong man to actualize the Somatocist pantheon, when the Ruíz brothers came to him with an idea. Like Moses, they argued, the sculptor might best connect with the cosmos by entering a wilderness. To Gerard it sounded plausible, and so the next day the three men ventured out under the midday skull—El Cráneo, the locals called it—first driving Gerard's pony cart to the barren, blasted foothills of the Sierra Madre Oriental, then hiking through the ash fields, and finally starting up the southern slope of the Volcán de Catemaco. Experienced hikers, Pelayo and Fulgencio whistled merrily throughout the ascent. Gerard wished they would speak instead, encouraging him the way Virgil had encouraged Dante during the difficult climb from Ante-Purgatory's first terrace, abode of the excommunicated, to its second terrace, repository of the late repentant.

His words so spurred me that I forced myself
To follow him with desperate scrambling feet
And crawl and strain until I'd gained the ledge.

Both he and I then sat upon the rim
And faced the east, the way from which we'd come,
For looking back will give a traveler joy.

It took them three hours to get from the base of Catemaco to the inner crater, where an immense lake of lava seethed and steamed like metals mingling in an alchemist's retort. After strapping on their war-surplus gas masks—a necessity, given Catemaco's noxious vapors—the three men stared into the bubbling broth, trolling for enlightenment.

Fulgencio found the cat-god first.

"There! Do you see it?"

"No," said Gerard.

"Half man, half jaguar!"

"Where?"

"There! There!"

At last Gerard saw the shape-shifter, a smiling feline head surmounting a humanoid trunk that rippled with muscles.

During the glory days of the Olmec civilization, Fulgencio explained, every community harbored its own divine werejaguar. A shape-shifter's identity, however, was unknown to the villagers themselves, so that the average native lived his whole life in reference to a mystery: Who is it? My uncle? My neighbor? My best friend? Eventually the werejaguar would disclose himself to the most beautiful wife in the village, and one night woman and beast would go off together and couple beneath the full moon. A conception always occurred. His destiny fulfilled, the werejaguar soon transmuted, his feral half claiming him as he disappeared forever into the rain forest. The god-touched woman would meanwhile return to her hut, wake her husband, and arouse him, her true intentions readable only in the faint trace of a smile on her lips.

Gerard beheld the god and gasped. He shivered with epiphany. This was Soaragid, master of the revels, avatar of celebration. Taking out his sketch pad, he set about capturing the manifestation before it returned to geologic chaos. By sundown he was back in his studio, sweating profusely and singing "Amazing Grace" as he drove his C3 cleaving chisel into the ten-ton reubenite block where the deity lay imprisoned.

"I couldn't be more delighted," said Lucido at the start of their regular Sunday-afternoon encounter.

"I'm rather pleased myself," said Gerard.

Lucido had insisted on their meeting in the private aviary adjoining his Mount Tapílula mansion: a thoroughly unpleasant place, in Gerard's view—hot, stifling, and reeking of parrot droppings. Twice the height of a human being, the werejaguar stood midway between their fan-back wicker chairs, Pelayo and Fulgencio having trucked it up Calle Huimanguillo to the aviary that morning. El Cráneo imparted a buttery sheen to Soaragid's coral flesh. Rising, Lucido ran his fingers along the biceps and massaged the firm stomach.

"Listen, all you *demonios.*" He lifted his eyes skyward and spoke in a gritty whisper. "Your reign is ending. The Somatocist pantheon has come to Earth!"

Gerard contemplated the idol. The eyes weren't right: the next time, he would provide a predatory gleam. "And did you frighten the *demonios*, Adrian?" he asked in a mildly chiding tone.

"I hear skepticism. Good." Lucido settled into his chair and removed a panatela from a teakwood humidor. "What you must understand, Gerard, is that in metaphysics a phenomenon needn't be empirical to be true. By believing in the new gods, our acolytes will bring them into nonrational reality. You're not convinced."

A rainbow-hued parrot sailed across the aviary and landed atop Soaragid's head. "When people believed in the Judeo-Christian monogod," said Gerard, "that didn't keep them from getting sick. Faith is therapeutic, no question, but only up to a point."

"You're forgetting that abulia is not, at base, a physical illness. Its locus is the soul, the domain to which our pantheon is so finely attuned. You're still not convinced."

"I'm still not convinced."

Lucido flicked his butane lighter and ignited his cigar. He blew a smoke ring, the carbon halo drifting toward his brow and disintegrating above his head. "Don't get stuck in obsolete categories, Gerard. Live in your own time. It's the only era you can truly occupy."

Over the next three months the remaining deities arrived, first in molten lava, then in solid reubenite, each conjoining the beautiful with the bizarre. Orgasiad, queen of passion, adapted from an Olmec serpent-goddess, featured a sensual reptilian face—smiling mouth, double eyelids, crescent pupils—set atop a female torso that in turn surmounted a spiral of scaly coils. Risogada, lord of the jest, a variation on an aboriginal crocodile-god, was playfully but not inaccurately described by Fiona as "an ambulatory grin." Idorasag, mistress of milk, derived from an indigenous ape-goddess, suggested what might have resulted if King Kong had somehow consummated his lust for Fay Wray.

Among Lucido's many entrenched opinions was his view that Somatocism would succeed only if its temples "positively dripped with deities." Thus did the spring of 2005 become the most productive period of Gerard's entire career. Each time his workshop yielded another affirmation god, he sent word to Hubbard Richter, Somatocism's chief deacon, whereupon the sour and unimaginative bureaucrat would arrive with several assistants and haul the idol away. For reasons that defied Gerard's comprehension, Richter fancied himself an art critic, and the chief deacon rarely took an idol into his keeping without commentary. "A god of laughter should smile, yes, but this is the grin of a psychotic," he remarked after receiving the third Risogada. "You were too generous with her breasts," he said while packing up the newest Orgasiad. "She lives in a grove, not a bordello."

Lured by rumors, impelled by desperation, plague victims began filtering into Coatzacoalcos during the last week of June, each family offering horrific testimony to the collapse of those manifold enterprises—colleges, museums, churches, laboratories, factories, shopping malls—that had once constituted Western culture. Prior to this mass immigration, the Coatzacoalcos natives had greeted Lucido's project enthusiastically, the skilled laborers receiving fair wages for building Tamoanchan, the artistically inclined enjoying ample rewards for fashioning robes, ciboria, and other temple accoutrements. In a matter of days the city became a refugee camp—plague families from the American Southwest swarmed everywhere, draining the food supplies and straining the sanitation facilities—and suddenly the locals wanted no part of Somatocism. Many fled to Chiapas and Campeche, seeking to live off the rain forest's dwindling game and the bay's remaining bounty rather than risk the typhus and cholera that were certain to arrive as Coatzacoalcos turned into a necropolis.

"Our sisters just took off for Ciudad del Carmen," Pelayo informed Gerard and Fiona. He strode across the outdoor studio, put on his protective goggles, and pressed a cleaving chisel against the spinning grindstone. A spray of sparks arced away like the trail of a skyrocket.

"If the fish don't bite, they'll try Isla de Aguada, then Champotón," said Fulgencio, daubing ochre pigment on an Idorasag's comforting eyes.

Fiona slapped an Orgasiad's coils with her paintbrush, giving the deity golden scales. "*You're* not leaving, are you?" she asked Fulgencio.

"A clash is coming, *un encuentro estupendo*, abulia versus the new gods. What true artist would miss an event like that?"

Grasping his carving hammer, Gerard ascended the scaffolding, pulled a bushing chisel from his safari jacket, and began bestowing a snout on a Risogada. "I want your honest opinion. Do you think we're going to win?"

"Hard to say," said Fiona.

"Difficult question," said Fulgencio.

"One thing I do know, Señor Gerardo." Pelayo slowed the grindstone and removed his goggles. "The Olmec gods are as jealous as Jehovah—and every bit as fierce."

"They don't like rivals?" said Gerard.

"Rivals make them furious," said Pelayo.

Fiona set down her brush and smiled. "Especially, I should imagine, when those rivals wear stolen faces."

On first hearing Nora's plan to plunder Arborway Cemetery, her brother rejected it as sacrilegious and illegal, but when the night of the foray arrived—a sweltering July evening alive with cicadas and crickets—he went along anyway. The main gate was padlocked, so they had to heave their wheelbarrow and tools over the wrought-iron fence, then scale it using the scrollwork for footholds. Reaching the top, Nora apprehensively surveyed the metal pickets, reminiscent of the arrows that Eric had used in "The Martyrdom of Sebastian," his grisliest trick. She steeled herself, thinking of her left knee, which had knitted improperly after a tenth-grade lacrosse accident. At last she jumped—and was fortunate to fall, along with Douglas, into the embrace of a barberry bush.

Scrambling to their feet, they collected their tools, dropped them into the barrow, and started across the graveyard.

"We shouldn't be doing this," Douglas whispered.

"Who's watching us?" she replied, countering the pain in her knee by tightening her grip on the barrow handles. "Santa Claus? The Tooth Fairy? God?"

"God is watching us, yes."

"In school I learned that eyeballs are among the minimum requirements for vision."

"When you look at the Cranium Dei, Nora, you see God's face. When I behold it, I see Satan's mask."

With abulia's ascent, the art of gravedigging had fallen into amateur hands, and Arborway Cemetery was now an unsightly mass of pits and heaps, like a prairie-dog town built by insane prairie dogs. Wandering amid the maze, Nora noticed that many of the plague victims were only partially buried, their black and rigid limbs jutting grotesquely into the air. Finally she reached Dexter Gansevoort's resting place, with its exquisite Korty Madonna cradling a sickly marble Jesus. A bouquet of gardenias leaned against the elaborate monument—nothing like the floral cornucopia Nora had delivered almost three years earlier, but impressive by plague-era standards.

They set to work. Nora dug furiously, undaunted by her exhaustion, hunger, and knee pains. Douglas, too, threw himself into the task, and by 11:00 P.M. a third of the buried Cadillac Catera lay exposed to the foul summer air. Through brute luck they'd chosen the gas-cap side. Their good fortune got Douglas humming. Nora giggled like a teenager. Collapsing against the cool dirt wall, they put down their spades, gathered their strength, and listened to the low, hoarse sound of poplar branches scraping granite mausoleums.

"I thought he'd smell," said Douglas.

"The windows are rolled up," Nora explained, rubbing her sore knee.

Predictably, the gas cap was locked, but they'd come prepared. Nora held the flashlight while Douglas wielded the hammer and chisel. Seven blows, and the fuel tank was theirs. Eagerly they inserted the rubber tube and switched on the Siemens siphon, powered by four C batteries from Kevin's toy robot. When the first ounces spurted into the milk jug, brother and sister cheered in unison. The gasoline kept coming, and within five minutes they had successfully pirated an entire gallon.

As the night deepened, they repeated the procedure, again and again, until nine jugs of Gansevoort high-test sat along the edge of the hole like severed heads ringing a chopping block. The graverobbers were filling jug number ten when a male voice exploded from the darkness.

"Hold it right there!"

Nora directed the flashlight beam toward the intruder. A young man, stripped to the waist and skinny as a whippet's fetch, stood on the far edge of the pit, gripping a revolver. His smile, like God's, was scornful.

"Guess you had the same idea as me," said the young man. "These rich people, they can afford the really good embalmers. The best-preserved meat in Massachusetts." His face suddenly contorted, a caricature of astonishment. "Hey—you're Mrs. Burkhart. I had you for ninth-grade English. Remember me? Curtis Padula?"

"I remember you," said Nora, climbing out of the grave. Though not fondly, she was tempted to add. Curtis had been one of those semiliterate slouch masters who read *Strumpet* magazine under his desk and fell asleep in class. "Stop pointing that gun at me, Curtis."

"Mrs. Burkhart, wow, I never imagined meeting *you* here."

For Nora it was a familiar phenomenon: the student who was amazed to discover that his teachers had lives outside the classroom.

"The gun, Curtis."

The revolver remained frozen. Cradling the Siemens siphon, Douglas exited the hole and joined his sister on the grass.

"You don't need that," said Curtis, indicating the siphon. "I've done experiments. Hang the corpse upside down from a road sign, slit the throat, and the formaldehyde runs out like sap from a maple tree."

"Like sap from a maple tree," echoed Nora. "An impressive simile, Curtis. What did I give you?"

"A fucking C minus."

"You could've earned a B." Cautiously she began loading the milk jugs into the wheelbarrow. "Did anything from our Greek mythology unit stay with you?"

" 'Fraid not."

"Nothing at all?"

"I remember Zeus had a really busy pecker." Keeping his gun trained alternately on Nora and Douglas, Curtis approached the monument and leaned against the Korty Madonna's hip. "Your husband?"

"Brother. What about Jason and the Golden Fleece? Icarus and Daedalus?"

"Go home, Mrs. Burkhart. These burgers belong to me."

"We came for the gasoline."

"The *gasoline*? Maybe you didn't hear, but the world has ended. There's no place worth visiting anymore."

"Put your gun down, Curtis," she said firmly. "I mean it."

Evidently she'd hit the right note, for Curtis now engaged in the atavistic action of obeying his former teacher, slipping the pistol into his pants pocket.

"You're probably disappointed in me," he said.

"I admire your initiative," she said.

Throughout the rest of the week, Nora and Douglas pursued their careers as gasoline ghouls, exhuming a different Gansevoort each evening and plundering the coffin: motorcycle, speedboat, private plane, stock car. By midnight on Friday they'd stolen the last of the lot, for a total of fifty-two gallons. Assuming she drove Phaëthon slowly and efficiently, she had enough gasoline to reach the Texas-Louisiana border.

"And *then* what?" asked Douglas, siphoning the final ounce of Gansevoort high-test.

"I'll commandeer a horse and buggy," said Nora.

"I don't know where you get your ambition, Sis. Mom didn't have any. Dad neither."

"Heredity is not destiny."

"Martin Luther would agree with you there. We're all born equally depraved, regardless of chromosomes." He set the jug inside the barrow and groaned. "I want you to promise me something. That thing Curtis Padula has been doing—you'd never resort to that, would you?"

"'Better sleep with a sober cannibal than a drunken Christian.' Herman Melville."

"You've got a quote for everything," said Douglas. "It's going to be the death of you."

PART TWO

Gilgamesh in Greensboro

The God's Ear Brigade

NORA HADN'T DRIVEN the Mass Pike since 1994, when she and a select group of her ninth graders went to see Diana Rigg play Medea at the Longacre Theater on Broadway. Except for Wendy Katzenbaum and a few other teacher's pets, the students had reacted doltishly to Euripides' tragedy, finding it boring and pointless. But Nora was shaken to the core. Killing your own children to spite their philandering father... to Nora it was unthinkable, and yet two weeks after seeing *Medea*, she'd learned that her divorced friend Elyse Phillips had seriously contemplated this very crime, and the following year an Arkansas woman had captured headlines by going through with it. Abominable fantasies of revenge, Nora had concluded at the time, were probably more common than most people cared to admit.

Seagulls wheeled across the ubiquitous skull, looking for dead abulics not yet picked over by the buzzards and crows.

Maybe she'd made a mistake in taking only her smartest students to *Medea*. Perhaps a future cannibal like Curtis Padula would have better grasped its essence. Dining on the Gansevoorts each night, he had probably, like Medea, concluded that a life lived in extremis was better than one of inertia and resignation. In the end Curtis, too, would doubtless feed on gall and wormwood, but at least he'd said no to the Fates.

Nora owned the turnpike. The concrete stretched nakedly before her, mile after mile. The impulse to speed was strong, but her circumstances argued against it. Phaëthon was a traveling bomb, the cargo bay loaded with forty gallons of Gansevoort premium confined by HDPE recyclable plastic. Complementing this cache were thirteen additional milk jugs, still empty despite her recent raids on a dozen derelict cars in Cambridge—but she refused to regard that failure as ominous. Surely some unguarded gasoline lay between Massachusetts and Texas, free for the stealing.

Kevin lay in the cargo bay, sprawled across a Posturpedic mattress and guarded by his old stuffed monkey, Rodney, central to a trick called "Tarzan and the Witch Doctor." With the arrival of the boils, he'd become too flaccid for the wheelchair, but she'd brought it along in case his recovery included a temporary return to stage two. Besides placing his mattress as far from the gasoline jugs as possible, she'd surrounded him with plastic pots of hyacinths. The hydrocarbon stench prevailed, but that hardly mattered: he seemed oblivious to olfactory data these days, along with visual, auditory, and tactile data. Only the subtle rising and falling of his chest differentiated him from those abulics whose fetches had consummated the relationship.

Reaching her exit, Sturbridge, Nora enjoyed the trivial thrill of cruising through the tollbooth without paying, snapping off the crossing gate like the lead runner breaking the tape at the Boston Marathon. As she headed south along Interstate 84, a thundershower broke, sheets of rain cascading out of the macabre sky. She turned on the wipers. The surrounding funeral pyres blazed through the storm like signal beacons, their flames writhing and guttering beneath the squalls. Nora knew that the roasting corpses stank, but between the ghastly familiarity of that aroma and the gas fumes filling the cab, the sensation barely registered. In a peculiar way she drew comfort from the pyres, a rational public-health measure undertaken by a civilization otherwise in chaos.

Normally a motor trip from Boston to Manhattan would last only four hours, with Nora reaching the George Washington Bridge well before 2:00 P.M., but normalcy had long since succumbed to abulia.

A mile outside Hartford, she pulled over preparatory to the lengthy business of feeding Kevin his lunch, dressing his pustules, and exercising his limbs. As the rain slackened, she dumped some uncooked macaroni into a saucepan of water and set it on her Sterno stove. While the macaroni softened, she changed her son's diaper. His stool was bilious, the color and consistency of guacamole. During her first months of motherhood, Nora had vaguely enjoyed diapering Kevin—it was earthy, reassuring, and imparted a certain order to the universe—but now she could extract no pleasure from the process.

She fed him, attended his boils, and had just begun his physical therapy when the rear doors swung back, releasing a flood of damp gray light into the cargo bay. A young woman stood in the drizzle, wearing a black motorcycle jacket studded with silver nodes, her neck encircled by a long white aviator's scarf that hung down her chest like a tallith. She glared at Nora and spoke, her voice resonant with a confidence that doubtless sprang from the Uzi machine gun balanced on her arm.

"Got anything to eat?"

"Macaroni," said Nora nervously. She was pretty sure Curtis Padula wouldn't have shot her, but she couldn't predict the behavior of this total stranger. "Also beef jerky, raisins, baked beans, and chili."

"I'll take the jerky." Glossy chestnut hair framed the stranger's face, the tresses pasted to her cheeks by the rain.

Nora reached into her picnic basket, removed the plastic-wrapped package of Tillamook Country Smoker, and reluctantly surrendered it.

"Where're you heading?" asked the stranger.

"South."

"How far?"

"Pretty far."

"You're not with the Anglos, are you?"

"Who?"

"My worst enemy. Yours too, maybe. I'm Rachel Sorkin. Your truck says Ray Feldstein, but that probably isn't your name."

"Nora Burkhart."

"Hey, Nora Burkhart, can you give me a lift as far as Jersey?"

"What if I said no?"

"I'd probably shoot you." Tearing open the package of Tillamook Country Smoker, Rachel took out a jerky hunk and chewed it with the zeal of a child devouring a candy bar.

"Come out of the rain. You'll catch"—a smile twisted Nora's lips—"your death."

Rachel snorted, shouldered her gun, and climbed into the cargo bay, her sharp leathery fragrance mingling with the gasoline fumes. "Clever idea you've got here, turning your truck into a hearse." She pointed toward Kevin and the hyacinths. "I didn't know anybody still bothered with funerals. How much're they paying you?"

"This isn't a hearse, and we aren't going to a funeral," said Nora, annoyed. "Our destination is the Lucido Clinic in Mexico."

"Never heard of it."

"My son happens to be alive. The flowers are a deodorizer."

Rachel grimaced. "People say callous things these days. I'm sorry." Her tone was more defensive than apologetic. "Thected, right? My father's fetch entered him last month"—she patted her gun—"so I'm going to Paramus in his place. You got any more beef?"

"There's a war in Paramus?"

"Among other towns. I'm still hungry, sweetie."

"Nora."

As Rachel consumed her second piece of jerky, she explained how the entire metropolitan New York area was presently convulsed by civil strife. The Greater Manhattan B'nai B'rith had dispatched heralds to the farthest reaches of Connecticut and New Jersey proclaiming that all decent people, regardless of ethnic or religious heritage, should arm themselves and come fight the good fight. Rachel intended to enlist in the Army of Northern New Jersey, whose commanders were committed to engaging and defeating the Anglo-Saxon Christian Brotherhood, currently inflicting pogroms on Jewish communities throughout the northeast.

"Look, I'm sympathetic to your cause," said Nora. "I'm half Jewish myself. But I can't get involved in a war right now."

"Nobody's asking you to get *involved*," said Rachel. "Just drive me to Paramus."

"One stray bullet could turn this truck into a fireball."

"Drop me off in Emerson, and I'll walk the rest of the way." Rachel climbed into the passenger seat, locking the Uzi between her knees. "Now let's get going, okay? If I miss the big battle, I'll never forgive myself."

All during the trip to New Haven, Rachel chattered, placing the pogroms in historical context. Among the collateral insanities accruing to the Black Death that had devastated fourteenth-century Europe, she explained, was a systematic attempt to assuage the Almighty's wrath through Hebrew blood. Still angry over the Jews' role in His son's assassination, per Matthew 27:25, God would purportedly lift the bubonic plague only after the Gentile nations demonstrated a serious commitment to anti-Semitism. In Basel, thousands of Jews were locked inside wooden buildings and burned alive. In Spyer, the victims were sealed in wine casks and rolled into the Rhine. Now history was repeating itself. For the past six months, the Anglo-Saxon Christian Brotherhood—which had first gained public attention when its terrorist arm, the Sword of Jehovah Strike Force, appointed itself the Corpus Dei's guardian during the great trial—had been sending its divisions north, mostly to New York City, "where the Jews are," in the words of the coalition's commander-in-chief, a West Virginia snake handler named Durward Montminy. At the moment Manhattan was besieged: traffic arteries severed, tunnels barricaded, rivers patrolled. Additional Anglo-Saxon regiments had penetrated what Montminy called "the Jew-contaminated strongholds" of northeast New Jersey and the Bronx peninsula, but the communities had mounted impressive counterattacks. From Nutley to Englewood, Mount Vernon to Scarsdale, the two sides had fought each other to a standstill.

A profound sense of dislocation overcame Nora, as if she'd walked into her apartment and found a family of bears in residence—except it was not her apartment but a significant portion of her country that had fallen to invaders.

"When we leave Connecticut, be sure to get on 287 north toward the river," said Rachel.

"Wouldn't the George Washington Bridge be faster?"

"Anglo saboteurs dynamited the G. W. last week. The God's Ear Brigade. God listens only to them. The Whitestone Bridge and the Throgs Neck are open, but Long Island is now in enemy hands."

"So it's the Tappan Zee Bridge or nothing?"

"You're lucky I came your way, Nora Burkhart. Without my guidance, you'd be driving right smack into Hell."

At noon the rain stopped. The storm clouds lifted; the skull resumed its celestial hegemony. New Haven came and went. An elaborate yawn seized Rachel Sorkin, traveling the length of her body.

"You need a nap," said Nora.

"Can I trust you not to steal my gun?"

A tempting thought, Nora had to admit. An Uzi was probably exactly the sort of gift that would get Kevin into the clinic. "You'll have to take your chances."

Weapon in hand, Rachel crawled into the cargo bay, stretched out on the floor between the wheelchair and the empty milk jugs, and drifted into an unquiet sleep. Snoring and twitching, she held the Uzi to her breast like a child clutching a rag doll.

Nora didn't know what to make of her companion. She suspected that Rachel's coarseness disguised an essential fragility: sandpaper giftwrapping a china figurine. No doubt the young woman could fire her Uzi, but she'd probably never drawn blood with it.

Absently Nora flipped on the radio and rotated the tuner knob. Pops, crackles, wows, and whines filled the cab. She left the receiver fixed on a rhythmic discharge of static, oddly soothing, like electric surf caressing a platinum beach.

A mile outside Bridgeport, a new sound arose, a pathological *thump, thump, thump*. The steering wheel jerked left, fighting her attempts to straighten it as the truck lurched toward the shoulder. "Damn," growled Nora. "Hell." Pulling over, she killed the engine and hopped out. Her guess was correct: the driver's-side front tire had become a shapeless mass of rubber. Nora was up to the task—during her nine years in Ray Feldstein's employ, she'd changed as many flats on Phaëthon—but the uncertainties always rattled her. The wrench might be missing, the lugs frozen, the ground too soggy to support the scissors jack.

She opened the cargo bay doors, inhaled the mixture of gas fumes and hyacinths, and got the necessary tools. The tire swap went smoothly, and soon she was reversing the scissors jack and lowering the chassis. She paused briefly to eat two handfuls of Sun-Maid raisins, then shoved the box back into her Celtics jacket, picked up the lug wrench, and gave each nut a final twist.

On the opposite side of the highway a banana-yellow bus emblazoned with the words SCHOOL DISTRICT OF PROVIDENCE pulled over, its tailpipe spouting black exhaust. Oddly, the school bus's passengers were all adults, their expressionless faces pressed against the windows, eyelids drooping, irises milky.

Throwing his transmission into neutral, the bus driver activated the pneumatic double door. An unearthly stink wafted across the road. The driver grabbed a battered suitcase and eased his bulk onto the gravel. He was middle-aged and bushy-bearded, with the belly of a man whose pre-plague exercise regimen was probably limited to separating six-pack cans from their plastic tethers. A baseball cap protected his head, a ratty fisherman's sweater warmed his chest, and a double-barrel shotgun teetered in the crook where his left hand entered his pants pocket, the dual muzzles angling toward Nora's knees.

Why was everyone pointing guns at her these days?

"Let me offer my services," said the driver.

"I'm really just finishing up," said Nora, struggling to place the stink. She had a theory, but she hoped it wasn't true. "Thanks for stopping, though."

"I'm not talking about lug wrenches. I'm talking about everlasting life." He leaned his shotgun against the bus, then set his suitcase on the ground and lifted the lid. A hundred paperback books spilled forth. Like a miser fondling gold coins, he pushed his hands into the mass of recycled pulp and buried his arms to the elbows. He extracted two volumes with a theatrical flourish. "Look, I wrote these—*The Myth of Oblivion* and *The Mortality Hoax*, both best-sellers!" A staccato giggle, at once vain and desperate, issued from his throat. "That's *my* name on the cover, Harvey Sheridan, award-winning spiritualist and president of the Institute for Afterlife Studies!" He displayed another pair of paperbacks. "*E-Mail from the Dead*, that's mine too, and look here, *Postmortem Phone Calls*!" Dipping into his suitcase a third time, he pulled out a cluster of audiocassettes. "Eleven hundred hours of recorded conversations with departed spirits! There is no death, dear lady, and I've got proof—*proof*!" He flung the cassettes aside and seized his shotgun. "Mortality is a fraud, do you understand? The skull is a lie. Right before they passed over, my passengers all grasped that essential truth."

Nora's gaze drifted toward the bus windows. She groaned. Whatever their individual differences in personality and socioeconomic background, everyone in Harvey Sheridan's charge shared the conspicuous condition of being dead.

"You . . . killed them?"

"I *immortalized* them." The spiritualist cracked the breech of his shotgun, fed a red shell into each chamber, and elevated the twin muzzles to the height of Nora's chest. "I dispatched them to the Higher Realm."

As her heart crashed against her ribcage, Nora pulled the Sun-Maid box from her jacket. "Would you like some raisins? I'll bet you're hungry."

"The world we see around us is but an elementary school, preparing us for the Angelic Plane beyond. In a few seconds—ten, to be exact—you'll hop aboard the Bus of Providence and travel to an infinitely wider and impossibly glorious reality. Raise your arms, please. One! Raise them, dear lady. Two!"

Nora reached skyward. A pool of bile welled up in her stomach. I'm about to die, she thought. A lunatic with a worldview is going to murder me.

"Three! Four!"

"Please! *Please!* I'd love to enter your terrific afterlife, but not *now!*"

"Five! It's beautiful on the Other Side. Six! Peace past human ken. Seven!"

"No, Mr. Sheridan!"

"Eight! Nine!"

Shots rang out, and there was red blood. But the blood came not from her, it came from Harvey Sheridan. He spouted and spurted. He leaked like a perforated wineskin. Smoke curled away from his shattered chest as, spinning around, he collapsed on the gravel, dead.

Nora, gasping, turned toward Phaëthon. Rachel stood by the rear doors, her Uzi cooling in the afternoon air. Her face looked like cheese, white and mottled. She licked her finger and rubbed it along the barrel. The spittle sizzled.

"Shit," she muttered. "I never killed anybody before. I'll be thinking about this all week."

"Of course."

"It hasn't even *begun* to sink in."

"He deserved to die."

"It was so damn easy. I feel sick."

Nora stepped toward her friend, and they embraced. A minute passed. As the odor of Sheridan's blood filled her nostrils, Nora tried unsuccessfully to imagine circumstances under which two people might need to hug each other more fiercely.

"We've got work to do," she said.

"You want to bury him?" said Rachel.

"No, I want to raid his gas tank. Diesel fuel guarantees admittance to the Lucido Clinic. I have a Siemens siphon and thirteen empty jugs."

"After that, will you drive me to the war zone?"

"I'll drive you to the goddamn *moon*."

"Just get me to Paramus by sundown."

Up north the season was autumn, a vacuous concept in tropical Mexico, and yet the world somehow felt different to Gerard. The air smelled of change. If the rumors were true, Lucido was finally satisfied with Somatocism's manifold components—its temples, idols, clerics, and rites—and he would soon open Tamoanchan to the plague families thronging Coatzacoalcos.

Although Gerard had given them forms and faces (perhaps even psyches), he felt no affection for the Somatocist deities. They were a severe and forbidding race, conceived in lava, gestated in dreams, and born from chisel strokes that partook more of desperation than of art. These gods were not his friends.

Fiona was his friend—his beacon, his Beatrice, his bulwark against the despair inherent in his Nietzsche-positive status. Pelayo, too, was his friend, as was Fulgencio. And yet Gerard ached with a need that none of them could satisfy. He longed for philosophical discourse; he required a cerebral massage. Thus did his off-hours find him devising intellectual peers. He sculpted a basalt Karl Marx, gleefully informing the statue that history had been unkind to his theories of class warfare. He fashioned his own private Sigmund Freud, subjecting the ingenious neurologist to a feminist critique of depth psychology. With a nod to his old Cinecittà scheme, he carved a fifteen-foot reubenite statue of Desiderius Erasmus, then gave the Dutchman a German sparring partner, the chronically constipated, colonically obsessed Martin Luther. In the night's deepest hour, Gerard would pour a glass of mescal, sit at the theologians' feet, and listen.

LUTHER: Is that you, Satan? Begone, Evil One. Begone, or I unleash the most withering anal blast a man can summon.

ERASMUS: Hold your fire.

LUTHER: Desiderius? In the flesh?

ERASMUS: In the stone.

LUTHER: Logic's trollop! The whore of Aristotle! Splendid! Where are we, anyway?

ERASMUS: Some sort of afterlife, I believe. I'd call it Purgatory, but you'd start ranting about unscriptural Catholic fabrications.

Luther tries without success to discharge a gas bubble.

LUTHER: I hate being a statue.

ERASMUS: On what topic shall we disagree today? Free will? Salvation? Jews?

LUTHER: Let the Jews improve their opinion of our Savior, and I shall improve my opinion of the Jews. I don't want them murdered, mind you. Banished, yes...

ERASMUS: Once, in Palos, I saw thousands of them perish. They were trying to cross the Mediterranean after Isabella's General Edict of Expulsion.

LUTHER: ...disenfranchised, enslaved...

ERASMUS: Not all the drownings were accidental.

LUTHER: ...but I can find no scriptural warrant for extermination.

ERASMUS: Instead of behaving in a Christian fashion, the hired captains tossed their charges overboard.

LUTHER: I feel one coming.

ERASMUS: A scriptural warrant?

LUTHER: A blast. Beware, Satan! Get thee behind me!

An intestinal tornado reverberates through Purgatory.

LUTHER: Take that!

ERASMUS: Did you catch him?

LUTHER: Listen carefully. He sprints away on cloven hoofs. I haven't dealt him such a blow since my ninety-five theses.

ERASMUS: Feces?

LUTHER: Against indulgences. A man cannot buy his way into Heaven, Desiderius. God decided each man's fate before the beginning of time.

ERASMUS: Whenever you tell me how salvation works, I grow weary in the soul. In the misty distance I see a glass of wine and a copy of the *Ethics*. They call to me like the beguiling sirens of old.

LUTHER: Be honest. It's my flatus, not my philosophy, that sends you away.

ERASMUS: Not so. Give me the stink of your bowels over the stench of predestination any day of the week. Fare thee well, monk. I am off to commune with the divine Aristotle.

On the last day of September, Gerard drove his pony cart along Calle Huimanguillo and up the slopes of Mount Tapílula for his regular Sunday-afternoon meeting with Lucido, an event he anticipated with all the jollity of a cancer victim beginning radiation therapy. The last three such sessions had been utterly unproductive and not a little embarrassing, with Lucido getting wired on hyperion-15 and loudly defying abulia to appear before him in humanoid form so the two of them could wrestle like Jacob and the angel.

Lucido's private apartments—his conservatory, gymnasium, bedchamber, study, and library—reminded Gerard of a child's set of plastic nesting blocks, rooms within rooms within rooms, a configuration culminating in a *sanctum sanctorum* known only to the psychoanalyst, his immediate staff, and the ghosts of various Veracruz governors. Today, for the first time, Chief Deacon Hubbard Richter guided Gerard all the way to the center. The space was hexagonal, each wall featuring an arched portal and a gigantic television screen surrounded by red velour drapes. In the center: a sunken hot tub, steam rising from the swirling waters. Powered, presumably, by Tamoanchan's underground generators, a hidden array of VCRs flooded the hexagon with six separate transmissions. Lucido's present tastes ran to vintage black-and-white horror movies, so Gerard now confronted a kaleidoscope of mad scientists and resuscitated corpses.

"Your last Risogada was unsatisfactory," said Hubbard Richter, sidling out of the hexagon. Predatory, humorless, and deficient in affect, with bony limbs and bad skin, the chief deacon was the sort of man whose sculpted portrait would be most fittingly rendered in dirty ice. "His grin was menacing when it should be jocular."

"What the fuck do you know about jocular?" snapped Gerard.

"I'm rejecting it," said Richter, and he vanished.

A plush gold divan overshadowed the hot tub. Dressed in his customary black caftan, Lucido lounged on a pile of satin pillows, puffing on a panatela. As Gerard approached, the psychoanalyst opened a drawer beneath the divan and retrieved the Moroccan leather case in which he kept his syringe and his phials of hyperion.

"Horror movies are like sex," said Lucido, injecting himself with two cubic centimeters. "It's a terrible experience, but you know you have to keep on going because there's this astonishing *thrill* waiting at the end."

"I would like to make a complaint," said Gerard.

"Throughout my early youth I could imagine no pleasure more

supreme than seeing a classic horror film revived on late-night television." Lucido, rising, blew a smoke ring shaped like a Möbius strip. "In becoming a therapist, I sought to tame the dark side of the psyche as thoroughly as Universal Studios had domesticated the denizens of Transylvania and Vasaria." He pressed his palm against the nearest screen, which currently displayed a deranged descendant of Victor Frankenstein working furiously in his laboratory, mimicking God. "It was all so simple. Wooden stakes for vampires, silver bullets for werewolves, torches for ambulatory mummies."

"Mr. Richter's credentials as an art critic are unfamiliar to me. I want him to stop editorializing on my sculptures."

"Then I treated my first pedophile, next a necrophile, and I realized that the sociopathic mind is a thousand times more miasmic than anything in the Universal vaults." Lucido slid his palm from the scientist's lab toward the Creature from the Black Lagoon. "The Gill Man touched me deeply. He had an aptitude for abducting women but no genitals, so what did his talent avail him?" Placing his index finger against the screen, he momentarily endowed the Creature with a penis. "Meanwhile, I had genitals but no aptitude for abducting women." He sucked on his cigar. "The priciest panatela in the world. Each puff costs me two dollars. I shall instruct Mr. Richter to keep his opinions to himself."

"I'd appreciate that."

Taking Gerard's sleeve, Lucido led him across the hexagon and into the vicinity of a green velvet curtain embroidered with a snarling Soaragid. Lucido lifted the veil, disclosing a dim alcove dominated by a hospital gurney. A comatose adolescent in a blue smock lay on the pad, her pasty skin marred by the pocks and grooves of stage-four thexis. Her mother sat on a footstool, keeping watch, a small, hunched woman in her fifties, head bowed, fingers interlaced in prayer. The woman inhaled and exhaled in time with her daughter, as if the young abulic might otherwise neglect to breathe.

"Meet Anna Fergus, mother of Malvina Fergus," said Lucido. "Mrs. Fergus, meet Gerard Korty, the man who makes the gods."

"We came all the way from Victoria, Texas"—Anna Fergus stood up and lifted her outstretched arm to the height of her heart—"seven hundred and fifty miles. I carried Malvina in a hay wagon, plus eleven gallons of diesel fuel."

Gerard supposed that Anna Fergus meant to shake his hand, but then he perceived a more intimate intention. The desolate woman hugged him, mutely but passionately, swinging both arms around his trunk like Orgasiad trapping a monkey in her coils.

"The great war has begun," said Lucido, locking his emerald irises on Gerard, "and the first battle will be fought within Malvina Fergus's soul. She spends tomorrow on a hyperion drip, and then she goes to the temples."

As Anna relaxed her embrace, tears of gratitude coursed down her cheeks. "Right now we see only our Creator's skull," she told Gerard in a thick whisper, "but He's mostly good, I *know* it. With God's grace, your art will deliver my daughter."

"With God's grace," Gerard echoed feebly.

"With Soaragid's grace," corrected Lucido, releasing a two-dollar smoke ring, "and Risogada's—and the others."

Throughout the next week, Gerard submerged himself in his work, harvesting three reubenite chunks from Oswald's Rock and turning them into serpent gods, but he couldn't shake Anna Fergus and her dying daughter from his mind. He knew that if Malvina failed to recover, he would convene a mental tribunal and ruthlessly interrogate himself. Why didn't you create a more soothing mistress of milk? the judges would ask. Why not a funnier lord of the jest, a merrier master of the revels, a hotter queen of passion?

Saturday afternoon found him perched atop a tower of scaffolding, stripped to the waist, detailing the fangs on a thirty-foot Soaragid. Crimson dust coated his fingers; sweat speckled his brow. In the studio below, Fiona worked on the sequel to her unpublished novel, while the Ruíz brothers collaborated on a 5′ × 10′ oil of an erupting volcano spewing out choirs of angels.

A young woman with the complexion of a Dresden shepherdess walked into the jaguar-god's shadow, singing the Beatles song called "Octopus's Garden." Her porcelain skin held faint traces of stage-four lesions. Her awkward gait suggested an eleven-month-old taking her first steps. To her breast she clutched four crude mahogany renditions of the Somatocist pantheon, each the size of a Barbie doll.

Gerard clamped his frosting chisel between his teeth and scrambled down the ladder. "Dear child, how *are* you?"

"No longer a child, Mr. Korty," said Malvina Fergus in a mellifluous voice. "On Wednesday, I entered Orgasiad's grove and left my innocence behind. Thanks to your gods, I have experienced the raptures of reality."

"No more fetch? You've thrown her off?"

"The last time I saw Gwendolyn, she was wandering around a coffee plantation, blind as God, totally confused."

"*Maravilloso!*" said Pelayo.

"*Fabuloso!*" said Fulgencio.

Glory be to the wereserpent, thought Gerard. Hosannas to the jaguar-god. All hail Idorasag and Risogada.

"I'd like to become your apprentice," said Malvina.

"It's not much fun," said Gerard. "Sharpening chisels, hauling rocks . . ."

"I need to serve you."

"As you wish."

"*Gracias.*" Malvina's eyes expanded like bubbles of lava rising from Catemaco's flow. "I carved these myself," she said, setting her inept idols on the ground. Her face acquired a luminosity that Gerard did not find entirely benign. "In every human psyche, four mythic energies flow like rivers. At Tamoanchan, the affirmation gods took my hand and led me to the waters' sacred source. The world gland suckled me. I kissed the serpent, laughed with the crocodile, danced in the jaguar's arms."

Fulgencio set down his brush and cried, "*Mamó y chingó!*"

"*Rió y bailó!*" shouted his brother.

"*Sí, sí, sí, sí!*" sang the acolyte.

A queasiness spread through Gerard. What had Lucido wrought, exactly? A pagan fundamentalist? A fool for Soaragid? He prayed that

Malvina's faith was spongy at the core—adolescent enthusiasm, not full-bore fanaticism.

"I hope Gwendolyn stays away forever," said Fiona.

"How could it be otherwise?" asked Malvina.

Because every god has a dark side, thought Gerard. Even the king of the risible. Even the mistress of milk.

A treacherous fog enshrouded the Eastern seaboard as Nora drove over the New York state border and north along the Cross Westchester Expressway toward the Tappan Zee Bridge. She firmed her grip on the wheel and brooded. Given their volatile cargo—the Gansevoort premium plus the thirteen gallons of diesel fuel they'd pilfered from Harvey Sheridan's bus—prudence demanded that she stop until the mist lifted. Screw prudence, she thought. Every minute she spent between here and Coatzacoalcos was sixty seconds ceded to Kevin's fetch.

"You awake?"

"Uh-huh," said Rachel, slouching in the passenger seat, her white scarf draped across her face.

"It's foggy, but I want to keep going."

"No argument from me."

"You still thinking about . . . ?"

"The man I murdered? Of course."

"That wasn't murder," said Nora. "It was fumigation."

As they approached the Hutchinson River Parkway, a deserted Texaco station appeared, and Rachel asked Nora to stop. Swathed in fog, two defunct service islands rose above a sea of fractured concrete, each pump as useless as the udder on a dead cow. After grabbing one of Kevin's diapers—to clean the seats, she explained—Rachel marched up to the ladies' room, opened the rusty door, and, braving whatever vermin resided within, entered.

Five minutes later, she emerged holding a small aluminum can, sealed, its label stained with dribbles of blue enamel.

"Look what I found." Rachel flourished the can. "Would you mind if I painted something on your truck?"

"What?" asked Nora.

"The Star of David. I want us to enter Paramus in style."

"Be quick about it."

Rachel went to work, using her white scarf as a paintbrush, and soon both of Phaëthon's panels glistened with garish blue Mogen Davids.

"There's something I've never understood," said Nora as they left the Texaco station. "In Chinese culture, once you save somebody's life, you're obligated to protect that person forever."

"No offense, Nora, but I'm glad we don't have that rule in America."

"But isn't it a strange rule? You'd think it would work the other way around."

"I don't know about Chinese culture. It's hard enough being Jewish."

"Such a strange rule."

Two miles beyond White Plains, the fog lifted to reveal an impressive spectacle. Banners flying, three Connecticut regiments—the Norwalk Irregulars, the Greenwich Grenadiers, the Bridgeport Berets—poured onto the Cross Westchester Expressway. Armed with everything from bazookas to hunting bows, assault rifles to slingshots, they paraded down both shoulders whistling John Philip Sousa's "Washington Post March." They were prepared for a long campaign, their backpacks stuffed with bedrolls and bristling with pots and pans. As Phaëthon cruised past these tired but determined volunteers, they pulled off their berets and cheered, evidently heartened by the Mogen Davids and—Nora mused sadly—by the possibility that a motorized Jewish division was not far behind.

Around five o'clock, the Hudson River swung into view, its waters sparkling in the late afternoon sun as they broadened to become the Tappan Zee. The amateur army soon doubled in size, squad after squad of New York volunteers spilling from the marshes and onto the expressway, melding with the Connecticut troops.

Only on seeing the burning bridge did Nora finally and fully believe Rachel's story of an Anglo-Saxon invasion. It was really happening: armed combat, civil war—war with its tactics and body counts, its suicide missions and saboteurs. The present conflagration, said Rachel, was almost certainly the work of the God's Ear Brigade, those professional demolitionists who'd managed to cut Manhattan off from the outside world. A dozen pockets of flame rose along all four spans like burning sheaves of wheat, crackling and hissing as they ate the asphalt. Smoke billowed upward, obelisks of roiling blackness. And yet the volunteers were not deterred. Eyes flashing, throats erupting in war cries, they advanced across the bridge, dodged the fires, and rushed pell-mell toward the west bank of the Hudson.

"Pedal to the metal," ordered Rachel.

"Pedal to the metal?" wailed Nora. "Are you crazy? We've got—"

"A bay full of gasoline, right. Let's get it over with."

"Remember the Chinese rule? You're responsible for me! You're not allowed to endanger my life!"

"Come on, Nora!"

"No!"

"Mexico, Nora! They have the cure! You can't get to Mexico unless you cross the goddamn Hudson River!"

Nora floored the accelerator, bringing the truck to the threshold of the first span. The heat arrived as a searing wind. Honking furiously, she improvised a path among the soldiers and around the fires. Smoke filled the cab. The women coughed and wept. A worst-case scenario unspooled in Nora's mind: melted tires, trapped truck, exploding gasoline.

"Keep going!" cried Rachel.

Approaching the second span, Nora heard a low, grinding, insectile drone. The soldiers gestured skyward. She lifted her eyes. An air attack had begun. A propeller-driven dirigible cruised back and forth above the westernmost span while, leaning out a cabin window, a God's Ear saboteur hurled down a clutch of Molotov cocktails. The bombs hit their target and detonated, turning the asphalt into a bright orange fireball. Through the clearing smoke Nora saw that the explosion had ripped a ten-foot crater in the roadway. She slowed to a crawl, reaching span number three as the saboteurs passed overhead.

"You're doing great!" yelled Rachel. "Don't stop!"

Seeing the dirigible in her side-view mirror, Nora fixed on the logo and thus learned the source of the brigade's name. This bulbous vehicle was in fact the famous Goodyear blimp, the letter Y and one of the O's erased by splotches of black paint, so that the word read GO*D*EAR.

"One more span! You can do it!"

The Greenwich Grenadiers counterattacked. In her mirror Nora observed some twenty soldiers tear off their coats and start beating the flames while a handful of their fellows pulled out the components of a portable cannon, assembling the weapon with the frantic efficiency of auto mechanics performing a pit stop at Le Mans.

"Blow them out of the sky!" screamed Rachel.

Having completed one bombing run, the God's Ear blimp languidly reversed direction. The instant the war balloon cruised within range, the Greenwich Grenadiers fired their bazooka, but the shot proved as impotent as the US Navy's recent efforts to eradicate the plague with Polaris missiles.

"They're just warming up," said Rachel.

And in fact, as the dirigible bore down on the center of the bridge, the Grenadiers fired again. The helium envelope ruptured, six thousand cubic feet of inert gas whooshed into the air, and the blimp dropped toward the Hudson like an immense tear shed by the Cranium Dei.

With nowhere to go but forward, Nora urged Phaëthon along the final span. The fires bellowed; the burning blacktop stank like fear syrup. She drove on, swerving past the smoking crater, pedal to the metal, just as Rachel wanted.

At last the tollbooth appeared, a comforting image, like the sight of Kevin's bicycle chained outside Meadowbrook Manor: evidence that he was safely home. Entering the shadow of the booth, she disengaged the transmission and applied the brakes. For two minutes she simply sat there, shaking. As her nerves settled, she retrieved a quarter from her Celtics jacket, rolled down her window, and tossed the coin into the basket.

"What did you do *that* for?" asked Rachel.

"It's not a toll," said Nora. "It's an offering."

"Huh?"

"Of thanksgiving."

"Who're you thanking, Mr. Smiley Face up in the clouds?"

"No."

"We're not even in Jersey yet. If I were you, Nora, I'd save all my money for Mexico."

Nora Joins the Circus

After the carnage at the Tappan Zee Bridge, the remainder of their Paramus journey seemed blessedly uneventful. Nora drove Phaëthon west on Route 87 for about five miles to the Garden State Parkway, motoring past a volunteer regiment called the Stratford Spearshakers, then turned south and crossed the border into Jersey. Empty as a fetch's womb, the parkway afforded the privacy Nora always preferred when ministering to Kevin. She pulled off near a pine grove and began the grim rituals of prevention: dressing his boils to head off infection, feeding him to forestall malnutrition, exercising his muscles against atrophy. She locked her gaze on Kevin's. His pleading stare horrified her, and yet she maintained eye contact. It was the one sort of connection he could still apparently feel.

"Are you Nietzsche-positive?" asked Rachel.

"Not yet," said Nora. "You?"

Rachel nodded. "I shot her. The bullets had no effect, but I gave the bitch quite a fright."

"I doubt that."

"I scared the shit out of her."

Having bandaged, nourished, and massaged her son, Nora replenished the fuel tank with five gallons of Gansevoort premium and guided Phaëthon back onto the highway. As dusk fell over the Garden State, a significant detachment of the Army of Northern New Jersey emerged from the shadows. Two dozen brigades were bivouacked in Beth-Elohim Cemetery, their flimsy pup tents rising incongruously amid the marble tombstones and granite mausoleums, their banners proclaiming their homes: East Orange Historical Society, Passaic Art Appreciation Guild, Montclair Book Discussion Group, Hackensack Kennel Club, Ridgewood Softball League. Like their Connecticut counterparts, the New Jersey volunteers took heart at the sight of a motorized vehicle decorated with Mogen Davids, and for a fleeting instant Nora considered contributing Phaëthon to the cause. A noble sentiment, but impossible, she decided. It was the truck, and only the truck, that elevated her Coatzacoalcos scheme above the level of a pipe dream.

Entering the Montclair Book Discussion Group's headquarters, a collapsible aluminum-and-vinyl gazebo originally designed to shield well-fed suburbanites from the midday sun, Nora and Rachel explained themselves to a rawboned black woman wearing a lieutenant's bars and camouflage fatigues. The lieutenant directed them toward a vehicle that, thanks to her familiarity with Kevin's plastic models, Nora knew to be an "ontos," a caterpillar tractor with a triad of recoilless rocket launchers swivel-mounted on both sides. Perched atop the turret was the brigade's recruiting sergeant, Nathan Kitman, a tightly wound little man who, it developed, had taught Jewish studies at Columbia before the plague struck. After gratefully accepting Rachel's services, Sergeant Kitman explained that she was now in the Army of Northern New Jersey's newly created Third Division, one of five poorly equipped but resolute corps committed to engaging the enemy the next day on the Arcola Golf Course. In Kitman's view, the battle would prove decisive. Either the Christian Brotherhood's main body would be destroyed (with a subsequent lifting of the siege of Manhattan) or the Army of Northern New Jersey would go down fighting (with a consequent collapse for the average Jew of all meaningful distinction between Durward Montminy's America and Adolph Hitler's

Europe). At one point in his narrative the sergeant leaned forward, drummed his knuckles on a rocket launcher, and observed that the ontos had seen its last battle, its fuel tank being empty.

"Diesel?" asked Rachel.

"Diesel," said Kitman.

"Interesting," said Rachel, inflicting a pointed glance on Nora.

Rachel was pleased to report that not only were the Stratford Spearshakers moving down the Garden State Parkway, but three additional Connecticut regiments had recently marched over a sabotaged but passable Tappan Zee Bridge. Assuming they avoided the Anglo-Saxon brigades, Rachel theorized, these spirited volunteers would probably reach Beth-Elohim Cemetery by 11:00 P.M.: they would have plenty of time to pitch their tents and enjoy a decent night's sleep. Casting a covetous eye on Phaëthon, Kitman remarked that the key to Rachel's reconnaissance work had obviously been the panel truck. How lamentable that Nora intended to leave at dawn. Normally he wouldn't think twice about commandeering her vehicle, but the Third Division's fetches had threatened to murder them the moment they violated any part of the Decalogue save the law against killing.

Right after supper—a feast of baked beans and boiled cabbage reminiscent of nearly every meal Nora had consumed since the plague hit its stride—the brigade's commanding officer, a retired Marine colonel named Sol Weiskopf, assembled his troops. The five hundred volunteers gathered in concentric circles around the ontos. The Coleman lanterns imparted a ghostliness to the soldiers, as if Beth-Elohim Cemetery had recently experienced an epidemic of resurrection. Although Weiskopf failed to fit Nora's mental image of a marine—his shoulders were narrow, his stature diminutive, his uniform ragged—he radiated both courage and competence. Even without her diesel fuel, she felt, the Army of Northern New Jersey stood a good chance of winning.

The colonel's speech began with a question. "How many of you have ever killed anyone?"

Only three raised their hands, a chubby youngster wearing a

blaze-orange hunting jacket, a burly middle-aged man dressed in camouflage fatigues, and Rachel.

"Tell me about it."

The young hunter related how he'd accidentally shot and killed a farmer's wife on the first day of antlered deer season in central Pennsylvania. "Worst thing that ever happened to me." The middle-aged vet revealed that he'd machine-gunned thirty-one Iraqi tank crewmen during Operation Desert Storm. "I was just doing my job, but I still have nightmares." Rachel told of dispatching a devout spiritualist with her Uzi earlier that day. "It was so *easy.*"

"Most of you are probably asking if you have what it takes," said Weiskopf, walking back and forth on the ontos. "When the battle begins, will you be able to pull the trigger? Were the technology available, I would now run video clips from the siege of Manhattan, images that would galvanize the self-doubters among you. Luckily, we have the next best thing. Sergeant Kitman's sister-in-law, the celebrated *New Yorker* cartoonist Donna Szydlowski, has spent the past week creating a presentation called *The Way of the World.*"

From his duffel bag Sergeant Kitman obtained a stack of glass slides and an antique brass-and-wood projector that Nora immediately recognized as a magic lantern. (Eric had employed one at the start of his act, using it to display Victorian placards such as SPITTING IS PROHIBITED and LADIES, PLEASE REMOVE YOUR HATS.) Kitman ordered the Colemans doused, then set the magic lantern on an engine louvre, ignited the kerosene lamp, and aimed the beam toward the side of a mausoleum housing the Goldstein family. While a Playwrights Horizons actor read the narration and a New York Philharmonic musician played Hebrew folk melodies on his violin, Kitman projected the paintings. The tepid titles scarcely conveyed the horrors they depicted: a dozen atrocities perpetrated by the Anglo-Saxons during the siege of Manhattan. Nora was especially moved by *Firebombing a Synagogue,* with its terrified congregants leaping through the windows, *Looking for Swallowed Diamonds,* which documented a mass evisceration, and *War of Attrition,* a tableau of starvation, each victim so bereft of fat and muscle that his skin had become an organic ossuary, bones poking out in stark detail: femur, ulna, radius, pelvis, ribcage.

"The Anglos are a formidable foe, but they aren't invincible," said Weiskopf as Kitman cranked down the wick and stifled the flame. "Even as I speak, over a thousand Connecticut volunteers are racing to join us. When the sun rises tomorrow, we shall match the enemy soldier for soldier."

On this encouraging note, the colonel dismissed his brigade.

Ten minutes later, holding two milk jugs by their handles and cradling two more against her chest, all four gallons sloshing to and fro, Nora approached the ontos, where Rachel and Sergeant Kitman were packing up the magic lantern. The nine remaining gallons from Sheridan's school bus, she reasoned, would probably be sufficient to purchase Kevin's treatment.

"As luck would have it, Rachel and I came into some diesel fuel today," Nora told the sergeant, setting the milk jugs on the mud shield.

"May your fetch keep her distance," said Kitman.

"I'll help you get the other gallons," said Rachel.

"No, that's it," Nora told her.

"Don't you remember? We siphoned thirteen."

"They're my ticket to the clinic."

"Thirteen gallons would probably last us the entire battle," said Kitman.

"Listen to the sergeant," said Rachel.

Head to foot, Nora bristled. Yes, Rachel had delivered her from Harvey Sheridan's Angelic Plane—but her friend had no right to make such a request. "I'm already taking a risk giving four away," said Nora.

"May God forgive you," said Rachel.

"Didn't you watch His trial?" Nora pointed to the Cranium Dei. "God reprimanding His creatures for selfishness is like a door-to-door serial killer criticizing his victims for having illegible numbers on their houses. I don't want *God's* forgiveness, Rachel. I want yours."

"You'll have to settle for God's."

"If you were a mother, you'd understand."

"Well, I'm not, so I don't," Rachel replied. "Now get out of my sight. If I never see you again in my life, it will be too soon."

Dawn spilled softly into the cargo bay. Nora awoke sheathed in sweat. She rose and exercised Kevin's limbs. Hunger rumbled in her stomach, a need she assuaged with beef jerky and raisins. Her head ached, her back hurt. It was not her true self, she felt, but some enfeebled, fetchlike facsimile who now got behind the wheel and drove Phaëthon out of Beth-Elohim Cemetery.

Her plan was simple. She would take the Garden State Parkway to Interstate 80, pursue 80 into Pennsylvania until she hit 81, then follow 81 south through Virginia.

She never even reached the parkway. The Third Division jammed the road from shoulder to shoulder, a sea of unsmiling volunteers. Grabbing her Triple A Atlas, she turned to the relevant map and plotted her alternatives. Her next two attempts to connect directly with 80, Pascack Road and Highland Avenue, also failed; both thoroughfares were clogged with brigades from the Second Division. She implemented plan three, steering Phaëthon west on Linwood Avenue into the tidy little town of Ridgewood, where she easily attained Prospect Road, a promising escape route from the war zone.

Twisting and turning, the highway cleaved to the meandering Saddle River, whose waters rushed southward along the perimeter of the Arcola Golf Course. As the air vibrated with drum cadences and bugle calls, the two armies took up strategic positions on the fairways, thousands of infantry troops pouring into opposing mazes of trenches and foxholes. Fearsome walls of wooden stakes guarded the forward redoubts of the Anglo-Saxon line. Barbed wire defended the Jewish salients, the clawed coils unraveling across the field like some vast demonic Slinky.

The instant Nora shifted into fourth gear, two supernatural events caused her to slam on the brakes: the sudden materialization of a naked Quincy Azrael on the front seat, exuding a loamy fragrance, and the equally abrupt transformation of the steering wheel into a red snake, its tail fixed in its mouth, a perfect circle. Screaming, she stopped the truck and removed her hands from the snake, which proceeded to slither around the gearshift lever, turning it into a machine-age caduceus. The reptile, yellow-eyed, stared directly at Nora, its forked tongue flicking about like a miniature dowsing rod.

She yanked on the emergency brake, opened the door, and, without bothering to shut off the engine, escaped into the crisp September air.

"You were right to jump ship," said Quincy, joining her on the shoulder. "That species is famous for its neurotoxic venom."

"Give me back my goddamn steering wheel!"

"One bite, and the victim becomes so stiff, he makes the average stage-two abulic look like Fred Astaire in *Swing Time*. Let's watch the battle, Mrs. Burkhart. If a cavalcade of organized killing has nothing to teach us, I don't know what does."

Nora shuddered. She had to say this for the fetches: they weren't phony. You could, if so inclined, organize an incandescent cult around them. Death, when done right, became as grand and fierce a religion as anyone could want. Look at ancient Egypt. Look at Christianity. On this Prufrock I shall build my church.

Even if it were not occurring on a golf course, the Battle of Paramus would have initially seemed more like a team sport than a military engagement. For twenty minutes the armies attempted to outflank each other, but the intimidating presence of the Jews' ontos and the Anglos' equivalent machine—a Brinks truck bristling with machine guns and emblazoned with an amateurishly painted Crown of Thorns shedding droplets of blood—prevented either force from securing any ground. Although most of the fighters were foot soldiers, a few platoons had managed to improvise vehicles. One Christian Brotherhood unit controlled a squadron of steerable hot-air balloons, their various commercial logos (Blockbuster Video, Tru Value Hardware, Burger King) partially hidden by the Crown of Thorns insignia, while another Anglo group had converted thirty aluminum mulch barrows into war wagons, each pulled by a team of Rottweilers and outfitted with crosscut saw blades projecting from the hubs. On the Jewish side, a full brigade mounted on apprehensive-looking quarter horses unfurled a banner reading TEANECK RIDING ACADEMY. Another such detachment, proud possessors of a hundred electric shopping carts, prepared to do battle under a flag heralding the BLOOMFIELD CONSUMERS LEAGUE.

"Did I tell you the big news?" said Quincy. "I've decided to write a joke book. What do you think of *Charnel Chuckles* as a title?"

Upon realizing that their flanking maneuvers had failed, the armies decided to engage each other head-on, and the Battle of Paramus turned bloody. The first clash pitted the mulch barrows against the shopping carts, both divisions of latter-day charioteers charging across the fairways with elemental antipathy and primal rage. For ten minutes the golf course darkened beneath a merciless storm of bullets, buckshot, grenades, Molotov cocktails, arrows, bottles, and stones. "Kill the plague bringers!" screamed the Anglos. Bodies fell everywhere, littering the links—the wounded, the dying, the dead, the fear-frozen. The two sides seemed equal in firepower, and Nora guessed that the outcome would depend on the vehicles themselves, with the mechanized troops quickly outclassing their biological counterparts. She was right. Ignoring their drivers' commands, the Rottweilers ran off madly in a dozen directions, whimpering and yelping. If the Jewish charioteers drew any satisfaction from besting a German breed, their countenances did not betray it; with grim lips and steely eyes they accelerated their shopping carts and fired at the retreating mulch barrows, systematically slaughtering the drivers and gaining all the acreage from the tenth hole to the Bing Crosby Tavern. The links ran red, a deluge of blood blotching the fairways and staining the sand traps.

Beholding the fallen troops, Nora gasped at the monstrous inadequacy of the post-theistic world. All these wounded soldiers, and no resources to treat them—no antibiotics, disinfectants, plasma, morphine, anesthesia, or surgical instruments. A sour wave of nausea washed through her. Her knees buckled, and she embraced the nearest road sign, SPEED LIMIT 45.

As the Jewish charioteers regrouped, the Anglos deployed their hot-air balloons. The pilots guided their craft in low, a maneuver that left the squadron vulnerable but turned the shopping carts into easy targets. "Death to the plague bringers!" At first the tactic worked, the bombardiers dousing the charioteers in flaming sheets of charcoal lighter. "Kill them all!" Shrieking like the victims in *Firebombing a Synagogue,* the burning charioteers leaped from their shopping carts, tore across the links, and hurled themselves into the Saddle River. Now the Teaneck Riding Academy joined the fight, rupturing the balloon bags with volleys from their assault rifles. One by one the gondolas succumbed to gravity, hitting the ground and splitting open like pumpkins dropped from skyscrapers. Pilots and bombardiers spilled forth. The majority suffered broken legs, and the Teaneck cavalry exterminated them on the spot. Struggling to their feet, the remaining balloonists retreated toward their lines, a futile move that merely inspired the equestrian rifles to gun them down.

"I'll bet the Third Division could really use their ontos now," said Quincy. "Too bad it's out of fuel."

"I gave them what I could spare," said Nora.

"I'm sure. If you'll go back to the truck, Mrs. Burkhart, you'll find that our reptile friend has decided to become a steering wheel again."

Having failed to win the day at a distance, each army now undertook to destroy its enemy in hand-to-hand combat. As the carnage unfolded—a noisy welter of shouts, screams, gunfire, hemorrhages, and dismemberments—Nora staggered toward Phaëthon. The gearshift lever was free of snakes. The steering wheel had returned. She climbed in.

"Your ethics elude me," said Quincy, joining her in the cab. "Aren't you aware that leaving the scene of an accident—"

"Ten thousand accidents."

"—is both illegal and immoral?"

"Don't speak to me of morals, you demented slug." She stomped on the accelerator.

"My Nora Burkhart dossier reveals that you learned first aid in Girl Scouts. If you act quickly, you can save somebody's life."

"If I act quickly, I can save *my* life."

"Tourniquets, splints, CPR."

Nora glanced toward the golf course and winced. The fetch, God damn him, had a point.

She stopped the truck.

It was an Anglo bombardier who delivered Nora from her conscience, a barrel-chested, apish man whose hot-air balloon displayed the Wal-Mart logo. Gliding past the beech trees that lined the Saddle River, the aircraft headed straight for Phaëthon. The bombardier leaned over the edge of the gondola, his right hand gripping a Molotov cocktail.

"Plague bringer!" he howled. "Christ-killing Jew plague bringer!"

Putting Phaëthon in gear, Nora gritted her teeth and zoomed down Prospect Road. The bombardier hurled his cocktail. It landed thirty feet behind the truck, the explosion filling Nora's side-view mirror like a Florida sunset. She jammed the transmission into second gear, floored the accelerator, advanced to third, then fourth, soon putting five miles between herself and the Wal-Mart balloon.

"If you don't like *Charnel Chuckles*," said Quincy as the interstate ramp appeared, "maybe a better title would be *Funny Bones*. What's your opinion?"

Nora guided Phaëthon down Route 80.

"*Funny Bones*," repeated the fetch. "What do you think?"

"What do I think? I think the Lucido Clinic terrifies you, Quincy Azrael. I think it gives you nightmares."

Nora got all the way to Hackensack before realizing she was driving in the wrong direction. She turned around and headed west, eventually crossing the Saddle River Bridge. Dead soldiers clogged the stream, their wounds tinting the water the hue of Hawaiian Punch. The nearest Jew lacked a body from the waist down. The chest of an adjacent Christian Brotherhood infantryman had a crater instead of a cardiopulmonary system.

She stopped, jumped from the truck, and approached the bridge rail, eyes locked on the river. God's reflection rode the water, His grin folding and stretching as the crimson current flowed south toward the Passaic. Crazed with hunger, a stray dog sniffed the heartless Christian.

Nora looked down. A lithe female form in a motorcycle jacket floated amid a stand of cattails. Her forehead displayed a black pendant: crusted blood surrounding a hole the size of a bottle cap. Rachel's Uzi lay across her chest. Everything about the scene shocked Nora, and nothing about it surprised her. In the age of abulia, there were no happy endings.

"You really believe the answer lies in Mexico, don't you?" said Quincy as Nora, weeping, settled back behind the wheel.

"I don't know what I believe."

"Give up, Mrs. Burkhart. There is no Mexico. It doesn't exist. The ants have devoured the jungles. The condors have stolen the children. The cities are on fire."

As Quincy descended into his host, Nora turned the ignition key. No Mexico. The wraith made sense. She could see it all. Ants and condors, quite so. Burning cities, yes.

She depressed the clutch, shifted into first gear, and headed toward Pennsylvania.

In Allamuchy, Nora decided that her top priority, more important even than her son's next physical therapy session, must be to remove the Stars of David from Phaëthon's panels. She parked, soaked a diaper in Gansevoort premium, and got to work. The gasoline made a reasonable solvent, and after fifteen minutes of strenuous rubbing she'd become a less tempting target to whatever Anglo brigades might lie between the Delaware River and the Rio Grande.

Over the next two days, she managed to put six hundred miles between herself and Paramus, but the battle still cascaded through her mind, one searing tableau after another: an infantryman from the Passaic Art Appreciation Guild impaled like an insect specimen on a Christian Brotherhood stake, a male flag bearer from the Norwalk Irregulars chopped to pieces by the serrated hubs of a mulch wagon, a female shopping-cart charioteer running across the golf course with flames shooting from her hair, a sharpshooter from the Stratford Spearshakers clutching his externalized intestines like a housewife holding a grocery bag. Nora's sin tortured her. It tied her soul in knots. *The Way of the World*, slide number fourteen: *Half-Jew Hoarding Diesel Fuel.*

She lived by her wits and on her toes. No danger eluded her senses; no resource escaped her gaze. Whenever another vehicle appeared in her side-view mirror, she immediately improvised a detour. Each time a babbling brook or an unharvested apple tree emerged from the landscape, she stopped the truck and reprovisioned.

All along Route 81, from Pennsylvania to Maryland to West Virginia to Virginia, America's death throes presented themselves in grisly detail. For every abandoned McDonald's restaurant there was a funeral pyre; in some cases the McDonald's *was* the pyre, jammed with corpses and set ablaze, the golden arches rising above the inferno like the haunches of a dead abulic. Starving livestock roamed at will, searching for the meals their deceased keepers could no longer provide. Unmilked cows lowed. Ecstatic carrion birds ruled the sky, convinced that some vulturine paradise, a corvine Second Coming, was at hand.

About half the roadside billboards were painted over with ads for local treatment methods.

ALDERFER FARM THIS EXIT
FETCHES PERMANENTLY EXTRACTED
FOR CANNED GOODS
DRINK FROM OUR WELL OF WELLNESS

And six miles later...

107 CURED SO FAR BY MIRACLE HEN GERTRUDE
SWAP SURPLUS GAS FOR RESURRECTION
OMELET AND COFFEE
ELSIE'S DINER TWO MILES EAST

And just beyond the Virginia town of Mount Jackson . . .

JOIN US UNDER THE BIG TENT!
REVEREND DOCTOR SILAS CONNOLLY'S
CHRIST-O-RAMA
&
24-HOUR HEAL-A-THON!
(ALL FAITHS WELCOME IN JESUS' NAME)
LET SISTER ABIGALE MASSAGE AWAY ABOOLIA PROBLEMS!

Five miles south of Route 64, Nora recalled that, while the Stars of David no longer decorated Phaëthon, both panels still displayed the name FELDSTEIN. She pulled over, climbed into the cargo bay, and looked around for an implement capable of defacing the Tower of Flowers motto, quickly settling on the scissors jack.

No sooner had she finished scraping away the F in the driver's-side FELDSTEIN than an enormous war machine appeared, popping out from behind a crumbling stone barn. Kudzu vines drooped from the cannon barrel. The turret sported a Crown of Thorns insignia. Firing repeatedly, each shell exploding closer to Phaëthon than the one before it, the deadly tractor moved parallel to the highway, rolling through a cabbage patch and across a moribund cherry orchard. Nora knew what she was up against, an M-46 Patton tank: her brother had given Kevin a radio-controlled replica for his ninth birthday.

She could identify her enemy's weapon, but could she read her enemy's mind? When it came to blowing away a Jewish soldier versus blowing up a Jewish panel truck, which target would the Anglos choose first? The truck, she decided. A Jew was just a Jew, but a truck these days was an unending inspiration.

Heart thumping, she sprinted to the rear doors, flung them wide, and leaned into the cargo bay. Her eyes adjusted to the gloom, settling on the diesel fuel. The keys to Lucido's kingdom, and now she must abandon them. No, not all nine. She stuffed two jugs inside her backpack and shouldered the load.

Ten feet away, a shell detonated, gouging a pit in Route 81.

The manufacturers of the Posturpedic mattress had equipped their product with handles. She wrapped her fingers around the closest pair and dragged the pad to the edge of the bay. Sliding one hand under Kevin's back, the other under his knees, she lifted him free of the truck and turned toward a field of cornstalks: a difficult objective, blocked by a drainage ditch and a barbed-wire fence, but the field and its adjacent haystack were the only sanctuaries in sight.

Pulling Kevin's limp body tight against her chest, she started across the road. Her bad knee spasmed. The Patton tank rumbled behind her. As she reached the gully, the Anglos scored a direct hit. With a thunderous roar Phaëthon exploded. Nora screamed but kept on moving. Everything lost. Groceries, gasoline, wheelchair, Mexico. Smoldering hunks of panel truck fell to earth, a hail of crashing glass and resounding metal that lasted almost a minute.

But then: a straw to grasp. In destroying Phaëthon, the Anglos had inadvertently obscured their quarry. A screen of thick black smoke rose from the burning chassis, enveloping Nora and Kevin as it blew across the gully and drifted through the barbed-wire fence.

"Bastards!" cried Quincy, climbing out of Kevin and facing the Patton tank. "He's not yours! How *dare* you think he's yours?"

As much as Nora loathed the leveler, she was not above accepting his help. Together they lifted Kevin over the fence and, still cloaked in the dark cloud, carried him through the cornfield—the stalks brown and withered, their husks crinkled like parchment—to the haystack. Nora wasted no time. As the smoke dissipated, revealing the skull above and the mud below, she buried Kevin in the hay, shoring up the airway with a dead branch and a discarded hoe handle.

"I suppose I ought to thank you," Nora whispered as she and the fetch joined Kevin inside the stack.

"Our rapport will improve significantly," said Quincy, "when you realize that death is actually a blessing. But for the gift of oblivion, you humans wouldn't be here."

"Keep your voice down."

"Ask Charles Darwin. Without death, life on planet Earth remains a carpet of pre-Cambrian slime: immortal, unchanging, and as boring as the rushes for *Last Year at Marienbad*."

"Quiet!"

For the next sixty minutes, an eternity, Nora breathed as quietly as possible, but she could do nothing about Kevin's wheezing. Sweat trickled down her chest and arms. Her knee throbbed. Besides being intolerably hot, the haystack was horribly alive, home to ladybugs, aphids, crickets, and weevils. Stoically she brushed the insects from her limbs and face, crushing them when they ventured inside her ears.

Nora would never know why the Anglos abandoned the hunt. Perhaps they were simply embarrassed about destroying one of America's few remaining fossil fuel supplies. In any event, when she finally peeked outside, the only evidence of the Patton tank was the flattened cabbage patch and charred truck.

"This calls for a joke," said Quincy. "Harry answers the telephone, and it's an emergency-room doctor. The doctor says, 'Your wife was in a serious car accident, and I have bad news and good news. The bad news is that she's lost the use of both arms and legs, and she'll need help eating and going to the bathroom for the rest of her life.' Harry says, 'My God. What's the good news?' The doctor says, 'I'm kidding. She's dead.'" The fetch plucked a ladybug from his hair and flicked it into the core of the haystack. "One of these days, Mrs. Burkhart, I'll get a laugh out of you."

"Don't count on it."

"It may interest you to know that the Army of Northern New Jersey has accomplished its objective. They defeated the Christian Brotherhood handily."

"I wish I could believe you."

"I bring plague, but I never lie. The Anglo regime will fall in less than a year."

"Wonderful."

"If you want my opinion—"

"I don't."

"—those nine gallons of diesel fuel would've cut Jewish casualties in half." Chuckling, Quincy began his customary descent into Kevin. "Did I ever tell you how much that Harvey Sheridan fellow offended me? If there's one thing we spirits can't stand, it's spiritualism. The hottest places in Hell are reserved for those who trivialize death."

As the wraith and the child became one, Nora left Kevin to the safety of the stack and advanced gingerly across the deserted highway. With mounting despair she surveyed Phaëthon's remains. The melted wheelchair was easy to identify. The adjacent black glob had probably once been the carburetor; the amorphous mass, a tire; the carbonized threads, Kevin's mattress, possibly his monkey. It made no sense to continue south—not when a huge population center lay only ninety miles east on Route 64. There must be kind and generous people in Richmond. Surely the entire city hadn't succumbed to plague-era selfishness. Perhaps she would find a fellow wayfarer, some resolute parent preparing for the pilgrimage to Coatzacoalcos. With any luck, this person would have a stalwart heart, an iron will, a functioning car, and a hundred gallons of gas.

Would have cut Jewish casualties in half.

She lifted her weeping eyes toward Jehovah's grin, intent on begging Him aloud for whatever forgiveness her soul deserved and His dwindling powers permitted, but her strength deserted her, and the words lodged unspoken in her throat.

The Catemaco Miracle, Gerard called it. The Mexican Resurrection. The Tehuantepec Apocalypse. In the sculptor's view, recent events around the smoldering volcano partook no less of the supernatural than did the malignant wraiths who'd started it all. Malvina Fergus was the first of her kind, a thected abulic in seemingly permanent remission, but she was not the last. By the time Columbus Day rolled around (try as he might, Gerard couldn't shake off the U.S. calendar), the Church of Earthly Affirmation was curing fifteen plague victims per week.

Initially it seemed that the dispossessed fetches might be a problem, not because they consumed too many resources—a leveler knew no appetites beyond its lust for someone else's life—but simply because they took up space. Throughout that amazing autumn, it was difficult to find a fetchless plaza or park in Coatzacoalcos. But then, as if following the example of Malvina Fergus's doppelgänger, the parasites simply removed themselves, stumbling blindly into the jungle and vanishing amid the vines and ferns. When he heard that the plague was in retreat, a wave of self-satisfaction rolled through Gerard's breast. He hadn't felt so pleased with himself since receiving the Order of Saint Matthew Medal for his Madonna. Pride was a sin, of course—Dante disciplined its practitioners by consigning them to ledge one of Purgatory and placing heavy rocks on their necks—but it was probably too late for him to mend his ways.

Have you not learned that we are lowly worms,
Born to become angelic butterflies,
Destined to sail to Judgment all unveiled?

Say wherefore does your puffed pride soar so high,
Since you are naught but insects incomplete,
Like to the grub of unperfected form?

"Adrian, my hat goes off to you," Gerard told Lucido.

They were sitting in the psychoanalyst's aviary, descending cup by cup through a punchbowl of sangría, and for once the stench didn't bother Gerard. Birdshit, he decided, was simply the price you paid for birdsong.

"I'm not sure which affords me greater delight," said Lucido, his brain afloat on red wine and hyperion-15. "Defeating the levelers or humiliating those hidebound eggheads who have for so long monopolized the Western philosophical tradition."

"The former, I should imagine."

"Quite possibly the latter." A cockatoo landed atop Lucido's outstretched forearm. The bird hopped onto the tea table, dipped its beak into the punchbowl, and imbibed half an ounce of sangría. "From Pascal to Kierkegaard, it has been axiomatic among intellectual reactionaries that a Deosuicide would be a bad thing. For all His failings—His evil aspect, if you buy Judge Candle's theology—the idea of an interventionist God is so powerful, so inspiring, that any effort to replace it must *ipso facto* fail. And, indeed, until this moment, all attempts at such a swap have proven catastrophic." He removed a panatela from his humidor, ignited his butane lighter, and touched flame to tobacco. "The whole pathetic story begins with Immanuel Kant's categorical imperative, a feeble ideal at best, no more capable of sustaining the transcendent than my cockatoo is capable of sustaining a conversation. After Kant, of course, we get the vapid Deist vision of a scientific utopia and the French *philosophes'* oxymoronic Church of Reason. Then come Hegel's specious dreams of high culture fused to modern industry, Comte's pathetic positivism, Nietzsche's inhumane humanism, the calamity of totalitarian Communism, and the vile nationalistic occultism of the Third Reich. Finally, there's America's special contribution, the worship of mass-produced material goods. But here on the Isthmus of Tehuantepec, we have accomplished the impossible. We have superseded God, Gerard. God Almighty. Jehovah Himself. Does that sound absurdly Promethean and impossibly vain?"

"Yes, Adrian, it does."

"The traditionalists say, 'If God wanted man to fly, He would have given him wings.' To which I reply, 'If God *didn't* want man to fly, he would have strangled the Wright brothers in their cribs.'"

"The Jehovah to whom I once subscribed didn't strangle people. I hope the same can be said for Soaragid and Idorasag and—"

"Rest assured, Gerard." Lucido took a drag, blew a figure 8, and smiled. "The Somatocist pantheon is as benign as your lame-duck Trinity."

Gerard would have regarded his patron's high opinion of Somatocism and its gods skeptically but for the fact that Lucido's views were evidently correct. Besides exhibiting no symptoms whatsoever, the recovered abulics were proving to be an astonishingly charitable population. Almost without exception, they used their new leases on life to promote the common good. True, their devotion to the affirmation deities partook of zealotry, but it was at base a thinking zealotry and, just as important, a loving zealotry. A third of the acolytes and their families set out for Tamulipas, Nuevo Leon, Coahuila, and the continent beyond, determined to locate as many thected abulics as possible and lead them south to treatment. Of those pilgrims who stayed behind, about half dedicated themselves to helping recently arrived plague families find donations acceptable to the Church of Earthly Affirmation. Chief Deacon Hubbard Richter took charge of the other half, directing them to augment the gods' terrestrial domains: more cul-de-sacs in Idorasag's labyrinth, additional alcoves in Soaragid's cave, a second palace for Risogada, an expanded Orgasiadian grove—projects made essential by the religion's astonishing success.

From this pool of industrious pilgrims, Gerard was permitted to draw a dozen additional assistants, so that (counting Fiona, Malvina, the Ruíz brothers, and himself) the number of El Dorado godmakers now stood at seventeen. He could have employed twice that many. The larger Tamoanchan grew, the greater the number of niches there were to fill, and before long the studio was producing twelve graven images a week. Slowly but surely, El Dorado changed from a workshop into a factory, even as Gerard's role evolved from master sculptor to plant manager.

Although he despised his administrative duties, Gerard couldn't deny that humankind's future depended on the mass production of Somatocist idols. The time was not far off, he suspected, when Lucido would be anointing missionaries, arming them with the pantheon, and exhorting them to spread the faith. Beset by earthly affirmation, the fetches would eventually become as extinct as the dinosaurs whose extraterrestrial nemesis had brought Lucido and his collaborators to Mexico in the first place.

"I'll admit it—at first I was a doubter, but now I'm convinced Lucido's some sort of genius," he told the Ruíz brothers as the three of them rolled a huge hunk of Oswald's Rock onto the sledge. "Wouldn't you agree?"

"Up to a point," said Fulgencio.

"Yes, the man has his appalling side, I won't deny it," said Gerard. "And yet I can't help admiring him."

"Appalling," echoed Pelayo approvingly as he hooked the sledge to the donkey's harness. "We talked to Lucido just once in our lives, when he interviewed us for this job."

Fulgencio urged the animal down the hill. "We remember a disturbing remark he made. He said, 'Give me a long enough prick and a place to stand, and I'll fuck the world.'"

"Perhaps you missed the allusion," said Gerard.

"Archimedes," said Fulgencio. "Our nuns were classicists to the bone."

"Then what's the problem?"

"The problem, Señor Gerardo," said Pelayo, "is that he wasn't joking."

Every time Quincy describes the scene, I get tears in my eyes. Here's Mother, all hunched over from the two gallons of diesel fuel on her back, sometimes carrying and sometimes dragging her son down Route 64. She's hungry. Her bad knee is killing her. She has to stop every five minutes to catch her breath. But she keeps on going, mile after mile.

The worst part is the heat: the sun's rays combined with the funeral pyres burning on both sides of the highway. The logs crackle. The dead abulics pop and sizzle.

Night brings creepy sounds and spooky shadows, but at least Mother gets some relief from the sun. She finds a dry culvert, then makes us a bed out of fallen leaves and uses clumps of kudzu for pillows. A coyote would be proud to own this den. Mother is so hungry and tired, she doesn't bother with my physical therapy. Beyond the culvert, the pyres keep blazing. Even though I'm locked inside my head, helpless as Vincent Price chained to the basement wall in *Tales of Terror* while Peter Lorre bricks him up, I can still smell the roasting meat.

In the shank of the hot October afternoon, Nora stumbled into Charlottesville—the corpse of Charlottesville, she decided, for there wasn't another human in sight. She started up Fifth Street, searching for a good Samaritan, or even an amoral Samaritan—anyone who might part with a crust of bread, a bit of cheese, a gulp of potable water. Where was everybody? Dead? Thected? Had the plague hit Virginia especially hard?

A rangy, unshaven man sat in a bus-stop hut at the corner of Fifth and Main, hunting rifle on his lap, pulling apart a skinned rabbit. He greeted Nora's approach with an inhospitable glance, sidled silently to the far end of the bench, and began eating. Once she was beside him, however, Kevin draped across her knees, the rabbit hunter softened for some reason and made her the object of his chivalry. After proudly explaining that he'd shot, flayed, and boiled the animal himself, he offered her half the breast plus the remaining swallows in his can of Diet Coke.

The rabbit meat tasted like ambrosia. No lactating angel had ever produced milk to equal the hunter's aspartame elixir.

"God bless you," she said.

"We're better off than most towns. Lots of game up and down the Rivanna River. Rabbits, porcupines, pheasants, a few deer. Lord knows what we'll do if the animals get the plague."

"Where is everybody?"

"McIntyre Park, watching the matinee. Me, I'm not much for theater. Football, that's a different matter. I used to be the world's greatest Falcons fan, back when there were Falcons. I'm sorry about your boy."

"I'm taking him to the Lucido Clinic."

"Is that in Virginia?"

"Mexico."

"Hell, lady, you've got a long walk ahead of you."

It took the revived Nora only twenty minutes to bear her son the length of Main Street. McIntyre Park was an agreeable conjunction of groves, fields, and picnic pavilions surrounding a bandstand that currently functioned as an arena theater. Roaring and bellowing, a brawny actor stomped across the stage wearing a huge papier-mâché mask, eyes burning, nostrils flaring, tongues of flame darting from the mouth hole. Two bare-chested heroes dressed in leather aprons and copper greaves bounded into view, the first one stabbing the monster with a dagger, the second decapitating it with a sword. Hollywood blood spurted everywhere.

Nora shed her backpack and laid Kevin along the last row of seats, right beside an elderly woman who greeted each Grand Guignol effect with applause. Settling down to absorb the show, Nora soon realized that the drama derived from the world's oldest epic poem, *Gilgamesh*. She had just witnessed the celebrated slaying of the giant Khumbaba by the hero and his stalwart friend, Enkidu.

Act one came to a visceral conclusion with Gilgamesh and Enkidu washing Khumbaba's dried blood from their limbs. During the intermission, four troupers moved up and down the aisles carrying Rubbermaid garbage cans and asking for donations. The audience paid generously for its amusement, offering up everything from Hershey bars to smoked trout, raw broccoli to trussed rabbits, crab apples to a box of Wizard of Oats.

"Who are these people?" Nora asked her neighbor.

"The Great Sumerian Traveling Circus," answered the old woman.

"You mean they . . . move around?"

"In the morning they break camp and head south."

"How far south?"

"Couldn't say."

Act two commenced, developed, and reached a climax—the king's famous lament over Enkidu's corpse, culminating in his vow to find the secret of immortality—but the details were lost on Nora, whose brain now buzzed with a plan. A second intermission-cum-solicitation occurred, and then came act three: Gilgamesh walking a hundred miles through a fiery desert, killing a Man-Scorpion, and making love to the divine wine maker, Siduri. For Nora it was all a blur. As the hero sailed across the Waters of Death, she shouldered her diesel fuel, picked up her son, and headed for the park's outdoor lavatory.

In the ladies' room, a putrid cinder-block bunker that, oddly enough, still had running water, she steeled herself and stared at the mirror. Dirt freckled her brow and jaw. Her hair looked like the Gordian knot. Her cheeks and eyes were baggy, as if she'd recently removed her face and slept with it under her pillow.

Like Gilgamesh and Enkidu, she washed herself head to foot. She straightened her hair, pinched her cheeks, and cleaned her teeth with a fingernail.

The performance was over, the sun setting, by the time she emerged into the warm Charlottesville air. She carried Kevin past the bandstand, through a cluster of cottonwoods, and entered the troupe's encampment, a circle of five weather-beaten and decrepit Gypsy wagons, hillbilly shacks on wheels, each paired with an equally weather-beaten and decrepit horse. Spotting the actor who'd played Enkidu, she inquired whether the Great Sumerian Circus was indeed heading south, and, receiving an answer ("at least as far as Greensboro"), asked him where she might find the troupe's manager. Enkidu pointed to the jewel of the caravan, its windows hung with lace curtains, its chassis decorated with gilded scrollwork.

"Ask for Percy Bell," he said.

"Do you think he'll let me hitch a ride?"

"No, but what the hell do I know? I never thought he'd give me a decent part, but I ended up with almost as many lines as him."

Nora mounted the stepladder to Percy Bell's wagon and rapped her knuckles on the window. The door opened, and there stood Gilgamesh—not surprisingly, the Sumerian Circus's beefy and handsome leading man was also its manager—saying, "I gave at the office" in an accent that wonderfully combined South Carolina and Sean Connery. His only unattractive feature was his beard, a mass of black whiskers that he wore in overwrought Mesopotamian ringlets.

She introduced herself and explained why she wanted to reach the Isthmus of Tehuantepec as soon as possible.

"Your troupe needs me," she said.

"I rather doubt that," said Percy Bell.

Reluctantly he ushered Nora into his quarters, then lifted Kevin from her arms and laid him on the couch. Theatrical posters papered the walls, each displaying Percy Bell's name above the title of a play. Before the plague, he'd evidently divided his time between children's productions and off-Broadway Shakespeare, so that one month might find him portraying the Reluctant Dragon, the next month the reluctant Dane, one month the Hunchback of Notre Dame, the next month the crookbacked Duke of Gloucester.

"I'll mend your costumes," she said. "I'll make your posters and collect your donations."

"Those jobs are taken," said Bell, smearing lard on his face.

She scanned the actor's dresser, soon spotting an untitled script—an adaptation of the Orpheus myth, she concluded after leafing through several pages, skewed to the realities of the abulic age. "If you could just take us to Greensboro..."

"Sorry, Mrs. Burkhart." He continued to apply the lard, soon becoming as pale as a fetch. "I already have too many mouths to feed."

Nora flourished the script. "Your next production?"

"If I can talk the troupe into doing it. The title is *The Lyre of Fate*, or maybe *Orpheus Underground* would be better."

"In college I wrote a parody for my drama teacher. *Waiting on Godot.* Beckett's hobos are working in a restaurant. The menu is blank. There's no furniture. One afternoon Godot appears and orders an empty glass of absinthe."

Percy cracked a smile. "I can't hire you. I simply can't."

"Nobody understood the sadness of it all like the Greeks. They got it better than the Sumerians, better than the French absurdists."

"Tragedy without self-pity," he said, nodding. "Defeat with dignity. The instant Orpheus learns he mustn't look back on his lover, you know he'll never get her to the surface."

"The woman who played Inanna tonight..."

"Elizabeth Darby."

"She'd make a good Eurydice."

"Indeed."

"But isn't the outcome too upbeat for you?" asked Nora. "Orpheus and Eurydice together again, frolicking through subterranean meadows?"

Percy rubbed away the dissolved makeup with a scrap of fabric. "It's obviously a fake, like the framing story in the Book of Job. My version will climax with the nightingales singing over Orpheus's grave."

"Brilliant."

"All right, you and Kevin can ride in Elizabeth's wagon. She talks too much, but she has extra room."

"You won't regret this, Mr. Bell."

"Yes I will, but that's the story of my life." He reached out and squeezed her arm. "We break camp at dawn. Welcome to life on the road, Mrs. Burkhart. It has nothing to recommend it."

The Flagellants of Montrose

FIVE MILLENNIA AGO, when the world was new and the gods were young, there ruled in high-towered Uruk a courageous king, two-thirds divine, one-third mortal. His name was Gilgamesh, and his subjects did not love him. Gilgamesh exhausted the men of Uruk, exhorting them to gird the city with jewel-studded walls. The women he abused as well: maids and matrons, daughters and dowagers—all were prey to his royal ardor. At length the gods took pity on the people, creating for them a physically cruder but spiritually superior version of their king, a warrior with strong muscles, hooves for feet, and untamed flowing hair.

Wild in his soul, free in his heart, noble Enkidu roamed the Sumerian plains and woodlands. He romped with the gazelles; he talked to the wolves; he ate grass. And still the citizens of Uruk endured their king's daemonic energies, until one day a palace courtesan named Shamhat went in search of the promised champion. Spotting Enkidu swimming in the Euphrates, she anointed her breasts, shed her garments, and enticed him into her arms. For two days and nights the mortals coupled atop the very clay from which the gods had fashioned Enkidu. At dawn on the third day, Shamhat rose abruptly and returned to the city.

Enkidu, lovestruck, pursued her. Passing through a series of mighty gates guarded by stone lions, he wandered the city streets, eventually encountering not his beloved but his king. Still in thrall to his loins, Gilgamesh stood poised to enter a marriage house and claim the bride in advance of the groom. Enkidu blocked the doorway. Encouraged by the thronging courtiers, the two men wrestled, until at length Gilgamesh prevailed, leaving Enkidu lying breathless in the street. The king's fury abated. Here, Gilgamesh realized, was someone equal to himself. Here was a brother and friend.

The following night, Enkidu had a frightening dream. In his vision, an enormous black bird swooped down from Heaven, sank its talons into Enkidu and Gilgamesh, and bore them to the world below.

"Shuffling among the dead, who lay everywhere in great heaps, we reached the House of Dust. We entered the banquet hall and beheld the princes of long ago seated at a table, their crowns set aside for all eternity. The princes' food was mud. Bitumen was their drink. Peering through the gloom, we saw Belit-Sheri, keeper of the Book of Death, who pointed to us and cried, 'Who has brought these ones here?!'"

Enkidu's nightmare shook Gilgamesh to the marrow. The gods, he believed, were exhorting the two friends to fill their lives with glorious adventures, for death would claim them soon.

Now it so happened that the royal architects were planning many new temples and civic buildings for Uruk, projects requiring vast quantities of timber, a resource that grew abundantly on the Cedar Mountain to the east. When Enkidu reminded Gilgamesh that a giant guarded this forest—the fire-breathing Watchman, Khumbaba—the delighted king decreed they must depart immediately.

The friends buckled on their weapons and struck out for the rising sun. After a journey of many days, they reached the eastern forest with its timber stockade, lair of Khumbaba. Gilgamesh shouted over the stockade walls, commanding the monster to meet them in open combat. Suddenly Khumbaba appeared, releasing ferocious roars that bowed the cedar trees and blew the heroes to the ground. Regaining his feet, Gilgamesh stabbed the giant with his dagger while Enkidu beheaded him with a sword.

The triumphant adventurers made sacrifices to the gods. Taking up their axes, they stripped the Cedar Mountain and set the trees afloat on the Euphrates, knowing that the current would bear the booty to Uruk. Covered with sweat, dirt, and Khumbaba's blood, they dove into the river and washed.

One month later, as Gilgamesh walked alone through Uruk's burgeoning temple complex, the evening breeze brought him sweet whisperings from Inanna, Queen of Heaven, the rollicking goddess of love. Following her call, Gilgamesh came to the largest of Uruk's sacred gardens, where Inanna was pruning a huluppa tree that she intended to carve into a throne for herself. But a sickness had infected the tree, turning its branches as bare as bone. The cause was obvious. A vicious viper was wound around the huluppa's roots, the vampire Lilith inhabited the trunk, and the sinister Imdugud bird had nested in the crown.

Acting on Inanna's orders, Gilgamesh killed the viper, evicted Lilith, and frightened off the bird. Moved no less by his beauty than by his bravery, the goddess made advances to the king. He spurned them: his days of profligacy were over—and besides, everyone knew that Inanna's lovers came to grotesque ends.

The rebuffed goddess swore vengeance. She convinced her father—Enlil, king of the gods—to curse Uruk with seven years of drought. The disaster climaxed with the arrival of the Bull of Heaven, a terrible behemoth that raged through the city's streets, leveling the marketplace and trampling thousands under its hooves.

Gilgamesh and Enkidu charged into combat. Closing on the Bull of Heaven, Enkidu grabbed its tail and hurled it against a masonry wall. As the beast recovered its balance, the king drove his sword deep into its brain. Victory seemed certain. But then, unexpectedly, thrashing about in its death agonies, the Bull of Heaven gored Enkidu with a sharp, serrated horn.

Shocked and horrified, Gilgamesh directed that his friend be carried to the palace, laid on the royal bed, and attended by the wisest physicians in Sumer. Their medicine proved futile. Enkidu's wound festered, and he died in Gilgamesh's arms.

Day after day, night after night, the desolate king brooded beside the corpse, refusing to let the embalmers do their work. Only after the worms claimed Enkidu's flesh did Gilgamesh give his brother up for burial.

Insane with grief, the king fled Uruk and rushed into the burning desert. For an entire month he wandered beneath the fiery sun and slept under the remorseless moon. He cried out to all the gods.

"When I die, shall I be like unto Enkidu? Shall I descend to the House of Dust and dwell among shadows? Will mud be my food, bitumen my drink?"

Gilgamesh conceived a plan. If the legends were true, there lived in fabled Dilmun two humans who had achieved immortality: King Ziusudra and his wife, favorites of Enki, god of wisdom. The hero of Uruk vowed to cross the sea of Ocean, find Ziusudra, and learn his secret.

Thus did Gilgamesh begin his second journey, to the west this time, domain of the sun god, Utu. After many days of wandering a scarred and barren wilderness, he reached twin-peaked Mount Mashu, portal to the Ocean Sea.

A Man-Scorpion guarded Mashu, armed with a venom-tipped sword. The ensuing fight was arduous, but at length Gilgamesh slew the Man-Scorpion and passed into the mountain's dark heart. For an entire day and night he stumbled through the tunnel, until finally, directly ahead, a shaft of dazzling light appeared. Inspired, he dashed outside, strode along the shore, and entered the golden garden of Siduri, the divine wine maker, who many people believed was Inanna in another form.

Learning of her visitor's ambition, Siduri laughed. The idea of a mortal eluding death was both sacrilegious and ridiculous.

"O Gilgamesh, to where do you run? When the gods created

man, they allotted to him death, but immortality they retained for themselves. Come, Gilgamesh. Drink my wine. Enjoy my body. And after you return to Uruk, let your days be filled with feasting, your nights with merriment. Take a wife, sleep with her, and cherish each little child who holds your hand. For this, too, is the lot of man."

Gilgamesh did as Siduri bade, imbibing her wine and visiting her bed. Awakening the next morning in the goddess's embrace, Gilgamesh again declared his intention to reach Dilmun. Before they parted, Siduri unfurled her hair and rubbed the paint from her cheeks. Now Gilgamesh saw the truth: Siduri was indeed Inanna.

He raced down to the beach, soon encountering Urshanabi, King Ziusudra's faithful boatman. Urshanabi agreed to unmoor his skiff and bear Gilgamesh beyond the pellucid sea and over the Waters of Death, but only if the king would first equip their expedition with 120 staves harvested from twin-peaked Mashu. Acceding to this odd condition, Gilgamesh returned to the mountain, felled six score trees, and smoothed them into poles. Not until he and the boatman had sailed beyond Ocean did Gilgamesh appreciate their peculiar cargo. Every time Urshanabi dipped a stave into the Waters of Death, thereby moving them closer to their destination, the corrosive currents ate the wood.

Finally Gilgamesh reached paradisiacal Dilmun, where he found the immortal king and queen seated on their thrones. Hearing about the hero's mission, Ziusudra revealed that the path by which he'd attained everlasting life was now closed.

"Enlil granted us immortality only because I acted with courage and resolve during the Great Flood he sent to punish humankind for its impieties. Following orders from our divine benefactor, Enki, I built a boat and stocked it with a breeding pair of every species. Never again will one man be given the opportunity to save an entire world."

Gilgamesh wept. Taking pity, Ziusudra's wife told the hero a closely guarded secret. Beneath the River of Immortality grew the sharp-thorned Flower of Youth, a miraculous plant that restored vitality to anyone who ate its petals, leaves, or roots.

Pledged now to Gilgamesh's service, Urshanabi piloted him far up the River of Immortality. Gilgamesh lashed boulders to his feet and plunged into the waters. Descending to the river bottom, he entered a grotto and found the Flower of Youth, protected by the Crab of Hell. A furious struggle followed, but Gilgamesh eventually killed the monster with a sword thrust, then used the same weapon to uproot the plant. The thorns pierced his arms and chest as, cutting the boulders from his ankles, he shot to the surface.

Urshanabi poled Gilgamesh back across the Ocean Sea. The sun pounded on the western desert as the two men set out for Uruk. Fearing death by thirst, Urshanabi wanted to partake of the magic flower then and there. Gilgamesh answered that it would be ignoble to do so before his subjects received their portions.

Late one afternoon, the travelers reached an oasis boasting huge palms and deep wells. Gilgamesh and Urshanabi hid the plant behind a rock and stretched out in the shade. While the travelers slept, disaster struck. Attracted by the plant's fragrance, a Woman-Serpent appeared and clamped her jaws around the Flower of Youth. As the sun set, Gilgamesh awoke to behold the serpent and her treasure vanishing down a well.

Overcome by despair, Gilgamesh and Urshanabi attempted to console each other. The king grew pensive. Perhaps Siduri was right. The wise man feasts, dances, and makes love while he can.

"Now let us sleep, Urshanabi, for tomorrow we reach fair Uruk! Do you know my city? Its walls shine like polished copper, its gates glow with lapis lazuli, and its foundations are of burnt brick!"

Before bringing *Gilgamesh the King* to the McIntyre Park bandstand, the Great Sumerian Traveling Circus and Repertory Company had been touring for nearly five months, systematically bypassing big cities in favor of towns and villages. Their motive was simple. Any settlement larger than Charlottesville still lay under the tyrannical administration of the Anglo-Saxon Christian Brotherhood, whose devastating defeat at Paramus had yet to impact its southern brigades. Rare was the Anglo-Saxon who did not regard itinerant acting troupes as havens of satanism and sexual deviancy. Thus did Nora find herself inhabiting a series of Virginia hamlets and farming communities, innocuous backwaters with vaguely sinister names like Bent Creek, Rustburg, Lynch Station, Motley, and Dry Fork.

Her duties were many. If hooligans had ripped down the placards posted by the advance man — Fritz Wexler, a former puppeteer who'd designed the play's various masks, trick props, and mechanical effects — it was her job to replace them. If the venue of the moment was dirty, be it a bandstand, hatch shell, high school auditorium, or abandoned movie theater, she must arrive two hours early with bucket and mop. Whenever a baby wailed during a performance, Nora was expected to escort both parent and child out of the audience's hearing. She had, additionally, a small but crucial role in the production itself. By yanking on a fishing pole threaded to an Imdugud-bird marionette, she made the insidious creature flee the huluppa tree in act two, a bit of technical wizardry whose execution the overworked Fritz was happy to place in the newcomer's hands.

In a matter of days Nora learned to despise unconditionally what Percy Bell called "life on the road." The Gypsy wagon's incessant bumping, lurching, and rolling jangled her nerves and unsettled her stomach. Unlike Phaëthon, the conveyance lacked air-conditioning, and she spent the transit between successive gigs at the mercy of the year's final heat wave. As a roommate, Elizabeth Darby was the near-total disaster Percy had predicted: a stern, stately, Nietzsche-positive Marxist who, when not keeping Nora awake with her snoring, accomplished the same result by laboriously recounting her pre-plague career as a writer and director of "progressive radical feminist pornography videos," products of her belief that women, too, had the right to indulge their raunchiest fantasies.

What really annoyed Nora about Percy was not his vanity or his bossiness but his views concerning the Lucido Clinic. His skepticism ranged from denials that the place even existed to diatribes against its presumptuousness.

"I don't see how a made-up religion can begin to defeat the levelers."

"Somatocism is polytheistic," Nora explained. "If Jehovah is merely one god among many, His orbiting skull becomes fundamentally innocuous."

"But the new gods don't exist."

"It's a matter of faith."

"I have none," he said. "Do you?"

"I have faith in faith," she said firmly.

"The skull never would've bothered my Sumerians," he conceded. "Enlil is dead? How sad. But we can still turn to Ninhursag—can't we?—and Enki and Utu and Inanna."

"There, you see? Quod erat demonstrandum."

"Quod erat baloney."

Whenever the troupe hit a new town, Nora looked around for a better situation—ideally, a Coatzacoalcos-bound plague family with a gassed-up minivan and room for herself and Kevin. No such miracle occurred. But then one day a startling though evidently accurate piece of gossip spread through the Great Sumerian Circus. Instead of veering north when they reached Greensboro, they would continue south, all the way to New Orleans, a city that in its proverbial quirkiness and perennial Catholicism had long ago kicked out the Anglo-Saxons. In the Big Easy, Nora reasoned, she'd have a good shot at finding a ship captain willing to ferry her across the Gulf of Mexico. And so she renewed her commitment to the *Gilgamesh* circuit: a tortuous but apparently trustworthy route to her goal.

"You're stuck with me," she told Percy. "'The straight course is hacked out in wounds, against the will of the world.' D. H. Lawrence."

"There's wisdom in that," he said.

"Especially now, when the will of the world is all we have."

Living night and day with Gilgamesh's adventures did nothing to lift Nora's spirits. The drama's central theme, the inescapability of death, was an idea of which she'd already grown heartily sick. By offering up this particular story, which he'd adapted himself from various translations of the Akkadian clay tablets, Percy was hoping to help humankind face its fetches with dignity. As the epic unfolded, people would come to perceive an ennobling universality in their plight—though for most audiences, Nora sensed, the production merely added angst to anguish. Even Percy admitted that *Gilgamesh*'s popularity had less to do with its message than with its being one of the few theatrical diversions available in the abulic age.

Beyond the enervating subtext, the play troubled Nora for its lack of fidelity to the seminal tablets. Percy had made cuts, imposed elisions, and pillaged other Sumerian myths.

"In the original poem, the Bull of Heaven doesn't gore Enkidu," she informed him. "Inanna causes him to fall sick."

"Who wants to see a play about somebody catching an awful wasting disease?" he replied. "My treatment preserves the basic concept, Inanna's cruel vengeance."

"In every surviving version," she persisted, "Gilgamesh talks the Man-Scorpion into letting him enter Mount Mashu. He doesn't battle the guard to the death."

"The audience has been sitting on its ass for over two hours. The fight wakes them up."

"I've never read any rendition in which Siduri seduces Gilgamesh."

"It's romantic."

"It's distracting."

"Dramatic license."

"Dramatic licentiousness."

Nora decided that, up to a point, Percy was enjoying her unsolicited critique. At least she was taking his play seriously, which distinguished her from almost everyone else in the company. "Near the end you give us a totally fabricated— "

"A totally fabricated Crab of Hell. I know."

Among Kevin's favorite bad movies, she remembered, was Roger Corman's 1957 *Attack of the Crab Monsters.* "Three monsters weren't enough? You had to have *four?*"

"Gilgamesh's Flower of Youth foreshadows a hundred subsequent legends in which a hero steals a dragon's treasure."

"Giant crabs are hokey."

"So are giant skulls. We live in hokey times."

Shortly after they crossed into North Carolina, Nora realized that her attitude toward the Great Sumerian Circus had changed. Whatever else one might think of these eccentrics, they were not—Elizabeth Darby excepted—boring. Not since her days of hanging out with Eric's magician friends had Nora run with such an energizing crowd. Bruno Spangler, cast as the drama's quartet of supernatural monsters, was a retired Indiana University football coach who also functioned as the company's bouncer, deftly extracting drunks and hecklers from the audience. Harold Ratcliffe, who acquitted himself brilliantly as the neurotic boatman, Urshanabi, had once been a carnival barker, convincing country bumpkins to patronize an armless man who threw daggers with his feet. Cyril Avalon, the handsome black actor who each night played both Enkidu and Ziusudra, was a former stage magician who'd known Nora's husband back when both men were doing the Lions Club and bar mitzvah circuit. Then there were the twins, Vicky and Valerie Lotz, who between them essayed four roles: the harlot Shamhat, the vampire Lilith, Ziusudra's queen, and the Woman-Serpent who devours the Flower of Youth. Whenever the company collected around the campfire, these versatile young actresses would tell tales of pressing their twinness into the service of revenge scenarios, such as the time they convinced Valerie's mean-spirited boss at Pompeii Pizza that he was losing his mind.

But it was the Sumerian Circus's treatment of Kevin that ultimately won Nora over. Not a day went by without a cast member volunteering to feed the sick boy his lunch or dinner. Whenever Nora was about to massage Kevin's muscles or dress his boils, a trouper invariably stepped in and offered to help. They even found Kevin a minor part in the show itself: the corpse that Khumbaba displays on his stockade as a deterrent to trespassers. To Nora the child seemed quite pleased every time the monster carried him on stage.

Crammed together in the Greensboro First Baptist Church, the opening-night audience gave *Gilgamesh the King* a standing ovation, and Percy easily convinced the city fathers—father, actually, his colleagues having all died of the plague—to approve an extended run. As it turned out, this particular residency marked a new chapter (a fresh clay tablet, as it were) in Nora's personal epic. During the first three Greensboro performances, she realized that whenever Percy was on stage, a phenomenon comprising 178 of the play's 192 minutes, her gaze never left him. After the fourth performance, she understood why.

God had died; Kevin had been thected; the future belonged to the fetches. And yet here she was sitting in the back pew of a ramshackle church in North Carolina, eating peanuts, sipping sassafras tea, and counting the curls on Percy Bell's beard.

Nobody liked to discuss the subject, but during the early days of the company's tour the plague had taken a severe toll on the Great Sumerian Circus. It was by disease, not design, that half the troupe had ended up playing multiple roles. Only in the night's deepest hours, as Percy and Nora lingered around the campfire tossing dry twigs into the flames, was he willing to talk about his losses to the Cranium Dei.

Among the victims was Percy's old drama coach from Duke, Terence Sterling, who'd joined the cast shortly after the fetches succeeded in making higher education as uncommon as costume balls.

"What part?" asked Nora.

"Khumbaba the Watchman." Percy poked the fire with a birch stick. "The weird thing is, in real life Terry was the sweetest man you ever met."

"Our dark sides always find outlets, don't they?" she said. "Your teacher played Khumbaba. My father drank. *His* father hunted African lions."

"God unleashed epidemics."

Nora laughed. "The school psychologist thought Kevin's magic was cathartic. He actually used that word. Cathartic."

Jabbing the fire again, Percy raised the glowing ember to his lips and blew away the ash. His acting that evening had been particularly forceful, their final Greensboro performance. Nora hadn't been so impressed since Eric, crouching over her on their wedding night, had drawn a blooming red rose out from between her thighs.

"I wish you'd seen Mason Yates, an absolutely amazing Ziusudra," said Percy. "The minute he walked on stage, you knew exactly why Enki appointed him to save the human race." The flames bestowed an amber glaze on his rugged face and shaggy arms. She thought of Talos, the bronze giant who menaced the Argonauts during their return to Greece. "Then Mason got thected and died, and I had to put Cyril in the role. He's good, but he's not a natural like Mason."

"Your concept of Ziusudra is delicious, the way he keeps thinking Enki didn't *mean* to pick him to build the ark, it was all a dreadful mistake."

"I thought you hated my play."

"Yes, but when it came to Ziusudra, you were really on your game. Reluctant leaders make the best heroes."

Despite her carping, he clearly valued her companionship. Of all the people in the troupe, she alone shared his passion for myth. Once they got started, the two of them would discuss Orpheus's descent, Icarus's fall, Leda's parturition, and Medea's murder spree as excitedly as if these bizarre events had occurred in their own families.

"I hope Dr. Lucido isn't like Ziusudra, torn by feelings of unworthiness," she said. "I want him to believe he's a wonder-worker."

"Monomaniacs who set up self-aggrandizing empires in Third World countries," said Percy, "do not generally suffer from low self-esteem."

Yawning in tandem, they rose, kicked out the fire, and started toward the wagons, clustered on the grounds of the Greensboro Rotary Club. Sycamore trees lined their path; the shed leaves crunched and crackled underfoot. A crescent moon hung behind the Cranium Dei, giving Jehovah a pair of goatish horns.

Percy's wagon loomed out of the darkness. Despite November's chill, sweat formed in Nora's palms. What if he invited her inside? Would she assume the usual risks—learning that he coveted only her flesh, admitting some pathogenic spirochete into her body—merely for a passing thrill? She knew one thing for certain: it was a problem she wanted to face.

"May I walk you home?"

"All right," she replied evenly.

"Something's bothering you?"

"No, no."

"I thought it went well this evening," he said, "especially the seduction."

"You seemed to have your heart in it, among other components."

Arriving at her wagon, they hugged each other good night—a nuanced hug, and they both knew it, as carnal as anything they might accomplish without fusing their mouths or removing their clothes. Percy walked away whistling. Nora departed humming. She climbed the stepladder, opened the rear door, and tiptoed inside. Kevin wheezed musically. Caught by the skull, its silvery rays streaming through the windows, the Imdugud-bird marionette glowed with a beauty she'd not noticed before. I'm in love with a Sumerian king, she thought.

A disquieting and familiar fragrance reached her nostrils: the stink of fresh sartre sauce. She turned toward Elizabeth Darby. The dead woman's stage-four symptoms were vivid, the pocks like bullet holes, the grooves like saber cuts. Eyes open and vacant, she lay in a pool of fear syrup mixed with pus. Nora laid her palm against the corpse's cheek. What she felt was not an external chill, imposed by the autumn air; this chill traced to a gratified fetch. It was the frost that starts from within.

Nora bolted from the wagon and started across the encampment, alternatively praying she was mistaken about the actress's condition and wishing she'd been more appreciative of her paeans to feminist pornography. Just then she could recall only one of Elizabeth's plotlines, about a Wiccan priestess who traded her witch's broom for an elongated windup dildo.

Percy was in the corral, feeding his mare, a skittish roan named Dolly.

For forty-five minutes they performed CPR on the actress, Percy pressing her sternum, Nora inflating her lungs. When it was obvious that her leveler had won, they wrapped Elizabeth in a tarpaulin and laid her beneath a sycamore tree, gnarled as an arthritic's hand, bare as Inanna's huluppa. Percy enshrouded her speckled face with his white linen handkerchief.

"She became Nietzsche-positive in Manassas, saw her fetch again in Culpepper," he said. "She told me they'd made a deal."

"Fetches don't make deals," said Nora.

"They make them, and then they break them. Elizabeth was supposed to reach New Orleans."

"Have you met yours, Percy?"

"Only once. Horatio. He came to our world première, front row, gasped in all the right places. An unnerving experience, seeing my double like that. I suddenly knew how Gilgamesh felt when he first laid eyes on Enkidu." He exhaled, his condensed breath forming a spectral cloud over the blanketed corpse. "What I'm about to say might sound unfeeling, with Elizabeth not even in the ground yet, but on Tuesday we open in Asheboro, and..."

"And you want me to play Inanna? You're right, Percy. It sounds unfeeling."

"I'm sorry. Will you play Inanna?"

"I'm not much of an actress."

"We're not much of a troupe."

"I'd probably get stage fright."

"It's milder than reality fright, the condition we all endure these days."

At first the idea of acting opposite Percy appealed to Nora almost as much as the idea of becoming his lover. Memorizing her lines would be a snap: she'd seen the show twenty-four times. But then she considered the nature of the part. Night after night, Gilgamesh spurned Inanna in act two. Inanna subsequently bedded him in act three, but only by virtue of wine and shapeshifting, not because he found her irresistible. What subliminal effect, Nora wondered, would Inanna and Gilgamesh's dysfunctional relationship have on Percy's feelings toward his costar?

"Let me think it over."

"Of course."

At dawn, Bruno and Fritz dug a shallow grave with the small spade Inanna used for transplanting huluppas in Uruk's sacred gardens. Elizabeth's coffin was a Magic Chef refrigerator box that Vicky and Valerie had salvaged from a Dumpster behind the Rotary Club.

Later that morning, Percy called his troupe together and led them in a succinct but dignified burial rite. For a eulogy, he quoted the lament that Gilgamesh delivered over Enkidu: the world's oldest funeral oration, Nora realized. "The path we followed through the dark forest weeps for you," he intoned, staring at the coffin. Bruno had covered the Magic Chef logo with Elizabeth's prize possession, a scrapbook containing favorable reviews of her feminist pornography. "The mountain we climbed where we slew the Watchman weeps for you. Your companions, the ibexes, shed tears. The wolves grieve. The deer mourn. The gazelles leap no more."

He concluded on a bitter note, chastising Elizabeth's fetch for terminating her career as Inanna and also for depriving her of Eurydice, the role she was slated to assume in *The Lyre of Fate.*

"All right, sign me up," Nora told Percy after the funeral. "I'll play that shifty bitch, and I'll do a good job of it, too."

Nora had never believed the theatrical truism whereby a disastrous dress rehearsal augurs a successful opening night, but in the case of her debut, aphorism and actuality proved identical. While the run-through in the Uwharrie National Forest was a debacle, with Nora forgetting a quarter of her lines and garbling many of those she remembered, the following evening's performance in Asheboro contained only one minor fluff—"I shall harness for you a chariot of lapis" emerged from her mouth as "I shall harness for you a chariot of apples"—and when the show was over, Percy presented her with "a token of his regard," the silk-and-wire immortality plant that Gilgamesh retrieves from the river bottom.

Midnight found Nora drifting into the sort of deep and gratifying sleep she hadn't known since the skull's advent. In her dream, she became Leda, the Spartan whom Zeus, assuming the form of a swan, seduced one night—a human-avian union destined to produce Helen of Troy and the Dioscuri, Castor and Pollux. Nora's subconscious provided a memorable denouement: when she went to give birth, an enormous egg emerged from her womb. The shell cracked, and out popped a particularly obstreperous Imdugud bird, noisily demanding a bigger part in *Gilgamesh*.

She awoke feeling vaguely immortal and oddly content—attitudes certain to pass, she knew, but she succeeded in savoring the moment. That evening Percy Bell would spurn her Inanna half, after which her Siduri persona would seduce him though guile and grape, and the following evening in Samarcand the same events would unfold, as they would the next night in Ellerbe and the next night in Rockingham. It could be worse. Better a drunken hero in your bed than no hero at all. And besides, a Queen of Heaven should not squander her energies dallying with demigods when there were plagues to conquer and destinies to undo. Beware, abulia. Take heed, contagion. Here comes Inanna, who is also Ishtar—and Astarte—and Aphrodite—and in a weird Jungian way the Virgin Mary too. Here comes Nora Burkhart, deliverer of flowers, before whom all fetches tremble.

In Gerard's view, the one truly troubling facet of the Catemaco Miracle was El Agujero, "the Hole," a concrete fortress erected outside Tamoanchan's main gate as a detention center for those seeking admittance to the temples. Architecturally the building was a crime, its walls so featureless and sterile that they made the Bauhaus seem heir to the Baroque, but he reserved his deepest disgust for the behavior that the detention center contained. He'd explored the place only once—it had piqued his curiosity, luring him into its depths much as Hell had both captured and captivated Dante—but that single visit was sufficient to outrage him. Touring a succession of stifling, windowless rooms jammed with petitioners, he quickly realized that El Agujero served a purpose far more sinister than the mere screening of true abulics from those occasional pilgrims whose symptoms traced to either depression or schizophrenia. The detention center was a world unto itself, a fiefdom ruled over by Chief Deacon Hubbard Richter and his drones, all of them apparently committed to placing as many bureaucratic barriers as possible between plague families and the Church of Earthly Affirmation.

Although they varied in detail, the pilgrims' stories cleaved to a single theme: the impossibility of finding justice within El Agujero's walls. An Iowa pig farmer and his thected sister had so far spent two weeks in the center, sleeping on the floor and subsisting on quesadillas. Each morning a supercilious assistant deacon would appear and promise a noon interview with Richter, but at the appointed hour the deacon simply moved them to a different holding area. A famous New York trial lawyer, keeper of her dying son, had managed to lug eleven gallons of diesel fuel all the way from Milwaukee. Upon the lawyer's arrival in El Agujero, Richter confiscated the donation, subsequently claiming that she'd never brought it. A best-selling children's author, his life now dedicated to curing his young bride, had actually received and filled out a coveted "blue certificate" (the patient's passport to Tamoanchan), but the guards sent the abulic back to the center on a technicality: because of a defective printer ribbon, the serial number was illegible.

Conscience throbbing, indignation burning, Gerard raced the pony cart up Mount Tapílula to Lucido's mansion. In the vestibule, he encountered the psychoanalyst's private chauffeur, the annoyingly ingratiating Leopold Dansk, who revealed that Lucido was presently in the basement, cataloguing the Chardonnays and burgundies through which various plague families had purchased their loved ones' salvation.

Entering the wine cellar for the first time, Gerard noticed dozens of archaeological treasures emerging from the musty darkness: earthenware pottery, obsidian idols, gigantic baby-faced stone heads crowned with gear suggesting rugby helmets. A basalt disk the size of a tractor wheel leaned against the doorjamb, its facets swarming with arcane numerals and cryptic icons. In the far corner rested a four-legged granite altar that had evidently commended itself to Lucido as a bar, its surface littered with goblets, split limes, and wine corks.

Dressed in a green silk kimono, Lucido acknowledged Gerard's arrival by setting out two champagne flutes and filling them with Moët et Chandon. "An unexpected visit, how flattering." His brittle enunciation of *unexpected* implied that further such surprises would be unwelcome.

Gerard rested his hand on the basalt disk and looked at Lucido quizzically.

"An Olmec calendar," Lucido explained. "Impressively accurate, though difficult to nail to a kitchen wall. This cellar abuts the ruins of an Olmec temple, locus of rituals whose precise nature continues to defy scholarly speculation. Care for some wine?"

Instead of answering, Gerard explained why he'd come to Tapílula.

Lucido drank the first flute of Moët et Chandon in a single breath, then began sipping the second. "Are you aware," he said, "that I am perhaps the last man on Earth who enjoys access to *le vrai champagne*?"

"I don't want to talk about champagne. I want to talk about Hubbard Richter."

"My patients treat me well. There are rare vintages in my cellar, porterhouse steaks in my freezer, Italian suits in my closet . . ." Lucido finished the second flute of champagne. "You must understand—we're seeing thirty new cases of abulia a day around here. Richter is our man at the floodgates. His stringent standards forestall chaos."

"Not stringent. Sadistic."

Lucido offered a smile of begrudging assent. "My lieutenant has his enthusiasms."

"And if you refuse to dampen them, I might just have to—"

"To what? Quit? Go ahead, Gerard. I dare you. Walk away from the only full-time job a sculptor can get these days."

"What do you see in a man like Richter?"

"Opportunism, officiousness, and an appalling lack of imagination. I shall accept your resignation whenever you wish to tender it."

Gerard did not resign that day, or the next day, or the next. He did not resign at all, in fact: a shameful matter, no question—so shameful that he confessed it to his reubenite companion, Erasmus. Not surprisingly, the principled humanist refused to let Gerard off the hook. In their own way, Erasmus argued, the excesses of El Agujero were as evil as the sixteenth-century religious violence against which he'd so vociferously dissented. When Gerard suggested that this analogy was extreme, Erasmus left in a huff and started chatting with Martin Luther.

ERASMUS: I still believe that people possess freedom of thought and action. Even now, postmortem, I believe it.

LUTHER: Once again you hope to convince me that free will exists?

ERASMUS: I do.

LUTHER: Your compulsion to persuade me is irresistible? In fact, you have no choice about it?

ERASMUS: Very funny. If there's no freedom, monk—if no man picks a fight, a mistress, or his nose independently of the divine will—then doesn't God become responsible for every act of savagery on the planet?

LUTHER: Our Creator's wrath cuts deep. His mercy, deeper.

ERASMUS: I wrote *De Libero Arbitrio* to discourage Protestant fanatics from purchasing God's omnipotence at the price of His goodness.

LUTHER: And I wrote *De Servo Arbitrio* to discourage papist Grecophiles from elevating Scholasticism above Scripture.

ERASMUS: This is between you and me, Martin. Let's leave Aristotle out of it.

LUTHER: If freedom is the lot of man, why can't I unblock my bowels at will?

Luther strains, attempting to break wind.

ERASMUS: Too many turnips.

LUTHER: A man's soul is like a horse. When God takes the reins, the horse goes where God chooses. When Satan takes the reins—always with the Almighty's permission, of course—the horse goes where Satan chooses. The two riders dispute the destination between them, but the steed must obey whichever power occupies the saddle.

ERASMUS: I already knew you regarded the Pope as the Devil's deputy, but I hadn't realized you viewed the Devil as God's lieutenant.

LUTHER: Not His lieutenant. His instrument. Like a pruning hook, or a hoe—a tool for cultivating His divine garden. There *is* progress, Desiderius. Even you are less a papist than when I nailed up my theses.

ERASMUS: I shall die a Catholic.

LUTHER: Endorsing Mariolatry, Purgatory, Transubstantiation, and a hundred other absurdities.

ERASMUS: I am as opposed to Mariolatry as you, Purgatory happens to be our present venue, and Transubstantiation is by no means absurd.

LUTHER: How can you imagine that the bread and wine convert completely into Christ's body and blood, when it's patently obvious that His body and blood combine with the substance of the bread and wine?

ERASMUS: Transubstantiation enjoys the virtue of tradition.

LUTHER: Consubstantiation enjoys the virtue of being true.

ERASMUS: Transubstantiation is a divine mystery.

LUTHER: Consubstantiation is an undeniable fact. And constipation too, poor me.

Again Luther tries to pass the gas bubble.

ERASMUS: You'd think that in Purgatory, of all places, purgation would come easily.

LUTHER: And then there are fools such as Zwingli, who believes only in Christ's *spiritual* presence during the Eucharist. But I shall not speak of the unspeakable.

ERASMUS: Unless, of course, the Devil compels you to.

The following Monday, Gerard's mood hit bottom when Hubbard Richter appeared in the god factory with orders from Lucido to halt all idol production, immediately and totally. To Gerard the decision made no sense. True, the temples were now jammed with deities, but what about the ancillary Tamoanchans so desperately needed throughout North America and Europe? Logically, Gerard and his apprentices should be carving idols for years to come, until nothing but a pebble remained of Oswald's Rock. Where was the bold thinking, the grand designing, by which Lucido had conceived Somatocism in the first place?

Gerard tracked down Lucido in the mansion's central hexagon, where the psychoanalyst lay relaxing amid the swirling waters of his hot tub. A different martial-arts movie unspooled on each television screen (or possibly unsynchronized moments from the same martial-arts movie), so that the men's conversation progressed amid a mélange of flailing limbs and somersaulting bodies.

"Why are you shutting us down?" Gerard asked.

"The temples are full," Lucido replied. "Don't worry. You'll still be fed and pampered. When your fetch attempts to claim his prize, I shall supervise your cure personally."

Gerard stared into the hot tub, fixing on a frothy mass of bubbles. In Canto VII of the *Inferno,* Dante had revealed the fate of "the sullen," mired beneath the Stygian marsh, their gurgled speeches turning to meaningless foam on the surface. "Shouldn't we be sending out evangelists? Exporting Somatocism to every pocket of plague in the world? Oswald's Rock is good for a thousand more idols at least. We'll never eradicate abulia by sitting on our asses in Coatzacoalcos, complacent and visionless."

"My dear Gerard, do you know nothing of metaphysics? You speak of evangelists. In point of fact, our church boasts an *army* of evangelists, and it grows larger by the hour. I refer, of course, to the legions of parasites we have driven from their hosts. Even as I speak, they are wandering the Earth, informing their fellows that a cure exists. It won't happen today, or tomorrow either, but in time all the world's fetches will become demoralized to the point of dematerialization."

"I find that difficult to believe."

Lucido rose from his hot tub, the steamy water trickling down his simian chest and hairy legs. "I agree with you on one point. We must have a vision for the future. What do we want Western civilization to look like a hundred years from now? To what absolutes should the post-abulic world pledge its heart? The Bergsonian Life Force? The Cosmic Christ?"

"We've *got* to take Somatocism on the road."

"This conversation has grown boring. My insights have proven correct in days gone by, and they will prove correct in the days to come."

Sauntering out of the hexagon, Gerard right behind, Lucido

padded through his library, a jumble of psychology books, medical texts, metaphysical treatises, sacred writings, and—a collection doubtless supplied by plague families—first editions of literary masterworks. He entered his bedchamber, approached a tall carousel outfitted with mirrors and hooks, and, spinning the wardrobe ninety degrees, drew forth his emerald kimono. Languorously, he cocooned himself in imported silk.

"I can offer you a new commission," said Lucido. "El Agujero's architect, you may recall, provided the main foyer with a sculpture niche. The present statue, a Soaragid, must be replaced."

"With a Risogada?"

"No."

"An Orgasiad?"

"The niche, dear fellow, cries out for a statue of me."

Gerard chewed pensively on his lower lip. "What medium?"

"Reubenite." Lucido retrieved a manila envelope from his writing desk. "I have no time to pose. This package contains a dozen full-face photographs. How long from brainstorm to finished piece?"

"Five weeks."

"I'll give you three."

"Do you want a mere statue, Adrian, or do you want something that captures the soul beneath the skin?"

"All right. *Four* weeks. No, take all five. But I expect you to go farther beneath the skin than you've ever gone before."

As the Great Sumerian Circus tramped through the ruins of Georgia, revealing to each successive village the face of *arete* and the shape of stoicism, Nora realized that acting had less in common with teaching, and more with sex, than she'd previously supposed. In the classroom you could never feign a competence you didn't possess; the students would see through you, catching you in a contradiction or stumping you with an impish question. The theater, by contrast, tolerated pretense. On most nights, Nora gave herself completely to her role, becoming Inanna body and soul. But a performance, like an orgasm, could be fudged. When beset by a sore throat or knee spasms, she merely went through the motions, and nobody except Percy seemed to notice.

What most delighted her about a trouper's life was its encompassing sensuality. Up on the stage, everything looked brighter, felt hotter, tasted sweeter, smelled sharper, resounded more deeply. Her role enabled her to wear two enthralling costumes, the white silk gown in which Inanna propositions Gilgamesh and the red satin robe in which Siduri seduces him, and they both caressed her skin even as they clothed it. The Inanna costume in particular comprehended Nora: not so much a dress as a kind of ghostly lover. Climbing into it night after night, she came to understand the unholy desire that fetches felt toward their hosts, the raging wish to assume another entity.

Come, Gilgamesh, and be my lover!
Grant to me your seed,
And I shall harness for you a chariot
of lapis and gold,
Whose wheels are brass and whose ornaments
are burnished copper.
You shall have storm-demons for your horses
And a great serpent shall be your whip.
Before you kings, lords, and princes shall
all be humbled.
The bounty of the hills and plains they shall
bring to you as tribute!

On a warm mid-December morning, Nora awoke in the throes of a severe menstrual flow, a deluge to challenge a homuncular Ziusudra. She had just finished replacing her homemade rag tampon and was about to start on Kevin's bandages—his boils still leaked copiously—when Percy unexpectedly graced her doorstep, tugging agitatedly on his beard. He hadn't looked so distressed since losing his leading lady. Fritz Wexler, he explained, had just reported that the Chattahoochee was impassable, a crisis that jeopardized the evening's scheduled performance in Tuskegee. Apparently some "nameless idiots" had built a funeral pyre near the woods, and now an inferno was "raging uncontrollably" for miles up and down the Alabama border.

"I'd like your help," he said.

"I've never put out a forest fire," she said.

"I'm hoping to find a way through. Vicky said she'd check on Kevin, change his bandages, whatever."

She wondered if Percy understood how erotic it was when a man arranged child care for you. "Count me in."

Later, as Percy swung onto his mare, she saw that the rising sun had painted the Cranium Dei a shimmering orange, as if the skull had somehow caught the light of the Chattahoochee holocaust. She settled behind her costar, the saddle forcing them into unavoidable intimacy. Sliding her arms around his waist, she leaned forward and pressed against his spine.

They felt the fire before they saw it, each gust rushing toward them like an exhalation from the great dragon Fafnir. Coils of smoke rode the air. Sparks nicked their faces. And then the beast itself appeared, a roiling red-and-black hulk, thundering and crackling as it feasted on Lakepoint Resort State Park. The odor was pungent but tolerable, the corpses' stench evidently neutralized by the sweet fragrance of boiling sap. In perfect synchronization Percy and Nora removed their jackets and crammed them into Dolly's saddlebag. Nora looked toward the Chattahoochee, clogged with burning branches. God's bony face lay reflected in the copper waters. He wore a crown of fire.

Steering the horse south, Percy followed the course of the river. The La Grange Railroad Trestle was a tumult of smoke and flame, as were the Lake Harding Dam and the Barletts Ferry Bridge. Two miles beyond Mulberry Grove, the blaze finally dwindled. On the outskirts of Columbus, it became a feeble collection of brushfires.

Percy pointed to the anonymous but intact bridge that bore Route 82 into Alabama. "Mission accomplished."

He wheeled the mare around and guided her back through Mulberry Grove, then onward to Barletts Ferry and the dam beyond. At the railroad trestle the fire still seethed at full power. Masses of smoke filled the sky like obese phantoms. Eyes smarting, the riders wept. The heat was savage. Nora tightened her hold on Percy, as if she feared the Hephaestan blasts might unseat her, though her motives were more lustful than practical. They sweated profusely, continuously, like two Sumerian mariners attempting to pole their raft across the Ocean Sea in record time.

"I've got to cool off." Percy vaulted from the saddle, then placed a steadying hand on Nora's thigh, their connection reverberating through her body as he led the mare down to the riverbank.

He tethered Dolly to a trestle pylon, fed her a carrot stub, stepped onto the sand bar, and took off all his clothes. His self-possession did not surprise Nora. This was a theater person, after all, a free spirit. He hung his clothes on a spindly hunk of driftwood. His navel was large, an alluring black vortex. She thought of a favorite myth: Zeus setting the two eagles loose at opposite ends of the Earth, knowing they would eventually meet and mark the omphalos, the center of Creation, deep within the temple at Delphi.

Naked as a fetch, Percy entered the river and began treading water.

The Delphic oracle itself was delivered by a priestess, the Pythia, originally a maiden but in later years a woman past fifty. After bathing in the waters of the Castalian spring, she would seat herself on a tripod over a cleft in the ground, breathing in the intoxicating vapors that poured from the heart of the Earth. Thus entranced, the Pythia prophesied, while the priests of Apollo wrote down her words and turned them into hexameter verse.

Nora dismounted. She stripped slowly, littering the beach with jeans, blouse, underpants. The inferno licked her flesh. December became August. She removed her bra. Her nipples hardened. She stepped into the Chattahoochee, laughing as the cool currents reached first her calves, then her thighs, hips, and breasts. Firebrands splashed down everywhere. Embers sizzled as they hit the river. She'd never known a stranger environment, this sanctuary hedged with menace.

Half walking, half floating, she approached Percy. Their lips met; their tongues performed a Dionysian dance. She reached down, found the string, removed the tampon. They kissed voraciously: two escapees from the House of Dust reveling in the liquidness of things, the outside world with its muddy rivers and wet membranes. They caught their breath and kissed again. Like a curious fish, his submerged prick probed her thigh. She tossed the tampon aside. Planting his feet on the river bottom, he encircled her waist with his arms and clasped his hands behind the small of her back. The inferno bellowed. Sparks cascaded through the air. She seized Percy's shoulders, her legs drifting upward.

"Sweet Inanna, I know that you destroy your lovers, but I must take my chances," he said, ducking under the water. He suckled her immersed nipples, came up for oxygen, went under again. Surfacing, he said, "I'm yours, Inanna. Turn me into a jackal. Send me to the Seven Fierce Judges."

She took his cock in her hand and guided it toward her reedy delta, the Chattahoochee's flow combining with her own to smooth the way.

It had been well over two years. Almost three. Ben Sawyer, who'd made Kevin a plywood doghouse for his "Fangs of Cerberus" trick.

"And I shall harness for you a chariot of lapis and gold," she whispered, bobbing to Percy's rhythm, "whose wheels are brass and whose ornaments are burnished copper."

"Lapis and gold," he echoed, gushing inside her blood-stained temple.

That night, strutting around on the auditorium stage in Jubal Early Junior High School in Tuskegee, Nora gave a singularly passionate performance. It was the dead of December, but everyone could feel the heat.

Until two weeks ago, the dreams Quincy sent me were sweet: mental music videos featuring my cousin Cindy wearing nothing but a bowler hat. Now he sends me nightmares.

I'm lying on a bed, naked, bound with leather straps like John Kerr fastened to the torture slab and being menaced by Vincent Price. ("You are about to enter Hell, Bartolomé. Hell! The netherworld, the infernal regions, the abode of the damned, the place of torment, Pandemonium, Abaddon, Tophet, Gehenna, Naraka, the Pit . . . and the pendulum!") The anesthesia wears off gradually. At first I think nothing's wrong, but then I realize the surgeons have filled me with large holes. They're mouths, actually: forty brand-new mouths, carved into my chest, back, arms, and legs—drooling, puckering, fat-lipped mouths, complete with thirteen hundred teeth that clatter like castanets.

A nurse arrives with a washtub of oatmeal. She slops it all over my body, like a little kid dribbling syrup on a waffle, and then my mouths start eating, and it's the strangest sensation I've ever had, all these big living holes in my body, opening and closing as they gobble up the oatmeal.

When feeding time is over, the nurse washes me with a bath towel. The instant she leaves, I feel sick to my stomach. Suddenly it all comes up, forty-one rivers of oatmeal pouring out of me as I lie on the mattress screaming through my eighty-two lips for a nurse who never comes.

The worst part is knowing that, tomorrow night, the whole thing happens again.

"Are we lost, dear?" Nora asked.

Percy, seated beside her atop his Gypsy wagon, said nothing, his mind focused on guiding Dolly amid the docks of Montrose, a once prosperous fishing community spread along the eastern shore of Mobile Bay. According to the two aging Nietzsche-positive tramps they'd met that morning at the local pyres, an abandoned movie palace, ideal for staging *Gilgamesh the King*, lay in the center of town. For a full hour they'd crisscrossed the heart of Montrose without spotting the promised Casper Theater, whereupon Percy had steered them, on impulse, into the labyrinthine wharf area.

"We're lost, aren't we, darling?" she persisted.

Percy maintained his silence. Nora ate a boiled potato. She stared at his heroic face and saw once again why she adored him, his unaffected bewilderment, his natural sweetness. What did it mean to love a man, and to have that love returned, when everything was dissolving around you? It was a fundamentally ludicrous situation, partaking less of grand romantic tragedy than of some dopey Roger Corman postapocalypse melodrama, *The Day the World Ended*, perhaps, or *The Last Woman on Earth*.

"Maybe the Casper Theater burned down," she said. "Maybe those hobos haven't laid eyes on it since the Montrose première of *The Day the World Ended*."

Kevin's embattled body rose in her imagination. Two days earlier, his boils had transmuted into classic stage-four symptoms: a network of pocks and grooves suggesting a connect-the-dots puzzle solved by a lunatic. The act of discarding his bandages had brought Nora no comfort, for beyond this phase of thexis, she knew, lay only death.

An immense oil tanker loomed out of the mist, moored to a concrete quay. At first she assumed that the *Exxon Bangor* was a derelict, another casualty of the collapsed infrastructure—quaint as a milk wagon, obsolete as a steam locomotive—but then she noticed the lamps blazing in the wheelhouse and the sailors scurrying across the weather deck. Four tugboats approached from the south, their skippers evidently bent on towing the *Bangor* into the bay.

"I know what you're thinking," he said.

"There's no harm in asking," she said.

"I don't want to burst your balloon, honey," said Percy, "but I doubt that they're getting her ready just in case somebody shows up needing a ride to Mexico."

"Fatalist."

For a man committed to sailing his tanker out of the harbor by sundown, the master of the *Exxon Bangor*, a muscular African-American named Marbles Rafferty, seemed peculiarly unperturbed—pleased, actually—when Nora and Percy appeared uninvited on his bridge. The explanation proved simple. Rafferty had caught *Gilgamesh the King* two nights earlier in Barnett Crossroads, and he'd loved every minute.

"You were brilliant," he told Percy. Spiffily attired in dress blues, the captain was an imperially serious man, with soft dark eyes and a slight stammer. "Act three was the best, all those nautical scenes." He guided them into his private quarters, a cluttered cabin dominated by a desk holding a brass sextant, a pack of Camels, and a cloth-cover edition of a book called *The Gospel According to Popeye*. "I'd never realized how much of *Gilgamesh* is a sea odyssey. The Crab of Hell had me on the edge of my seat."

"Not everyone cares for the Crab," said Percy, smirking in Nora's direction. He brushed the gold piping on Rafferty's sleeve. "We're hoping you can point us toward the Casper Theater."

"This isn't my town." Rafferty retrieved the Camels and with a flick of his wrist caused a single cigarette to emerge from the pack. "Smoke?"

"No, thanks."

"We're also trying to reach the Bahía de Campeche," said Nora.

The captain removed the exposed Camel, slid it between his lips, and, giving the pack a shake, coaxed out a second cigarette. He offered it to Nora. She declined.

"That seduction scene of yours, Mrs. Burkhart—sensational!" Rafferty lit his cigarette and scowled. "Palermo's my port of call. Would either of you like a beer? I feel like I'm entertaining royalty."

"I might be tempted," said Percy.

"Sure," said Nora.

Rafferty opened his refrigerator and took out three damp brown Budweiser bottles. "These may be the last three Buds in America," he said, distributing the beers. "Normally I'd never use the *Bangor* as a passenger liner, but somehow they found enough bunker fuel for an Atlantic crossing, plus they're paying me in gold. Once we reach Europe, I'm converting to Islam and heading for Turkey. No abulia there. Why Mexico?"

"My son's been thected. There's a treatment facility in Coatzacoalcos, the Lucido Clinic. Heard of it?"

"'Fraid not."

"I hope to find a ship in New Orleans."

A smile spread across a face that seemed unaccustomed to the merest grin. "When you get there," said Rafferty, "scour the docks for my good buddy, Anthony Van Horne. You've heard of him, the guy who hauled God from Gabon to the Arctic. He got a book out of it. Anthony, I mean, not God. I was his first mate." Taking a hearty swallow of beer, he lifted *The Gospel According to Popeye* from his desk and showed Nora the back cover: a photograph of a rugged but vulnerable-looking sea captain—a New Age Ahab, she decided, prepared to make peace with the universe. "Lately he's had a run of tough luck, I heard, reduced to managing some sort of oddball whorehouse."

"Has he got a ship?" asked Nora.

"One way or another, Anthony always gets a ship." From his refrigerator Rafferty obtained a Skippy peanut butter jar filled with a gray, moist, arcane gunk. "When you find the old gooney bird, give him this, and he'll know you're my friend." He handed Nora the jar, colder even than the Budweiser. "It's called glory grease, an ointment we used to make on the *Valparaíso*: Corpus Dei blood and lymph, good for what ails you—sunburn, hemorrhoids."

"Will it help my bad knee?"

"Worth a try. Tell him Marbles Rafferty thinks your Great Sumerian Circus has done the world a few favors, and he should bust his chops trying to get you across the Gulf."

As Nora tucked the glory grease into her Celtics jacket, Rafferty's first officer, a man reminiscent of Khumbaba in bulk and loudness, appeared in the doorway and announced that their "weirdo passengers" had arrived. The captain glowered, obviously more inclined to discuss *Gilgamesh the King* than to address practicalities. He introduced his visitors to the mate, who bore the incongruously fey name of Delbert Florence, then grabbed his binoculars, donned his Hemingway cap, and ushered everyone back onto the bridge.

"Ever hear of a movie palace called the Casper?" Percy asked Delbert Florence.

"It went belly-up a few years after VCRs came in," said Florence. "New owners stripped it clean and turned it into a Wal-Mart."

Fingers locked tight around the glory grease, Nora followed her companions out of the wheelhouse and onto the starboard bridge wing. The noonday sun shone brightly, collaborating with the skull to burn off the last of the mist. When Nora saw Rafferty's passengers, her first impression was that some progressive insane asylum had accorded its inmates a field trip. Despite December's cold, or possibly because of it, the pilgrims were naked to the waist, their abdomens girded by iron bands, their attention fixed not on the temperature but on the task at hand: lashing one another savagely with leather thongs, bandsaw blades, and strands of barbed wire. The air vibrated with whipcracks. Smiling through their tears, answering one another's yelps and groans with inspirational laughter, the flagellants marched across the docks and up the gangway, a parade of happy masochists.

"Three hundred from Pensacola, seven hundred from Bay Minette, over a thousand from Mobile," said Rafferty.

"I don't get it," said Percy.

"If they make a pilgrimage to the Cinecittà Reliquary, whipping themselves all the way, God will lift the plague—or so they believe."

Nora snorted contemptuously. "*Who* will lift the plague? *God?* Don't they ever glance at the sky?"

"The skull, they claim, is a snare set by Satan, rather like the dinosaur fossils," said Rafferty. "To tell you the truth, I'm not looking forward to this trip."

As the flagellants swarmed over the weather deck, Nora beheld their piety in all its grisly particulars, a crazy quilt of weeping wounds and exposed bone.

"Are you two screwing in real life," asked Rafferty, "or do you just do that on stage?"

Percy slipped his arm around Nora's waist and said, "Have you noticed how straightforward people are these days?"

"Our era's only virtue," said Rafferty.

"We're screwing in real life," answered Nora.

"Good for you," said Rafferty.

Repulsed by the martyrdom on deck, Nora turned toward the water. A dozen fishing trawlers plied Mobile Bay, accompanied by squawking entourages of cormorants and seagulls. She reached into her jacket and removed the peanut butter jar. If she rubbed glory grease all over her son, would Quincy go away? Doubtful. And yet the balm was precious: her entrée to Anthony Van Horne and, by extension, her passport to Coatzacoalcos.

Later, as Nora and Percy stood on the dock watching the tugboats drag the *Bangor* seaward, she asked, "Why was Gilgamesh so foolish as to leave the Flower of Youth unprotected?"

"Hard to say, honey," replied Percy. "Perhaps he knew, unconsciously or whatever—he knew that no mere mortal could possess the plant for long. If the Woman-Serpent hadn't stolen it, a lion would have, or a wolf, or an eagle."

While Nora pondered Percy's analysis, the tugs shot free of the *Bangor*. The tanker's engines kicked in, their guttural groans rising above the laughter of the flagellants and the clatter of their lashes.

"I see what you mean," she said, squeezing the jar. "Even so, if the Flower of Youth ever comes my way, I'm going to guard it with my blood."

Inanna Unbending

The wet and gloomy morning of December 29 found Nora, Percy, and the rest of the Great Sumerian Circus on fabled Bourbon Street, moving amid swarms of gaudily costumed revelers, most of them sipping Hurricanes and bathtub-gin fizzes through red plastic straws inserted into sequined masks adorned with peacock feathers. Dixieland trumpet solos vibrated the winter air. Banjos sang; snare drums rattled; sybaritic shouts resounded among the ornate hotels, doorless restaurants, and iron-brocaded balconies. It made no sense, she decided. Carnival season always started on January 6, never before. Not until the Sumerians reached Jackson Square did she understand that a celebration even grander than Carnival was in progress, an everlasting Mardi Gras convened in decadent defiance of the skull. High above the stratosphere God enacted His perpetual laugh, and the city of New Orleans laughed back.

The entire French Quarter had become a red-light district. Everywhere Nora looked, streetwalkers unveiled their wares, as if Storyville, Louisiana's fabled experiment in legalized prostitution, had returned from history's mists to spread its ethos throughout the town. Given the scope of the bacchanal, Nora predicted a poor turnout for that evening's performance. Who had time for the Sumerian Circus's three-act paean to stoicism when the Vieux Carré roiled with communal rye, free love, and gratis jazz? And yet attendance proved substantial—a consequence, she supposed, of Percy's canny decision to saturate the town with handbills emphasizing not only the show's many sword fights but also its glamorous venue, the legendary Superdome. In fact it was their largest audience to date, over two thousand violence aficionados and carnage connoisseurs who probably hadn't visited the moribund sports complex since abulia's ascent, each now seeking the satisfactions he'd lost when NFL games went the way of gladiatorial combat and public executions.

Even if *Gilgamesh the King* ran for a decade, it was unlikely that the Sumerian Circus would ever again play to a house packed with people dressed as fire-breathing dragons, dead American presidents, penises the size of canoes, and the entire menagerie of Noah's ark. Distracted by all this ostentation, Nora had trouble staying in character. She screwed up three lines. She missed two cues. The audience didn't mind. Indeed, they rewarded their entertainers handsomely, filling the troupe's Rubbermaid cans with bags of raw crayfish and boxes of Cajun rice. Nothing, it seemed, not even abulia, could dim the city's renowned *lagniappe.*

Act three was well under way, with Gilgamesh battling the Crab of Hell, when Nora, surveying the spectators from behind a scrim, spotted a squat, sixtyish man in the second row, wearing a tattered pea jacket and a baseball cap embroidered with the word VALPARAÍSO. Stern eyes, weathered skin, beard resembling a Brillo pad: a colleague of Van Horne's, surely. The crab fight took forever. Gilgamesh's final speech went on and on. The curtain call seemed interminable. But then, at last, as the houselights brightened, Nora moved inconspicuously into the bearded man's vicinity, drew him aside, and asked whether he might be a sea captain.

"Right church, wrong pew. Crock O'Connor, engineer on the *Natchez Queen.* Can I buy you a drink, Inanna?"

"Who runs the *Natchez Queen?*"

"Anthony Van Horne."

Her heart leaped. "Author of *The Gospel According to Popeye*?"

The engineer gave a knowing nod. "People thought it was fiction, but I knew different. When Van Horne sank his hooks into God and started towing Him north, I was right there, making sure we didn't blow a boiler."

As her conversation with Crock O'Connor progressed, Nora learned that the *Natchez Queen*, once the flagship of a proud fleet devoted to hauling tourists up and down the Mississippi, had fallen on hard times. Shortly after discovering that her owners had died of the plague, Anthony "commandeered" the old sternwheeler, outfitting her with wood-burning boilers and turning her into an extension of the city's eternal Mardi Gras: a floating bordello catering to a clientele that favored aquatic sex over landlocked. Twice a day Van Horne and his crew made their tautological voyage, ferrying the fornicators down to Belle Chasse then up to Harahan and back to the French Quarter. For a can of soup or ravioli, a man received admittance to the general orgy on the cargo deck. Two cans got him a free Hurricane and a private stateroom with the tart of his choice.

"And what would a customer get for *this*?" asked Nora, producing the peanut butter jar she'd obtained three days earlier on the *Exxon Bangor*.

O'Connor's jaw dropped. He yanked off his baseball cap, revealing a large, livid steam burn etched on his pate like a nautical mark of Cain. "I haven't seen that stuff in years."

After explaining how she'd come by the glory grease, Nora asked whether Van Horne might be willing to meet her that night.

"Sorry, ma'am," said O'Connor. "We're doing a wee-hours cruise, and then he always goes home to his wife and kid. A sad story. The boy got thected in March. Thirteen years old."

For the first time ever, the word *thected* made Nora smile. "Thected? Then he'll definitely want to see me."

"Tell you what. Come down to Riverwalk by eleven-thirty, pier 24, and the boss might spare you a minute."

If Percy had known about the perils of Bienville Street, he probably would have insisted on accompanying her, with Cyril Avalon or the Lotz twins looking after Kevin. Instead he took the boy in hand, kissed Nora so hard that his beard enveloped her jaw, and wished her good luck.

Maneuvering along the crowded thoroughfare, brushing past hookers and winos, she endured the entreaties of a half-dozen men with dirt under their fingernails and ejaculation on their minds. On four occasions she had to brandish the plywood sword Percy employed each night to butcher the Bull of Heaven (easily mistaken for the real thing under the city's sallow lamps) and threaten to separate the accoster from his testicles. The deterrent worked in every case.

Battered but stately, the *Natchez Queen* lay cozily in her berth, lashed to a dozen bollards, the celestial death's-head hovering between her twin smokestacks like a field goal suspended in time. Although the boat wouldn't be leaving for an hour, the evening's entertainment had already begun, and Nora's progress across the cargo deck became a matter of picking her way through a pulpy landscape of naked, contiguous, writhing bodies. Such a pathetic spectacle, she thought. If an antidote to abulia existed, it surely wasn't this. You couldn't simply fuck the plague out of existence.

She entered the casino, walked past a raucous craps table and a solemn blackjack game, then ascended to the saloon deck using the broad central staircase, its brass banisters and plush carpet evoking the luxury hotels of pre-plague Paris. A second staircase brought her to the observation deck, a third to the texas deck. The door to the captain's stateroom stood ajar. She crossed the threshold.

In contrast to Marbles Rafferty's spartan cabin aboard the *Bangor*, Van Horne's private sanctum boasted gilded mirrors, oil paintings of sailing ships, and red taffeta drapes: the sort of elegant Victorian salon in which Henry Jekyll, his dark side waxing, might have sought to seduce a music-hall prostitute. The captain himself lay sprawled on a green velvet sofa, clean shaven, eyes closed, not so much asleep as dazed. Hearing Nora approach, he swung his legs outward and set his feet on the fake Persian carpet.

"I've got no job for you," he grumbled, then added, with a laugh, "All the sexual positions are taken."

Nora, nervous, absently unsheathed her sword. The captain glanced at the plywood blade and smiled.

"My name is Nora Burkhart," she began, "and you are Anthony Van Horne, father of a thected child."

Van Horne stood up, smoothing the front of his New York Mets windbreaker. Fifteen years after the fact, he was still fundamentally the trim, attractive man of his *Gospel According to Popeye* author photo. "How did you know that?"

Presenting the glory grease, Nora told her tale. Kevin's illness, the alleged Mexican clinic, the Sumerian Circus, her encounters with Rafferty and O'Connor.

"Sailing with you would be lovely, I'm sure," said the captain. "Do you play chess?"

"Not very well, but I can recite six Shakespearean sonnets by heart. I'm hoping we might leave sometime tomorrow."

"Impossible."

"The next day, then. It's not easy getting admitted. I've lugged two gallons of diesel fuel all the way from Virginia. If I were you, I'd offer something from this vessel—the roulette wheel, your binoculars."

"The *Natchez Queen* is a riverboat, Mrs. Burkhart. It's intended for rivers. The Mississippi River, for example. The Gulf of Mexico, by contrast, is part of the Atlantic Ocean. Storms arrive without warning, and the waves get big as houses."

"So you'd rather have a dead boy than a swamped boat?"

Searing anger claimed the captain's face. His jaw tightened. "Do you know how many cures Cassie and I have tried?" he whispered with fearful intensity. "Do you? Give Stevie a pound of mashed cantaloupe rinds a day, that's sure to drive away his fetch. Take him to the Creek Indian medicine men over in Andalusia, they whip those old wraiths every time. Check out the hoodoo priests in the bayous, they never fail. Sorry, Mrs. Burkhart. We've heard it all."

"The Lucido Clinic is different."

"No doubt. And the children still die. It's time you were running along. I start work in fifteen minutes."

"Do you like your job, Captain?"

"I hate my job. I hate this stateroom, this cathouse, this whole sleazy setup. I'm a pimp with a sextant. A man has to feed his family."

Nora sheathed her sword, sidled toward the door, and offered Van Horne the precise stare with which her Siduri side nightly seduced Gilgamesh. "The Circus is in town until next Friday," she said, leaving the captain's quarters. "You haven't seen the last of me."

For two deplorable and wholly unproductive days—forty-eight hours of alternately sipping rum and reading Dante Alighieri, Emily Dickinson, and Thomas Ockham—Gerard ignored his commitment to carve a heroic statue of Adrian Lucido. On the third day, the obligation took hold of him, claiming his conscience like Soaragid seizing a goat in his jaws, and he performed the first step: riding down to El Agujero to inspect the niche in which the projected sculpture would reside.

He entered the despicable detention center, got out his tape measure, and obtained the needed dimensions. He fled. Dusk found him at Oswald's Rock, scanning the asteroid in search of a suitable protuberance to harvest for the statue. Lucido's vanity appalled but did not surprise him. From the very first, Gerard had sensed the analyst's ambition to promote himself to the same ontological status enjoyed by his contrived pantheon.

As his fingers skittered along the asteroid's surface, he felt as if he were somehow journeying through this great fragment from space, touring it layer by layer. He imagined that its core was molten, seething with melted reubenite and the liquid screams of its Late Cretaceous victims. Like a conch replaying the pounding surf, Oswald's Rock poured out the anguished cries of the ankylosaurs . . . the hadrosaurs' moans, the gallimimuses' laments, the iguanadons' death rattles.

At last he discovered the required lump—and something far more compelling. Could it be? Had all the random amputations to which they'd subjected Oswald's Rock ultimately wrought a representational image? He stepped back ten paces, studied the asteroid. Yes. Another ten paces. Yes! Once he'd extracted the Lucido material, the remainder would precisely resemble, in all its convoluted beauty, a ten-meter-high human brain.

I agree with you on one point, Lucido had said when Gerard came to him arguing for a more evangelical form of Somatocism. *We must have a vision for the future.*

The sculptor shuddered. He sweated. His body felt like a musical instrument, a wonder of jeweled keys and golden strings, and now some ineffable presence was starting to tune him. The plague, Lucido believed, was destined to pass. The skull would disintegrate. And then... the grand experiment, act two. Son of Western civilization. But what should it look like? What sort of world ought to emerge in abulia's wake?

For Gerard there could be only one answer. The future that made sense was a certain dead Jesuit's vision of short eternities and little myths: Father Ockham's republic of warm reason, free of the old order's "terrible transcendent truths," a democracy consecrated to the lobes and hemispheres (wider than the sky, deeper than the sea, counterbalancing the cosmos pound for pound) of the human brain.

The Hebrew tribes had received unending inspiration from their Ark of the Covenant. The American abolitionists had drawn boundless energy from the Philadelphia Liberty Bell. Throughout the history of Islam, the pilgrims' rough road to Mecca had been smoothed by the shining promise of the Ka'ba, that inscrutable black cube, forty feet high, housing a sacred meteorite.

Confront the human animal with a sufficiently numinous artifact, and he will astound you every time.

The presence began to play Gerard, wringing a concerto from his ligaments. Laughing like the giddiest disciple of Risogada, he spun away from Oswald's Rock and rushed down the hill into the jungle's sultry embrace. He didn't stop running until he'd reached El Dorado, where he sought out his C9 cleaving chisel and his heaviest soft-iron hammer, just the right tools for molding brains, whittling dreams, and carving a portal to the future.

As Anthony Van Horne ascended the back stairway of the Jean Lafitte Arms, he thoughtfully reviewed the two offers he'd rejected that evening, one from a whore hoping to swap her body for a bottle of rye, the other from a mother seeking a passage to Mexico. In both cases he'd made the right decision, but it behooved him to tell Cassie about the second solicitation. On the day Stevie became thected, Anthony and his wife had made a pact: regardless of where it lay or how fraudulent it sounded, they would reject no therapy out of hand.

He reached the top landing, inserted the key, and entered the apartment, its shabbiness subdued by the anemic light of dawn. Cassie sat dozing at the kitchenette table, head on the checkered oilcloth, fist squeezing a wooden pencil angling upward like the joystick component of *Fetchkiller,* a video game from the pestilence's early months. Pages torn from a yellow legal pad lay on the floor, each covered with dialogue from Cassie's newest play, *The Martyrs of Circumstance,* a project she was hoping might intrigue Le Petit Theatre du Vieux Carré—what was left of it, anyway, the plague having decimated the local arts scene.

As envisioned by Cassie, *The Martyrs of Circumstance* would tell of Hezrai, a cataleptic Jewish dissident living in first-century Judea. Arrested during Passover for tearing Roman medallions from the Temple in Jerusalem, Hezrai is crucified alongside a rabble-rouser named Jesus. Most of the drama would consist in a convoluted conversation between Hezrai and Jesus, who manifest a striking physical similarity to each other. In the end, misreading Hezrai's catalepsy, the Romans remove him prematurely from his cross. Entombed, the medallion thief regains consciousness beside the corpse of his doppelgänger.

Stumbling out of the sepulcher, Hezrai creates quite a stir among the assembled mourners.

A migraine aura hovered at the edge of Anthony's vision. Pulling the Zomig bottle from his windbreaker, he shook two pills into his palm, then swallowed them dry. He kissed his wife gently on the head, pressing his lips into her silky gray hair. She awoke.

"Profitable night, Captain?"

"Six pounds rice, two pounds crayfish. Soon we'll be the fattest couple in town. You didn't have to wait up."

"I was on a roll." Cassie took a gulp of cold tea and gestured toward the strewn manuscript. "Somewhere in that mess is the first draft of act one."

Drifting toward the cot, Anthony removed the wool comforter from his son and began the physical therapy. Gently he flexed Stevie's arms and legs. The stage-four abulic breathed in fitful gusts, as if his lungs were bellows operated by an epileptic smith.

"A theater troupe just hit town," said Anthony. "The lead actress visited me tonight."

"Would she like to play Mary Magdalene in a dazzling new drama about the birth of Christianity?" said Cassie.

"Her kid's been thected. She wanted me to run her across the Gulf. There's a new treatment in Coatzacoalcos, the Lucido method."

Anthony pulled back the French doors and shuffled onto the balcony. Six A.M. and yet the streets were wild as always, the shouts, songs, jazz, and party horns blending in festive cacophony. Dominic, naked, stood in the far corner, a stubby cigarette perched on his upper lip, one hand resting on the scrollwork balustrade, the other holding a bathtub-gin fizz.

"Care for a Marlboro, Dad?"

"Shut up," said Anthony.

He looked Dominic in the eye. How strange that a creature could replicate Stevie down to the smallest detail and yet bear no resemblance to him.

"Want to hear a bedtime allegory?" asked the fetch.

"No."

"I call it 'The Parable of the Petri Dish.' A brilliant scientist has long dreaded his approaching death, and his fear spurs him to great heights of biotechnical achievement. Eventually he succeeds in cloning himself. Several months later, entering the elderly genius's lab for the first time, the Grim Reaper finds ten identical scientists facing him. The startled Reaper contemplates each scientist in turn, but he cannot tell which is the prototype..."

Anthony's impulse was to hurl Dominic off the balcony, but he knew from experience that the leveler would simply exempt himself from gravity, hovering in the air like a Day of the Dead helium balloon blown over from Tampico.

Dominic finished his gin fizz. "At last a gambit occurs to the Reaper. 'Excellent work, Doctor,' he says. 'In fact, you made only one mistake.' 'Mistake? What mistake?' the original scientist demands to know. The Reaper points a skeletal finger at the one who has spoken and says, '*That* was your mistake!'"

Hawking a gob of phlegm from his lungs, Anthony transferred it to his tongue and spat it into Dominic's face. The fetch sneered and wiped away the sputum.

"Wait till my therapist hears about this, Dad."

Anthony stepped back into the apartment. Cassie sat on the floor beside Stevie, rubbing a salve into the boy's pocks and grooves.

Glancing up, she asked, "Is there really a new treatment in Mexico?"

"So she claims," said Anthony.

"The Lucido method?"

"Flat-bottom boats can't handle the Gulf."

"I know."

"The first serious roller would swamp us."

"Yes."

"Lucido is probably a charlatan," said Anthony.

"Probably," said Cassie.

He looked directly at his wife. Cassie stared back. Their eyes were wide, the veins in their necks engorged.

"We need to bring a donation," he said. "The woman thinks binoculars might do it."

"When do we leave?"

"Monday morning, on the tide."

Outside the hospital, famine rules the land. I'm imprisoned in the operating room. The mouths in my body have healed, but that hardly matters. In a nightmare by Quincy Azrael, you never win.

A starving family fidgets in the far corner. Their eyes are sunken, cheeks hollow. The nurse gives me a spinal. I go numb from the neck down. The doctors take up their saws. They remove my left arm and present it to the little girl, who eats it. The surgery continues. The little boy gets my right arm. The parents get my legs. It's all very slow, like church.

My eaters are grateful. They pat my forehead and kiss my cheek. I cough so hard that I fall off the table and start flopping around on the floor like a fish, begging Quincy to wake me up.

"We have control over this thing," said Nora, strolling hand-in-hand with Percy along the Riverwalk levee. Pier followed pier; the paddle-wheel steamers rocked in their berths. "It doesn't have to end badly."

"Maybe it doesn't have to end at all," he said.

"You know it does."

Spontaneously they stopped walking and fell into each other's arms. They kissed. Even in the age of abulia, she decided, people were able to arrange romantic moments. No, more, they were *obligated* to arrange them. It was everyone's duty these days to etch sonnets on moldering bones, dance atop dung heaps, and embrace beside poisoned seas.

"But is it me you love," she asked, their hug dilating, "or merely your image of me?"

"And what is my image of you?"

"Heroine of an unwritten myth," she said. "Inanna with a heart of gold."

They separated.

"An accurate list," he said.

"I'm none of those people."

"I love the real Nora too," he insisted. And then he added, with surely more scorn than he intended, "The stubborn, mule-headed English teacher who thinks she's going to find the Flower of Youth in Mexico."

"Let's not start on *that*."

They continued past the *Black Magic*, the *Becky Thatcher*, and *Cajun Witch*, this last steamer now a corpse barge. Dead abulics clogged the cargo deck, each body blanketed in quicklime, the whole grisly shipment probably destined for the river bottom. As Nora and Percy hurried through the stench, a tall woman in a green decontamination suit maneuvered a wheelbarrow onto the vessel and tipped it sideways, adding a fresh victim to the pile.

"So what about you, my dear?" he said. "Do you love both the Percy Bells, the real and the fabulous?"

"Both, yes."

He massaged his black Sumerian beard. "The anguished playwright, the daring bull slayer—he's easy to love. But what about the neurotic second-rate actor who thinks he can bring a dash of *arete* to a despondent world?"

"I love him too."

"Why?"

"He's honest."

They reached pier 24 and the *Natchez Queen*. The pilothouse window offered occasional glimpses of Van Horne pacing fretfully, no doubt pondering his folly in agreeing to challenge the Gulf. The mighty paddle wheel hung from the stern like a rotating drum built to exercise the Giant Rat of Sumatra. In an effort to minimize flooding on the cargo deck, the captain and Crock O'Connor had nailed a palisade of wooden planks to the bulwarks, so that the once aristocratic

Queen now evoked a working-class neighborhood whose inhabitants defined their properties with scrap-lumber fences. Kevin and Stevie were already on board, pursuing their hellish stage-four lives in adjoining staterooms.

"After *Gilgamesh,* we're doing *The Lyre of Fate,*" said Percy. "You'd make a great Eurydice."

She stepped onto the narrow catwalk, gingerly following it down to the wharf. "You, of course, will play the hero."

"Orpheus is my alter ego. I'm always looking back."

"I'm not."

"I know. I envy you. Me, I have nothing but regrets." Percy joined her on the wharf. "I'm going to try the Lotz twins as Inanna, though I don't expect any miracles. For a while I considered making it a drag role for Bruno, but I couldn't wrap my mind around it."

"Valerie might surprise you. That child has an edge. I can imagine her doing Medea someday."

Unhitching his backpack, Percy set it down and reached inside. He pulled out the white silk gown that Inanna wore for the seduction scene.

"Thanks for everything, Nora." He pressed the gown into her hands.

"Severance pay?" she asked, her throat growing hard as a stone.

"Souvenir."

"Someday I'll be too fat to wear it." The silk absorbed her tears. "But I'll never, ever throw it away." She draped the gown over her arm and made an abrupt about-face, stepping onto the gangway.

"Track me down, okay?" Percy called after her. "I'll cast you as Eurydice."

A steam-powered shriek issued from the *Natchez Queen* as Nora brushed the tears from her face, crossed the gangway, and marched into the sternwheeler without looking back.

Plutocrat Preserves

THE CRANIUM DEI SMILED fiercely, carrion clotted the Mississippi, and yet Nora felt oddly alive. For six months she'd been buffeted about by the death throes of the West, but now she'd made her break, reveling in the peculiar sense of freedom that only open water can provide. Although Kevin's symptoms were more dramatic than ever—his pocks growing wider by the day, the fissures deeper—the proximity of Coatzacoalcos buoyed her spirits and bathed her soul in hope.

They were a skeleton crew, four adults running a boat that normally needed seven, a fact Nora rarely forgot as she chopped firewood on the cargo deck, carried water down to Crock O'Connor in the boiler pit, or cleared away the detritus from the sternwheeler's previous career as a whorehouse. The *Natchez Queen* was disheveled beyond belief. Empty liquor bottles littered the companionways, exuding the saccharine fragrance of stale rum and cheap bourbon. Used condoms drooped over the rails like Dali watches. Diaphragms lay beside the sinks like amputee jellyfish. Nora spent the better part of the afternoon attempting to turn the observation and saloon decks into livable spaces, a project she abandoned upon realizing its futility. Even Hercules, who'd scoured the Aegean stables in a trice, would have balked at this mess.

The trip down the river took an entire day, their progress impeded by floating trash and waterborne bodies. It seemed that the *Queen* was not so much a sternwheeler as an icebreaker, her massive prow pushing through floes of flesh and bergs of pale putrescence. The boilers groaned; the engine grunted; the drive shafts squealed. As the boat steamed forward, the great carousel of paddles—eternally churning, forever dripping—became in Nora's mind an immense spinning wheel, as if some enterprising river god were transmuting the Mississippi into a single shining thread, long enough to weave a winding-sheet for all humanity.

At dusk, posted in the bow on orders from Van Horne, she stood and watched the Mississippi delta draw into view, portal to the tempestuous Gulf. As the sun descended to starboard, the captain's wife, Cassie Fowler, a regal woman with a strong-boned face, joined Nora on the foredeck. They contemplated the approaching sea and talked. Autobiography, reminiscence, confession. By the time Venus appeared in the sky, sparkling above the Cranium Dei like a bright idea, the two of them knew all about each other.

Cassie had met her future husband on the *Carpco Valparaíso*, their love affair periodically interrupted by Anthony's efforts to haul God's body to a tomb at the North Pole, a destination demanded by a pair of terminally ill angels. Eventually Anthony succeeded, but not before Cassie, communicating secretly with her atheist boyfriend in New York, had arranged for a bombing raid on the *Valparaíso*'s consecrated cargo.

"Our plan was doomed from the start," she told Nora. "We barely put a dent in the thing."

"Too much meat?"

"Too much meaning. The Corpus Dei was never supposed to end up in the Mohns Trench, or in an Arctic tomb either. Thomas Ockham was probably the first to figure that out. Have you read his book? 'By orphaning the human species, God has cleared its path to maturity.' Chapter two, last sentence."

"And by unleashing abulia, He has cleared our path to extinction," said Nora.

"I subscribe to Martin Candle's theory. The Almighty in His day was a duality." Cassie pointed toward the orbiting skull. A full moon had risen behind God's dome, making Him appear mildly hydrocephalic. "Abulia obviously comes from His demonic half, but I like to believe there's a benevolent side too, and it'll have the final say. I *have* to believe that."

"Stevie's an amazing kid, I can tell."

Cassie pretended to smile. "You should hear him play the clarinet."

"Kevin's into magic. His father, may he rest in peace, was a professional."

"Plague?"

"Heart attack."

"I'm sorry."

Nora's throat constricted. "Kevin used to have a live rabbit, Penelope Cottontail. In one trick she would eat a bunch of silk and leather, and then Kevin would reach into her mouth and— "

"Pull a hat out of a rabbit?"

"Exactly."

"Wonderful."

"I never found out the secret."

"Magicians never tell, do they?"

The crossing began after dark. Waves pounded the *Queen*'s gunwales, but the scrap-lumber palisade kept her from shipping more water than her crew could bail away. Winds rattled her beams and blew foam as high as the observation deck, yet the superstructure held firm. Her smokestacks vibrated like a tuning fork. Staring out to sea, watching the moonlit rollers, Nora mused to Crock O'Connor that at least the Gulf wasn't acid like the Waters of Death.

"I must admit, I didn't understand that scene." Crock sipped a gin fizz from a Texaco coffee mug. "If the Waters of Death could dissolve all those wooden poles, why didn't they eat the skiff too?"

"Myths and epics work that way. Dream logic. Such stories aren't factual, but they're metaphorically true."

He drained the coffee mug and said, "No wonder I hated English."

Later, lying in her bunk, lulled by the rhythmic thumping of the paddle wheel, Nora sifted through her brief but rewarding career on the stage. The evening's performance would be over by now. So what was Percy doing? Knocking back Hurricanes with Bruno Spangler? Shagging the Lotz twins? Sleeping, most likely. He'd never been much of a reveler.

She resolved to meet him that night in the land of Morpheus, but when she awoke the next morning, she realized that her subconscious had been cruel, taking her not to Percy's side but to the New Orleans Superdome.

In Nora's dream, the Circus was doing *The Lyre of Fate*. Cast as Eurydice, she'd somehow missed all the rehearsals and hadn't learned a single line.

Her first cue arrived. She faced the audience. She opened her mouth.

And she said, "Come, Gilgamesh, and be my lover! Grant to me your seed, and I shall harness for you a chariot of lapis and gold!"

When Gerard finally got around to assembling his apprentices on the studio grounds and explaining how their jobs no longer existed, Somatocism's temples being at capacity and its founder indifferent to evangelization, the dismay that emanated from the acolytes' loved ones did not surprise him. What he hadn't anticipated was the pain of the acolytes themselves. How strange that these saved souls, these delivered psyches, should be vulnerable to ordinary disappointment. But soon he came to perceive an essential humanness in their anger: what was the point of returning from the dead if you weren't then allowed to worry about taxes, dandruff, or water in the basement?

One by one, the apprentices drifted away. A few, such as Malvina Fergus, moved into El Agujero with the aim of helping plague families get through the ordeal of waiting. Others, including Pelayo and Fulgencio, headed north to find unhealed victims and guide them toward treatment. Gerard was especially sad to see the Ruíz brothers leave his employ: they were credible artists and energizing companions, and without their knowledge of Mount Catemaco's theophanic powers, Somatocism's gods might never have burst into actuality. Eventually only Gerard remained—Gerard, Fiona, and the great reubenite brain.

Much to Fiona's distress, Gerard was practically living at Oswald's Rock these days. His project consumed their conversations, fueled their arguments, occasioned their silences, and wrecked their sex life.

"Now and forever, you are my Beatrice," he told her. "Inspired by your purity, I shall fashion the greatest tribute to human creativity since the library of Alexandria."

"I'm pure now? Is that why you don't fuck me anymore?"

"We'll make love tonight."

"Your prick will be inside me, but your mind will be inside this sculpture."

"Nolo contendere."

"You have the odd distinction, Gerry, of being the only man I know who can fake an orgasm."

Claimed by the ghost of Erasmus, inflamed by Ockham's shade, Gerard set about transforming the Cretaceous dinosaurs' gravestone into a contemporary Ark of the Covenant, a latter-day Liberty Bell, a postmodern Kaʿba—or so he hoped. Hour after hour, his chisels danced along the cosmic stone. Chips flew into the sultry air. Sparks shot upward, arcing away like seeds from which a thousand Burning Bushes might spring. As always, the reubenite proved sufficiently plastic to permit the effects he sought—mineral become animal, lithic tissue, the throbbing collective mind—yet the emerging hemispheres still possessed a gravity appropriate to their purpose.

By day ten, he'd completed not only the striated cerebellum, locus of balance, but also the mighty cerebral cortex with its majestic convolutions, ropy crimson veins, and great central commissure. Next he shaped the pituitary gland, breaching it with a rectangular portal suggesting the entrance to a pharaoh's tomb. At last he was ready to tunnel through the cerebrum. He would hollow out the left hemisphere, then the right, then the cerebellum, filling each chamber with vivid displays of Homo sapiens's ingenuity and sculpted incarnations of Ockham's little myths. It would be, he prayed, a shrine to make Erasmus proud.

ERASMUS: Have you seen Korty's newest project?

LUTHER: Is that really what cerebral convolutions look like, a brood of writhing snakes? Most men have satanic souls—do they also have satanic brains?

ERASMUS: He's got the physiology right—it's the philosophy that troubles me. This bloated brain of Korty's simultaneously aggrandizes Man and reduces him to mere flesh.

LUTHER: Dear Desiderius, at last we agree on something. If our friend's magnum opus succeeds in seducing the human imagination, he'll have much to answer for. Matter without spirit is shit.

ERASMUS: Better excrement on one's hands than blood.

LUTHER: Oh, that again.

ERASMUS: Even the blood of rebellious German serfs. That again.

LUTHER: You have a one-track mind.

ERASMUS: If a second chance presented itself, would you still call for their extermination?

LUTHER: I'm a reformer, not a revolutionary. The princes were right to crush them.

ERASMUS: I still have my copy of *Against the Murderous and Thieving Peasant Bands.* I keep it alongside your translation of the Beatitudes.

LUTHER: I'm prepared to defend both documents.

ERASMUS: Death toll, five thousand. If that's where your Road to Damascus leads, monk, give me Gerard Korty and his brave new church any day of the week.

LUTHER: His brave new godless church.

ERASMUS: He's scooping out the cerebrum even as we speak. He intends to fill it with iconography—a Nativity, perhaps, a Loaves and Fishes, a Sermon on the Mount.

LUTHER: You papists love your graven images.

ERASMUS: Mind as museum, brain as basilica—a powerful conceit, don't you think? Our Savior said, "The Kingdom of God is within you." I'd always believed he meant our souls. Perhaps he meant our synapses.

LUTHER: A Romanist quoting scripture. How novel.

ERASMUS: The Third Millennium is going to be an amazing time.

LUTHER: Thank God I'm dead, and thus fairly certain of missing it.

ERASMUS: That's the difference between us. I'd rather glimpse the future than behold a hundred naked courtesans. Say, look there. Do you see him?

LUTHER: Who?

ERASMUS: An angel sails toward us—Raphael, I think. Or Gabriel.

LUTHER: On shining wings!

ERASMUS: How they glow!

LUTHER: Feathers of flame!

ERASMUS: A question, monk. Imagine that our angel is presently weighing two alternatives. He can carry us straight to Heaven, or he can restore our youth and maroon us in the Third Millennium. Which fate would you implore him to seal?

LUTHER: I don't even have to think about it.

ERASMUS: Figures.

LUTHER: What about you? Which shall it be? Heaven, or the future?

ERASMUS: Difficult question.

LUTHER: Decide quickly. He's almost here.

ERASMUS: The future, monk. It probably has a better library.

From the very first, Gerard knew that when it came to appointing his brain, he would begin not with the right hemisphere's Hall of Artistic Passion nor with the left's Garden of Scientific Knowledge but with the freshly dredged Gallery of Decency. Much as he loved art and prized science, it was only his species's moral cerebellum, its priceless if underexercised faculty for counterbalancing impulse with obligation, anger with wisdom, that had kept the pages of human history from being written entirely in blood.

He molded a rabbi, two feet high, dressed in a crimson robe. Flowing hair, neat black beard, eyes like a lion's. A woman stood beside him, frightened but not cowed. Without especially intending to, Gerard carved her in the image of Fiona.

An indignant crowd encircled the rabbi and the woman, brandishing rocks, staves, and bits of broken pottery. They stared at the rabbi's outstretched hand. His palm held a chunk of basalt.

Above the tableau Gerard fixed a wooden plaque. It read LET HIM AMONG YOU WHO IS WITHOUT SIN CAST THE FIRST STONE.

"It's gorgeous," said Fiona.

"Thank you."

"He looks a little smug."

"You're right. I'll work on that."

"Maybe if the mouth were straighter."

"Good idea."

"Wisdom smiles," she said, "but it never smirks."

Nora saw it first. As she stood watch in the bow, her eyes scanning the foggy morning sea for tar balls, flotsam, and other debris that might damage the *Natchez Queen*'s paddles, a vessel emerged from the mist: an ancient square-rigger under full sail, prototype of the model Eric had used in one of his best tricks—ship here, bottle over there, and suddenly, abracadabra, the ship was in the bottle. She switched on the walkie-talkie and told Anthony of the intruder, and five minutes later he stood beside her, red neckerchief fluttering in the breeze, gripping the foredeck rail.

"Who's minding the bridge?" she asked.

As Anthony fixed on the horizon, a dreaminess clouded his eyes, and when he spoke, Nora realized he was looking not on the square-rigger but inward. "You should see that boy of mine take the helm."

"But who's steering her *now*?"

He blinked, tightening his hold on the rail. His muscles bulged, fattening the mermaid tattooed on his left forearm. His hands, she saw, were large and scored with scars—cable cuts, winch wounds, barracuda bites—each having its own tale to tell.

"My wife," he said. "Damn good quartermaster."

By 1335 hours, the *Queen* had cruised near enough for Nora to discern both the square-rigger's name, *Cornucopia*, and her triad of smokestacks: she was an antique steamship, built during the era when it was prudent to retain masts, ropes, and canvas in case your boiler exploded. The steamer's owners had their own peculiar ideas about propulsion. Her stacks were vacant, her engine silent, and the objects that Nora had initially taken for sails were in fact solar panels—thirty at least, wired to the yardarms. Evidently the panels didn't work. The *Cornucopia* was dead in the water.

"Ahoy, there!" cried a wiry, sunburned man from atop the forecastle—the only visible presence on deck besides the diminutive Asian man at the helm and the hefty African-American woman making ready to lower the dinghy. "Ahoy, *Natchez Queen*!"

"Ahoy, *Cornucopia*! Anthony Van Horne here, bound in ballast for Coatzacoalcos!"

The *Cornucopia*'s solar panels were not her strangest accessory. She was loaded to her gunwales with nearly a hundred upright steel cylinders, each encircled by an aluminum coil and featuring a stained-glass rose window from which a human face peered out. At first Nora assumed that the cylinders were diving bells, their contents oceanographers, but then she noticed the ice crystals crosshatching the windows and the corona of frost surrounding each face. Maybe the occupants had been oceanographers in the past, but now they were that most unremarkable of Third Millennium commodities, a collection of cadavers.

"Boris Lampini here, Institute for Lifespan Augmentation!"

"What're you carrying, *Cornucopia*?!"

"Ninety-four suspendees!" shouted Boris Lampini, slapping the nearest cylinder.

"Suspenders?"

"Suspendees! Can you help us, Captain Van Horne?! Our coal ran out this morning!"

Nora bristled when Anthony invited Boris Lampini onto the *Queen*, and she bristled again when the captain expressed a willingness to take the derelict in tow. A burden of such magnitude would add at least a day to their journey.

"It's a terrible idea," she told him.

"I agree," said Cassie.

"Let's hear the man's story," said Anthony.

"I'm happy to tell it," said Lampini.

They were sitting in Anthony's Victorian stateroom, Crock at the helm, the Maxwell House instant flowing freely, the four of them absorbed in a problem that seemed lurid even by contemporary standards: how to prevent the famished citizens of Houston, Texas, from stealing and devouring ninety-four frozen human bodies. After carefully establishing that he and his crew were cryonicists, not cryobiologists (the latter profession generally taking a dim view of the former's ambitions), Lampini explained that the "patients" in his care enjoyed a condition known as cryonic suspension. Years before the plague, each client had shelled out $165,000 to the Institute for Lifespan Augmentation in Bellaire. In return, Dr. Lampini and his colleagues promised the client that at the instant of his death specially trained technicians would artificially restart his heart, squirt glycerol into his veins to minimize freezing injury, and suspend his body in a vacuum bottle filled with liquid nitrogen. The client's tissues would drop to a temperature of –196° centigrade over a period of fifteen days, a state in which his remains might be preserved indefinitely, provided that the Augmentation Institute replenished the coolant as it evaporated. By this procedure the client stood a reasonable chance, in Lampini's opinion, of awakening in a future where medical science, blessed with nanotechnology, had no more difficulty reviving dead neurons than setting broken arms. Thus did the suspendee attain a qualified immortality. At the Augmentation Institute, the customer was eternally right.

"When the plague cut off our liquid nitrogen supply, we reluctantly converted to formaldehyde dunks combined with solar-powered electric refrigeration," said Lampini in a defensive tone. "This isn't good customer service, I'm the first to admit it, but we had no choice." His sunburn was more severe than Nora had realized, his nose a plump radish, his forehead so speckled with blisters that it suggested a swatch of bubble wrap. "Keeping the patients frozen was the *least* of our worries." He shivered, a symptom of either his disturbing recollections or his damaged skin, Nora couldn't tell. "Abulia hit Houston especially hard, no fuel, people starving in the streets. Then somebody remembered about the Institute and its suspendees, and soon we were under siege."

Cassie swallowed a mouthful of coffee, smiled, and said, "You can't ask a hungry mob to ignore a pile of frozen TV dinners."

"I find that remark offensive," said Lampini.

"I find cryonic suspension offensive," said Cassie.

Lampini resumed his tale, narrating how the Institute's security forces had beaten back the besiegers long enough for the twelve scientists to escape with their customers—every last suspendee, solar rigs included—under cover of night. They fled to Galveston. The besiegers gave chase, but before the two factions could come to blows, the Institute's staff loaded their customers onto the *Cornucopia* and steamed out of the harbor.

"We burned our last lump of coal three hours ago," said Lampini, sighing, "but we're not giving up. The Institute has taken on a sacred trust, and we intend to honor it."

Anthony stretched across the length of his green velvet sofa. "Are the cannibals still after you?"

"Two hours away, unless they're stopping to fish, which I doubt—they've got their hearts set on my patients. Racing yachts, catamarans, outrigger canoes, whatever they could lay their hands on. They think we're headed for Jamaica. Tow us to Coatzacoalcos, Captain, and this nightmare will end."

"Sorry, Doc. It's six hundred miles from here to there, and the *Cornucopia* will cut our speed in half, especially with all those cans of rich people you have on board."

"Stockbroker stew," said Cassie.

"Plutocrat preserves," said Nora.

"Cream of capitalist."

"Chief Executive Officer Boyardee."

"That's enough, you two," said Anthony.

"They aren't cans," said Lampini. "They're cryogenic Dewar vessels."

"What do your customers tell their children?" asked Cassie. "'Sorry, kids, I spent your inheritance on my immortality. I'm going to outlive you yet.'"

"What we *will* do is take you to the Yucatán," said Anthony. "We'll drop you off, then cruise west along the coast."

"Darling, we aren't responsible for this man's problems," said Cassie to her husband.

"When times are tough, people must go out of their way to help one another," said Anthony.

"Two hundred miles out of their way?"

"I've towed quite a bit of death in my day. I'm ready to start towing life."

"They're *corpses*, dear. This lunatic is hauling *corpses*."

"Suspendees," said Lampini.

"Suspendees," said Anthony.

"Give me a break," said Cassie.

"Look at it this way," said Anthony. "If we were out of fuel, wouldn't you be grateful if the doc here took us to our destination? I'm telling O'Connor to plot us a course for Puerto Chicxulub."

Nora scowled and finished her coffee. So the tow would happen. Very well. Maybe it was even the right thing to do. Maybe she should've robbed a bank when her husband died, sent the cash to the Augmentation Institute, and had him frozen instead of buried.

Oh, God, how she would love to see Eric's face when he thawed. Would the world still need stage magicians in A.D. 2500? Probably. As Eric liked to say, "Conjurers and concubines are invulnerable to automation."

Throughout the rest of that hot, long, dreary day and far into the sticky night, they dragged the defunct *Cornucopia*, her frightened crew, and her frozen passengers from the 27th parallel to the Tropic of Cancer, a journey punctuated by the clank and clatter of the tow chains. Everything aboard the sternwheeler seemed to occur in slow motion—the steering, the chopping, the stoking, the bailing—a situation that Nora decided to exploit.

Since first glimpsing the *Natchez Queen* in its Riverwalk berth, she'd wanted to know how the boat worked, and Crock, to his credit, believed she would make a good pupil. By sunset she could trace the "live steam" as it traveled from boiler to pump to drive shaft on its way to becoming "dead steam"—water—in the condenser. She could light the burners, stoke the fires, lubricate the pistons, and operate the throttle.

Nora's investigation of the engine room not only provided her with insights into nineteenth-century motive power, it gave her an opportunity to test Marbles Rafferty's glory grease. Ascending the narrow ladder that led from the boiler pit to the cargo deck, she banged her bad knee on the railing. The pain was immediate and excruciating, a red-hot iron spike driven into her patella, her worst such spasms since the original lacrosse accident.

She hobbled to her stateroom and opened the peanut butter jar, releasing a fragrance suggestive of Brussels sprouts boiled in molasses. With her index finger she extracted a blob of the holy unguent and smeared it on her knee. The grease was warm—and potent. Her pain vanished, quickly and completely. As she screwed on the lid, the grease continued to bless her, seeping through her flesh and bathing her nervous system in the sort of intense well-being she'd previously known only from Percodan and sex. She climbed into her bunk and fell asleep, dreaming of a post-plague world where Kevin, cured, had become a famous film director whose latest project was a sixty-million-dollar remake of Corman's *The Last Woman on Earth.*

As dawn suffused the *Queen,* Nora rose and visited her son. His stateroom stank, polluted by the fetch's exhalations. She kissed Kevin's spotted cheeks. His pajama top lay open, exposing the pocks on his chest—an array of darkening stars, she decided, a constellation allied to some ugly and depleting myth. Fully awake now, she gave him his first physical therapy session of the day, levering his legs and pumping his arms for a solid hour.

She left the stateroom and wandered aft. Cassie leaned against the starboard transom, binoculars raised, looking past the wake and the tow chains toward the *Cornucopia*.

"Good morning!" yelled Nora over the thunderous suck of the paddles.

"Christ almighty! I can't *believe* this!"

Groaning, Cassie shoved the binoculars into Nora's hands and bolted toward the pilothouse.

Nora lifted the binoculars and twisted the focus knob. The skull grew sharp, pouring down its monotonous mockery. She lowered her gaze and immediately saw the reason for Cassie's distress. During the night, a two-masted schooner loaded with famished Texans had overtaken the *Cornucopia*, and now they swarmed across her decks like pirates boarding a merchant ship. After neutralizing Lampini and his colleagues, a straightforward matter of knocking the distraught scientists unconscious and roping them to the masts, the invaders split into two forces and set about their ghoulish business. One group concentrated on the Dewar vessels, tipping them over and attacking the lids with crowbars and chisels. The others pulled down the photovoltaic cells, evidently seeking to improvise a cooking device.

She studied the nearest cylinder, horizontal now, stenciled with the name HOSKINS. Crowbars in hand, two Texans crouched over the top—a bearded, emaciated man wearing a ragged red blazer and a battered cowboy hat, and a spidery, athletic woman in a threadbare business suit. Together they wrenched off the circular lid. A wave of formaldehyde rolled out, an image that for Nora recalled the gush of amniotic fluid that had heralded Kevin's arrival. The refrigerated preservative splashed across the deck, meeting the warm tropical air to form billowing clouds of steam.

Reaching inside the Dewar vessel, the Texans retrieved the Institute's dead client and pulled him into the daylight. Ice crystals clothed the naked corpse head to toe. The Texans kissed—lovers evidently, possibly married. In one sense, their expedition was a kind of date, a dining-out experience they would both remember.

Nora fixed on the corpse, a bald, toothless man with a misshapen jaw. Quite possibly cosmetic surgery had figured in Mr. Hoskins's postresurrection plans.

The lovers surveyed the mess they'd made. Their expressions bespoke confusion, as if they'd expected Hoskins to arrive with microwaving instructions or a recipe card. They hauled their prize toward the solar oven. Already a plutocrat was under the heat, defrosting slowly, cold droplets raining from his flesh.

As Nora averted her eyes, Anthony and Cassie appeared on the *Queen*'s afterdeck. The captain grabbed the binoculars and handed Cassie a pair of canvas gloves. He brought a walkie-talkie to his mouth.

"Can you hear me, Crock? Over."

"Loud and clear!" came the engineer's voice, barbed with static. "You on the bridge? Over."

"Afterdeck! Helm's locked! Half ahead, okay?"

"Half ahead!"

The *Queen* decelerated.

"Set us free!" Anthony commanded his wife. He peered through the binoculars. "Lee side first, then the windward!"

"Aye-aye," said Cassie.

"What do you see?" Nora asked the captain.

"You don't want to know."

Cassie, gloved now, grasped the starboard loop of chain with both hands and lifted it off the cleat. She hurled the steel noose into the Gulf, then crossed the stern and unhooked the second chain. The disconnected *Queen* lurched forward like a bronco released from a rodeo chute.

"Full speed ahead!" screamed Anthony.

"Poor rich people," said Cassie, flashing a dark smile. "They can't even get their money back."

"Maybe they're better off dead," said Nora. "To wake up penniless and alone in a hostile future, that sounds like hell to me. Lampini's patients would probably get treated like slaves, or freaks. Like second-class citizens at best."

"Unless, of course," said Cassie, "they also froze their lawyers."

I am near death. That's what the new dream tells me.

My arms and legs are back, but only so the doctors can perform more surgery—a "somatodectomy," a body removal. In a matter of minutes they cut me down to nothing. Skin, organs, muscles—everything melts under their knives, as if I were just one big tonsil.

Now they start on my skeleton, lifting away each bone. I've become a game of pick-up sticks. Soon I'll be like God Himself, nothing but a skull.

The lights appeared at midnight, straight off the port bow, sixteen red and roiling masses speckling the black horizon like St. Elmo's fire. Anthony, staring through the pilothouse window, interpreted the phenomenon as signal beacons set by Puerto Chicxulub residents to warn fishing boats off the rocks, but Nora, stationed at the helm, found a more sinister meaning in the fires. She'd seen too many pyres between Boston and New Orleans to doubt that these flames served any purpose beyond corpse removal. It hardly mattered. The *Queen* had reached the Mexican coast. A thirty-degree turn followed by a half-day's voyage across the Bahía de Campeche would land them in Coatzacoalcos.

Anthony sipped instant coffee from a stained Exxon mug. "Tell me your darkest secret," he said.

Nora winced. Tightening her grip on the wheel, she reluctantly described her refusal to bless the Army of Northern New Jersey with the plunder from Harvey Sheridan's school bus.

"Now tell me yours," she said.

"Like yours, it involves fossil fuel."

For the first time Nora apprehended her captain's true identity. This was *the* Anthony Van Horne, the hapless skipper who'd cracked up the *Carpco Valparaíso.*

"Matagorda Bay?" she said.

"Five hundred miles of blackened beaches," he said, nodding. "Six hundred acres of ruined shrimp beds. Three hundred and twenty-five manatees got oil in their eyes and scratched them out."

"The grand jury exonerated you," she said vaguely, uncertain how to comfort her captain and equally uncertain whether he wanted comforting. "They said you weren't to blame."

"I am technically innocent. Like God."

How would history remember him? she wondered. As the adventurer who'd hauled the Corpus Dei to an Arctic tomb, or as the blunderer who'd dumped eleven million gallons of crude oil into a vital ecosystem?

"So here I am, back in the Gulf," he said. "The criminal always returns to the scene of the crime."

"You're not a criminal."

He started to respond when a deep, growling, superhuman voice rang out, filling the pilothouse with reverberations so violent that they cracked the glass in the compass binnacle.

TAKE OFF THY SHOES!

Anthony said, "What?!"

YOU HEARD US! SHOW SOME RESPECT! TAKE OFF THY SHOES!

Anthony removed his sneakers, leaving his feet clothed only in threadbare white cotton. Following his example, Nora pulled off her hiking boots but kept her socks in place.

STATE YOUR NAME!

The captain glanced in all directions, seeking the source of the command. "Anthony Van Horne, master of the *Natchez Queen.*"

AND WE ARE GOD ALMIGHTY, MASTER OF THE UNIVERSE!

"What?"

ARE YOU DEAF? GOD ALMIGHTY!

Acting on instinct, Anthony and Nora lashed the wheel and, slipping and sliding in their stocking feet, rushed out onto the signal deck. The Puerto Chicxulub air was cool. Myths flecked the heavens: Orion, Cassiopeia, Pegasus. Prickly with fear, Nora hugged herself, rubbing her hands up and down her biceps.

"God doesn't exist," Anthony announced to the watery blackness. "His body went to pieces while I was towing it through the English Channel."

WE ARE THAT WE ARE.

"Show Yourself."

USE YOUR EYES.

Nora and Anthony glanced skyward, fixing on the lambent death's-head.

NOT UP THERE, DUMMIES. DOWN HERE, IN THE GULF. THE DIVINE INTESTINES, YOU WILL RECALL, DID NOT DISINTEGRATE THAT DAY.

They leaned over the rail, Nora favoring the bow, Anthony looking aft. Suddenly she saw it, basking in the skullglow: a huge, pulpy, corpulent worm, festooned with algae and stippled with barnacles, the whole impossible beast coiled tightly upon itself and sealed at both ends like a sausage. Immediately she thought of Jormungand, the Midgard serpent, wrapped around the mortal world, tail in mouth, an organic equator.

"See anything?" Anthony asked her.

"I see it, but I don't believe it."

Anthony pivoted, sharing her view. "Holy shit."

PRECISELY. TELL ME, CAPTAIN, DO YOU KNOW WHERE YOU ARE?

"Latitude twenty-one degrees, forty minutes, north," said Anthony, closing his eyes. "Longitude ninety degrees—"

YOU ARE TWO KILOMETERS FROM THE LARGEST IMPACT CRATER ON THE PLANET, THE CHICXULUB, FORMED BY THE VERY ASTEROID THROUGH WHICH WE EXTERMINATED OUR CHERISHED DINOSAURS.

"I've heard about that."

IT'S A CONTROVERSIAL THEORY, BUT THERE'S LOTS OF EVIDENCE.

"How could a single asteroid destroy hundreds of species?"

WE HAVEN'T THE TIME. THERE ARE BOOKS.

"If You valued the dinosaurs, why did You kill them?"

DIDN'T YOU WATCH THE TRIAL? DON'T YOU HAVE CABLE? THE PROSECUTION CALLED IT RIGHT: WE POSSESS AN EVIL DIMENSION.

"What do You want with *me*?"

NOT *YOU*, CAPTAIN—YOUR AMBITIOUS PASSENGER OVER THERE.

Fear exploded in Nora's chest, her worst such jolt since the school-bus spiritualist tried to shoot her.

LOOK AT US, ENGLISH TEACHER.

"Where're Your eyes?" she asked. "Your mouth?"

WE ARE EVACUATING OUR WORDS DIRECTLY INTO YOUR BRAIN.

She flashed on Kevin's beloved *Attack of the Crab Monsters*, with its memorable scene of the mystified scientist—a hammy performance by Leslie Bradley—being lured to his death by the projected voices of two sailors, their brains still active even though they'd recently been devoured by giant mutant crabs.

"I get it," she said. "We're communicating telepathically."

YES. TELEPATHICALLY. LIKE THE TWO SAILORS IN *ATTACK OF THE CRAB MONSTERS* LURING THAT SCIENTIST PLAYED BY MEL WELLES.

"No, Mel Welles played the *other* scientist."

IT WAS MEL WELLES.

"It was Leslie Bradley."

SHUT UP. LISTEN, ENGLISH TEACHER, THE INSTANT YOU GET TO COATZACOALCOS, YOU MUST SEEK OUT A SCULPTOR NAMED GERARD KORTY.

"Korty of the Korty Madonna?"

THE SAME. HE WAS ALSO COMMISSIONED TO DESIGN THE CINECITTÀ RELIQUARY, BUT IT DIDN'T WORK OUT. HIS CURRENT OBSESSION IS THE HUMAN BRAIN HE'S CARVING FROM THE CHICXULUB ASTEROID. WE SHALL REMAIN SILENT CONCERNING ITS AESTHETIC VALUE. GOD DOES NOT FANCY HIMSELF AN ART CRITIC, THOUGH THE REVERSE FREQUENTLY OCCURS. OUR POINT IS THIS. THE PROJECT IS MUCH TOO BIG FOR HIM. MARK OUR WORDS, HEED OUR PROPHECY, READ OUR ENTRAILS: KORTY'S BRAIN WILL SHRED HIS PSYCHE AND CRUSH HIS SOUL. YOUR SACRED DUTY IS OBVIOUS.

"Warn him?"

WARN HIM. HE MUST ABANDON THE BRAIN OR GO MAD.

"Why do You care whether one pathetic sculptor retains his sanity?"

AT THE MOMENT, WE READILY ADMIT, YOU ARE ADDRESSING YOUR CREATOR'S EVIL SIDE, WHICH MEANS THAT YOUR QUESTION IS, ON THE SURFACE, ASTUTE. WHAT YOU FAIL TO APPRECIATE IS THAT OUR FACETS SPORT DUALITIES OF THEIR OWN. YOU MIGHT BE ADDRESSING THE EVIL SIDE OF OUR EVIL SIDE, OR YOU MIGHT BE ADDRESSING THE GOOD SIDE OF OUR EVIL SIDE—THERE'S NO WAY TO TELL. EVEN IF THE LATTER UNEQUIVOCALLY OBTAINED, YOU COULDN'T BE CERTAIN WHETHER YOU WERE ADDRESSING THE GOOD SIDE OF THE GOOD SIDE OF OUR EVIL SIDE OR THE EVIL SIDE OF THE GOOD SIDE OF OUR EVIL SIDE. METAPHYSICS IS A TRICKY BUSINESS. WE WANT YOU TO RESCUE THE SCULPTOR BECAUSE, ONCE ADRIAN LUCIDO DIES, KORTY BECOMES THE LOGICAL MAN TO CARRY ON HIS VALIANT MISSION.

"So the Lucido Clinic really exists?"

YOU'LL FIND OUT SOON ENOUGH.

"Do You want the Clinic to endure because it works—or because it *doesn't* work?"

THAT DEPENDS ON WHETHER YOU ARE ADDRESSING THE GOOD SIDE OF THE GOOD SIDE OF OUR EVIL SIDE OR THE—

"Last year somebody put a magnifying glass in my son's Wizard of Oats."

DON'T INTERRUPT US. OR THE EVIL SIDE OF THE GOOD SIDE OF OUR EVIL SIDE. HIS CONJURER CRUNCH, ACTUALLY.

"No, his Wizard of Oats. It took me to the Lobo mausoleum in Arborway Cemetery."

I BESEECH YOU, IN THE BOWELS OF CHRIST, THINK IT POSSIBLE YOU MAY BE MISTAKEN.

"Right."

GONERIL DID IT.

"Goneril?"

YOUR FETCH.

"I've always hated that name."

THAT'S WHY SHE PICKED IT.

"My fetch put the magnifying glass in Kevin's cereal?"

YES.

"Are You sure?"

ARE WE *SURE*? YOU ARE TALKING, MRS. BURKHART, TO THE LORD OF HOSTS AND THE ARCHITECT OF REALITY. IN OUR DAY WE COULD DO ANYTHING. PART OCEANS, JUGGLE PLANETS, IGNITE STARS, PLAY KASPAROV TO A DRAW. NOW OUR REIGN IS ENDING. TONIGHT WE DIVE INTO THE YUCATÁN FISSURE AND FROM THERE TO THE HEART OF OBLIVION. "THE OLD ORDER CHANGETH, YIELDING PLACE TO NEW." WORDSWORTH.

"Tennyson."

WORDSWORTH.

"Tennyson."

Anthony said, "If You have a shred of decency left, You'll tell us whether Adrian Lucido can help our children."

YOU STILL FEEL GUILTY ABOUT MATAGORDA BAY, DON'T YOU, CAPTAIN? DYING SEA TURTLES HAUNT YOUR DREAMS.

"I blinded three hundred manatees."

A TERRIBLE MIGRAINE POSSESSED YOU THAT NIGHT, SO YOU ABANDONED THE BRIDGE, LEAVING FOOLS IN CHARGE. YOU HAVE OUR SYMPATHY. WE ARE PREY TO MIGRAINES OURSELVES. THE 1527 GERMAN PEASANTS' REVOLT GAVE US A LOLLAPALOOZA.

"You mean . . . I'm forgiven?" said Anthony.

YOUR OIL SPILL WAS BAD, BUT OUR ASTEROID WAS WORSE. IF YOU'LL FORGIVE US, WE'LL FORGIVE YOU.

"It's not in my power to forgive You."

QUITE SO. DO IT ANYWAY.

"Really?"

YES.

"I forgive You, God."

DITTO.

"I've got something on my conscience as well," said Nora.

YOU SHOULDN'T HAVE HOARDED YOUR DIESEL FUEL. WE WON'T PRETEND OTHERWISE.

"Do I have Your forgiveness?"

The beast said nothing. A cold and abrasive Gulf breeze arose, spitting spray across the signal deck.

"I understand why Anthony abandoned the bridge," said Nora, zipping up her Celtics jacket, "but not why You're abandoning the world."

AND LEAVING FOOLS IN CHARGE?

"I'm not a fool."

THEN WE CAN VAPORIZE IN PEACE. FAREWELL, MRS. BURKHART. SAYONARA, CAPTAIN VAN HORNE.

"Don't go!" cried Nora.

"We have more questions!" shouted Anthony.

"How long will the plague last?"

"Why did You have to die?"

But already the beast had started to sound, its compacted coils paying out like a fire hose designed to douse the flames of Hell. For a brief instant the skull's floating reflection crowned a sinuous loop of bowel, a configuration suggesting an enormous grinning cobra. Twist following twist, turn following turn, the enigmatic mass plunged beneath the black waters off Puerto Chicxulub, until only a swirling skein of bubbles remained, and then the foam too was gone, leaving the humans alone on the signal deck, bound together in apocalyptic astonishment.

PART THREE

Little Myths

Waiting for Lucido

WITH ITS CRUMBLING PIERS, decrepit fishing boats, and unkempt beaches heaped with surf-borne trash, Coatzacoalcos Harbor partook of the abulic age as much as any vista in Nora's recent experience. The only exceptional feature was the smoldering volcano in the distance. Anthony identified it as Catemaco, adding that while its vents had smoked, belched, and oozed continuously since 1914, no one believed it would ever actually blow. Catemaco, he said, was like an aging, fangless, junkyard Doberman whose deterrent value depended entirely upon intruders mistaking him for a younger dog.

Only after they'd navigated the harbor and started up a murky jungle river called the Uspanapa did Nora fully grasp the incongruity that had marked their recent voyage. Sailing a flat-bottom boat across the Gulf of Mexico was like pressing a rubber band into service as a fan belt or using a fountain pen for an ice pick. Now, at last, the *Queen* was where she belonged, on waters strange but manageable.

"Last night—was that a hallucination?" said Anthony, steering around a bend in the river.

Raindrops fell, peppering the pilothouse windows. "What do *you* think?" said Nora.

"Well, it *felt* real. Except that my guilt is still intact, even though He forgave me."

"We probably weren't hallucinating. People don't hallucinate in tandem."

"Then you'll obey the entrails' command?"

"Eventually, yes. It certainly won't be the first thing I do."

"You'd defy God Himself?" said Anthony, eyebrows ascending. "I'm impressed."

"'I would persist in my indignation, even if I were wrong.' Ivan Karamazov."

As the jungle thickened, an embarcadero emerged from the drizzle, beyond which lay a cantina, La Sangre de la Serpiente, a two-story mass of rain-warped wood and corrugated tin. With only three sailors under his command, Anthony had trouble docking. It was the ultimate test of Nora's competence at the helm—ten degrees right rudder, now seven degrees left, now fifteen right—but at last the boat lay snugged against the wharf. Because the Uspanapa was a tidal river, Anthony insisted that they tie the *Queen* up tight, lest the rising waters lift her onto the dock. Nora was pleased with herself. Bring on the next maritime challenge, she thought. Let me brave the wrath of Triton and the hazards of Scylla. Let me bear Odysseus safely home.

The four travelers left the embarcadero and crossed the dusty yard, home to a dozen pigs, as many turkey cocks, four goats, and two donkeys. A charcoal-colored tapir observed the intruders suspiciously, decided that they intended no harm, and buried its snout in a pile of maize husks. Chickens clucked in wire cages. High in the treetops, a troop of howler monkeys roared their contempt at the Cranium Dei.

Presiding over La Sangre de la Serpiente was Esperanza Vargas, a statuesque mestiza who, with the addition of a bandolier across her chest, would have looked wholly at home during the Mexican Revolution. She ushered the travelers through the doorway and into the dark smoky cantina, then set four cold bottles of Cerveza Moctezuma on the bar. Nora drank some beer, steeled herself, and asked Señora Vargas the supreme question: Did she know of a local treatment facility called the Lucido Clinic?

"Know of it?" said Esperanza. "Every day a plague family parks their donkey cart in my yard, comes inside, eats my *guisado*, and asks me to point them toward the temples."

Delight filled the faces of the *Queen*'s company. Unless this woman was a better actress than anyone in the Great Sumerian Circus, Nora decided, the Church of Earthly Affirmation truly existed.

Upon learning that two stricken boys lay aboard the sternwheeler, Esperanza began offering advice. Were Captain Van Horne and his party equipped with "valuable gifts"? Then they had no cause to enter the city, where every alley concealed mercenary bandidos, most of them employed by plague families seeking "gold, gasoline, and other donations acceptable to Lucido." Instead they must go directly to the detention center—El Agujero, "the Hole," gateway to the temple complex—but only after allowing her to feed them "the best lunch you've had since El Cráneo jumped into the sky."

"Do you personally know of anyone getting cured up at Tamoanchan?" Nora asked Esperanza.

"Last week my cousin got admitted—no word yet, but in Coatzacoalcos there are many who swear Lucido drove out their *demonios*."

The rain stopped. Peering through the cantina's solitary window, El Cráneo gleamed His brightest. Esperanza went to the stove and, dipping her ladle into a scorched pot the size of a whiskey barrel, provided the pilgrims with steaming bowls of ginger-root *sopa*. Nora found the meal delicious, her opinion persisting even after their hostess explained that among the tasty morsels floating in the stock were the indigenous slugs called *gusanos de maguey*. In payment, Esperanza happily accepted a box of latex condoms from the sternwheeler's abundant stores. For a woman of "normal appetites," she explained, the present world's dearth of contraceptives verged on barbarism.

Shortly after Esperanza pocketed her compensation, Cassie disclosed that these prophylactics held personal associations. They were Shostak Supersensitives, invented by the father of her ex-fiancé, Oliver Shostak, mastermind behind the failed attempt to sink the Corpus Dei during its Arctic voyage. Cassie had never really been in love with Oliver, but she would admit that the idea of marrying into incalculable quantities of money had momentarily beguiled her.

During dessert, a stale banana pie, Nora inquired about Gerard Korty. Of *course* Esperanza had heard of the mysterious sculptor; how could Nora imagine otherwise? The man enjoyed celebrity, even mythic status, in Coatzacoalcos—not for carving a brain from an asteroid (Esperanza knew of no such project) but for fashioning the idols that adorned Tamoanchan. Korty's studio lay at least forty kilometers upriver, a fact that strengthened Nora's resolve to postpone her mandated mission until Kevin became an acolyte.

Not only did condoms make acceptable lunch chits, Esperanza explained, they were also good for the transport service she provided between the cantina and El Agujero, nine kilometers away. Crock O'Connor elected to stay behind and make sure the incoming tide held no surprises for the *Queen.* The party left at 2:00 P.M., Esperanza's bulk bowing the driver's seat of her donkey cart, the parents and children crammed into the load bed. Nora took poetic satisfaction in the fact that her fragmented journey via panel truck, Gypsy wagon, and steamboat had in the end placed her on the humblest vehicle imaginable. The donkey's name was Felipe, and while his stubby inelegance made him seem as disconnected from his equine ancestry as a Chihuahua was from a timber wolf, he got the job done, delivering the petitioners to the detention center in under two hours.

Bereft of windows, shorn of cornices, El Agujero resembled nothing so much as a pre-plague weapons factory producing some unimaginably deadly chemical. A battered urban bus, now operating as a shuttle between Coatzacoalcos and the Hole, was parked beside the front steps, its engine idling. A Brahman bull nibbled the surrounding weeds. The pilgrims climbed out of the cart, Stevie hanging from Anthony's arms, Kevin asleep on a litter borne by Nora and Cassie. Cautiously Nora opened the main door, a riveted iron slab. The foyer was cavernous and sterile, its appointments limited to a stone statue of a jaguar-headed man plus three metal desks ruled over by male functionaries in olive-drab suits. A line of exhausted plague families arced away from each desk toward the opposite wall. It took Nora but a minute to grasp El Agujero's protocol. Approaching the first available bureaucrat, you identified your thected loved one (name, age, nationality, birth date) and outlined his medical history, then opened your luggage to prove that you'd brought a donation.

The wait extended past 5:00 P.M., but at last Nora and Cassie stood before a squat middle-aged man who introduced himself as Roland Jackendorf, first assistant deacon of the Church of Earthly Affirmation. Both interviews proceeded efficiently, after which Jackendorf summoned a plump official whose name badge read SIMON BORK and told him to take Kevin, Stevie, and their parents to room 301. Saying nothing, Bork ushered them out of the foyer, through a tangle of corridors, and up three flights of stairs to a damp cell lit by bare lightbulbs and furnished with straw pallets. A thected young woman, no more than twenty, cheeks marred by stage-four pocks, lay along the far wall, her bewildered father crouching at her feet. Another victim, an elderly stage-three woman with cornsilk hair, sat catatonically in the corner beside her dozing husband. To Nora the cell felt like the waiting room of some backwater airport where the planes normally crashed on takeoff. Appearances don't matter, she told herself as they laid their children down, gently resting each boy's head on a pallet. If Jonas Salk's accomplishment had been judged solely by the looks of his untidy Pittsburgh lab, humankind might still be suffering polio epidemics.

"Welcome to room 301, known also as Limbo," said the young abulic's father. "It's gray and gloomy, and nothing ever happens."

Pivoting toward Nora, Bork disdainfully brushed her knapsack, as if it might contain manure. "What do you have for us?"

"Diesel fuel."

"How much?"

"Two gallons."

"Only two?"

"Only two," echoed Nora, beating back a wave of despair.

The official faced Cassie, massaging her knapsack in the same scornful way. "What about you?"

"We're a seafaring family," said Cassie, upending the canvas bag so that its contents poured forth: sextant, compass, binoculars, telescope.

"Anything else?"

"No. The sextant has gold in it."

"I'll relay that fact to Mr. Richter. He might accept these trinkets. Then again, he might not."

"The binoculars are powerful," said Cassie, repacking the knapsack.

"You can see the craters on the moon," said Anthony.

The fat functionary wasn't listening. He scooped up both knapsacks, bobbed his head in a manner that tripled his chin, and silently left the room.

Although Nora prayed that Simon Bork would soon reappear with a verdict on the diesel fuel—a plea she mentally broadcast to both El Cráneo and the divine entrails—they saw no more of him that night. Their only visitor was a frail, wrinkled woman who stopped by at 10:00 P.M., pushing a food cart laden with bean burritos, a complimentary but miserable snack that she disingenuously termed dinner.

The veterans of Limbo had nothing good to say about Lucido's lieutenant, Chief Deacon Hubbard Richter. Wilbur Loeb, devoted husband of Margaret Loeb for fifty years, had managed to reach Coatzacoalcos with his entire private collection of eleven Cézannes, the third largest such holding in the world. Every Friday for the past two months, Richter had summoned Loeb into his office and proceeded to belittle the pilgrim's donation. "My five-year-old nephew paints better apples," said Richter. "These people are supposed to be *bathers?* They don't even look wet." Norman Kitchen, whose comely daughter Elaine had become thected on her seventeenth birthday, told a much more troubling story. Although Kitchen's donation, an invaluable set of antique clocks, had impressed the chief deacon, he would admit Elaine only if her father agreed to leave Richter alone with "Sleeping Beauty" for an hour. Kitchen refused. Richter sent him back to room 301.

Shortly after dawn, an asthmatic but chipper young functionary breezed into Limbo: Mordecai Blassingame, son of Dr. Lucido's college roommate and private secretary to Hubbard Richter. Hearing Blassingame's announcement—"Deacon Richter intends to accommodate the Burkhart family today"—Nora's spirits soared, but then she remembered that Wilbur Loeb had already seen Richter eight times without gain. She grabbed her shoulder bag, took Kevin in her arms, and allowed Blassingame to guide her along a dim passageway terminating in a musty cubicle whose only amenity was a folding chair. At Blassingame's direction she sat down and waited, Kevin sprawled across her lap. Four hours went by. She exercised Kevin's limbs. Hunger clawed at her stomach. Another four hours elapsed. The food vendor arrived, furnishing Nora with a half-dozen flautas. She fed three to Kevin, ate the others, and, thus renewed, performed her son's physical therapy.

Twilight was fast approaching when Blassingame reappeared and led Nora on a twenty-minute trek past room after room jammed with plague families. At length she found herself in an unpainted plasterboard office cooled by a ceiling fan, standing before a fiftyish administrator who claimed to be Hubbard Richter. Brusquely, wordlessly, Richter placed Kevin on the couch and, bending low, gave the boy a cursory examination, looking into his eyes with an ophthalmoscope and whacking his knee with a rubber hammer.

"It's abulia, all right," said the chief deacon. He was a gaunt, cadaverous man, not many degrees removed from El Cráneo. "Occasionally we see a simple case of clinical depression." He turned his inert gaze on Nora. "Mrs. Burkhart, that diesel fuel you submitted is worthless. We tried it in three different generators."

A bolt of dread cut through Nora. "I siphoned it myself, right out of a school bus."

"You got the fragrance right. What did you do, mix witch hazel with lighter fluid?"

"I siphoned it myself!"

"Of course," said Blassingame snidely.

"I'm telling the truth!"

While Blassingame wheezed and Nora fumed, Richter repeatedly hit his open palm with the rubber hammer.

"There's an alternative," he said at last. He massaged his stubbled jaw and winked at Blassingame, who immediately vacated the office. "Here in Tamoanchan," Richter continued, "we have a goddess, Orgasiad, who blesses us with sexual gratification." He shot a furtive glance heavenward. "But what is sexual gratification? Its boundaries are continually shifting. Remove your clothes."

"What?"

"Remove your clothes."

When Nora was twenty-four, a man had come up behind her in a Cambridge alley—she was walking home after seeing *Casablanca* at the Brattle Theater—and thrown her to the ground. She screamed insanely. The stranger fled. The whole incident lasted less than a minute, but she still thought about it at least once a month.

"You . . . fetch," Nora muttered under her breath.

"What did you call me?"

Quivering, she pondered her options. They numbered two. She could assault the man, though that would surely ruin Kevin's chances of admission. Or she could close her eyes, clench her teeth, and detach, thereby turning a rape into mere coercive sex.

"Strip, Mrs. Burkhart."

Who was she kidding? There were no qualified rapes, any more than there were qualified thermonuclear explosions.

She stripped, her molars grinding together as she mentally chewed Richter's eyeballs to the consistency of fondue. The ceiling fan droned. Kevin snored. Richter hummed. The intermediate steps escaped her, each button, clasp, catch, and zipper erased from recollection, but somehow she reached the humiliating state her tormentor demanded.

"The Cranium Dei does terrible things to a man." Richter removed his shirt, unbuckled his belt, dropped his pants. "Dr. Lucido and I haven't quite solved the problem." His disenfranchised organ hung uselessly between his legs. "Orgasiad and I have a special relationship. Her priestesses understand my needs. They perform miracles with their mouths."

Nora didn't know how the inspiration arrived, but suddenly she was fishing through her shoulder bag in search of her knee medicine.

"Reliable miracles?" she asked.

"Quite reliable."

"But not totally reliable." She slammed the peanut butter jar onto Richter's desk and unscrewed the lid. "It's called glory grease, distilled from God's tissues during the Arctic tow." The room filled with the odor of Brussels sprouts boiled in molasses. "We must understand each other from the outset. If this is the elixir you seek, you may keep the whole jar, provided you leave me alone and make Kevin an acolyte."

"It can help me?"

"I think so."

"Might it work better than the priestesses?"

"If it does, will you admit Kevin?"

"All right," said Richter evenly.

She pressed three fingers together, inserted them in the jar, and extracted a scoop of glory. "Go ahead. Don't be afraid." She extended her sticky fingers, transferring the glob to Richter's open palm. "Rub it on."

"How do I know to trust you?"

"Plague families don't play games."

The grease proved efficacious. A mere thirty seconds after he'd applied the stuff, Richter's hapless organ flooded, angling into space like a flagpole bolted to a door frame.

"Now send Kevin to the temples," said Nora, hitching up her bra. She pulled on her cotton jersey, then climbed into her underpants and jeans. "You promised."

For a full minute Richter simply stood there, worshiping his erection. The thing persisted even after he began to dress, so that the restoration of his pants suggested a man trying to get a kayak into a sedan.

"Do you have any more?"

"An adequate cache," she said, telling Richter what he wanted to hear.

"Where are you staying?"

"On a steamboat docked beside La Sangre de la Serpiente."

"A first-rate donation, no doubt about it"—he buttoned his shirt—"but I'll need Dr. Lucido's approval."

"Then get it."

"In due time."

"Get it *now.*"

Pocketing the glory grease, Richter summoned Blassingame and instructed him to take Mrs. Burkhart and her son down to room zero.

Room zero, an ominous name—and appropriate, Nora discovered. The place was a musty dirt-floor cellar across which black scorpions and brownish-red cockroaches roamed at will. A wax candle burned atop an upended oil drum. Nora laid Kevin on the straw pallet, knelt beside him, and exercised his limbs, fully prepared to frighten away the vermin with the candle flame or crush them with her hiking boots, whichever defense proved more effective.

Two hours later, a zaftig woman in a flowing saffron robe appeared and identified herself as Vonda August, avatar of the world gland. "On your feet, Mrs. Burkhart—Dr. Lucido has approved your donation."

The joy that surged through Nora was tempered by her fear that this new functionary might be messing with her head, but her suspicions dissipated as, effortlessly lifting Kevin, Vonda August guided her out of room zero, up a marble staircase, and into a chamber featuring a pair of canopied beds covered with silk sheets.

"Tomorrow morning, you'll fill out his blue certificate," said Vonda, laying Kevin on the nearer bed, "and then he goes to Arcadia Lodge for his hyperion drip. We'll drive the Devil out of your fine young son. You have my solemn word."

The goose down certainly helped, but Nora would have slept peacefully that night on carpet tacks and broken glass.

The nightmare takes hold of me again. I am shucked, severed, pulled apart . . . and then suddenly I'm coming together. My bones reconnect, my muscles return, my flesh grows back.

I wake up . . . I mean, I *really* wake up. Somehow I've broken free of Quincy. After months in a tomb, I'm now in the outside world, resting on feathers and wearing a bathing suit. A hefty red-faced woman stands over me. She calls herself Vonda August, high priestess of Idorasag, goddess of suckling. She says it's Monday morning, and for the rest of the week I'll be staying here in Arcadia Lodge along with twenty-three other acolytes.

I tell the high priestess I'm hungry. She tells me a meal is coming.

I'm connected to an IV rig, the bottle filled with something blue and glowing. As an acolyte, Vonda August explains, I'm privileged to receive a drug called hyperion-15. It has blasted the fetch right out of me. By converting to Somatocism, I can guarantee he'll never return.

I glance around the dormitory. The other acolytes range from a little kid of Cub Scout age to an old woman with skin like a prune. After removing our IV needles, Vonda and three of her sister priestesses lead us to their deity's temple in the basement. Six statues of Idorasag—a big female monkey with an enormous smile and boobs like punching bags—guard the entrance. The statues are sitting. On the knee of each is a bronze bowl the size of a hubcap.

We explore the temple, which turns out to be a maze of narrow corridors and blind alleys. By midmorning we reach the center, where a surprise is waiting. Imagine a mountain of fur twice the size of that haystack Mother stuck me in when the Anglo-Saxons were after us. Eyeballs polka-dot the fur, and the mountain also has dozens of swaying arms—think of tree branches covered with Spanish moss—plus puffy lumps that remind me of Idorasag's boobs, each with a nipple like a baby bottle's. We dive in, and it's the best sensation I've ever had—that furry creature feels so warm and spongy against my bare skin. I can hear her heart beating, a peaceful *thump-thump-thump*. The priestesses tell us to suck on the nipples, and soon we're drawing this incredible stuff into our mouths. It's like a vanilla milkshake, and it takes my hunger away. We'd probably fall asleep right there if the priestesses didn't drag us to our feet so we could begin our devotions.

Our first duty is to praise Idorasag with a song. "Your fur is soft as soft can be," we chant. "Your milk is sweet and thick and free," and so on. Next we're required to "pour out libations." This isn't easy. The acolyte must fill his mouth with milk from one of the mountain's nipples and then find his way back to the maze entrance. He spits the milk into one of the bronze bowls, goes back for another libation, and then he does the whole routine over again. He's forbidden to swallow any mouthful meant for the goddess. It takes us all afternoon to fill the bowls. By the time the ritual is over, we know Idorasag's maze as if we'd always lived in Arcadia Lodge. Back in the dormitory, we collapse on the mattresses without bothering to remove our bathing suits.

A few hours later, there's a horrible scratching noise, as if a monster with huge claws is trapped under my bed, and I scream. The monster growls and roars. Jumping up, I realize that the other acolytes are screaming too (they've got monsters under *their* beds!), and soon we're tearing out of the dormitory like it's on fire. As we charge down staircase after staircase, a terrible storm starts raging, wind and rain, plus thunder booming like an artillery barrage. The lightning flashes phosphorescent white. We pour through the temple entrance. Luckily we're all maze experts, so it doesn't take us more than ten minutes to find the center. As the thunder rumbles, twenty-four frightened acolytes go piling into the fur mountain.

The mountain strokes me, hugs me, sings me a lullaby. She lifts me to her nearest breast, and I suckle. In a few minutes I calm down, and after an hour or so of drinking her milk and hearing her heart, I feel totally safe, not only from monsters and storms but from every danger in the world. I spend the night in the fur mountain's arms.

Was it rigged? As I wake up, the thought occurs to me. The priestesses could've piped in the monster's noises using a tape recorder;

they could've made the storm from trick fuses and sound effects. Fake or real, I don't care, because Idorasag is the most wonderful deity ever, and I plan on worshiping her for the rest of my life.

By the time Nora arrived for the mandatory orientation session, the Carl Jung Auditorium stood at capacity: plague families mixed with clinic personnel. Searching for a seat, she realized that the room was funnel-shaped, the crowd swirling around the rostrum like flotsam caught in Charybdis. A hulking man with a goatee shuffled toward the lectern, raised the cobra-necked microphone to the level of his jaw, and introduced himself as Dr. Adrian Lucido.

"The measure of any religion," he began, "is the quality of its gods." Lucido paused to shoot Nora a disapproving frown as, spotting a vacancy in the second row, she maneuvered through an obstacle course of feet, knees, and umbrellas. "Here at the Church of Earthly Affirmation," he continued, "we are proud of our pantheon." He snapped his fingers, and a wheeled dais rolled across the stage, bearing plaster images of the Somatocist deities. "As their education progresses, your stricken loved ones will open their hearts to the queen of passion, embrace the master of the revels, glorify the lord of the jest, and suckle the mistress of milk."

The rest of Lucido's lecture explicated the theory behind the clinic. Flood the patient with pharmaceutical euphoria, thus kicking his melancholia into remission, then teach him to tap his inner energies, his wellsprings of joy, so that he becomes immune to further nihilistic infections. In the end a new self emerges, a soul over whom El Cráneo holds no more power than would a Halloween skeleton decorating a drugstore window.

Nora wanted to love Dr. Adrian Lucido, but she simply couldn't manage it. Despite a demeanor that broadcast competence and an aura that advertised devotion, he did not inspire her trust. He reminded her of the oncologists who'd treated her father during his final year. With the exception of the inspiringly modest Dr. Irving Frankel, they seemed to fancy themselves a race apart—a different species, in fact, supernatural in heritage, stranded on Earth through a teleological error that God would soon correct.

The afternoon belonged to two articulate, hot-eyed, intermittently messianic speakers. Dr. Derek Scarron, a cultural anthropologist from the University of Pennsylvania, displayed sixty-three idols that he'd collected during his world travels, then delineated the compelling similarities and the equally compelling differences between the Somatocist pantheon and its predecessors. Dr. Constance Vogel, a chemist once employed by Bristol-Myers Squibb, recounted how she'd discovered the antifetch drug, hyperion-15. Her story was a biomedical thriller replete with cul-de-sacs and surprising turns, its climax occurring when Vogel injected her thected father-in-law with an auspicious formula and saw the impacted leveler leap from his flesh like a hooked marlin breaching the surface of the sea.

Returning to La Sangre de la Serpiente that afternoon, Nora summarized the day's developments for Crock, then proposed that they take the *Queen* upriver the following morning in search of Gerard Korty. Crock, indignant, pointed out that appropriating a man's thirty-ton steamboat wasn't exactly like borrowing his car. But Nora had arguments ready. Anthony, she noted, held no legal title to the *Queen*, and, moreover, the reason for this mission was not some whim of hers but a direct order from Jehovah's entrails.

The journey began shortly after sunrise. While Crock drank tequila in the engine room, Nora settled into the lofty pilothouse, one hand on the helm, the other clutching a map of the Rio Uspanapa supplied by Esperanza. Like the God of the imperiled Catholic faith, Nora was trifurcated, a third of her attention devoted to keeping the *Queen* off the sandbars, a third to hoping that Kevin was faring well in the Temple of Risogada, a third to wondering whether she'd come to Mexico only to place her son in the hands of a mountebank.

Deities were serious commodities. You couldn't simply legislate them into being. It wasn't a question of empiricism: the Norse, Greek, Hindu, and Sumerian pantheons were no more factual than Lucido's.

The gods who commanded your respect, however, the ones who could claim spiritual reality, enjoyed the weight of tradition. If Kevin walked away cured, she would forgive the new religion its excesses, but at present she doubted that Somatocism's ministers, with their confected cults and psychoactive drugs, had their patients' best interests at heart.

The Mexican sun flared and pulsed, turning the pilothouse into a stewpot. On both sides of the river, sugarcane fields and cacao plantations alternated with dazzling bursts of jungle. The rain forest proper evidently lay many kilometers to the south, but for Nora the immediate terrain—the broadleaf trees garlanded with morning-glory vines and magenta-blossomed bougainvillea—boasted a lushness no true flower woman could fail to adore.

After two hours on the river, she noticed a sandstone bluff rising to a rambling hacienda shielded from the jungle by a stockade fence, the side yard cluttered with scaffolding, hoisting gear, and massive stone blocks. A pair of carved giants dominated the outdoor studio, the nearer one indecipherable, the other depicting her brother's psychic mentor, Martin Luther. She committed the *Queen* to Crock's care, lowered the skiff, and poled her way to the beach. Swatting mosquitoes, she disembarked. Baked by the sun, the mud exuded a complex scent, fecundity leavened with decay. She ascended the bluff and marched across the studio grounds until she reached the sculpted Luther, who appeared to be battling an episode of constipation.

A door squealed opened. Nora turned. A slender, dark-haired beauty, with European features and tanned skin, stepped onto the veranda.

"This is obviously Martin Luther," said Nora, "but who's that fellow over there?"

"Erasmus of Rotterdam. My husband carved it."

"And now he's working on a giant brain."

"How did you know?"

"Long story. Call me Nora."

"Fiona."

They retreated to the shade of the veranda, whereupon Nora narrated the pertinent events in her life, most especially her conversation with the divine bowels. Each successive revelation caused Fiona Korty's jaw to fall a notch.

The women walked into the jungle, Fiona finding the path, Nora reveling in the orchids: clumps of delicate pink and mauve odontoglossum punctuated by flashes of purple cattleya. Hummingbirds sought out the blossoms, airborne syringes extracting the precious nectars. Bees flitted from flower to flower. Higher up, toucans and budgerigars darted amid the branches.

Beholding the reubenite brain, Nora gasped, perhaps even louder than when she first saw Eric convert a silk scarf into a live dove. The thing was huge—as huge, complex, and beautiful as the *Queen*. It lay atop a grassy hummock, looking somewhat like a golf ball on a tee, an impression reinforced by its stippled surface. Naked to the waist, Gerard Korty sat between the frontal lobes, eating garnachas and reading a book, the sort of civilized lunch break Nora had known only after losing her teaching job.

"Gerard, a visitor!" shouted Fiona. "With a message from God's bowels!"

Muscles in men had never done much for Nora, but she had to admit that Korty's physique was striking, if at odds with his sagging cheeks and drooping eyes. Monumental sculpting was evidently at once a passionate vocation, a spiritual ordeal, and an athletic event. He rose and descended a makeshift wooden ladder.

Absorbing Nora's autobiography, from her college days all the way through her various adventures reaching Mexico, Korty seemed more intrigued to learn that she'd once taught English than that she'd recently been deputized by Jehovah's colon to warn him against finishing the sculpture. When she incidentally professed an affection for *The Divine Comedy*—she'd entered the epic seeking the medieval perspective on antiquity, stayed around for the sheer beauty of it all—his fascination intensified.

"Dante and I have a lot in common," he said. "Catholicism, misanthropy, an intellectual hero named Thomas—Aquinas in Dante's case, a quirky Jesuit priest in mine." He pressed his book into Nora's hands: *Parables for a Post-Theistic Age,* by Thomas Ockham, S.J. "Borrow it. Read it. Come back and tell me whether I have a prayer of doing it justice."

"Aren't you troubled by the entrails' prediction?"

"Troubled, Mrs. Burkhart? I'm *exhilarated.* The God who whipped up this plague is obviously a criminal: of *course* He wants me to abandon my project. It threatens to help the world."

"The bowels have a dark side, no question—they even admitted it," said Nora. "But their arguments still sounded plausible."

"What does it profit a man if he retains his sanity but loses his reubenite brain?"

Korty, she decided, was like his project—formidable, overbearing, slightly deranged. For all his refined manner and verbal facility, he seemed to have difficulty inhabiting himself. He was the sort of man about whom Eric would have said, "He doesn't have both oars in the water," though Korty's problem appeared to be more like a superfluity of oars, propelling his psyche in a hundred directions at once. Nora liked him.

"This brain of mine will help make the Third Millennium civilized, perhaps even enlightened, perhaps even wise." Korty placed his palm against the left cerebral hemisphere, running his splayed fingers along a bulging vein.

"How can a mere piece of sculpture have such power?" Nora asked.

"The Philadelphia Liberty Bell had such power. So did the French Republic's Marianne and Picasso's *Guernica.*"

"But only because people invested them with meaning."

"Indeed." He massaged the medulla. "Fiona is my Beatrice, but you, Mrs. Burkhart—you are my Virgil. You've come to guide me through whatever Hell I must endure in completing my magnum opus." Extending his arms, he embraced both women and escorted them toward a doorway cut into the pituitary gland. "As you wade through his *Parables,* you'll see that Ockham imagines us moving beyond the 'terrible transcendent truths' of myth and religion. Ah, but what replaces them? you ask. Walk with me down the corpus callosum and into the cerebellum — my Gallery of Decency."

The instant Nora entered the cerebellum, a scintillating space lit by a dozen incandescent-mantle lanterns, her mood grew inexplicably buoyant. Carved from reubenite and inlaid with semiprecious stones, the decency dioramas glowed like braziers jammed with burning coals. The air seemed electrically charged, as if some Promethean science experiment had just been conducted here, leaving behind a whiff of ozone and an intimation of hot clay. The opening of the *Paradiso* sprang into her mind: Dante in Eden, imitating his Beatrice by daring to look directly at Apollo, the sun.

I suffered him not long, yet not so little
But that I saw him glowing all around
Like molten iron pouring from the forge.

And suddenly it seemed that day on day
Was superadded, as though God had sought
To with a second sun embellish Heaven.

Each tableau commemorated a great moment in the history of ethical obligation. In one niche, the Good Samaritan aided the beaten and abandoned traveler. In another, a congregation of Quaker abolitionists clothed a fugitive American slave during his escape along the Underground Railway. A third tableau depicted Warrant Officer Hugh Thompson and his helicopter crew rescuing Vietnamese villagers from the My Lai massacre.

"Wow, Gerry, it keeps getting better," said Fiona.

"You do beautiful work," said Nora.

"It's a book, Mrs. Burkhart." Korty's eyes flashed as brightly as the mantles on his lanterns. "A stone poem, a reubenite *Paradiso*, a bible for the Third Millennium." He led Nora and Fiona out of the cerebellum, through the rear portal, and into the muggy jungle air. "No wonder God can't stomach it."

"But why will people believe *this* bible?" asked Nora. "What makes it more convincing than the *Book of Mormon* or Mary Baker Eddy?"

"Maybe they *won't* believe it," said Korty. "All I know is, I have to finish the damn thing."

Bidding Korty farewell, Nora again expressed her enthusiasm for the Gallery of Decency—never before, she said, had she found morality so moving—then thanked him for his crucial artistic contribution to the Church of Earthly Affirmation.

"The clinic works," he said. "I've seen proof."

"Terrible things happened to me at El Agujero."

"It's a terrible place. Ahead of you lies a cured child."

"I believe that. A cured child. Yes."

That afternoon, sitting on the forecastle deck, the sternwheeler moored to Esperanza's wharf, Nora read chapter one of *Parables for a Post-Theistic Age.* She was especially impressed by Ockham's concept of "little myths," those unadorned ideals of kindness and creativity that Korty was currently reifying in stone. The words that most haunted her, however, were not Ockham's own but a passage he'd quoted from the Protestant theologian Dietrich Bonhoeffer.

"So our coming of age forces us to a true recognition of our situation vis-à-vis God," Bonhoeffer had written in *Letters and Papers from Prison.* "God is teaching us that we must live as men"—and as women too, she thought—"who can get along very well without Him. The God Who makes us live in this world without using Him as a working hypothesis is the God before Whom we are ever standing. Before God and with Him we live without God."

Lying in her bunk that night, she dreamed herself back to ancient Greece. She was sitting at Aesop's feet, listening enthralled as he spun a tale populated by the Somatocist pantheon. At the climax, attacking in concert, Soaragid, Orgasiad, Risogada, and Idorasag shredded Jehovah's large intestine, hungrily devouring the morsels of holy flesh. Suddenly the bowel beast retaliated, fatally crushing each god in its coils.

"The moral lies beyond my grasp," said Aesop to Nora. "Perhaps this fable foreshadows the coming worldview, a monotheism destined to stretch from the frontiers of India to the farthest shore of an undiscovered continent. Some people may prosper by this new God, others may deplore His advent, but one thing is certain. He won't die an easy death."

Approaching the palace of Risogada, god of laughter, I immediately see that this isn't your normal sacred temple. It looks more like a Las Vegas casino imitating a wizard's castle. The inside suggests one of those gaudy old-time movie theaters where they use red velvet ropes for crowd control. A dozen priests of Risogada lead us through the lobby, past the snack bar, and down a hall lined with funhouse mirrors. I see that my pocks are smaller, my grooves thinner.

We enter the main auditorium, its walls covered with murals of clowns throwing pies at each other. The stage holds a big Risogada: a fifteen-foot marble man wearing diamond-pattern tights and an enormous crocodile head, his jaws open in a gigantic laugh. As we settle into our seats, a fat hobo wearing baggy pants and a tattered coat appears before the idol and introduces himself as "Algernon Bembo, high priest of hijinks." He says that we'll be spending the next twenty-four hours "sniggering, snickering, chuckling, yukking, guffawing, and hee-hawing." Strutting off the stage, Mr. Bembo slips on a banana peel and falls. We laugh.

"Let the service begin!" cries the clown, picking himself up. "Time to worship Risogada with the sacred sound of laughter!"

For the rest of the day we're treated to a vaudeville show. The sketches range from knock-knock jokes, to sex gags I don't quite get, to stuff so rowdy it makes the Three Stooges seem like guidance counselors.

My favorite routine has an explorer getting lost in the Amazon jungle and ending up captured by bloodthirsty natives. "Oh, God, I'm screwed," he mutters to himself. Suddenly there's a ray of light from Heaven, and a voice booms out: "No, you are *not* screwed. Pick up that rock at your feet and crush the head of the chief." So the explorer picks up the rock and bashes out the chief's brains. As he stands panting above the dead body, surrounded by hundreds of natives wearing shocked expressions, God's voice booms out again: "Okay... *now* you're screwed."

Every hour or so, I visit the snack bar and load up on popcorn, soda, nachos, and candy bars. Risogada's priests pipe in the jokes using the PA system, so I don't miss anything. During my third trip to the snack bar, I see Quincy standing naked by the drinking fountain. He's eating a Hershey bar and gulping down a Dr. Pepper.

"Tomorrow I'll have you back in the hospital," he tells me.

"No way," I say.

My fetch coughs, ill with a bad case of hyperion-15. I'm reminded of a joke.

"Jack the Ripper goes to Heaven," I tell Quincy. "'How did *you* get here?' asks Saint Peter. Jack sneezes and says, 'Flu...'"

Quincy keeps on coughing. I tell him another joke.

"William Shakespeare once saw Ben Jonson sitting on the toilet reading a book. 'Poor old Ben,' said Shakespeare. 'His memory is so poor, he needs directions to shit.'"

Before I can tell him the one about the Amazon explorer, my fetch runs out the door.

During the dinner hour, the priests bring us trays of food (right to our seats, like we're passengers on a jetliner flying across the Atlantic), and then Mr. Bembo leads everyone in a hymn of praise to Risogada.

With a kick in the pants
And a pie in the face,
We end the skull's reign,
We break its embrace.

The high priest announces that it's time to make "offerings to the lord of the jest." This means walking up to the crocodile-man, climbing a stepladder, and whispering a funny story in his ear. I figure the idol must be hollow and there's a priest inside, because whenever Risogada hears a punch line, laughter rolls out of his mouth.

At last it's my turn. Leaning against the god's head, I tell him Quincy's story about the death-row prisoner who learns he can have anything he wants for his last meal. ("I'd like some mushrooms," he says. "I've always been afraid to eat them.") My joke gets an especially loud laugh from Risogada.

The sacrifice session ends, and we settle in for the final part of the service, a festival of Monty Python movies. All during *Life of Brian*, I giggle uncontrollably, even though I've seen it before. *The Holy Grail* has us in stitches. *The Meaning of Life* almost makes us wet our pants.

At midnight we stumble out of Risogada's palace and head for Arcadia Lodge, our sides aching. Suddenly I see Quincy, slumped against a marble fountain decorated with Idorasag statues. The spouting milk glows magically in the moonlight. My fetch coughs twice and staggers away. This church is going to cure me. I'm absolutely sure of it.

Not since he'd won first prize in the New Jersey Parochial Schools Arts Festival, wowing the judges with his ceramic interpretation of *Saint Francis Embracing a Fawn*, had an evaluation of his work thrilled Gerard as much as Nora Burkhart's message from the divine entrails. His Stone Gospel had earned the reprobation of the defunct Judeo-Christian God. What better proof that in transmogrifying Oswald's Rock he was creating an object of cosmic significance?

His mood remained high even after, later that day, Hubbard Richter delivered a petulant letter from Lucido, who wanted to know how his statue was progressing. At first Gerard chose to ignore the inquiry, but then Fiona reminded him that the deadline had passed eight days earlier. Through prodigious deployments of willpower, he returned to El Dorado, pulled out his set of Lucido photographs, and sat down to await his muse. After a long evening spent hunched over the drafting table, he teased out a concept that he suspected would please his patron: Lucido standing in *contrapposto* beside a healed abulic, the grateful adolescent rising from her sickbed to embrace her deliverer.

Much to his frustration, Gerard couldn't locate the scrap of paper on which he'd recorded the dimensions of the El Agujero niche. He inverted his pockets, scoured his studio, searched the Stone Gospel. Nothing. At last he resigned himself to the inevitable. Instead of finishing the Gallery of Decency (the final tableau, the Sermon on the Mount, still required at least six hours of effort), he would have to waste the day taking measurements at the detention center. He hitched up the pony and drove along Calle Huimanguillo through a warm steady rain, reaching El Agujero at 3:00 P.M. and setting to work amid the usual grim hubbub of pilgrims arriving with their thected loved ones. By 3:30 P.M. he'd secured the numbers. Although the niche was high enough to accommodate a piece even taller than the resident Soaragid, it measured only two meters across. Gerard winced: he would have to revise his vision, making the resurrected adolescent a little girl instead. Perhaps it was all for the best. Art always sprang from some ineffable mixture of epiphany and stricture, didn't it? Dante had needed the shackles of *terza rima*; one couldn't imagine *The Divine Comedy* without that iron scheme.

As he slipped the tape measure into his pocket, a commotion reached Gerard's ears—stomping feet, angry voices. Moved by a mixture of curiosity and unease, he hid behind the reubenite jaguar, crouched down, and peered into the foyer. A fiftyish, muscular African-American stood before Roland Jackendorf's desk, arms positioned like the prongs of a forklift, cradling a middle-aged woman, also black, her skin scored by stage-four pocks and grooves. It was a common El Agujero tableau—pilgrim petitioning assistant deacon—except for one grim fact: this particular plague victim, Louise Swinscoe of San Diego, had already been through Tamoanchan. She'd cheerfully and energetically apprenticed herself to Gerard two days after completing her therapy.

"You *have* to let her in!" screamed Louise's brother, Claude Swinscoe, an unemployed investment counselor who'd also worked briefly at El Dorado. Claude's fellow pilgrims observed his tirade with intermingled admiration and horror. "She needs a second treatment!"

Jackendorf's stare was blank, unreadable. "Her piety is incomplete, now and forever."

"She loves the gods! She made sacrifices every day!"

The assistant deacon grabbed a mallet and slammed it into a Frisbee-size gong. A dozen minions materialized, surrounding the Swinscoes like the devils besieging Virgil and Dante in Circle VIII.

"Remove this gentleman from the premises," said Jackendorf. "His sister lacks faith."

"That's not true!" wailed Claude as the minions escorted him and Louise past the queues of plague families.

The bulkiest functionary thrust open the riveted door—"The gods are not deceived!"—and banished the pair, forcing them out of El Agujero and into the steamy drizzle. Claude roared like a werejaguar caught in a steel trap. The celestial skull snickered. A groan shot from Gerard's throat, fortunately muffled by the crash of the closing door.

Later, back in El Dorado, he approached his open-air workbench and stared unhappily at the clay lump from which he'd planned to fashion a maquette of Lucido's statue. A rhythmic ticking permeated the studio, drippings from the recent storm. The clay pulsated in the skullglow. He steeled himself and got busy, and by 11:00 P.M. a miniature Lucido had emerged, along with the angelic preschool girl whose salvation the psychoanalyst had just accomplished.

"Come to bed," said Fiona, ambling into the studio.

Gerard wrenched the cap off a warm bottle of Cerveza Moctezuma. "I'm not tired."

"Sleep isn't exactly what I had in mind." She leaned provocatively against Erasmus's pedestal.

"Today a man brought his thected sister to the Hole." He took a swallow, passed the bottle to Fiona. "She'd already been through the temples."

Fiona filled her mouth with beer, the foam clinging to her lips. "Shit."

Facing the maquette, Gerard cupped his hands around the analyst's cranium. "Maybe it's an unusual case, but it froze my blood."

He rotated his wrist, snapping the neck in two, and tossed Lucido's head to Fiona. She nabbed the thing with her free hand, laughed, and threw it back.

"I do not love thee, Dr. Lucido," Gerard told the head, closing his fingers into a tight ball. Clay oozed between his knuckles.

For the next fifteen minutes husband and wife drank beer and played catch in the atelier. The violence energized Gerard; it pricked his id and heated his libido. Taking Fiona in his arms, he led her across the floor in a tarantella choreographed by Soaragid, then carried her to their bedroom. They performed like gods. Their orgasms came from the Volcán de Catemaco. As they drifted off to sleep, Fiona mumbled, half joking, half serious, that from now on they must always preface their lovemaking with a pagan dance, a symbolic decapitation, and a six-pack of Cerveza Moctezuma.

The Olmec Innovation

MIXED MOTIVES AND CONFUSED ambitions lay behind Nora's decision to volunteer at La Sangre de la Serpiente, sweeping and scrubbing and whatnot. It would make Esperanza's life easier. It would help pay for their docking privileges. But mostly Nora wanted to escape from herself. The acolytes' release still lay ninety-six long hours—over five thousand excruciating minutes—in the future. Cantina keeping might prove boring, but it should also take her mind, however fleetingly, off Kevin's pocks and grooves.

While mopping tables and washing dishes failed to soothe, soup making proved therapeutic, its fragrances a mental balm, its rhythms inimical to plague anxiety. But the best diversion lay in serving Esperanza's customers: not the newly arrived pilgrims, who rarely stayed more than twenty minutes after receiving directions to Tamoanchan, but the indigenous clientele. With the exception of two prostitutes and a half-wit seamstress, Esperanza's regulars were male: roughhewn fishermen and subsistence farmers who took Tuesday and Thursday afternoons off to indulge their fondness for dice, drink, tobacco, and brawling. Throughout Nora's first day on the job, her high school Spanish came creeping back, and while she rarely caught the nuances of the customers' conversations, she could often follow the drift. The men never spoke of the pestilence. Fishing was a major topic: who'd caught what, where, how many. Pigs and chickens made the cut. So did the weather, women's breasts, and the merits of Carta Blanca beer versus Cerveza Moctezuma.

But mostly the regulars talked about Catemaco. Some believed the mountain would blow any day now, a thought occasioning a kind of perverse joy in its adherents. The doomsayers' pleasure made sense. In contrast to abulia, a volcanic eruption had everything going for it: deafening explosions, spewing lava, flying debris, walls of flame. The bang was always better than the whimper.

At midnight, Esperanza shooed the last of the barflies into the jungle, closed the door, and asked Nora whether she wanted to be paid in beer or tequila.

"Make me the best margarita in Coatzacoalcos."

"I'll make you the best margarita in Mexico. Where does your son worship tomorrow? The temple of Risogada?"

"Orgasiad, actually. The priestesses are holy whores."

"Better he should lose his virginity in church than behind the corncrib, like happened to me. I shall pray for him."

Later, as Esperanza trod the stairs, heading for her room above the bar, Nora saw that the hotelier had an escort, a tall mustachioed man who'd been among the more vociferous prophets of volcanic doom. A sad smile curled Nora's lips. She took a substantial sip, wondering if she would ever see Percy again. The coarse salt rimming the glass burned her lips and stoked her thirst. She took another sip. The best margarita in Mexico: Esperanza was absolutely right.

"Good evening, Mrs. Burkhart," said a young male voice.

The speaker stood in the doorway, exuding the odor of humus.

"You'll be happy to hear I finished writing my joke book," Quincy continued, stumbling into the cantina. "I call it *Howlers from Hell.*" He wore black chinos and a hemp shirt. His left eye resembled a sphere of rubber cement, his right a charred Ping-Pong ball, both evidently ruined by hyperion-15. "I need a drink."

Nora's blood began to sing. Her bones laughed in delight. "Quincy, you've been dispossessed."

"Temporarily," he said, coughing.

Permanently, she prayed. Please, Soaragid. I beg you, Idorasag. "And blinded as well."

"A Cuba libre would do nicely."

She poured the fetch a tall glass of Bacardi, then mixed in several ounces of Pepsi-Cola. God, what a prodigy that man Lucido was! What a wizard! What a giant!

Quincy's searching fingers scuttled across the bar to the Cuba libre. He brought the glass to his lips, tipped it, guzzled. "What makes you so sure," he said, "that Kevin *wants* to come back?"

"Of course he wants to come back."

"I'll tell you something." Again the leveler coughed. "Long before my host contracted the plague, a severe melancholia had seized his soul."

"Liar."

"Adolescents are as vulnerable to clinical depression as adults—did you know that? Kevin hid it well." He slammed his Cuba libre on the counter. "Etiology? Hard to say. An undesirable gene? His absent father? Or maybe the problem was his overprotective mother. Speaking of depressing situations, I'm thinking of beginning *Howlers from Hell* with this one. George goes to his doctor for a routine physical. The doctor checks him out thoroughly and delivers the worst possible news: George is going to die. George asks, 'When?' The doctor says, 'Ten . . .' George cries, 'Ten? That's terrible. Ten what? Ten years? Months? Days?' The doctor replies, 'Nine . . .'" Backing away from the bar, the fetch floated across the room like a windblown shroud. "You simply refuse to laugh at these, don't you, Mrs. Burkhart? Why am I wasting my time? Good-bye."

Stretching out his arms, Quincy groped his way to the door.

Nora gulped the rest of her drink, finished off the fetch's. Kevin melancholic? No. Wrong. Morbid, perhaps, all those grisly tricks—"The Gourmet Ghoul," "The Giggling Mortician"—but the school psychologist thought them salutary, a way for the boy to confront his shadow side.

She left La Sangre de la Serpiente and walked into the steamy night. Quincy was gone, swallowed by the wet gloom. A hundred tree frogs chirped. A thousand cicadas trilled. She turned toward Tamoanchan, waiting patiently until a full-face portrait of Kevin consumed her inner vision.

"You want to come back," she told him. A plea, an admonishment, a question, a command.

Picture a rolling woodland meadow covered with soft green grass where hundreds of onyx-and-gold Monarch butterflies flutter among orange azaleas and blood-red hibiscus. Picture a stone idol atop each hill—a busty woman with the eyes and snout of a snake, her lower body winding around itself like a twist of soft ice cream. Picture willow glades, laurel glens, olive gardens, and a lagoon, its waters colored turquoise like a Holiday Inn swimming pool. You're seeing the Temple of Orgasiad—goddess of copulation, queen of passion—open to all acolytes over the age of fourteen.

The instant you step through the gateway, a rainbow trellis wrapped in grapevines, a high priest named Zachary Apple asks whether you prefer male, female, or both. He looks you up and down, then enters a kind of greenhouse and comes out a few minutes later with two people who could've easily gotten work as movie stars back when Hollywood existed. It's like being fitted for a suit, only more exciting.

I'm assigned to a priestess named Margo, a slender prom-queen type in a tight Friends of Fellatio T-shirt and cutoff jeans that give you ninety percent of her legs, and also to a priestess named Melody, who's a little heavier but has tits the size of softballs, which I figure out because her white gown is translucent like the wax paper inside a cereal box. Too bad I'm wearing the Bermuda shorts and Hawaiian shirt they gave me in Arcadia Lodge—I feel like a buffoon from the Temple of Risogada. At least my skin looks better. The pocks and grooves have faded into acne.

My new friends have prepared a picnic: wicker basket, checkered blanket, CD player. Our holiday starts immediately. The priestesses take my hands and guide me to a patch of meadow secluded by rosebushes.

Margo's legs scissor magically, Melody's tits shimmy like giant scoops of Jell-O. Melted chocolate goes rushing through my veins—that's how it feels, anyway. The three of us spread out the blanket, and when Melody bends over, I can see everything (a girl might show cleavage galore, but unless you catch a nipple, you're not atop Everest yet), so naturally I'm stiff as a pogo stick by the time we're sitting down.

"Here in the grove of Orgasiad," says Melody, opening the picnic basket, "hidden in the shadows of your soul, you will discover the secret well of Eros."

"Have you ever done it before?" asks Margo, turning on the CD player.

"Only in my dreams," I say.

The Doors song called "Light My Fire" spills forth as Melody takes a chicken thigh from the basket and begins munching. "Big day ahead."

The picnic is delicious but also painful, because the chicken, grapes, cheese, and rosé wine take so long to consume, but finally we're ready to worship Orgasiad, who has got to be the greatest goddess of all time. Margo lays me down and starts peeling off my Bermuda shorts, and suddenly my pocket rocket is on the launch pad, and it feels like T minus thirty seconds. Melody hikes up her white gown like she's about to wade across a brook, singing the goddess's name, "Oorgassiiiaaad," as she sits on me, and soon it becomes clear she doesn't bother with underwear.

"Quoits," she says, and right away gets a ringer, but I'm the person who feels that he's the winner.

"Oorgassiiiaaad," I sing.

"Put your gift on the altar, Kevin," says Melody. "Pour out your libation."

Over her shoulder, the skull is smiling its smile, and just then the thing looks ridiculous. Margo helps Melody pull her dress off over her head, so I can see Melody's water balloons completely. Her nipples are like two pink thimbles. And suddenly the countdown hits zero, we have ignition, we have liftoff, it's all jetting out of me, and I'm singing Orgasiad's name again, because now there's one less virgin in Mexico.

"You're young," says Margo, handing me a Three Musketeers bar. "You'll recycle in no time."

She's right. After I'm finished eating the candy, all Margo has to do is remove her T-shirt and climb out of her cutoffs, and I'm ready to make another sacrifice. Her nipples are totally different from Melody's, dark and wide like antique coins, but still breathtaking. She tells me to do her from behind, and I obey, because I want to try everything while I'm here, but I can't hold my libation back for more than a few minutes, which Margo says is normal under the circumstances.

Hand in hand, the three of us walk down to the lagoon and stretch out along the shore, and just when I've decided life can't get any better, Melody is treating my dick like a Fudgesicle, putting the whole thing in her mouth. She adds her hand to the procedure, up and down like she's opening and closing an umbrella, and I'm a dam that's about to break, or a volcano that's about to erupt, which of course I do, and Melody swallows everything.

As the afternoon goes on, we continue worshiping Orgasiad—on the sand, under the water, even in the cleft of a papaya tree. Sometimes the priestesses lick and massage each other, and at one point they rub my chest with a combination of spit and altar juices, saying, "We baptize you in the name of Orgasiad," and I'm happy it's official now, because Orgasiad is a goddess I'd follow into Vincent Price's torture chamber, if necessary.

Hours later, back in Arcadia Lodge, I ease myself onto the mattress, my dick sore and throbbing, and I decide it's the most wonderful ache a man has ever known. Are you there, Quincy? Can you hear me? Of course not. One skinny fetch against gods so powerful that each deserves his own comic-book series: it's no contest.

For three days Gerard managed to ignore the new gods' failure to cure Louise Swinscoe—the chinks in Soaragid's armor, as it were (the cavities in Risogada's teeth, the lumps in Orgasiad's breasts, the clay that constituted Idorasag's feet)—and fix his attention on the great work. He finished the Sermon on the Mount tableau, returned to El Dorado, and threw himself into a sketching session, drafting his ideas for the Garden of Scientific Knowledge. It rained voluminously, the droplets hitting the tin roof with the sound of popcorn blooming in a microwave oven. He hardly noticed. The science garden obsessed him. When finally rendered in reubenite and inlaid with jade and turquoise, the fifteen dioramas would rank with his most striking achievements, eclipsing even his *Paradiso* marbles. He took supreme satisfaction not only in his illustrations of Galileo discovering the Jovian moons and Darwin contemplating the Galapagos finches, but also in his concept of Einstein seated beside a window in the Swiss Patent Office, staring outward past his desk, the street, the city of Berne . . . beyond the Milky Way, beyond Newtonian physics.

On Thursday morning, while he was happily roughing out the penultimate diorama (Watson and Crick cobbling together their model of the DNA molecule), a haunted-looking young woman appeared at El Dorado and identified herself as Hannah Alport. She approached Gerard's drafting table with a despairing shuffle, her poncho shedding rainwater from the sleeves and hood, though her anguished face suggested that some of the droplets might be tears. Gerard offered her tea. She took the steaming mug, heaved a long sigh, and, slumping into a wicker chair, told her story.

Two weeks earlier, Hannah's eight-year-old, Joshua, had broken the grip of thexis in consequence of his journey through the temples, after which mother and son decided to stay in Coatzacoalcos, assisting newly arrived pilgrims. The previous evening, a terrible setback had occurred. Joshua's leveler returned, conquering the boy's will, invading his brain, festooning his body with stage-three boils.

As Hannah's narrative reached its climax, an icy nausea spread through Gerard. Damn. Hell. Louise Swinscoe's relapse wasn't unique.

Hannah said, "I thought maybe Somatocism was like chemotherapy, you need several doses, so we went back to El Agujero. The bastards kicked us out. Mr. Richter said Joshua lacked piety. Totally false. My boy made offerings every day." She pulled her poncho hood away, releasing a cascade of sandy hair. "You're the church's official sculptor. You have influence with Deacon Richter."

"Actually, the man hates me." Gerard turned toward his drafting table and began shading the double helix, but her pleading eyes continued to haunt him. "Lucido occasionally listens to me," he said at last. "If you like, I'll speak to him about Joshua's case."

Before Gerard could turn again, Hannah threw her arms around his waist and fervently embraced him.

"*Gracias!*"

The afternoon found Gerard driving dispiritedly toward Mount Tapílula, his mind filled with funerary images: Claude Swinscoe burying his sister, Hannah Alport burying her son. Calle Huimanguillo had become a carpet of mud, as thick and sticky as sartre sauce. The omnipresent ooze sucked at the pony's hoofs, seized the cart's wheels, and delayed Gerard's arrival by an hour.

Wandering through the mansion, negotiating the labyrinth of corridors, he finally located Lucido in the library. The psychoanalyst sat in an easy chair, dressed in his customary black caftan, his hyperion syringe and a bottle of Brunello di Montalcino resting on the adjacent tea table as his tired eyes scanned Sigmund Freud's *The Future of an Illusion*.

All during Gerard's tale, Lucido wore an expression as indecipherable as the Olmec calendar in his wine cellar. When at last he spoke, his tone proved likewise cryptic, somewhere between forced sincerity and oblique sarcasm.

"Two relapses," said Lucido.

"I suspect there may be more," said Gerard.

"Correct. I know of eleven such cases personally."

"Eleven? God."

"A twelfth is probably occurring even as we speak," said Lucido, infuriatingly placid. He closed the book and stabbed the cover with his pointing finger. "Sorry, Herr Doktor Freud. Religion is not an illusion. The believer doesn't *see* angels and demons zooming through the air. He doesn't need to *see* them, not when his faith tells him they enjoy metaphysical reality." He fixed Gerard with a gaze powered by certainty and hyperion-15. "Why does my church work so well? Because it's built on the mountain of faith, not the bog of illusion."

"But it *doesn't* work so well."

Lucido smiled darkly and filled a glass with rich crimson wine. "No treatment is totally reliable, though obviously some medicines are preferable to others." He sipped his wine and resumed speaking, slowly now. "Which is why I've started attacking abulia from a completely different direction. I call it Antidote X. Religion and science, inextricably fused. Still experimental, but the preliminary results are encouraging."

Gerard stared at the nearest shelf, jammed with Jane Austen first editions lugged to Coatzacoalcos by some desperate plague family. He had no inkling what Antidote X might be, but he did know that the idea of a backup church failed utterly to inspire him. "Even with its weaknesses, Somatocism is an astonishing achievement. Can you really invent something that effective all over again?"

"Through Antidote X, I intend to advance not only beyond the Church of Earthly Affirmation but beyond *all* churches everywhere, near and far, past and present."

"Okay, but meanwhile shouldn't we send the relapsers through Tamoanchan again?"

"What you're proposing is grossly unfair to those patients who still need a *first* treatment."

"We could train new priests and add a night shift."

Approaching his bookcases, Lucido shelved *The Future of an Illusion* with a condescending twist of the wrist. "I hate to say it, Herr Doktor Freud, but religion faces a far brighter future than depth psychology."

"Did you hear what I just said?"

"There's no need to keep Tamoanchan open around the clock. We're running a church here, not a laundromat. Besides, having personally examined several relapsers, I can say with confidence that they're in no immediate danger."

"Are you joking?" said Gerard. "They've been thected all over again."

"That's how it appears from the outside, yes," said Lucido. "Inside, a stalemate obtains between fetch and host."

"I don't understand."

"Blood tests. It's complicated. How is my statue progressing?"

"I've got a concept."

"A concept, that's all?"

"You're crouching before a sickbed. A healed child rises from the mattress, seeking to embrace her deliverer."

"Yes . . . only I'm looming over *two* beds," said Lucido, "one holding a child, the other an adult."

"The niche is too small."

"My dear fellow, are you still unaware of how we do things around here? When the niche is too small, we don't shrink the statue."

"I see."

"That's right, Gerard. We take down the wall."

To reach the Temple of Soaragid, master of the revels, god of dancing, you follow granite steps deep into the ground below Tamoanchan, then walk through a bunch of little chambers connected by tunnels. Suddenly a cavern opens before you, lit by candles and torches. The smoke curls upward for fifty feet and makes the ceiling as black as the night sky.

Smorgasbord tables line the far wall. Roasted pigs with apples in their mouths. Hams as big as fire hydrants. Bread loaves like pillows. Champagne bottles wedged into mounds of crushed ice. Seated inside a marble gazebo, a dozen musicians play fiddles, fifes, drums, and bagpipes. In the center of the cavern stands a mammoth Soaragid idol: a man with a jaguar's face, chin thrown back, arms raised. He is dancing.

As we acolytes come forward, two dozen priests and priestesses appear, each wearing a jaguar helmet and a cape of jaguar fur. My partner calls herself Luna, high priestess of Soaragid. Her face is almost as catlike as the god's, with large pouty lips and golden eyes.

Soaragid's servants lead us to the idol. A bronze basin sits at the right foot, "waiting to receive sacrifices," we're told. The cultists teach us a hymn of praise, and we chant it over and over, the musicians providing the tune.

He dances on the pounding waves
And eats the flying foam.
He waltzes on the whirling wind
And makes the clouds his home.

He pirouettes across the sun
And slips the moon a kiss.
He slyly tricks each dying fetch
Into the black abyss.

After we stop singing, the musicians keep playing, shifting into other melodies. I've never heard music like this before; it seems to come from another planet, yet somehow every note makes sense. "Your blood leaps up," says Luna as we begin to dance. "Feel the pulled plasma, the tide within." Sliding and stomping in time to the music, I can only guess at the steps, but what I do feels right. We dance mazurkas and mambos, tangos and fandangos, and then the real frenzy begins: sambas, congas, tarantellas, polkas, jigs. Our feet clatter on the stone floor; we sound like a stampede of happy buffalo. The food vanishes. The champagne flows. As the music gets faster, our revels get wilder ("every molecule alive," says Luna, "every organelle cavorting, every cell celebrating"), until our tapping, skipping, spinning, hopping, feasting, drinking, and singing pour into each other like the meeting of a thousand rivers ("the inverse agonies of the Temple of Soaragid," she says, "merriment's martyrs, racked by jollity, eviscerated by felicity"), and the sweat rolls out of us like cider from squeezed apples as we tear off our clothes ("nakedness knows nothing of shame, the true disciple wears only skin") and toss them aside, so we can move and breath better, our bodies all sleek and shiny in the torchlight.

The sacrifices begin. An acolyte dances up to the Soaragid idol, furiously shaking his arms and head so his sweat flies into the bronze basin. He goes back to the revels, works up a fresh cup, offers it to the god, returns to the revels, creates another cup, offers it, returns. Hour by hour, the basin grows fuller. We whirl and leap. The sweat level rises. We vault and soar. The basin overflows. We surrender our last drops and collapse—dizzy, exhausted, gasping. Then the great god Soaragid, pleased and appeased, climbs off his pedestal, creeps across the cavern, and, bending low over each acolyte in turn, whispers a promise in his ear. Soaragid vows to range through all the corridors of our minds, hunt down our wraiths, and hurl them "into Hell's most corrosive sea." And then suddenly, lying there with the blood thumping in my ears and the sweet mossy smell of the cavern floor filling my nostrils, I realize that I've truly thrown off my fetch—Quincy is gone forever.

My victory rushes through me like a double hit of hyperion, and I sleep.

When Hannah Alport heard that Gerard's attempt to intercede on her son's behalf had failed, she responded with a detachment more disturbing than the anger he was expecting. "These days, a person knows better than to get her hopes up," she said, her tone as affectless as the voice of the stone Luther. "Even after Joshua broke out of his coma, I didn't assume he was permanently cured."

"I simply can't connect with that man," said Gerard, gesturing toward his nascent statue of Lucido. That morning, in consequence of his labors, a recognizable head and shoulders had arisen from the block, but the limbs and torso, not to mention the two healed abulics, remained sealed in reubenite. "He's a great scientist, a genius really, but he lives inside his skull."

"I ask myself, if Dr. Lucido won't listen to his idolmaker, who *will* he listen to?"

"Good question."

Slogging across the muddy studio grounds, Hannah pulled off her Panama hat and set it on Erasmus's pedestal. "And then I think, 'He'll listen to me. He'll listen to a mother with a dying child in her arms.'"

"You're planning to visit Lucido?"

"This afternoon."

"It won't work."

She rubbed the humanist's calf, as if to relieve him of a charley horse. "And who is this?"

"Erasmus, sometimes called the Voltaire of the Renaissance. I talk to him."

"And does the statue talk back?"

"Yes. Lucido will rebuff you—I hope you know that."

Hannah indicated Erasmus's debating partner. "And this one . . . ?"

"Martin Luther. Good news, Mrs. Alport—the doctor is researching an experimental treatment. Your best strategy would be to stay in the city until the new cure becomes available."

"Or until Joshua dies." She wandered toward Gerard's workbench and picked up a tooth chisel.

Gerard said, "Lucido believes that Joshua's present condition, disturbing as it is, doesn't represent true thexis."

"Well, it sure-as-hell *looks* like true thexis." She approached the stockade portal, lifted the latch, and opened the right-hand gate. "I took History of Christianity in college. Luther suffered from constipation."

"One of the severest cases on record."

"Better blocked bowels"—she stabbed the chisel into the wooden lintel but failed to anchor the blade—"than a blocked mind."

"Erasmus would say that Luther had both."

Again she stabbed, successfully this time, and slipped into the jungle. Like the gnomon on a sundial, the chisel cast a long thin shadow across the open gate.

Gerard spent the rest of the morning completing his sketches for the Garden of Scientific Knowledge. He returned to Oswald's Rock and labored through the night, carving the contours of the Isaac Newton diorama by the roaring glow of his mantle lanterns. Gradually the scene emerged: the polymath in his Trinity College rooms, experimenting with pendulums and fiddling with prisms.

Dawn seeped into the left hemisphere. A voice said, "May I offer a bit of advice?"

Gerard looked up. A smiling man stood in the shadows, wearing a black felt hat and a tattered serape, an unlit clay pipe clamped in his jaws. At first Gerard didn't recognize the intruder, but then the man stopped smiling, and the sculptor realized he was looking at himself. A terrible apprehension clutched Gerard's soul. Was he about to die? Was the great work doomed? Personal obliteration he could abide, but the thought of losing his project was intolerable.

"Have you come to — "

"To foreclose?" said Julius Azrael. "At the moment I'm merely here to kibitz."

Gerard, grateful, laughed with Risogadan gusto. "Go ahead, Julius. Kibitz away."

"Use a real prism. Shine a light behind it. Flood Newton's rooms with a rainbow."

Gerard had to admit that he found the leveler's idea appealing. "There are no prisms in Coatzacoalcos."

"Use the bottom of a tequila bottle."

"That might work."

"I must say, you've been a productive fellow since I cut your cheek in the Forum. Me, I've accomplished almost nothing. Got my Christmas shopping done, opened a Mexican restaurant, read some Ayn Rand, that's about it." In a burst of fetchian playfulness, Julius caused a dozen steel pins to shoot from his hatband and fly into Newton's ceramic flesh, so that the figurine became a kind of Restoration voodoo doll. "This Stone Gospel is simply *terrific.* I'm proud to wear your face."

Despite Gerard's instinctive resistance, the wraith's praise truly touched him. "What I can't decide, Julius, is whether you are my enemy or my friend."

"It depends on your attitude toward death."

"I hate it."

"A stumbling block in our relationship, I'd say." The fetch lit his clay pipe. "When you're finished with Newton, what next?"

"Edward Jenner inoculating his children against smallpox."

"Jenner had the right idea. Prevention is always better than therapy. Lucido doesn't understand that. Night after night he slaves away in his wine cellar, struggling with Antidote X, when he should be developing a vaccine. Might I offer another suggestion? If you want Lucido to keep the temples open dawn to dusk, you must prove to him that the relapsers are in mortal danger. I can provide you with the evidence."

"Why would a fetch want to see Somatocism grow?"

"Death has many dimensions, Brother. We never met a paradox we didn't like."

Later that day, riding north in the pony cart along Calle Puesta del Sol, Julius holding the reins, Gerard absorbed the sorry fact that Coatzacoalcos, like so many cities before it, had suffered a dramatic reversal in the normal ratio between buried and unburied corpses. It was a city of the living, a city of the dying, but mainly it was a city of the dead. The corpses were everywhere: straight corpses, pretzel corpses, short, tall, thin, bloated, festering in the sunlight, decaying in the skullglow, the whole lot reeking like the shit-covered flatterers of Circle VIII. Flies moved across the death city in vast skittering clouds, their incessant drone suggesting a tone-deaf choir singing "Joy to the World" backwards. The air rang with the sound of grave digging, a carillon of steel shovels striking exposed rock.

"Eighty-five percent died of the plague before they could become acolytes," noted Julius, driving through an arched gateway and onto an expanse of vine-covered hills enclosed by a white adobe wall. "Their donations proved unacceptable to Richter." A public park in happier days—PARQUE CREPÚSCULO, the sign said—the space was now an improvised cemetery dotted with dead bodies, mounded earth, wooden crosses, and gaping excavations. "Ten percent died of natural causes while trying to get infected loved ones into treatment," the fetch continued. "Heart disease, cancer, diabetes—most especially the diarrhea endemic to cities with overburdened sanitation facilities."

"That leaves five percent."

"Five percent. Right." Julius reined up alongside an Indian laurel tree, jumped down, and tethered the pony to the handiest branch. "I'd like you to meet someone."

Behind a stand of acacias, beneath the noonday death's-head, a minimalist funeral—one corpse, one survivor—had just started. Gerard and Julius maintained a respectful distance. As the ceremony progressed, its solitary enactor, a bent woman with a narrow face and large bloodshot eyes, performed all the necessary functions: pallbearer, cleric, sexton, mourner. After depositing the corpse in the fresh grave, the woman marked it with a shabby cross assembled from two fence pickets. Gerard studied the cross, immediately noticing an epitaph burned into the transverse piece.

MALVINA FERGUS
1991–2006
SHE SANG LIKE AN ANGEL

He chewed his lip and moaned. This had to be the same Malvina Fergus who'd told him, "Thanks to your gods, I have experienced the raptures of reality."

The mother's grief peaked; tears flooded the creases in her cheeks. At length she approached the open grave, and for an instant Gerard imagined that Anna Fergus intended to throw herself atop her daughter's corpse. Instead, she took up the spade again and began shoveling back the dirt.

"Let me help you," said Julius, stepping out of hiding.

Anna Fergus looked the wraith squarely in the eye, then handed him the spade like a runner relaying an Olympic torch. "Malvina always liked you," she said.

"That isn't me," said Gerard, drawing abreast of Julius.

The woman's gaze alternated between parasite and host. "When the levelers come after someone of your status," she said at last, "what chance do the rest of us have?"

Striding up to the hole, Julius obtained a spadeful of dirt and solemnly continued the interment. The fetches, mused Gerard, had one point in their favor: they never shrank from menial labor. All during his trip to Mexico, he'd seen levelers weeding their hosts' gardens and walking their dogs.

"I'm sorry about Malvina," said Gerard, approaching the grave.

"Your gods aren't good enough, Mr. Korty."

He glanced at the body, largely obscured by pebbles, rocks, and hunks of dirt. Anna had dressed her child in a shroud improvised from a potato sack, interpenetrating the loose weave with freshly cut wildflowers. Lumps of crimson clay stained Malvina's brow and rouged her cheeks.

"Some people believe that in cases like your daughter's"—Julius dropped a spadeful of soil on Malvina's face—"a second treatment could spark a permanent remission."

"Since when are you bloodsuckers interested in remissions?" asked Anna.

Instead of answering, Julius set down the spade and uprooted Malvina's grave marker. "The proof I promised you," he explained, passing the cross to Gerard. He turned toward Anna and laid his frigid fingers on her shoulder. "Our godmaker has a problem. He wishes to persuade Dr. Lucido that relapsers are in mortal danger. Mr. Korty hopes you will permit him to thrust your daughter's cross in Lucido's face."

With an index finger Gerard traced the S in FERGUS. "How did you do the letters?"

"Screwdriver," said Anna, "heated over a Sterno stove. I burned myself four times—once on purpose, to honor Malvina."

"If you really want to honor Malvina," said Julius, "let Mr. Korty carry this cross to Mount Tapílula."

Anna made no reply. She picked up the spade and sealed the grave, silently sculpting the mound until it achieved a fitting symmetry.

"One condition," she said. "Her favorite song was 'Octopus's Garden.'"

"I know," said Gerard.

"I like it too," said Julius.

For the next five minutes they held hands beside the knoll, man, woman, and wraith, singing about a horticulturally talented cephalopod who delighted in welcoming children into his cave. He listened to their stories, taught them how to dance, and comforted them during storms. A paragon of his species, Gerard decided, a candidate for the Gallery of Decency.

The lobby of Arcadia Lodge was as featureless as a shoe box—no plants, mirrors, fountains, vases, or chandeliers—but filtered through Nora's heightened senses and jangled nerves, it quickly acquired a psychedelic vibrancy. A festive web of electric wires glowed behind the walls, pulsing blood-red as the volts ebbed and flowed. Copper pipes danced beneath the floorboards, channeling iridescent water throughout the hotel.

Clustered in the corners, hovering around the pillars, twenty-three plague families stood and waited, their hearts keeping the same anxious beat, their stomachs twitching synchronously. Nora observed a full range of coping strategies. Some pilgrims paced in fretful circles. Others consumed coffee and cigarettes. Many forced their fingers into Laocoönian tangles.

At 9:00 A.M., right on schedule, the acolytes appeared, singing a hymn to Idorasag as they paraded down the wide central staircase like debutantes entering high society. "Your fur is soft as soft can be. Your milk is sweet and thick and free." A succession of exultant thoughts rushed through Nora's brain—through every brain in the lobby. Lucido's patients could sing, could walk, almost certainly run . . . the *demonios* had been conquered! Each acolyte advanced gracefully, hobbled only slightly by the bulging canvas satchel that he carried at his side. The stage-four pocks were now tiny specks; the collateral grooves had become mere wrinkles. No acolyte was fancily dressed. Blouses, T-shirts, jeans—the very street clothes, Nora guessed, in which they'd entered Tamoanchan.

The singing stopped. Nora scanned the faces, her blood burning. The lead patient was a comely young Asian woman, and no sooner had she reached the middle stair than an elderly Asian man rushed forward, tore the satchel from her grasp, and swept her into his arms. An ecstatic mêlée followed, acolytes descending, family members charging upward. The air resounded with cries of happiness and whoops of joy as the two groups became one.

"Mother! Mother!"

It was he, no question. Mother, pick a card, any card. Mother, watch this clock turn into a cake. Mother, Danny Jacobowski has an extra guinea pig.

"Kevin!"

Canvas satchel swinging, he jumped over the seventh step and landed beside an easy chair.

"Mother!"

"Kevin!"

He dropped the satchel, and they connected, their embrace transcending clothing and skin, bones melding, lungs meshing, arteries entwining, hearts colliding. Nora was ready to extend the hug until one of them fainted from hunger.

"You look terrific," she whispered.

"I've got a million things to tell you."

The throng moved onto the hotel lawn, where the healed abulics, gesticulating like ringmasters and jabbering like Pentecostals, triumphantly opened their satchels and displayed their treasures: mahogany replicas of the four deities, carved in a style most generously described as unpretentious. Before bedding down in Arcadia Lodge for the last time, Kevin explained, they had all participated in an arts-and-crafts night. Note the tenderness in Idorasag's eyes. Look how smoothly Soaragid pirouettes.

The fact that these graven images were of the acolytes' own making did nothing to allay Nora's misgivings. How much, exactly, did Kevin owe his idols? What price would they ultimately extract?

Gods in hand, the reunited plague families boarded the Coatzacoalcos shuttle bus. Kevin followed Nora to the donkey cart, where he eagerly made Felipe's acquaintance, patting the animal on the nose. Nora climbed into the driver's seat and took the reins. Kevin scrambled up beside her. For a full minute mother and son sat together in the ferocious heat, waving good-bye as the rattly old bus turned around and disappeared into the morning haze.

"If Felipe ever gets stubborn," said Kevin, "you can borrow the riding crop on my Swiss Army knife."

As the day progressed—a day more glorious than any in Nora's memory—her doubts gradually fell away. Kevin seemed not simply fetch-free but worry-free, not just rehabilitated but reborn. Everything enchanted him. The cart with its comical donkey, the cantina with its seedy clientele, the sternwheeler with its echoes of *Life on the Mississippi* (a book he'd enjoyed no less than *The Adventures of Tom Sawyer* or *A Connecticut Yankee in King Arthur's Court*). Crock and Esperanza instantly succumbed to his charms, the engineer showing Kevin the steamboat's innermost secrets, the hotelier supplying props for Kevin's tricks. Esperanza burst into unaffected applause upon seeing the sand in her egg timer turn from brown to blue, then laughed uproariously as Kevin split open a fresh mango and removed a live tree frog.

On four separate occasions that afternoon he excused himself from the cantina for purposes of worshiping a god—a pattern that recurred throughout the subsequent weeks.

Depending on the deity, the ritual took between five and fifteen minutes. After securing the necessary offering, Kevin would head for the embarcadero, where his idols rose from the railing like the alabaster Marx Brothers on his bookcase back home in Cambridge. He honored Risogada by laying a millipede at the god's feet and bisecting it with Crock's screwdriver. Idorasag demanded a cockroach. Orgasiad received an ounce of semen. To praise Soaragid he pricked his index finger and smeared the idol's brow with blood. While the viscerality of these devotions disturbed Nora, she had to admit that Kevin performed them with a joie de vivre that bore no obvious relation to zealotry. For this acolyte, at least, sacrificing to the new gods was less a compulsion than a hobby, like collecting baseball cards or keeping tropical fish.

"I haven't become weird," he assured her. "It's just something I do."

"You *have* become weird," she said, "and that's perfectly okay."

Cured? Really? So it appeared. True, he was now a committed pagan, but what mother wouldn't prefer that to drug addiction or sexual promiscuity—not to mention the plague? Yes, he was exhausted much of the time, a condition that dictated both midmorning and late-afternoon naps, but this seemed reasonable in someone who'd recently ejected a fetch.

At the end of Kevin's third week as a cured abulic, Nora's lingering uncertainty vanished. Mother and son were returning to the cantina in the donkey cart after a long day of negotiating with Coatzacoalcos's cutthroat merchants and black marketeers, trading Esperanza's livestock for beer, tequila, and other necessities. Kevin was sullen. At one stall he'd come upon a jade Orgasiad, and his desire for the idol soon proved as ardent as the goddess's own libido. The vendor wanted an entire pig. Nora offered a chicken instead. The vendor laughed in her face.

"One lousy pig." Kevin took Felipe's reins from Nora. "Aren't I worth one lousy goddamn pig to you?"

"The pigs weren't mine," she said.

"Esperanza wouldn't care."

"Of course she would care."

"She's got *lots* of pigs."

"You have a perfectly good mahogany Orgasiad."

"It stinks."

"How about a little gratitude, Kevin? Got any gratitude in there? You think it was a picnic hauling your butt all the way here from Boston?"

"Quincy said you had wonderful adventures. You played a goddess and screwed an actor."

"A spiritualist almost shot me. The Anglo-Saxons blew up my truck."

"Am I going to spend the rest of my life hearing how heroic you were?"

"Am I going to spend the rest of my life hearing about some ridiculous jade statue?"

"Orgasiad isn't ridiculous!"

"I didn't say that!"

"You did!"

"I didn't!"

For fifteen long seconds, silence descended. At last he said, "We're having a fight, aren't we, Mother?"

Smiling, she retrieved the reins. "We're having a fight," she echoed. The cart passed beneath a canopy of trees arrayed in flaming bougainvillea. "I rather like it."

"Me too."

"Maybe we can get the statue on our next trip."

"It'll be gone by then," he said.

"Pessimism is a cheap attitude," she said.

"Stop lecturing me."

"Stop badgering me."

"I'm not badgering you." He offered her his most beguiling grin. "I'm needling you, but I'm not badgering you."

She laughed—a sustained, symphonic, jubilant laugh of the sort she hadn't produced since her students threw her a surprise thirtieth birthday party. "It's really you, isn't it?"

"Really me. The kid who likes Roger Corman movies. Kevin the Incredible. Let's go back for the idol."

"Incredible's the word, my son. Forget it."

"Poor child," said Adrian Lucido, cradling Malvina Fergus's cross as if it were a puppy he'd just decided to adopt. "Poor, sweet child."

The psychoanalyst's sympathy startled Gerard. It seemed too good to be true, which probably meant it was. "If you think it's a fake, I can show you her grave in the city."

"That won't be necessary."

Gerard stared at the hot tub, its motor dormant, its waters calm. "Will you open the temples to relapsers?"

Still holding the cross, which even now exuded the carrion fragrance of Coatzacoalcos, Lucido ambled around the hexagon, successively obscuring each television screen, his caftan rippling behind him. At the moment his affection for cinematic kitsch was flooding the room with biblical spectacles, the sort of approach-avoidance exposés of idolatry that Gerard had frequently consumed on late-night television shortly before fleeing to Indonesia. On each monitor a different woman of dubious redeemability officiated at a sybaritic rite, and to Gerard's surprise he easily identified all the actresses and most of their vehicles—Lana Turner in *The Prodigal,* Gina Lollobrigida in *Solomon and Sheba,* Claudette Colbert in *The Sign of the Cross,* Rita Hayworth in *Salome,* Hedy Lamar in *Samson and Delilah*—his memory failing only in the case of Anouk Aimée in something that looked vaguely Italian.

"For *you* this cross is a reason to give relapsers a second treatment," said Lucido at last, his flesh aglow with hyperion. "For *me* it's a reason to perfect Antidote X. A breakthrough is near. This is certain. You have your art, Gerard, and I have my science. If only I could convey to you the pure, primal thrill of basic metaphysical research."

"I'm sure it's a kick. The relapsers are dying."

"Is my statue finished?"

"Don't change the subject."

"Let me propose a bargain. If you'll return posthaste to El Dorado and complete my statue, I shall descend to my laboratory and submit Antidote X to a final round of clinical trials. Sound fair?"

"Perhaps."

"I assume you've made *some* progress," said Lucido.

"Once this new treatment is perfected," said Gerard, "will you make it available to the relapsers?"

"How could you imagine otherwise?" Completing his circumnavigation, Lucido paused before Gerard and pressed the cross into his hands. "Deal?"

Gerard pursed his lips. Antidote X was axiomatically a better course than abandoning the relapsers altogether, but the doctor's attitude still infuriated him. "Deal."

Lucido did an abrupt about-face and exited the hexagon, pausing briefly in the doorway. "Ever see any of these motion pictures? They're astonishing anthropological artifacts."

"What's the one with Anouk Aimée?"

"*Sodom and Gomorrah.*"

Despite the bargain he'd just struck, Gerard remained anchored to the spot, struggling to tease an intelligible thought from his brain. On the nearest monitor, a Hebrew farmer played by Edmund Purdom entered Lana Turner's caravan tent, a space forbidden to infidels, and became instantly smitten upon observing her pay obeisance to Astarte.

Spying, that was the right idea. To put his mind at ease, he must seclude himself in the wine cellar—locus of the Antidote X laboratory, according to Julius—and try to learn whether Lucido's enthusiasm for the new medicine was justified.

"Nahreeb, you said everything has its price," declared Edmund Purdom, indicating Lana Turner as he addressed Louis Calhern in the role of Astarte's high priest. "Name hers."

"She is not for a follower of Jehovah," said Calhern.

"I mean to have her," said Purdom. "One way or another."

Slithering along corridors and skulking down stairwells, Gerard made his way to the wine cellar. The door stood ajar. Firming his grip on Malvina's cross, he glanced inside. Although Lucido hadn't yet arrived, the former Olmec temple was luminous with oil lamps and Coleman mantles. Everything appeared as usual: the calendar disk, the giant head, the racked bottles, the stone altar strewn with jiggers, swizzle sticks, and wineglasses. He noticed only one novel feature. Hidden by a green tarpaulin, a rectangular object the size of an elevator car loomed over the altar: scientific equipment, he guessed, the technological nexus of Antidote X.

Footsteps resounded in the hallway. Gerard rushed into the cellar and ducked behind the basalt calendar, cloaking his body in shadows.

Lucido entered the laboratory accompanied by two El Agujero functionaries, the angrily phlegmatic Simon Bork and the annoyingly pert Mordecai Blassingame, both wearing shoulder holsters stuffed with handguns. The psychoanalyst's first action was to grab a corner of the tarpaulin and yank it. Instantly the mysterious object stood revealed, an iron-barred cubicle resembling an immense birdcage, its door secured by a padlock. Gerard stifled a gasp. The cage held two prisoners: Hannah Alport—bound with leather thongs, mouth sealed with duct tape—and an unconscious child, probably her son.

"This past month, I've administered Antidote X to thirty-four abulics, none of whom were ever acolytes," Lucido told his assistants. "Twenty-eight enjoyed complete remissions. Presumably we'll have even greater success with backsliders like young Joshua, but we won't know for certain until we perform the crucial test." Moving his forearm like a windshield wiper, he cleared the altar of bar paraphernalia, then produced a small brass key from his caftan and handed it to Blassingame. "Bring me the patient."

The functionary obeyed; he unlocked the cage, removed Joshua from his mother's side, and dragged him to the altar.

"Position the patient," Lucido commanded.

Bork grabbed Joshua's wrists, Blassingame seized the boy's ankles, and together they lifted him onto the altar and arranged him like a cadaver destined for dissection.

"The science of human sacrifice has a long and venerable history," said Lucido. "My research persuades me that the Olmecs conducted many of their classic experiments on this very altar. Without their pioneering work in cardiac ablation, of course, the great blood rites of the Aztec empire might never have evolved, and consequently none of us would be here now, giving birth to Antidote X." Reaching behind the altar, he drew forth a steel hunting knife, its blade serrated like a shark's tooth. "Watch carefully. The day may come when you must provide this treatment without my aid."

Methodically Lucido slashed an X into the comatose child's chest and, using the ragged grooves as a template, buried the knife to the hilt and sawed apart Joshua's rib cage. This isn't happening, Gerard told himself. It simply isn't. His muscles froze. His joints congealed. Decency demanded that he jump out and try to stop the crime, but decency lay helpless before his certainty that, if he acted, Bork and Blassingame would gun him down. Blood geysered forth. Hannah's moans, loud despite the duct tape, echoed through the wine cellar. Gerard gripped the basalt calendar to keep from fainting. Though visibly shaken, Bork and Blassingame stayed at their posts, holding the convulsing patient tight against the stone.

Within ninety seconds Lucido had exposed Joshua's beating heart. "The patient's loved ones typically fail to comprehend the scientifico-spiritual theory behind the treatment," he said, pointing the bloody blade toward Joshua's mother, "even after I've carefully explained it."

Pupils flashing, eyeballs expanding, Hannah flopped around on the cage floor like a beached mackerel. Her attempts at screaming produced only muffled gasps.

"The response you're witnessing is not uncommon. In some cases it becomes necessary to quell the relatives' skepticism by shooting them. With me so far?"

"With you," said Bork.

"Witness the miracle of Antidote X," said Lucido, thrusting his hands into the crimson cavity. "For a few precious seconds we can observe a child's soul poised between our own reality and the adjacent echelon, whereupon this imperishable spark"—he severed the blood vessels binding heart to chest—"begins its journey to the Olmec afterlife."

Like a naturalist extracting an exotic egg from a mountaintop rookery, Lucido removed the boy's quivering heart and placed it in an obsidian receptacle the size of a pasta bowl. A pathetic bleating emerged from the red excavation, followed by the resident fetch himself. Arms outstretched, legs splayed, the rising wraith hovered briefly above his host's remains, released a despairing gasp, and vaporized like a snowman cast into a furnace.

"The patient—can we doubt it?—is cured: completely defetched and bound for immortality," said Lucido. "What more could a young man want? Another success story for Antidote X, number twenty-nine, in fact. It's the synergy that does it. By amalgamating science and spirituality, the secular and the sacred, we can excise our patients' hearts with the full blessing of the cosmos."

"The mother remains unsympathetic," noted Blassingame.

Hannah Alport was banging her head against the iron bars as if attempting to debrain herself.

"Apply your guns to this situation," Lucido told his assistants.

Gerard never found out whether the two functionaries murdered Hannah that night or not, although he was fairly sure they did. By the time Bork and Blassingame opened the cage door, Gerard had abandoned his hiding place and ascended the stairs. Acid jetted up his esophagus, searing his throat, as he entered the vestibule, rushed outside, and stumbled across the plaza.

It had happened. All of it. Every drop of blood.

The acid settled back into his stomach. The Cranium Dei laughed gleefully. Gerard climbed into his pony cart, set Malvina's cross beside him, and started away, certain of nothing under sun or skull except one white-hot fact. Upon reaching El Dorado, he would take his sledgehammer and smash Lucido's emerging statue into a thousand meaningless shards.

Deus Absconditus

THREE TIMES A WEEK, while Kevin performed his oblations, Nora enacted a ritual of her own, driving the donkey cart down to El Agujero in hopes of learning Stevie Van Horne's fate. She never got past the foyer. Giving his clipboard a cursory glance, Assistant Deacon Jackendorf would glibly assert that Anthony Van Horne and his family had attained "level seven" or "station nine" or some equally impressive-sounding milestone. This was bullshit, and they both knew it, though Jackendorf persisted in the pretense. Lacking a gift commensurate with Gauguins or glory grease, her friends had clearly been condemned to a bureaucratic treadmill, fated to march in place until Richter's functionaries decided on a whim to make Stevie an acolyte. Whenever she demanded to see Richter himself, Jackendorf would reply that the chief deacon's schedule precluded contact with anyone not seeking admittance to Tamoanchan. Every tactic failed. Screams, tears, entreaties—even her threat to involve "Gerard Korty himself" in the situation. Nora's fellow *Natchez Queen* passengers were locked away in the detention center as tightly as Boris Lampini's suspendees had been sealed in Dewar vessels.

On days not consumed by yelling at bureaucrats, bartering in Coatzacoalcos, or helping to run the cantina, Nora normally took Kevin to visit Gerard Korty. Crock no longer allowed her to use the

Queen as her private vehicle, but she didn't mind: the overland journey by donkey cart proved easier than she imagined, and it was always rewarded by some astonishing new exhibit. Both the Gallery of Decency and the Garden of Scientific Knowledge were now complete, and the Hall of Artistic Passion already had three of the fourteen projected dioramas. How had the man done it? By what sorcery had he charged these chambers with so much light and heat? From whence sprang all this radical beatitude, this intellectual radiance, this aesthetic energy, this erotic wattage?

What most endeared the sculptor to Nora, however, was not his genius but his avuncular fondness for her son. Gerard Korty was the first real father figure in Kevin's life since Ben Sawyer. While she couldn't swear that the boy's interest was genuine, Kevin always seemed eager to absorb yet another lecture on the vast quantities of cultural history embedded in the Stone Gospel.

"Ever been to Rome?" Gerard asked Kevin.

"No, but I do a trick called 'The Roman Oracle,'" said Kevin. "I pretend to sacrifice a cat, and then I read its entrails, plastic Easter eggs with predictions inside."

"Oh, you *must* go to Rome," said Gerard. "I see the Stone Gospel sitting smack in the middle of Saint Peter's Square, displacing that boring Egyptian obelisk."

While Kevin's bond with Gerard delighted Nora, it was clear that some secret pain had taken root within the sculptor. She could read it in his face—his face, posture, gait, voice. If Kevin hung around Oswald's Rock much longer, she feared, he would witness his friend having a nervous breakdown. Gerard's agony was wholly different from the conventional artistic madness forecast by the bowels. Something ghastly was eating him, a private demon that made the average fetch a mere caricature of the uncanny, like a Vieux Carré voodoo queen or a horror host on *Chiller Theatre*.

Given the sculptor's torment, she hesitated to impose her own problems on him, but who else could conceivably help her fight the El Agujero bureaucracy? "I'm worried about my friends," she said.

"The Van Horne boy, Stevie—it's been two months now. Could you ask Richter about his case? Could you go to Lucido?"

"Lucido no longer includes me in his circle," said Gerard. "He lets me stay at El Dorado because he thinks I'm carving his statue."

"But surely he feels an obligation to you. Without your vision, there'd be no Somatocism."

"No, without my vision, there'd merely be somebody *else's* vision. I'll tell you a secret, Nora. Lucido's church has taken an ugly turn. Young Stevie would do well to avoid it."

"*Avoid* it?"

"I know far more than Lucido suspects."

He seemed about to elaborate on this cryptic remark, but instead he changed the subject, outlining his plans for giving the Hall of Artistic Passion an auditory dimension. So far, only one such tableau existed, a music box shaped like a harpsichord. He removed the fragile wonder, wound the motor, and returned it to the niche, whereupon Bach's Prelude and Fugue XXIV in B Minor wafted into the air. Whether by accident or design, the right cerebral hemisphere functioned as an amplifier, causing each delicate note to transcend the toy from which it sprang. Nora hadn't been so moved by a concert since age nine, when her father took her to hear the Boston Symphony perform *Peter and the Wolf.*

The third Sunday in February found her lounging in the prow of the *Queen*, alternately swallowing beer and browsing through *Parables for a Post-Theistic Age*. Time passed dreamily. Her thoughts drifted—from Kevin convalescing in his stateroom, to the river lapping at the dock, to Gerard Korty's odd opinion that Stevie might be better off without the Church of Earthly Affirmation. Hummingbirds hovered along the foggy shore, gorging on orchids. Cockatoos squawked in the trees. God ruled the sky. Nothing seemed particularly right with the world, but just then nothing seemed terribly wrong with it either.

Heavy leather boots creaked across the foredeck. A shadow obscured Ockham's book. Nora looked up.

"This river is full of pig shit." Despite the wretched heat, Hubbard

Richter wore a beige gabardine suit. Semicircles of perspiration fanned outward from his armpits.

"What brings you here?" she asked.

"You know."

She knew. Glory grease. Damn.

"I'll give you another jar," she said, snapping the book shut and setting it on the deck, "but first I need to hear about Stevie Van Horne."

"Who?"

"A stage-four abulic. He and his parents have vanished into El Agujero."

"The case has not yet come to my attention."

"*Make* it come to your attention."

Richter lifted the hem of his jacket and slipped his hand into his pants pocket, swollen with an emphatic bulge. "A Colt .45 revolver," he explained. "Loaded."

Her scalp prickled. The last time she'd been threatened with a gun, Rachel Sorkin had swooped to her rescue. Who would deliver her now? Her sleeping son? A drunken nautical engineer? God in His orbit?

"Stand up."

She obeyed. "We cut a deal once," she said. "Let's cut another. Return to El Agujero and get the Van Horne boy into treatment. When you come back, I'll hand over my other jars."

"How many have you got?"

"Four."

"That's all? Four? *Four?* Where?"

"Afterdeck hold."

"Lead the way."

Nora took a step. If she told Richter the truth—no more jars—he would probably shoot her . . . but at least her life would end on a positive note, with Kevin alive and healthy. She turned to the deacon and said, "Let me make a confession."

"I'm not going to like it."

"You're not going to like it."

Salvation arrived from an unexpected source. With a sound somewhere between a gurgle and a screech, a naked woman shot out of the river like an aquatic harpy, hurled herself over the transom, and thumped onto the deck. Richter screamed, frightening a toucan from a papaya tree. Water streaming from her arms and hair, Nora's fetch approached the quivering deacon, whose terror traced not to the wraith per se but to the five writhing cottonmouths coiled around her head. She came to within a meter of Richter, arranged her limbs in a demented rendition of Botticelli's Venus, and with icy nonchalance plucked a snake from her hair.

"His bite is worse than his bark," the fetch said, dangling the cottonmouth before Richter's widening eyes. "If I were you, I'd drop that gun."

The deacon did as instructed.

"She's *mine*, Richter," said the fetch. "Is that clear?"

He answered through chattering teeth: "C-clear."

"It's not her job to splint your dick. I can't kill you directly, but my pets have no such restrictions. Understand?"

Richter nodded.

The fetch restored the cottonmouth and said, "Get off the boat."

After the chief deacon had turned and run madly down the gangway, the leveler, grinning, pointed to her hair.

"I hope you appreciate the allusion," she told Nora.

"Not very subtle, Goneril."

"You know my name."

"The divine bowels told me." As Nora looked at her doppelgänger, an essential truth about mirrors hit home. A looking glass reversed you; it flipped you left to right. For the first time, she saw herself as others did. The distinction was subtle but real. "I suppose I should thank you."

"I suppose you should."

"Thank you."

"You're welcome."

"Are you going to kill me?"

"Death can perform many functions," said Goneril, "something you should have learned by now. Bearing you to oblivion is not among my immediate obligations."

"God said you're the one who put the magnifying glass in Kevin's cereal."

"True enough." Reaching up, Goneril patted her largest snake. "We need to have a serious talk, Sister. I'll meet you in the cantina tomorrow, stroke of midnight, and we'll go for a stroll. The jungle is full of marvels."

"A walk with death through a dark forest," said Nora.

Goneril climbed over the transom and started down the ladder, the river enveloping her pale body. "You may have enemies, Sister, but at the moment your fetch isn't one of them."

For ten minutes the Nietzsche-positive English teacher watched herself doing the Australian crawl toward the city, until mist and distance removed the apparition from view.

Yes, it was the age of abulia, Postmortem Dei with its middle-class cannibals roaming the streets of Western civilization, God's toothy grin supplying the whole spectacle with a mute laugh track—and yet Gerard could barely begin to assimilate the abomination he'd witnessed in the wine cellar. It touched nothing. It devoured everything. Adrian Lucido, lunatic and fiend, had ushered in the end of the world.

Gerard kept his vow. A firm whack with the sledgehammer sent Lucido's reubenite head flying across the studio. The head struck Erasmus's pedestal and split in two. Gerard pounded the halves repeatedly, converting Lucido's brains to rubble, then attacked the remaining block. Two dozen blows, and the torso crumbled into incoherence.

Rationalization worked fleetingly, affording him chimeric moments of peace. It wasn't as if Lucido had undertaken to inflict Antidote X on healthy people, he told himself. The doctor sacrificed terminal cases only.

"They would've died anyway," he told Fiona.

"Horse manure."

"This can't be compared to murder. It's closer to euthanasia."

"It's murder."

"So what would you have me do?" he said. "Kill Lucido?"

"You're the logical choice," she said. "No one gets suspicious when the godmaker comes to Tapílula."

"Circle Seven."

"What?"

"Dante places murderers in Circle Seven. He submerges them in boiling blood."

"And where does he place cowards?"

"Have you considered that there might be some validity to Lucido's approach?" said Gerard. "The people he binds to the altar, maybe they *do* achieve immortality. These things are fundamentally mysterious."

"You don't believe that," said Fiona.

"With any luck, Lucido's leveler will solve the problem for us."

"Not likely, given the amount of hyperion in his system. You're the man of the hour, Don Gerardo, whether you like it or not."

Eight days after witnessing the true nature of Antidote X, Gerard found himself leading Nora through the Hall of Artistic Passion while in the opposite hemisphere Fiona showed Kevin the Garden of Scientific Knowledge. It was an opportunity Gerard dared not squander. Nora seemed particularly impressed by the sculptor's homage to *Moby-Dick*, with its alabaster whale staving in a miniature *Pequod*.

"Ahab's mission was bound to end in disaster," he insisted. "He should've said to hell with the whale and gotten on with his life."

"People thought *my* mission was doomed too, but now I have my son back."

Gerard cleared his throat. "There's a fact you should know, Nora. I don't want to worry you, but occasionally, in rare instances, a cured abulic suffers a relapse."

She stopped, swallowed, forced a smile. "How rare is rare?"

"Promise me something. If Kevin ever gets thected again—"

"You think that's a possibility?"

"Not a strong one, no, but—"

"How many relapses have there been?"

"Two or three. Maybe more. Listen, Nora, if it happens to Kevin, you must flee Coatzacoalcos and take your chances with the disease."

"Flee? No, I'd try to arrange for a second treatment."

"When reinfection occurs, Lucido administers a new therapy—a dangerous therapy—against the family's will. Last month I told you his church has taken an ugly turn. Ugly was too mild a word. Monstrous. Depraved. Antidote X is lethal."

"Lethal?"

"Like a harpoon through the heart."

She rested her palm on Moby-Dick's hump, stroking the snowy crown as if the whale were a household pet. "Kevin's fetch is gone," she said in a thick whisper. "My son will never need Antidote X or any other medicine."

Nora's death was punctual, striding into La Sangre de la Serpiente at midnight precisely. Evidently the leveler had just finished plundering the *Queen*, for she now wore the souvenir Inanna gown from Percy. A madras shoulder bag swung at Goneril's side. Her hair was snakeless. Sucking up the last of her margarita, Nora realized that, for better or worse, she indeed possessed the courage to accompany the fetch into the rain forest.

"That's my dress you're wearing," said Nora.

"Tell me something, Sister." Goneril caressed her silken sides. "Don't you long to return to the stage?"

"I suppose so."

"Three kilometers from here lies an ancient theater. The resident troupe needs you—more than either you or they can imagine."

They left the cantina and headed north, walking along a narrow jungle pathway awash in natural light. The golden moon sat balanced atop God's skull, as if He were using the satellite to improve His posture. Orchids perfumed the air. Tree frogs chirped, advertising their intention to beget a new generation.

An hour's hike brought Nora and Goneril to a stone pyramid rising among the trees like a pygmy volcano.

"The finest piece of undiscovered Maya architecture in all Mexico," said the fetch. "Nobody knows what it's doing so far from the Yucatán."

A hundred steps towered before Nora. It could be worse, she thought, beginning the climb. Besides setting her bad knee to spasming, the exercise made her light-headed, though not so fuzzy that she failed to appreciate the temple at the summit, a squat building carved with writhing serpents and incomprehensible glyphs.

They went inside, moving through the cool, cavernous air toward a stone bench. They sat down, Nora's knee crying out for glory grease. From her bag Goneril produced three silver candlesticks holding bone-white tapers.

"Gerard Korty told me that cured abulics don't always stay cured," said Nora.

Goneril, lighting the tapers, didn't respond.

"Does Lucido really give relapsed abulics a lethal medicine?"

Reaching again into her bag, Goneril drew out a bronze cup and a green ceramic jug sealed with a cork. The instant she uncapped the jug, the air filled with a fragrance unlike anything in Nora's memory, a seeming mixture of boiling tar, decaying bananas, and tannic acid.

"Pulque, fermented agave milk," Goneril explained, pouring it into the bronze cup. "I've laced it with peyote buttons, morning-glory seeds, jimson weed, and those bitter psychedelic mushrooms the natives call *teonanacatl*, flesh of the gods." She passed the cup to Nora. "This cocktail will take you to places you've never been before."

"It smells like sheep dip."

"It smells like the future."

"You're trying to poison me."

"Drink deep, Sister, and learn the destiny of the West."

For reasons she couldn't articulate, Nora decided to trust her leveler. She lifted the cup to her lips and sipped. The pulque tasted variously tart, sour, and bitter, and she choked it down only by calling on the same fortitude that had once enabled her to jump into Walden

Pond on New Year's Eve. She was about to remark on the cocktail's protean flavor, when her immediate environment and the laws of physics parted company. The temple ceiling levitated, the walls flew away, and the floor vaporized, a dissolution accompanied by a clanging noise whose source she alternately located within the ambient flux and the depths of her throbbing skull.

The clanging stopped; the world congealed. Sunlight stabbed Nora's eyes.

"Where are we?"

"The City of Deus Absconditus," said Goneril, "circa 2101 Common Era."

"What happened to the night?"

"Pulque time keeps its own beat. I could detain you in Deus Absconditus an entire week and get you back to Coatzacoalcos by tomorrow morning."

One fact remained unaltered: they still occupied a bench—a convivial construction of molded plastic and vinyl cushions that would have probably struck the Maya as insufficiently austere. Gradually Nora absorbed her surroundings, an atrium of glass and steel, citizens bustling about in colorful cotton jumpsuits. A row of turnstiles spread before her, behind which lay a streamlined passenger train, doors wide open, its coaches balanced atop a monorail like an acrobat's unicycle hugging a tightrope.

"Here," said Goneril, handing Nora a metal token. "You can pay me back later."

Nora fingered the little disk, which bore the profile of Gerard Korty, then dropped it in the slot and pushed through the turnstile. They entered the nearest coach. The doors whooshed closed, and the train departed, gliding silently across the face of a vast city. No shining copper adorned its walls, no glowing lapis lazuli decorated its gates, but in its own way Deus Absconditus was as magnificent as Gilgamesh's Uruk. Crystalline towers aspired to the clouds, threaded together with monorails and tramway cables. Pedestrians and skateboarders moved along paved walkways and multilevel esplanades, a network as devoid of automobiles as the heavens were empty of death's-heads.

"In the bygone age, nature was under relentless pressure from an unholy conjunction of free-market economics, totalitarian socialism, and the Book of Genesis," Goneril explained. "Remember Who told the first humans, 'Be fruitful and multiply, and replenish the Earth, and subdue it'? Remember Who said, 'Have dominion over every living thing that moves upon the Earth'?"

"So ultimately God's death will have positive ecological consequences?"

"For the citizens of the Third Millennium," said Goneril, nodding, "the annihilation of His evil aspect will prove an unmixed blessing. But how, they will wonder, can we endure the loss of His benevolent side? They look around, and there's the Stone Gospel, exhorting them to embrace Thomas Ockham's little myths."

"God's entrails instructed me to warn Gerard off the project."

"A jealous colon's motives aren't difficult to fathom. Jehovah has always hated rivals. Korty's brain, if it survives the plague era, will help the West start believing in itself again." Goneril swept her arm across the passing scene, a gesture subsuming the entire metropolis. "Welcome to the land of the grown-ups, Nora, where philosophy ranks higher than folding money, and every politician is a poet."

A river flowed through Deus Absconditus from north to south, its waters as clear and bubbly as cream soda, its course shaped like a gigantic cursive W. "I gather we're in North America," said Nora, "so that's not the Uspanapa."

"North America, possibly Scandinavia, the British Isles, or Mediterranean Europe," said Goneril. "It's called the Erasmus, the purest river this side of the Jordan."

They got off at a station called Commissure Gardens, a plastic ziggurat perched on concrete stilts, descended to street level, and headed west across a scruffy urban terrain. Flanked by a branch library and a pizza parlor, an arresting edifice rose before them, a Gothic monstrosity with soaring belfries and garish stained-glass windows. The sign on the dirt lawn confirmed Nora's guess that the building was a church, as did the hundreds of anxious celebrants swarming through the arched doorway.

ASSEMBLY OF THE TURNED CHEEK
Dolores M. Feick, Shepherd
Today's Sermon:
"Can Francis's Bacon Be Saved?"

Goneril pulled a laptop computer from her bag, popped the screen, and called up a file. "Twenty-eight percent of the city's churches spring from the Sermon on the Mount—the Assembly of the Gift Cloak, the Assembly of the Beloved Enemy, and so on—while the rest boast Judaic and Buddhist roots." Closing the laptop, Goneril led Nora inside. "The first time I read the Gospel According to Saint Matthew," the fetch continued, "I said to myself, 'This is great stuff. Somebody should base a religion on the teachings of Jesus of Nazareth.' Here in Deus Absconditus, my wish has come to pass."

The instant Nora and Goneril found their seats, Dolores Feick—a hefty but energetic middle-aged woman wearing a silk muumuu adorned with newly harvested gloxinia—began speaking in a voice suggesting a sexually active viola. As the sermon progressed, Nora learned that (among their other missions) the city's churches aimed "to keep the intellectuals from doing more damage than absolutely necessary." If the God of Genesis was no environmentalist, Feick noted, then neither were many of history's most venerated thinkers. "Nature," Aristotle had evidently once argued, "has made all animals for the sake of Man." In Descartes's view, philosophy and science existed primarily "to make us masters and possessors of Nature." Francis Bacon, to whose ponderous opinions Nora had already been exposed in a college course on Renaissance philosophy, wanted scientists to bend Nature toward "the service of Man." The universe must be placed on "the rack" of empirical investigation, Bacon insisted, and forced to reveal its secrets.

After the service, Goneril guided Nora across the street to a Chinese restaurant, where they dined with Soaragidan gusto on vegetable lo mein and tofu family style. The waiter delivered a pair of fortune cookies.

"I'm starting to make the connections," said Nora. "The magnifying glass, the Lobos' tomb, the quote from Ling Po Fat, and now an actual fortune cookie." She cracked the shell and glanced at the slip. *I am indeed imprisoned in a Chinese fortune-cookie factory, but have you pondered the subtle cognitive snares in which you yourself may be trapped?—Ling Po Fat.*

Goneril nodded. "The magnifying glass was a hook." She retrieved two fortunes from her cookie. "By introducing it into Kevin's cereal, I tethered this journey to your old life, reality as you remember it, lest you imagine that you're simply dreaming." She displayed both messages. In her left hand: *I beseech you, in the bowels of Christ, think it possible you may be mistaken.—Oliver Cromwell.* In her right: *The absence of God is God enough.—Saint Clair Cemin.* "This isn't a charade, Nora. It's not a hallucination. Assuming the Stone Gospel pulls through, Deus Absconditus will become as real as your bad knee."

Goneril paid the bill by passing her signet ring across a sensor embedded in the table, then guided Nora back to Commissure Gardens. They climbed the stairs to the monorail station, hopped aboard the local, and rode downtown to Medulla Junction. Detraining, Nora followed her fetch into a district even seedier than Feick's parish (broken windows, fractured sidewalks, drainage culverts dammed with wet paper), though she'd certainly seen worse neighborhoods in Boston.

"So we're not in Utopia after all," said Nora.

"Utopia?" said Goneril, sounding genuinely perplexed. "No, not *that*, thank God." She guided Nora into a crumbling brick schoolhouse. "Show me a Utopia, and I'll show you the back door to Perdition."

Slipping silently into wooden desks set against the far wall of an eighth-grade classroom, the time travelers observed fifteen adolescents grappling with a twenty-second-century curricular offering called Elementary Adulthood. The teacher, Bonnie Canzoneri, whose girlish freckles and swaying pigtails made her seem little older than her students, led a discussion that managed to be simultaneously spirited and focused.

"Okay, here's another one. You run a corporation that nets six hundred million a year selling chlorofluorocarbons. Two scientists come to you with evidence that your product is damaging Earth's ozone shield. This crisis threatens to increase the skin-cancer rate, double the incidence of cataracts, and destroy the phytoplankton anchoring your planet's food chains. As an adult, how do you respond?"

A stocky African-American boy wearing granny glasses raised his hand. "Assuming the scientists have their facts straight, I guess I start phasing out production."

"You simply phase it out? Nothing more?"

"I also try to reemploy all the people who used to make chlorofluorocarbons."

"A truly grown-up reaction, Farley. Did the scientists in question—Rowland and Molina—have their facts straight?" The teacher pointed to a willowy Caucasian girl waving her arms like a castaway signaling a rescue plane. "Phoebe?"

"In 1995, Rowland and Molina received the Nobel Prize in Chemistry for warning the world about increased ultraviolet-light levels."

"Who can describe DuPont Corporation's reaction to the UV menace? Hyuk-Jun?"

"DuPont launched a massive campaign to convince legislators that no real danger existed," said a lanky Korean boy with dimpled cheeks.

"How do we account for this bizarre behavior? Didn't DuPont's board of directors care whether their grandchildren got skin cancer or their great-grandchildren inherited a sterile planet?"

Without waiting to be called on, a sallow young woman with hazel eyes said, "According to Thomas Ockham, many people in the theistic era regarded Earthly existence as a mere rehearsal for immortality. The environment didn't matter, because everyone was ultimately going to Heaven or, in certain cases, Hell."

"Okay, but was that necessarily the attitude of the DuPont executives?"

"I'll tell you my mother's theory," piped up Phoebe. "People who draw gigantic salaries for running large corporations have trouble thinking straight."

Bonnie Canzoneri now changed the subject, inviting her students to consider the topic of "affirmative fornication." Much to her disappointment, Nora didn't get to hear the subsequent discussion.

"The pulque has run its course," Goneril said as the classroom began to dissolve.

"But I don't want to leave." Even as Nora grabbed hold of her desk, it transformed into the familiar stone bench. "Damn."

Dawn's anemic light permeated the Maya temple. "We'll take another trip tonight," promised Goneril. "Your education is far from complete."

Woozily, uncertainly, Nora rose from the bench. Her head ached. Her tongue and eyeballs throbbed.

"Impressive," she said.

Goneril returned the pulque jug to her bag. "Homo sapiens is an amazing animal, Sister. Get God and Aristotle off its back, and miracles start becoming the norm."

As Gerard steered the pony cart through Coatzacoalcos, a rubber gas mask and Malvina Fergus's cross in his lap, two questions consumed him. Should he tell Anna Fergus that the grave marker had failed to move Lucido? And should he terminate the psychoanalyst's reign of terror by killing him?

To kill a man. To stop his heart, desiccate his veins, obliterate his mind: for Gerard such an action was inconceivable. Even in the post-theistic West, a world overrun by ectoplasmic assassins, the concept of murder revolted him. He was a creator, not a destroyer—a sculptor, not a hit man.

Braving the stench of the unburied abulics, he entered El Parque Crepúsculo. Eyes downcast, scores of mourners swarmed over the hills. A hundred gravediggers stabbed the earth with their spades.

Only one landscape in Gerard's experience could match this field of open tombs: the burning cemetery for arch-heretics that, in Circle VI, Dante discovered behind the subterranean walls of Dis.

I now beheld within each sepulchre
A ceaseless fire, a casket all aglow,
Like metal ready for the blacksmith's stroke.

The coffins lay uncovered; from them poured
Loud piercing groans that terribly revealed
The anguish of the tortured souls within.

As he parked the cart beside Malvina's grave, Gerard saw that his first question had become irrelevant. Anna Fergus lay across the mound, eyes locked open, limbs stiff.

He pushed Malvina's cross into the soft ground and, rotating slowly, addressed the crowd in the loudest voice he'd used since castigating the cardinals at the Cinecittà opening.

"Get out while you can!"

A handful of mourners and sextons—those whose despondency didn't preclude curiosity—looked up. Their faces seemed carved from basalt.

"Lucido's gone crazy!"

They watched him with impassive eyes.

"He's planning to kill you all! Get out!"

His audience stared at the wormy earth.

Gerard fled the rotting metropolis, hurrying the pony south along Calle de la Aguila past adobe churches, stucco houses, banana farms, and a coffee plantation. The Mexican sun pummeled his brain; he sweated like a follower of Soaragid. His plan was simple. During his early days at El Dorado, he had periodically visited the lava lake atop the Volcán de Catemaco, seeking within its languid swirls the forms and faces of the Somatocist deities. He would go to the mountain again, consulting it now on an entirely different matter.

The noon hour found him tethering the pony to a papaya root and ascending the smoldering slopes. He reached the inner crater, pulled the gas mask over his head, and stared into the crucible, looking for a sign. Nothing coherent emerged: the blobs remained amorphous, the bubbles meaningless. But then, at last, the contours of a man appeared in the lava—stark, emphatic, one hand gripping a chisel, the other raising a hammer. A sculptor. Himself.

The augury seemed unambiguous. Assassinating Lucido was not his job. He was obligated instead to take up his tools and finish his magnum opus.

Compounding the message's urgency was the status of the volcano itself. Gerard was no geologist; he knew nothing of seismic events. And yet he sensed that a fatal impatience had seized the mountain. Its sulfurous fumes seemed thicker than usual, its ashes heavier, its lava more turbulent. Like a frustrated artist or a fecund breast, Catemaco needed to express its juices, and soon.

He untied the pony, departed through a swirling mass of volcanic dust, and reached Oswald's Rock at twilight. Marching into the right hemisphere, he immediately set to work. It was his finest frenzy ever, and when it was over, the Hall of Artistic Passion had acquired a celebration of Vincent Van Gogh: the artist beholding Saint-Rémy by night—a heavenscape comprising a bright horned moon, eleven blazing stars, and a spiral nebula coiling across the sky like a dragon encrusted with a million jewels.

Forty-eight hours after Nora's first pulque odyssey, Goneril led her back to the Maya temple and took her on a second voyage. This new cocktail carried Nora not to Deus Absconditus itself but to the verge of an outlying wetland. Heaped between marsh and beach like mounds of raw sugar, a line of sand dunes sheltered the ecosystem from the crashing sea beyond. She was leaning against the balustrade of a wooden platform crowded with reverent bird-watchers and amateur watercolorists. Goneril stood beside her, peering through binoculars as intently as a piano prodigy's mother observing her daughter's first recital.

"Migration season," said the fetch as a flock of herons rose from the nearest mudflat. "The nomads are heading south."

They spent the morning contemplating the marsh—a dense biological symphony of terns, egrets, terrapins, scallops, horseshoe crabs, moon jellyfish, sea cucumbers, eelgrass, and thriving phytoplankton—then hiked to the nearest monorail station and jumped aboard an express train. Settling into the plush velour of the parlor car, the time travelers grew hypnotized by the passing terrain, the wetlands yielding to forests, the forests to dome-covered hydroponic gardens.

"Private transportation did not die an easy death," Goneril said, removing the laptop from her shoulder bag. She opened a file. "*Homo Sapiens versus the Internal Combustion Engine* was the World Court's most significant case since the trial of God." She consulted the screen. "All told, the two sides submitted 1,947 documents and solicited 5,419 pages of testimony over 211 days. When the fight was over, the justices issued a unanimous opinion, making automobiles as illegal as land mines."

In the seat across the aisle, two preadolescent boys swapped trading cards evidently inspired by the reubenite brain. Nora glimpsed Isaac Newton adjusting a prism, Charles Darwin studying the Galapagos finches, and Moby-Dick torpedoing the *Pequod*.

"Once automobiles disappeared," Goneril continued, "the world was halfway toward checking the greenhouse effect, with its threat of coastal flooding, massive crop failures, and devastating epidemics."

Now they were within the city limits, sailing across parks and promenades, bridges and levees, shops and theaters, synagogues and mosques, housing projects and sports complexes. Commissure Gardens came and went, as did Medulla Junction and seven other stops, until at last they reached Cerebellum Square, where Goneril had them detrain.

"You have a question," said the fetch. "You ask, 'It's all very well for the privileged West to reinvent itself as a wildlife preserve, but what about the remaining three-quarters of the world? Are pauper nations supposed to forego automobiles and industrialization for some nebulous squid-kisser ethos?'"

"That problem did occur to me, yes."

"The solution will surprise you."

Strewn with litter, Cerebellum Square opened onto a waterfront replete with collapsing docks, abandoned warehouses, and gamey fragrances—more picturesque than depressing, Nora decided, like a set for a Bowery Boys movie. Goneril hustled them across a concrete quay toward Harry's Sports Bar, a saloon perched on pylons above the Erasmus River. The sign in the window read DEONTOLOGY BOWL PARTY TODAY!!!!

"I hate sports," said Nora.

"It's not what you imagine," said Goneril, leading her inside.

For an establishment occupying a strange and far-flung future, almost everything about Harry's Sports Bar felt familiar to Nora: the squall of the jukebox, the clack of the billiard balls, the waitresses ferrying pitchers of beer from the kegs to the crowded booths—even the air itself, heavy with alcohol fumes and torpid conversation. The only surprise was the scale of the TV monitors; they were as large as picture windows, one suspended over the kegs, the other commanding the riverside wall. Both screens displayed the same shot, a Latino announcer sitting in the bleachers of an outdoor sports arena, speaking inaudibly to the camera.

"Live from Santiago, Chile—the Deontology Bowl!" noted Goneril, pointing to the riverside screen. "The whole world is watching. No athletic event on planet Earth matters more."

The scene shifted to the pregame parade. Banners flying, arms waving, hundreds of athletes, male and female, dressed in splendid liveries and wielding various point-scoring tools, strutted along a savanna of barbered grass. The off-screen orchestra played a march that managed to be stirring without sounding militaristic.

Guiding Nora into a vacant booth, Goneril suggested that they split a pitcher of black and tan. The beer arrived promptly, dark as molasses and crowned with foam. Sipping, Nora tried to hear the announcer's words, but the thumping music and the chattering barflies drowned him out.

Jesusball, Goneril explained, differed from pre-plague sports in that four teams competed in a single game, each team representing one of the planet's major geopolitical spheres: the European Economic Community, the New Russia Consortium, the Industrialized Asia League, and the Confederated Provinces of America. The real competition, however, occurred not during the game itself but throughout the previous seven months, when the four spheres made secret monetary donations to various United Nations funds devoted to international poverty relief, Third World debt forgiveness, global-warming mitigation, and rain-forest salvation. After assessing a given sphere's generosity, the International Jesusball Commission equipped that sphere's team proportionately. Among the assets distributed by the Commission were performance-enhancing drugs, including vitaloids and hallucinogens; defensive gear, most especially body armor and force-field generators; also jetpacks, tear gas, stun guns, bolas, and other offensive devices. Until the start of the game, no team knew how well its arsenal compared with its rivals'—at least not officially. In point of fact, espionage was not only rife, the Commission encouraged it, as such intrigues inevitably increased each sphere's clandestine largesse. Normally, the best-outfitted franchise won—the rules allowed only brief and intermittent alliances—and yet, just as the history of organized warfare contained instances of underdogs emerging victorious, from David's trouncing of Goliath to North Vietnam's humiliation of the United States, so did the annals of jesusball record a handful of famous upsets.

"Here in the post-theistic age," said Goneril, "securing its franchise a victory in the Deontology Bowl is the best way for a government to make its citizens feel proud." She blew the foam off her beer. "Nobody knows exactly when ethical patriotism eclipsed the territorial variety, but that shift stands tall among the Stone Gospel's many legacies."

Another unusual feature of the Deontology Bowl, Nora soon learned, was that it lasted twelve hours, from noon to midnight. The idea of a sane person spending a whole day watching any sort of ball sport struck her as ridiculous—but then the game itself got under way, and she immediately became entranced. Although Goneril tried to explain the numerous rules, strategies, and rituals, the whole mêlée remained as opaque to Nora as a Noh drama. She didn't mind. The surface aesthetics of jesusball, its peculiar mixture of ferocity and finesse, brutality and ballet, were enthralling in themselves.

It was a contest of byzantine complexity, conducted on a rolling pasture twice the size of Central Park. Beyond many types of balls, the game employed pucks, discuses, Hoberman spheres, boomerangs, and shuttlecocks, all shunted about by means of sticks, bats, rackets, mallets, and air rifles toward targets that resembled baskets, hatch shells, bear traps, satellite dishes, and African termite hills. At any given moment, a franchise typically had sixty men and women on the field, their efforts focused simultaneously on three or four different goals. An army of referees was required to guarantee the fair awarding of points and penalties. Covering the event for home viewing must have been a television director's nightmare. Split screen was the favored technique, supplemented by triptychs, fish-eye pans, helicopter shots, and instant replays.

The entire clientele of Harry's Sports Bar rose to its feet whenever the Confederated Provinces Capitalists scored a goal, whether it was against the EEC Marketeers, the Industrialized Asia Tigers, or the New Russia Consortium Bears. Blood pounding with chauvinistic ardor, the loyal fans cheered until the beer steins rattled on their trays. The fans' patriotism was equally intense when the Capitalists executed a successful defensive play. Nora cheered too, not so much for the home team as for the fact that Gerard's magnum opus held such marvelous power.

In keeping with hallowed Deontology Bowl tradition, lunch and dinner both consisted of pizza, nachos, and chicken wings. Nora was about to dig into the second feast when to her great frustration the pulque evaporated from her neurons. The score stood at 311 points for the Tigers, 304 for the Capitalists, 298 for the Marketeers, and 290 for the Bears, with five hours left to play. A close game.

"This isn't fair," she protested as Harry's Sports Bar dissolved in a morass of green mist.

"Life is like that," said Goneril.

"Do you know who's going to win?" asked Nora, collapsing against the wall of the Maya temple.

"Yes."

"Who?"

"Three billion wretches. The Stone Gospel must survive, Nora. Everything depends on it."

Whereas Anthony Van Horne likened their monotonous and debilitating life in El Agujero to the circumstances endured by preplague prison inmates, his wife believed their situation was even worse. As a charter member of the moribund Central Park West Enlightenment League, Cassie Fowler feared and mistrusted all enterprises that regarded themselves as churches. An institution that answered only to God ultimately answered to no one.

"If you ask me, Lucido is nothing more than a fanatic with an education," she said. "We should've stayed in New Orleans."

"Fanatic, maybe, but evidently he's getting results," said Anthony. "The logic is brilliant, don't you think? Somatocism fills the abulic with hope, and the fetches lose their grip."

Cassie caressed her son and sneered. "The problem with most religions is that they sound reasonable while remaining irrational."

As their incarceration continued, the days congealing into weeks, the weeks into fortnights, Anthony found himself agreeing with his wife's pessimism. But then, unexpectedly, on the last evening in February, a beefy functionary in a quasi-military uniform appeared—Leopold Dansk, Lucido's chauffeur—and said he had orders to drive them to the psychoanalyst's mansion on Mount Tapílula.

"I thought the therapy happened in Tamoanchan," said Cassie.

"You're thinking of the *old* cure. We have something more effective now, Antidote X, administered personally by Dr. Lucido."

Dansk commanded one of the few usable automobiles in Coatzacoalcos, a battered 1998 Lincoln Continental with mismatched tires and unlubricated brakes. He drove maniacally, slicing through the nocturnal fog at eighty miles an hour, so that Anthony and Cassie felt fortunate to reach the mansion alive. In the flagstone plaza a wiry man greeted them, Chief Deacon Hubbard Richter. With the exception of Cassie's ex-fiancé, Oliver Shostak, Anthony had never before so intuitively disliked a person. Foreboding gripped his soul. The more he thought about this turn of events, the uglier it seemed. What, exactly, was Antidote X? Why couldn't Stevie receive the proven therapy instead?

Following Richter's instructions, Cassie lifted Stevie from the backseat and laid him in Anthony's arms. Stevie's diaper needed changing. Far more distressing was his mass: even with Dominic inhabiting him, the boy felt almost weightless, bones of bamboo. Richter led the party, chauffeur included, along a columned portico and into the mansion. They crossed the vestibule, its plaster walls decorated with murals depicting the Somatocist pantheon, then walked down a spiral staircase, the steel helix curling into the mountain's core for two hundred and twenty steps.

The cellar door stood open. Anthony saw hundreds of wine bottles lying in their racks like captives filling the hold of a slave ship. He stepped inside. Among the room's several curiosities was a ponderous granite slab suggesting a primordial billiard table, a pre-Columbian calendar disk, a gigantic Olmec stone head, and two adjacent cages welded together from boiler plates and iron bars. The far cage was empty. The near one, padlocked, held a plague family: a gray-haired thected father and his middle-aged daughters, both women handcuffed and manifestly upset.

"Why are they in a cage?" Cassie demanded.

"Immortality is worth waiting for," Richter replied unhelpfully.

A familiar El Agujero functionary, Assistant Deacon Roland Jackendorf, dressed as always in an olive business suit, strode into the wine cellar. Without warning, he lunged at Anthony and tore Stevie from his arms. Richter and Dansk joined the fracas; they manacled Anthony and slammed him against the calendar disk, as if attaching an hour hand to the face of a clock. When Cassie lurched toward her son, Richter produced a second pair of manacles, clamping them around her wrists. Anthony and Cassie were soon locked in the far cage, Stevie sprawled at their feet.

"What the hell are you doing?" screamed Anthony.

"Where's Lucido?" shouted Cassie.

Instead of answering, Richter, Dansk, and Jackendorf draped a green canvas tarpaulin over the cage. A sudden gloom descended.

"Let us out, you fuckers!" yelled Anthony.

"We want to see Lucido!" cried Cassie.

Silence fell over the wine cellar. Anthony fixed on the tarpaulin, marred with a stain shaped like a ram's head. The canvas stank of mildew. A cockroach scuttled across his boot. Depleted, depressed, Cassie sat down on the cage floor, a grid of rusted iron suggesting a sewer grating.

The darkness augmented Anthony's hearing, or so it seemed. As he tuned his ears to the events beyond the cage, footsteps announced the entry of a fourth antagonist—a formidable person, judging by the heavy tread. "I am Dr. Adrian Lucido," the new arrival declared, presumably addressing the abulic's daughters. "Let me begin by saying that, while Antidote X is still experimental, its cure rate approaches one hundred percent. Initially you may find our methods perplexing, harsh even, but before long you will understand. Mr. Richter, kindly release the patient." For Anthony, comprehending what followed was like interpreting the action in a radio drama. A metallic jangle: key into padlock. A squeaking sound: hinges rotating. A scraping noise: the patient being dragged from his cell. "Our objective is simple," said Lucido. "We seek to transport your father to the Olmec paradise. First we lay him atop the sacred altar." Scuffling noises and heavy breathing combined to give Anthony a mental picture of Lucido's minions placing the old man on the slab. "Next we expose his chest"—cloth ripping—"and with this knife—"

A woman shrieked, "No!"

Her sister shouted, "Stop!"

"Shut up, both of you! By employing the serrated part of the blade like so"—a sawing noise—"I gain access... to the cardiac cavity."

"Please! *Please!*"

"Silence!"

Anthony and Cassie exchanged horrified looks.

As the daughters' screaming reached a crescendo, Lucido ordered their cage covered. The functionaries did as instructed—footsteps, a grunt, the rustle of the tarpaulin, each sound punctuated by the women's cries.

A stench stung Anthony's nostrils, the same ferrous fragrance he'd experienced many months earlier when the divine heart disintegrated over the English Channel.

"Finally, we use the tip of the blade to sever the blood vessels, and, *voilà*, the heart is free. But it appears that once again a plague family has failed to grasp the theory behind Antidote X. Mr. Dansk, Mr. Richter, will you kindly...?"

Footsteps, six gunshots, silence.

"My God," wailed Cassie.

"Jesus," rasped Anthony.

"Well done," said Lucido. "Mr. Jackendorf, will you deposit the heart in the proper receptacle?"

"Yes, sir."

"Perhaps you gentlemen have questions?"

"How long before the fetch exits his host?" asked Dansk.

"Usually the phenomenon occurs instantly, though sometimes—ah, look, there he goes!"

Fifteen seconds of quiet followed, during which Anthony pictured the old man's leveler ascending like a puff of smoke.

Dansk said, "So the patient has now achieved immortality?"

"That's what our best evidence suggests," said Lucido.

"Does this mean we're shutting down the temples?" asked Jackendorf, apparently concerned about his job security.

"Somatocism still has certain advantages over its successor," said

Lucido. "Whereas Somatocist acolytes remain in this particular world, with its predictable pleasures and satisfactions, Antidote X affords entrance only to the terra incognita of the Olmec paradise. As our knowledge expands, we'll be able to determine which cases would benefit more from Tamoanchan and which should go directly to the altar. And now, if you gentlemen will excuse me, I must write up this latest experiment."

"There's something I should tell you about the other family," said Jackendorf. "They know Korty. Or at least they know somebody who knows him—Nora Burkhart, always pestering me about the Van Horne boy. She makes me nervous. I think we should get it over with."

"No," whispered Cassie.

"No," echoed Anthony.

"Tomorrow's sun, Mr. Jackendorf," said Lucido, "will rise soon enough."

When Goneril casually announced that the third and final pulque cocktail wouldn't be taking them to Deus Absconditus, Nora made no effort to hide her disappointment. After two trips to the enchanting metropolis, she'd come to feel like an honorary citizen. She longed for Deus Absconditus as if it were her one true home.

"Tonight," said the fetch, "I shall show you a rather different sort of world. Its inhabitants call it Holistica."

Nora stepped into the Maya temple, sat on the stone bench, and apprehensively accepted a cup of pulque from the fetch's cold hands. Jungle sounds filled the room, an amalgam of overlapping chirps, caws, screeches, and drones. She drank.

"Is Holistica another city?" asked Nora as the hallucinogens took charge of her brain.

"More like a village," said Goneril. "A relentlessly pleasant place. The people have no meanness in them."

Once again the temple dissolved, a phenomenon that deposited Nora in the cleft of a mammoth cedar tree, Goneril beside her. The surrounding hills quivered with wild grasses and mulberry bushes. A solitary sun warmed Nora's face. In the valley below, the Erasmus River (she recognized its cursive W shape) gamboled toward an unseen delta. Larks and thrushes glided through an orange grove, singing on the wing. Cottony masses of cloud rode the sky, a wide blue vault as free of God's skull as were the heavens above Deus Absconditus.

As Nora and her fetch descended from the cedar tree and proceeded into the valley, it occurred to Nora that a trek like this would ordinarily start her bad knee vibrating. Among their many impressive properties, pulque cocktails were evidently potent analgesics.

In the misty distance rose Holistica, a clutch of mud huts suggesting immense bran muffins. Reaching the river, the time travelers started along a dirt road rutted by the traffic of countless carts and wagons. As the sun reached its zenith, they passed through a wooden portal bearing an inscription written with a length of vine, MODERNITY-FREE ZONE, below which hung a sign quoting the American naturalist John Muir.

> LET THE CHILDREN WALK WITH NATURE, LET THEM SEE
> THE BEAUTIFUL BLENDINGS AND COMMUNIONS OF DEATH
> AND LIFE, AND THEY WILL LEARN THAT DEATH IS
> STINGLESS INDEED, AND AS BEAUTIFUL AS LIFE.

"If Korty's brain perishes," said Goneril, "we can expect a world dedicated to neither Old-Time Theism nor Elementary Adulthood, but to something else entirely..."

A slender and attractive woman emerged from the nearest hut and introduced herself as Theodora Shaman, first assistant matriarch of Holistica and chair of the Welcoming Committee. Not since meeting Kevin for the first time—a warm, moist, wrinkled baby lying on her chest—had Nora found another person so immediately appealing. With her grass skirt, calico chemise, and hair arrayed in daisies, Theodora seemed as integral to the landscape as the omnipresent honeybees.

"We don't get many time travelers," said the matriarch after

Goneril explained where they came from. "Stay with us as long as you want. Our brother, the sacred river, will give you his fish. Our sister, the hallowed grove, will feed you her oranges."

As Nora's sojourn elapsed, each day passing in a mere Coatzacoalcos hour, she readily adapted to the pulse of Holistican life. The people devoted their mornings to prayers and hymns, including a predawn chant of gratitude to the Universal Energy Entity for delivering them from linear thought and unfeeling reason. Afternoons were given to practical pursuits: weaving, gardening, harvesting, mulching. Each evening, the villagers gathered around the campfire to share communal myths. Nora was especially impressed by Jared Shaman's heartfelt performance of "The Little Engine That Achieved Higher Consciousness," a parable about a steam locomotive that, realizing it was a machine, did the honorable thing and disassembled itself.

On the fifth night, Nora's hosts asked her to enliven their gatherings with what Sasha Shaman called "horror stories from the Nightmare Age." Nora happily complied: her first opportunity since leaving the Sumerian Circus to command center stage. "Tell us the legend of the Singer sewing machine," the Holisticans requested. "Spin us a tale of fluorescent lighting, and hold nothing back." "Chill our blood with Web browsers—go ahead, we can take it." At first Nora tried giving her improvisations a conventional narrative form. She reimagined Arachne as an aboriginal artisan destroyed by the Industrial Revolution, made Orpheus a symphony orchestra conductor driven mad by Western competitiveness, and turned Narcissus into a casualty of rationalistic individualism. But her audience, she soon realized, required nothing of such pointedness or complexity. She had merely to articulate a phrase like "pocket calculator," "digital watch," "fetal heart monitor," or "dual carburetors" to get the villagers swooning with the thrill of the forbidden.

On the first weekend of every month, the Holisticans held their Feast of Remembrance, a joyous celebration devoted (in the words of Second Assistant Matriarch Suki Shaman) "to the creative destruction of the four false gods." Representing these detestable deities were fifty male mannikins crafted from straw and outfitted with wooden plaques specifying their identities. One scarecrow collection bore labels reading THE ILLUSION OF PROGRESS. Another bunch was captioned MECHANISTIC MEDICINE. A third, ALL TECHNOLOGIES EMPLOYING METAL OR PLASTIC. A fourth, THE 18TH-CENTURY ENLIGHTENMENT. On Saturday morning, the celebrants embedded large rocks in the thirteen ILLUSION OF PROGRESS scarecrows, loaded the heavy effigies onto canoes, and sent them to the bottom of the Alph River (as the locals called the Erasmus). Turning next to the eleven scarecrows captioned MECHANISTIC MEDICINE, the celebrants spent the afternoon systematically dissecting them. At dusk, the Holisticans set fire to the fourteen ALL TECHNOLOGIES EMPLOYING METAL OR PLASTIC scarecrows, using these humanoid torches to illuminate a five-hour marathon of mutual massage.

Sunday morning brought the eagerly awaited Sky Dumping contest, which Gareth Shaman called "a noncompetitive athletic event keyed to Nature's rhythms." The game began shortly after the referees placed the dozen 18TH-CENTURY ENLIGHTENMENT scarecrows in three piles at the bottom of a ravine. Spanning the gorge was a platform supporting three sets of seven wooden chairs with saucer-size holes in their centers, each set suspended over a scarecrow cluster. Team Alpha, Team Beta, and Team Omega strode across the platform, dropped their various trousers and underclothes, and assumed appropriate positions on the perforated chairs. Theodora Shaman blew on her elk horn, and the excited athletes proceeded to defecate, groaning and straining as the other Holisticans encouraged them with nonfavoritistic cheers. At last a winner emerged, Team Beta, which had buried the dreaded Enlightenment in under seven minutes.

"It's not a very sophisticated argument," commented Nora's fetch, "but it boasts a certain piquancy."

During the week that followed, the sympathy that Goneril had initially shown toward Holistica turned into undisguised antagonism. Each night around the campfire, aided by her laptop computer, she attempted to embarrass her listeners with selected bits of regional history.

Though initially scandalized by Goneril's rudeness, Nora soon realized that such information held no power to perturb the villagers.

With supreme aplomb, Cecily Shaman addressed the issue of the Great Typhus Outbreak of A.D. 2096. "Our ancestors taught us never to use that word, *typhus.* Such language, along with *syphilis, polio,* and *scarlet fever,* bespeaks a nonspiritual, mechanistic understanding of the human body. In Holistica we believe in natural healing, counting our germs and viruses as essential to the divine harmony."

"But don't they sometimes kill you?" asked Nora.

"As Saint Muir revealed, rationalist concepts like *kill* give death an undeserved authority."

Silas Shaman smoothly fielded Goneril's question about the Great Drought of 2115 and the famine that had followed. "Obviously you've never seen a person transmogrify through starvation. It's an authentic spiritual experience."

"Starvation, or watching it?" asked Nora.

"Both. True, the hungernaut suffers momentary discomfort, but then a flood of cosmic awareness arrives."

On the day before their scheduled departure, Nora and her leveler went canoeing on the Alph. The entire river valley was a latter-day Eden, dotted with tranquil glades and fecund glens, each habitat hosting its own appealing combination of birds, deer, rabbits, and butterflies.

"So what do you think?" asked Goneril.

"Holistica is beautiful," said Nora. "The skies are clear, the rivers pure, the people happy. I can't stand it."

"It's settled, then? You'll guard Korty's brain?"

Nora nodded thoughtfully.

"When human beings aspire to the intellectual condition of woodchucks," said Goneril, "they are no longer in touch with their potential."

"It's not the primitivism that bothers me, or the childishness, or the sentimentality, or any of those things."

Using her paddle as a rudder, Goneril turned the canoe around, pointing the prow toward the village. "So what bothers you?"

"Heaven is boring," said Nora.

"It could use a jazz band."

"A jazz band, a chamber ensemble, a comedy troupe, a softball league, a Ferris wheel, a Charles Dickens novel, a recording of *Rhapsody in Blue,* a print of *Casablanca.* Take me back to Mexico, Goneril, before I go insane."

Matters of Life and Death

METICULOUSLY HE TAPED the handle of his soft-iron carving hammer. Methodically he sharpened his T7 tooth chisel, B4 bushing chisel, and F9 frosting chisel. If he got the details right, Gerard believed, then his mad, impossible plan might work.

He took particular care in selecting a coign of vantage. Slipping into Lucido's library, he positioned himself behind the Henry James first editions. He would not sully Homer, Shakespeare, or his beloved Dante by making them accessories before the fact.

The lava picture from Mount Catemaco—a muscular sculptor brandishing the tools of his trade—had never left him. But what, exactly, had the sculptor been about to carve? Entwined lovers? A smiling saint? An angry god?

"Something violent," Fiona had insisted.

Peering outward, Gerard hefted his valise. The carving hammer clanked against the chisels. Lucido shuffled into the central hexagon. All six video screens were alive, each displaying what Gerard took to be a 1950s Hollywood science-fiction movie, the black-and-white images dramatically offsetting the blood that slicked Lucido's fingers and the red stains that blotched his caftan.

"Violent but necessary," Fiona had added.

"Entirely necessary?" Gerard had asked.

Lucido stripped down to the skin, filled a glass with red wine, and removed his Moroccan leather syringe case from the drawer beneath the divan. He injected himself with his usual dose of hyperion, then activated the hot tub. The waters whirled. Bubbles flew away like spindrift. Easing himself into the maelstrom, he positioned his weighty frame on the submerged seat.

"Good evening," said Gerard as he stepped away from the bookcases, heart pounding, valise in hand. He felt bisected, a riven block of Makrana marble, so that the person thinking Gerard's thoughts and the insensate Angel of Vengeance now entering the hexagon seemed two entirely different creatures.

Lucido scowled. "Do you have an appointment?"

"No, but you do."

"What are you talking about? Is my statue finished?"

"I found a suitable chunk of reubenite. The maquette now satisfies me, but I'm planning to employ an unprecedented technique, and I want your approval."

"I don't understand."

"A unique type of chisel blow," Gerard elaborated as the Angel of Vengeance placed the valise on the hexagon floor and drew out the hammer and the tooth chisel. "A bold stroke."

"You're not making sense," said Lucido.

"Whereas ripping out children's hearts makes a lot of sense."

Lucido's pudgy fingers curled around the wineglass. "I admire your talent, sir, but you know nothing of metaphysics. The post-theistic man has broken free of rationalist inhibitions. William Blake said it well. 'May God keep us from single vision and Newton's sleep.'"

"Joshua Alport wasn't suffering from Newton's sleep. He was suffering from abulia, and you murdered him."

"You're a despicable little spy, Gerard Korty." Lucido raised the glass to his mouth and sipped. The wine reddened his lips. "This quarrel has turned tedious. Please leave at once."

"Not before I show you my stroke."

On the nearest screen a beleaguered man, his body reduced to the size of Tom Thumb, used a construction nail to battle a tarantula.

A different tarantula occupied the opposite screen, a mutant twenty feet high. Hairy, twitchy, and evidently enraged, it was industriously disassembling a large house with its front legs, much to the occupants' distress.

"I understand your skepticism concerning Antidote X, but it has a more honorable lineage than you imagine." Lucido set his wineglass on the tiled deck. "Every important religion is predicated on blood. Burnt offerings may fuel the engines of faith, but plasma oils the gears. A father, the Hebrew God, contrives the murder of His son, Jesus, for the sake of a greater good. Some people would say that's an ugly story, but I, for one, am moved to tears. Do you know the problem with the world today? People fear the greater good. The Hebrew God didn't fear it. He welcomed those Roman nails, chewing through His son's wrists. He welcomed that crown of thorns, that thrusting spear."

"You demented pig," muttered Gerard while the avenging angel licked the tip of the tooth chisel and advanced toward the hot tub.

"I'll tell you an unpleasant truth," said Lucido. "Metaphysics prospers in *spite* of men like you."

The angel kicked over the wineglass, shattering it, then crouched down beside his enemy. He pressed the chisel point squarely against Lucido's left shoulder, and then he—

Eyes widening, Lucido stared at the steel blade. "You wouldn't dare."

"*I* wouldn't, no, but *he*—"

—struck the chisel hard. The blade followed a true course, burrowing five inches into Lucido's torso, lodging amid muscles and fat. The accompanying cry was so loud, it frightened both Gerard and the angel.

Lucido, screaming, stood up, bathwater streaming from his legs and abdomen. Before his enemy could remove the chisel, the angel wrapped his palm around the handle and, like young Arthur freeing sword from anvil, pulled out the blade. A ribbon of fresh red blood rolled down Lucido's chest. It hit the whirlpool, tinting the waters the color of a jaguar's tongue.

"O divine Agoridas," hissed the analyst, gritting his teeth and staring heavenward. "O prince of pain." He faced the angel, addressing him in a voice that probably owed its uncanny tranquillity to hyperion-15. "I've never had an experience like this," he said, sounding strangely grateful. "Astonishing." Swerving, he fixed on the combat between the little man and the ferocious tarantula. The hero suddenly triumphed, impaling the spider on the construction nail. "Mr. Richter, come here! There's someone I need you to kill!"

Gerard felt the angel wipe the tooth chisel on a velvet drape, lunge toward the hot tub, and pound the blade into Lucido's right breast.

Again Lucido screamed, though amazingly his curiosity continued to eclipse his pain. "Wondrous wounds!" The analyst clasped the chisel with both hands, tearing it loose like a staked vampire attempting self-resurrection. Blood fountained forth. "Beautiful Agoridas!" Shivering, spasming, he jerked his weight from one leg to the other, the *contrapposto* of the doomed, then heaved himself out of the tub. "I am become art!"

Lucido pitched forward, spitting blood as he fell prone on the deck. No further work remained for the angel beyond a few flourishes and embellishments. He ripped the tooth chisel from Lucido's hands, retrieved the bushing and frosting tools, and delivered the finishing taps.

Gerard analyzed the analyst. He embroidered him with lesions. He sculpted him to death.

"Nel mezzo del cammin di nostra vita"—he gave one last blow, driving the bushing chisel through Lucido's left eye and into the meat beyond—"mi ritrovai per una selva oscura." Rising, he kicked the bulky corpse repeatedly, moving it inch by inch until it flopped over the edge of the hot tub and hit the churning pink waters. "Tant'è amara che poco è più morte."

Until his arrival in Lucido's wine cellar, Anthony hadn't believed he would ever suffer an experience more harrowing than the wreck of the *Carpco Valparaíso*, but now such an ordeal was upon him: captivity by lunatics who excised live human hearts as casually as altar boys lit candles. Gasping, the captain lifted his manacled hands and wiped the sweat from his eyes—the enveloping tarpaulin had turned the cage into an oven—then stared skyward and addressed El Cráneo aloud. His vow was succinct. He would attack Lucido's minions with fist and tooth the instant they laid hands on Stevie.

"Amen," said Cassie.

Lucido, Richter, and Jackendorf had long since departed, leaving the chauffeur in charge. With the approach of midnight, Leopold Dansk, motivated by a combination of immediate boredom and habitual cruelty, subjected his prisoners to the worst verbal abuse his talents permitted, placing particular emphasis on Stevie's impending death. "Let me offer a suggestion," he said, his voice muted by the canvas. "When your boy goes to the slab, pretend to be delighted he's bound for the Olmec paradise. Lucido might spare your lives. It's surprising how few plague families use that strategy. You probably think I'm insane, but I'm actually the most rational man on Lucido's staff. Do you imagine I buy his metaphysics? Antidote X won't take you to the Olmec paradise any more than the Coatzacoalcos shuttle bus will take you to Tahiti."

"Then let us go free," snarled Cassie.

"Rational men don't antagonize psychopaths, especially psychopaths like Lucido. They don't—"

Dansk's speech abruptly transmuted into a shriek—shock, outrage, pain. Anthony heard a body hit the floor. Moans followed. A woman spoke, her tone lilting, her accent American.

"You all right in there?"

"We're suffocating," said Cassie.

The tarpaulin rustled, slid downward, fell away. Dansk lay on the floor, writhing and grunting as he tried to extract the sacrificial knife, which projected from his abdomen like a croquet stake planted in a suburban backyard. His pistol, a Smith & Wesson, lay at his feet. A slender, gorgeous, middle-aged woman stood beside the wounded man, gripping the tarpaulin in her bloody hands. She dropped to her knees, rooted through Dansk's pockets, and, retrieving a set of keys, backed away from the chauffeur as if he were a leper.

"Thank you," said Cassie.

"Thank you," said Anthony.

"Fiona Korty," said the woman, quavering as she systematically tried each key in the padlock. "Married to Gerard Korty."

"The man who's sculpting the dinosaurs' asteroid?" said Anthony.

Fiona Korty, perplexed, said, "Yes. He's the one."

"I was on the scene when God told Nora Burkhart the project could drive your husband mad."

"No, Gerry's stronger than that." Fiona seemed calmer now. "Right now he's killing Lucido with a chisel."

The image of a steel chisel penetrating Lucido's granite heart gave Anthony intense pleasure, but the feeling dissolved as his gaze drifted toward the second cage. His ears had not deceived him: both of the elderly abulic's daughters lay slumped against the iron bars, black wounds dotting their foreheads like the perforations in a pepper shaker.

Fiona found the right key. She opened the cage door and began testing the remaining keys on Anthony's handcuffs. In one minute, he was free. In two minutes, Cassie.

"If you hang around Coatzacoalcos, Richter and the others will hunt you down. How did you get to Mexico?"

"On my steamboat, from New Orleans," said Anthony. "But it won't survive another Gulf crossing."

Fiona pressed the oily keys into Anthony's palm. "Here, take Lucido's car."

"No, we're staying," said Cassie. "As long as the temples are still curing people—"

"The temples are worthless," interrupted a compact, powerfully built man, striding into the cellar, his right hand gripping a valise. A chisel lay clasped against his breast, and his white cotton shirt displayed an archipelago of bloodstains. "Somatocism is a fraud."

Rushing from the cage, Fiona lovingly embraced the intruder, then pressed her open palm against the chisel point. "It's done?"

"It's done." Gerard Korty gestured toward the convulsing chauffeur. "If our upbringing counts for anything, we're both headed for—"

"Circle Seven?" said Fiona.

"Circle Seven," said Gerard. "Ring One."

"Is Somatocism really a fraud?" asked Anthony.

"The remissions last a few months at most," said Gerard.

"No exceptions?"

"With Lucido dead, the matter is academic. His church is unlikely to survive him."

Slowly, tenderly, Anthony lifted his ethereal son off the cage floor. He and Cassie stared at each other. Their eyes negotiated a silent pact. They would leave the Isthmus of Tehuantepec immediately, leave Mexico altogether, crossing into whatever nightmarish landscapes now constituted the United States of America.

"Perhaps we should get him some medical attention," suggested Anthony, indicating Dansk.

"Perhaps we should let him bleed to death," said Cassie as she followed Anthony out of the cage.

The chauffeur gurgled unintelligibly.

"This plague family knows of you," said Fiona to her husband. "They're friends of Nora's."

"Don't worry about Hell," said Cassie, giving Korty a hug. "Or Heaven either, for that matter. They're both closed for repairs."

Twenty minutes later, sitting behind the steering wheel, studying the embossed keys logo by logo, Anthony quickly identified the one belonging to the Lincoln Continental. The engine sprang to life on the first turn. He watched with satisfaction as the fuel needle arced toward FULL like the baton on a metronome.

Slumped in the back with Stevie in her arms, Cassie waved to their rescuers as Anthony guided the Continental across the nocturnal plaza. During their imprisonment the fog had become an opaque broth as hazardous as anything he'd ever encountered at sea, and it took them all night to drive down the mountain and through the jungle to La Sangre de la Serpiente. On five occasions they had to stop altogether and wait for the cloud to thin. Anthony took advantage of the second delay to inspect the Continental's trunk, discovering to his delight that it contained thirty-six cans of gasoline.

The fog had lifted by the time the *Natchez Queen* swung into view, transformed by dawn's faint light into the sort of phantom steamer the Flying Dutchman might have captained in his declining years: a decrepit ship, but functional. Anthony parked beside the cantina and, leaving Cassie to exercise Stevie's limbs, marched across the dock and up the gangway. Crock sat in a director's chair on the afterdeck, holding a fishing pole. A half-full bottle of Cerveza Moctezuma rested on the transom. Spotting Anthony, the engineer jumped up, flung out his arms, and knocked over the beer bottle; it hit the paddle wheel and ricocheted into the river. The men embraced.

"Tell me about Nora and Kevin," said Anthony.

"Nora's asleep," said Crock. "The boy became an acolyte and got cured."

"I'm afraid it's temporary."

Crock scowled. Rapidly but precisely, Anthony recounted their ordeal at Mount Tapílula—the death of Lucido, the near sacrifice of Stevie—then asked Crock to join their escape: if the car broke down, they would need his skills.

"Besides, do you really want to loll around on this boring river," said Anthony, "when you could be dodging gunfire from Adrian Lucido's henchmen?"

Crock reeled in his line. An energetic eel wriggled on the hook, twisting itself into a succession of commas, question marks, and tildes. He freed the creature, threw it back, and announced that he'd decided to go along. Yes, he would miss the good old *Queen*, but he would miss his captain more.

Anthony proceeded to Nora's stateroom. She lay facedown on the mattress, glorying in the peaceful morning sleep of a mother who believes her child's fetch is gone forever. Reluctantly he shook her. Seeing her old friend, she sprang awake and laughed exultantly.

"Anthony, thank God. Oh, please, *please* tell me they made Stevie an acolyte."

"They didn't."

"Damn. I'm sorry."

"I'm afraid I've lost faith in the temples."

"You mustn't. The treatment works. Kevin's doing fine."

"A lot has happened since El Agujero. Lucido went insane, and your sculptor friend killed him."

"Gerard killed Lucido? *What? What?*"

"Cassie and I are leaving. Crock too. There's nothing for us here. We can't risk another crossing in the *Queen*, but we've got a car now and plenty of gas. I think you should come. If you stay in Coatzacoalcos, there's no telling what Richter—"

"Remember the entrails' message, how Korty was sculpting the Chicxulub asteroid into a human brain? It turns out the thing is essential to humanity's future."

"Hanging around Korty is the stupidest thing you could possibly do."

"It's hard to explain." Nora rose from the bed, smoothing her nightshirt against a body made muscular by many hours of lifting her son. "These last three nights I've had visions."

"Visions?"

"I've been appointed to protect Korty's sculpture."

On the edge of Anthony's awareness, a migraine aura flashed like an electric storm. He reached into his pocket, felt the comforting contours of his Maxalt bottle. "You're serious about this, aren't you?"

"Let me give Stevie a farewell kiss."

With a snort of frustration, Anthony exited the stateroom, Nora marching resolutely behind him. He headed toward the cantina. A green lizard scurried across the veranda and disappeared into the jungle. An unseen howler monkey roared. Carta Blanca beer in hand, Crock peered under the raised hood of the Continental. Cassie stood leaning against the driver's door, swabbing her brow with a red neckerchief.

Somberly Anthony informed his wife of Nora's peculiar relationship to Korty's sculpture, a commitment that Nora herself attempted to clarify via a bizarre account of a futuristic city called Deus Absconditus. Although her friend's decision to stay behind ultimately proved as incomprehensible to Cassie as it was to Anthony, she unequivocally declared that Nora's sense of destiny deserved everyone's respect.

Close to tears, Anthony, Cassie, and Crock hugged their former shipmate good-bye. Nora opened the back door and, bending low over Stevie, brushed her lips against his pocked forehead.

Later, as they sped away from the cantina, Crock asked, "Will we ever see her again?"

"Those crazy visions," said Anthony, "not to mention her obsession with the sculpture. I'm afraid she's about to get in trouble. Maybe she's brave, maybe she's nuts. I can't decide."

"She's nuts," said Crock.

"She's brave," said Cassie.

"Where're we headed?" asked Crock.

"I don't know," said Anthony. "North. There must be treatments we haven't tried yet. Let's aim for California. In California they can cure anything."

Three days after Nora saw her friends vanish in the ballooning dust of Calle Puesta del Sol, a naked Goneril entered her stateroom, climbed into the white silk Inanna gown, and invited the flower woman to step outside and study the Volcán de Catemaco.

"What's happening now is just foreplay," said the fetch as she guided Nora across the embarcadero. Sulfur fumes wafted through the yard behind La Sangre de la Serpiente. "The explosion comes in a week, a day, an hour—who knows?"

Even before Goneril offered her ominous analysis, Nora perceived that Catemaco was building toward an eruption. She could see the volcano's billowing gray smoke, hear its bassy groans, smell its stink. Esperanza and her regulars had gathered outside the cantina in a tight, frightened knot. The turkey cocks gobbled nervously. The tapir grunted. Some customers said that El Cráneo was the main influence on Catemaco, agitating the volcano the way the moon pulled at the river, and so everyone should simply resign himself to his divinely ordained fate, be it lava, boulders, or poison gas. Other customers believed that they would not only survive but prosper, for the coming cataclysm most surely heralded the end of the plague and the dawn of a golden age. Still others maintained that the mountain was going through one of its usual innocuous fits, and there was no fundamental reason to attend the rumblings.

"I'm hearing lots of crazy talk today," said Esperanza to Nora. "Some people think we have nothing to worry about."

"Remind them that the boy who cried wolf ultimately spoke the truth." Nora swallowed a mouthful of air, coughing as the sulfur scraped her throat. "What will happen to the brain?" she asked Goneril.

"There's still time to save it," said the fetch. "Step one is to steam upriver to El Dorado."

Esperanza clasped Nora's shoulders, pivoting her so that their eyes met. "Don't listen to your *demonio.* If Catemaco blows, the lava will pour into the gorge, and you'll be roasted."

"I have every intention of avoiding that fate," said Nora.

"Take to the high ground, *amiga.*"

"I can't."

The cantina keeper closed her eyes. "Tell your fine young *mago* that his friend Esperanza is praying for him."

An adolescent pagan, an unemployed English teacher, a doppelgänger from another dimension: did a steamboat ever have a more unlikely crew? Nora doubted it. Thanks to his apprenticeship with Crock, Kevin knew the *Queen*'s inner workings, her boilers and condensers, her shafts and cranks, and he readily assumed the role of engineer. After declaring herself "navigator and first mate," Goneril appointed Nora "captain, quartermaster, and ship's conscience." The three of them functioned well together. In less than an hour they had cast off, achieved a head of steam, and cruised ten kilometers up the Uspanapa.

The instant they drew within view of the studio, Goneril became oddly obsessed with the *Queen*'s position. They must fix the boat in the exact center of the river, she insisted, prow facing Coatzacoalcos.

"I don't get it," said Nora.

"Trust me."

They came about and dropped one anchor from the port-side paddle-wheel housing and the other off the starboard bow—effective moves, but not sufficient to prevent lateral drift. Goneril fretted and cursed. She spat into the river. Eventually Kevin got the idea of outfitting the cargo deck with mooring lines—four in the stem, four aft—and running them from the boat to the jungle, securing each rope around a tree. The strategy worked, and by noon the *Queen* was locked in place, as immobile as if she'd run aground.

On Goneril's orders, they boarded the skiff and poled their way toward shore, Kevin clutching his Idorasag idol, Nora hacking from the sulfur. They disembarked and, sitting on the beach below the bluff, surveyed their handiwork and collected their strength.

A thundering reached their ears, a sound suggesting the Bull of Heaven crashing through Uruk.

"Catemaco?" asked Nora.

"No," said Goneril.

"Storm?"

"No." Goneril, rising, shook her head and rubbed the sand from her silk gown. "Good news, Sister—the plague is passing. El Cráneo's days are numbered. Even as I look you in the eye, my inner gaze travels to the beckoning abyss from which I first emerged. Do you want your gown back?"

"It was a gift, but the guy probably found somebody else by now."

The fetch took off her sandals and stepped into the water. She kept on moving, humming softly as the river covered her calves... knees... thighs... abdomen.

"You're deserting me?" asked Nora.

"My part's played out." The water reached Goneril's chest. "An admonition. For the next hour you must stay off the boat. Understood?"

"Understood," said Nora.

"Good."

Kevin clamped his palms over his eyes. "It's like watching you drown," he explained to Nora. "It's like watching my own mother drown."

The thunder continued to boom.

"Fare thee well, Sister." The river lapped at the fetch's shoulders. "I enjoyed our relationship, strained though it often was."

Nora observed Goneril's descent with schizoid emotions. She welcomed this reprieve from the Footman, of course, but in recent days she'd also come to depend on her death. "Can I save the brain without your help?" she asked.

"I have great faith in you."

The Uspanapa closed over the fetch. A mass of scummy foam rose to the surface, the bubbles popping into oblivion one by one, and then the waters grew perfectly still, home to a mystery.

Whenever Gerard needed a respite from his labors, he would join Fiona and his doppelgänger atop the reubenite brain and watch the luminous crimson carpet creep down the mountain and into the jungle. The lava's glow tinted the droplets of sweat speckling Fiona's face. She seemed to be perspiring rubies. Every hour the flow advanced at least twenty meters, turning the bougainvillea vines into burning fuses and forcing the cockatoos, budgerigars, monkeys, anteaters, and armadillos to evacuate. As far as Gerard could tell, the Stone Gospel would be spared the present outpouring, the lava confining itself to gullies and creek beds as it dribbled toward the Uspanapa. What he feared was a full-scale eruption—an event no mere reubenite sculpture could withstand. In his mind he saw the hot gases sear the Gallery of Decency, the burning winds melt the Garden of Scientific Knowledge, the boulders pulverize the Hall of Artistic Passion . . . and then, finally, an inexorable tide of molten earth reduced the brain to a smoldering lump of nothing.

Dressed in his felt hat and ragged serape, Julius lit his clay pipe, puffed three times, and faced Gerard. "Protectors are on the way," said the fetch, a promise he'd been voicing in one form or another ever since Gerard's return from Mount Tapílula. "Once you finish your magnum opus, the means to preserve it will become apparent."

"And what if Catemaco tosses her cookies before help arrives?" asked Gerard.

The fetch winced and sucked silently on his pipe.

Gerard's remorse tormented him even more than his seismic anxieties. Until the moment of Lucido's death, he hadn't realized just how deep within him the hooks of Holy Mother Church resided. He'd committed a mortal sin. His soul was suppurating. Condemned to Circle VII, he would be eternally scalded by hot blood while Dante, Virgil, and the Centaur looked on.

So with our faithful escort we set off
Along the shore that flanked the scarlet stream,
The boiling wretches moaning in our ears.

Some saw I all blood-covered to the brow,
Of whom the Centaur said, "Vile tyrants, these,
Grown fat on booty bought with murderous hands . . ."

Gerard's mentor, the renowned portrait sculptor Louis Endicott Frye, had once theorized that urgency aided the creative process, preventing the artist from sacrificing essences to details, but a volcanic eruption was hardly the sort of deadline the old man had been imagining. And yet somehow Gerard kept on working, despite the pressure (or because of it), despite his guilt (or because of it), and on Friday morning he declared the project finished. As he gave Fiona a Cook's tour, he couldn't help feeling intimations of posthumous glory. People would remember Gerard Korty. His name would live in the annals of passion. Entering the right hemisphere, Fiona took immediate joy in the *Romeo and Juliet* diorama: Juliet standing on the balcony above her father's walled orchard, unaware of Romeo concealed in the shadows below, her famous speech suspended on a nearby plaque. ("What's in a name? That which we call a rose by any other name would smell as sweet. So Romeo would, were he not Romeo called, retain that dear perfection which he owes without that title.") Fiona was equally moved by the Sermon on the Mount featured in the cerebellum, each beatitude emblazoned on a separate cloud.

They returned to daylight, the air laden with noxious vapors, and started into the jungle, reaching El Dorado by noon. While Fiona lingered on the studio grounds, trying to comfort their pony—evidently the animal could sense imminent eruptions—Gerard stumbled into the kitchen, weary but exhilarated. He removed the last bottle of Monte Albán from the liquor cabinet, slumped into a chair, and poured himself a generous amount of mescal. He'd done it, by damn. He'd translated *Parables for a Post-Theistic Age* into jade, turquoise, gold foil, and reubenite. Little myths would illumine the human future.

He was about to reward himself with a second mescal when Hubbard Richter scuttled scorpionlike into the kitchen gripping a Colt .45 and wearing a leather cartridge belt stuffed with dozens of rounds.

"Thanks to our association," said Richter, "I've become adept at recognizing chisel marks. In marble, reubenite, and Adrian Lucido."

Gerard's intestines tightened; his bladder autonomously emptied itself. He considered screaming for Julius to appear and save him (according to Nora, fetches readily intimidated Richter), but instead he simply said, with a nonchalance that astonished him, "Would you care for a mescal?"

"You used a tooth chisel, a bushing chisel, and—"

Before Richter could say "frosting chisel," the kitchen began to vibrate . . . the kitchen, the house, the grounds, the forest. The volcano's fury had seemingly seized the entire state of Veracruz. Frying pans rocketed off their hooks; wine bottles vacated the pantry; crockery shot from the shelves and broke. As Richter's gun hit the floor, Gerard shouted his gratitude toward Heaven, though he suspected that El Cráneo had spared him not from benevolence but merely to inflict a subsequent punishment far worse than bullets.

Catemaco's wrath increased, ejecting Gerard from his chair as the floor pitched upward like the lid of a jack-in-the-box. Airborne, he hit the window, which promptly shattered, flecking him with broken glass. He tumbled into the yard, gained his feet, and started across the studio grounds, glancing back in time to see Richter, gun in hand, climb through the jagged frame.

An apocalyptic thunder shook the air, like the rumble of an immense bowling ball hurled by God's own hand. Gerard ran for the stockade gate. Richter fired. Pain blossomed in Gerard's side. He stumbled and hit the dirt, pressing his hand against the screaming hole. Warm blood seeped between his fingers.

"You have no talent, Korty!"

The volcanic tremors continued, booming in counterpoint to the mysterious thunder, fissuring El Dorado, crack breeding crack until the studio grounds resembled the face of a shattered mirror. Gerard looked up. Richter charged toward him, bobbing his head and laughing insanely as he struggled to negotiate the shifting terrain. The deacon drew within twenty feet, aimed his pistol. Gerard steeled himself for Circle VII. Already he could feel the scarlet stream encircling his neck and trickling hotly down his throat.

"Your crocodiles look like chameleons!"

It was Martin Luther, of all people, who rescued Gerard. A particularly ferocious vibration possessed the statue. Uprooted, the Great Reformer struck Richter squarely and slammed him into the dirt. The statue followed him down but retained its momentum, a full metric ton of sculpted reubenite rolling across the deacon's legs with a noise suggestive of a bear dancing on dead twigs.

"I'll kill him!" wailed Fiona, snugging her fists into Gerard's armpits. "Where's my fucking knife? I'll kill him!"

She dragged the sculptor out of range, behind an Idorasag that Richter had refused to export to Tamoanchan. Gerard's wound was excruciating, a preview of the inferno to come.

The incessant thunder drew Gerard's attention to the south stockade wall. Seeing the source of the noise, he released an astonished cry, louder even than his howls of pain. It was the Stone Gospel, his magnum opus, shaken from its perch atop the grassy hummock and launched on a course toward El Dorado. Relentlessly the massive rock rolled through the jungle, severing vines and mowing down trees. Within seconds it breached the stockade wall, the pales tendering no more resistance than a house of cards would offer a hurricane, and now it was in the yard, heading straight for Richter.

God knows what the deacon thought as, flailing around in the dirt, he flopped over and beheld a gigantic human brain bearing down on him like a runaway locomotive. His features contracted into quintessential bewilderment. A high-pitched whimper broke from his throat, he got off a final, impotent shot—and then it was over, Richter gone, pulped, demoted to a condition somewhere between roadkill and creamed corn. The juggernaut rolled on, smashing through the south wall.

"Holy Mother of God," gasped Fiona.

Smeared with Richter's blood, the Stone Gospel reached the bluff and, behaving as would any thirty-ton object under the circumstances, fell. A terrible spasm pierced Gerard, as if the Lucifer of Canto XXXIV had inserted a frozen finger in his wound, and yet his perplexity absorbed him no less than his pain. Had Julius lied about the brain having protectors? Where were they? How could a sculpture change the world from the bottom of a minor Mexican river?

He fainted, overcome by blood loss and the limits of human reason.

Even if she lived to be a hundred—a real possibility now that Goneril had left for parts unknown—Nora knew she would always retain a searing mental picture of the reubenite brain, curiously bloodstained, as it sailed off the bluff and plunged toward the Uspanapa, inevitably making noisy and destructive contact with the *Queen*.

Shackled by gravity, the sculpture descended. It snapped both smokestacks, pulverized the pilothouse, and sent the helm spinning away like a discus. It hit the texas deck . . . the observation deck . . . the saloon deck, crushing the cabins and staterooms like an elephant sitting on a wicker commode. Planks and rails pinwheeled away, littering the river with flotsam. Eventually the thing came to rest on the cargo deck, medulla socketed into the hull, hemispheres extending over the water on both sides, an image that to Nora suggested an egg of infinite significance occupying an immense waterborne nest.

Miraculously, the steamboat stayed afloat, her hull evidently intact. Whether the whole impossible event traced to God, chance, the Fates, or some equally quixotic force, Nora suddenly understood how Gerard's magnum opus would escape the volcano. True, the vital connection between helm and rudder had probably been severed, but jerry-rigging an alternative surely lay within their collective competence.

"Jesus!" gasped Kevin, clutching his Idorasag as he might a teddy bear. "Bull's-eye!"

"Bull's-eye," echoed Nora, wonderstruck.

"My Soaragid!" wailed Kevin.

"We'll dig her out."

"My Orgasiad! My Risogada!"

Almost as astonishing as the Stone Gospel's flight was the fate that now claimed the reubenite Erasmus. Torn from his pedestal, in thrall to the ceaseless tremors, the humanist theologian somersaulted over the bluff and hit the steamboat's stem, his scholar's cap acting as a spearpoint. He punctured the foredeck, met the hull, and stopped. Nora blinked in bewilderment. Yes, it was true. The *Queen* had just acquired a figurehead, positioned unconventionally with feet in the air: Erasmus as yogi, humanism tempered by Hinduism, West meets East.

As the midday skull pounded down, Nora and her son sat huddled together on the shore, transfixed by the odd sight of a steamboat that had not only a brain for a superstructure but a theologian for a bowsprit. Nora was about to suggest that they paddle over and inspect the damage when a shadow crept across the beach. She looked up. Gerard stood amid the reeds, eyes glassy, leaning on a distraught

Fiona. His breathing was shallow and fitful. Blood marred his blue denim shirt.

"Richter shot him," said Fiona, easing her semiconscious husband onto the soft sand. She pointed toward the *Queen* and its peculiar cargo. "At least the bastard got punished. That's part of him on the cerebrum."

Nora, rising, moved toward Gerard, knelt down, and lifted his shirt. The hole in his side was deep and purple, ringed by petals of torn flesh. There was no exit wound.

"Is he dying?" asked Fiona.

"I don't know," said Nora.

Operating on some felicitous combination of instinct and reason, as if her mind had been molded by long sojourns in both Uruk and Deus Absconditus, Nora took up her stave and ferried Kevin over to the *Queen*. He must raise the anchors, she told him, then light the boilers and hunt up medical supplies. She returned to the beach. Gerard was as white as coconut meat. His brow burned with fever. Working in silent accord, the women loaded him onto the skiff. Briefly he awoke, mumbled something incomprehensible—Nora caught "buckets" and "syllable"—and returned to darkness.

They bore him over the Uspanapa, Fiona cradling her husband's head between her knees while cooling his brow with handfuls of river water. As Nora worked her stave, she gave her companion a short, breathless account of her visions: the Assembly of the Turned Cheek, the Deontology Bowl, Holistica, all of it.

"Gerard's brain must be protected at all costs," Nora concluded.

"Obviously," said Fiona.

"Unless, of course, it was a dream."

"No, friend. The brain must be protected *especially* if it was a dream."

Boarding the steamboat near her prow, they removed a dozen shattered planks blocking the pituitary portal, then carried Gerard into the Hall of Artistic Passion—his favorite part of the sculpture, Fiona said. The exhibits were in disarray, though surprisingly coherent given the fury of the Stone Gospel's fall. They deposited Gerard alongside the Van Gogh tableau.

Fifteen minutes later, Kevin entered the right hemisphere, proudly displaying a first-aid kit he'd salvaged from the wreckage, as well as his Soaragid and his Risogada. The engine, he was happy to report, had survived the *Queen*'s encounter with the reubenite mass. The paddle wheel seemed functional. The burners were lit, and soon they'd have two hundred pounds of steam pressure. He'd even restored steering to the boat by transforming a dislocated ceiling beam into a tiller, lashing it at right angles to the rudder post.

"When you pull the throttle, will the paddles move?" Nora asked him.

"Idorasag willing."

Dropping to her knees, she opened the first-aid kit—the brain's descent had scrambled the contents, but nothing appeared cracked or broken—and examined her unconscious patient. The bleeding had stopped, but the wound still looked dreadful. Carefully she disinfected the torn tissues, swabbing them with a cotton ball soaked in iodine, then bandaged the hole with linen.

The kit included a large glass-and-steel syringe plus a dozen vials of penicillin and seven hits of morphine. When Fiona insisted that they administer the antibiotic right away, Nora ran her index finger along the barrel of the hypodermic needle and shuddered.

"You can accidentally kill a person with one of these," she said. "Force too many air bubbles into the bloodstream, and..."

"I can do it," said Kevin evenly.

Automatically Nora asked a question that, in over a decade of mother-son interactions, had never once produced a negative answer. "Are you sure?"

He reminded her of how Kevin the Incredible had periodically employed a large syringe to inject a dead, defoliated rosebush with "the elixir of life," thereby making it sprout a dozen blossoms. He filled the glass barrel with penicillin, expelled a single drop, rubbed alcohol on the thick blue vein traversing Gerard's forearm, and inserted the needle. Retracting the rubber stopper, he sucked a drop of blood into the barrel. He winced and pushed the plunger.

"Teach me how to do that," said Fiona to Kevin.

"Later," said Nora. "We have a volcano to conquer."

The instant the three fugitives stepped through the pituitary portal and into the daylight, the long anticipated explosion occurred, so loud it seemed to shatter the air itself, tearing each oxygen atom from its twin. Boulders flew in all directions; they bounced off papaya trees, mashed banana plants, and slammed against the Stone Gospel, lodging in the cerebral convolutions. No sooner had the rocks landed than the ashes came, a mass of dark particles spiraling outward from Mount Catemaco like a tornado made of hornets. The sun vanished. El Cráneo went into eclipse.

Gradually the ashes settled, sifting into the jungle like negative snow and turning the Uspanapa black. The *Queen* became as grimy as a coal barge, her crew as sooty as chimney sweeps. Cinders filled their mouths and clogged their ears.

As radiant red lava streamed down Catemaco's slopes, Nora got to work. Spitting out ashes, she ordered Kevin to the engine room, then scanned the ruins of the forward galley. She spotted a fire ax and pulled it from the rubble. Tightening her grip on the handle, she raised the ax high. Bits of flaming rock attacked her like kamikaze cicadas. One spark struck her neck, eating into the skin. A second branded her brow. A third seared her cheek.

Nora brought the ax down hard, severing the nearest bow rope.

The lava advanced relentlessly, Gaia's own menstrual flow, the viscous mass burbling and glowing as the foothills of the Sierra Madre Oriental channeled it toward the river basin. Nora hadn't been so terrified since the Anglo-Saxons tried to gun her down with their Patton tank. Reaching the bluff behind the *Queen*, the lava continued to roll, dribbling onto the beach like incandescent oatmeal boiling over the sides of an immense cauldron. Nora severed another bow rope. The viscous earth started coming in long serpentine waves, each comber sending up plumes of steam as it fell sizzling into the Uspanapa. She cut another rope. A lava wave shot off the bluff, arced over the beach, and splashed down within ten meters of the *Queen*'s stern. Nora cut the last bow rope, expelled a mouthful of ashes, and, passing the ax to Fiona, commanded her to run through the brain and stand ready by the aft lines.

Nora needed height—perspective. The debris yielded a wooden ladder. She leaned it against the left frontal lobe and ascended. Ashes covered the crown of the brain, gusting along the cerebral commissure like dead New England leaves, but otherwise the Stone Gospel made a reasonable pilothouse. Smoke poured from the jagged metal stumps that had once been the *Queen*'s stacks: a hopeful sign—the boilers were functioning. To the north lay the open river. Nora's burns ached and her bad knee throbbed as she hobbled down the commissure, ashes padding her footfalls, and glanced toward the stern.

The recent barrage of ejecta had ripped away the remainder of the cargo deck and its superstructure, exposing the engine, boilers, burners, and pipework to the gritty air. Ax in hand, Fiona leaned against the transom. Kevin crouched above the boiler pit, his right arm feeding wood scraps to the flames, his left wrapped around the improvised tiller. Covered in ash, the four mahogany idols sat atop the gunwale like starlings on a power line. As far as Nora could tell, the only serious damage caused by the flying boulders were the two holes in the starboard boiler, one large, the other small, both releasing trickles of water into the hull.

A lava wave descended, missing the *Queen* by barely five meters.

"Steam?" she called down to Kevin.

"Steam!"

She lifted her eyes just in time to behold the flaming deluge destroy El Dorado. The lava swallowed the stockade wall, flooded the hacienda, and engulfed the studio grounds, toppling the winches and hoists as it rushed toward the river.

"Half ahead!" she shouted.

"Half ahead!" Kevin answered.

Offering Nora a brisk salute, he opened the throttle. The paddle wheel squealed like a tortured automaton. It groaned and grunted. It moved. Forty-five degrees . . . ninety . . . one hundred eighty . . . a complete revolution, then a second revolution, a third.

"Now!" screamed Nora. "Cut them now!"

Fiona severed both port-side ropes, dashed across the afterdeck, and hacked apart the two remaining lines. The *Queen* cruised forward.

"Steady as she goes!" cried Nora. Kevin tightened his grip on the tiller. "A bit to the left! That's it! Now to the right!"

A lava wave curled toward the *Queen*'s roiling wake, spattering the afterdeck with fiery mud as it hit the water. Clouds of hissing steam arose, obscuring the churning paddle wheel.

"Full ahead!" cried Nora toward the mass of hot vapor, and her boat lurched desperately away, bound for Coatzacoalcos Harbor and the Gulf beyond, racing the satanic red flood.

Gerard awoke with the exalted taste of mescal in his mouth. He was supine, he realized, his shoulders and hips pressed against the Stone Gospel's reubenite floor. The chamber was bright with lantern globes. Sulfur fumes thickened the air. Crouching in the shadows, Fiona held a bottle of Monte Albán to his lips. Sipping slowly, he focused on the Vincent Van Gogh diorama. The thing was disheveled—hardly a shock, given the brain's recent roll through the jungle—and yet its essence shone through: the painter poised above Saint-Rémy, absorbing inspiration for *Starry Night*.

"Do you feel the bullet?" asked Fiona.

"I don't feel anything."

"I gave you morphine." She flashed a glass syringe. "You're allowed another dose in four hours."

He blinked, his eyes adjusting to the blazing light of the mantle lanterns. Three meters away, Romeo skulked beneath Juliet's balcony. "The brain sank. Are we underwater?"

"It landed on the *Queen*. We're cruising down the Uspanapa."

"What astonishing luck. 'The brain is just the weight of God . . .'"

"Luck is only half the story."

"For, heft them pound for pound . . ."

Fiona said, "The other half is fetchian intervention—Nora's leveler told her where to park the boat. 'And they will differ, if they do, as syllable from sound.'"

He removed the Monte Albán from her grasp and took a substantial swallow. "The displays, I guess they're pretty banged up."

"But not beyond repair." She dipped a scrap of cloth in an aluminum bowl filled with a cloudy, pungent pint of the Uspanapa. "Not all the news is good. Catemaco blew. We're barely keeping ahead of the lava."

"Also, I'm dying."

"Not a chance of it." She wrung the cloth and laid it across his forehead. "Listen, darling, Nora's fetch showed her a city of the future, Deus Absconditus. It was all there, the kingdom of decency, Ockham's little myths. Do you understand?"

"My brain works?"

"It works, Gerry." Two tears, one from each eye, glided down Fiona's cheeks. "We can't stop in Coatzacoalcos, too much poison gas, but Nora swears she can get us to Texas—Corpus Christi or Galveston, maybe Port Lavaca." She flicked the tears away. "We'll find you a surgeon, and then it's on to Saint Peter's Square!"

Her enthusiasm didn't fool him. He was dying, pure and simple, a fact he greeted with ambivalence. The imminence of eternal nothingness stupefied him—and yet he'd always believed it behooved artists to check out at the height of their powers, lest their final gestures merely augment the collective crap heap.

He smiled, an exhausting exercise. His soul surged with inner peace and processed opium. The little myths were coming! Deus Absconditus! A gray mist obscured his thoughts, as if he'd been projected into his tableau celebrating the invention of anesthesia. He was T. S. Eliot's patient, etherized upon a table.

Ten minutes later—ten hours, ten days, impossible to say—he broke free of his dream (a courtroom melodrama in which he stood trial on charges of having plagiarized the Korty Madonna) and returned to the far stranger reality of sailing down the Uspanapa inside a reubenite brain, his stomach aflame with a polyp of lead. The sulfur stank. The paddle wheel churned. Fiona lay beneath the Bach exhibit, submerged in uneasy sleep. Julius Azrael, naked as a newborn, stood over her, winding up the tiny harpsichord.

"How's the wound?" asked Julius.

"It burns."

"I've lost my vocation, Brother. Richter's bullet has thrown me onto the job market. When I accosted you in Rome, I thought you were mine to keep." Julius became muzzy, fragmented, like a reflection in a polluted pond. "Not everybody gets to bid his death adieu. Relish the moment."

"Go away."

"Is that all you can say? 'Go away'? How about thanking me for letting you live long enough to build this brain?"

"Thank you," said Gerard, tonelessly. "Is it true that Nora traveled into the future?"

"Is it true? Do hippos fart in the Nile?"

"A future that won't exist unless . . . ?"

"Relax, Brother. If anybody can get your magnum opus to Rome, it's that stubborn English teacher from Boston." The fetch continued to fade, until nothing remained but his raspy voice. "Au revoir, Homo sapiens. We leave the planet to you."

The miniature harpsichord began to play. It was out of tune, Gerard decided, but that could be corrected. He stared at the *Starry Night* miniature. The great spiral nebula rolled through the sky like the river of divine grace that Dante beheld in the tenth and final Heaven.

A flowing radiance like a river shaped
I saw all golden glowing between banks
Arrayed in spring's most bright and wondrous blooms.

And from this river living sparks came forth
Which, falling toward the flowers on every side,
Became like precious rubies set in gold.

As the last notes of the Prelude and Fugue XXIV in B Minor dissolved in the humid air, Gerard grew vaguely aware of his wife bending beside him.

"Fiona?"

"Right here, Gerry."

"Where's Nora?"

"On the bridge."

"If I die before she visits me, give her a message."

"You aren't dying. What message?"

"When she goes to site the brain in Saint Peter's Square, she must tilt it upward. Just slightly. A few degrees."

"Tilt it?"

"Toward the stars, and mystery—toward the God beyond God."

"I'll tell her."

A liquid darkness seeped through Gerard Korty's brain, bathing each neuron, sheathing each synapse, and then came the cold, and then the silence.

Engine chugging, paddle wheel turning, fractured stacks gushing, the *Natchez Queen* steamed down the river, one step ahead of the lava. Nora thought of Gilgamesh and Urshanabi crossing the Waters of Death, grimly observing the acid waves consume one wooden pole after another. Minutes after they cruised past La Sangre de la Serpiente—a deserted place, Esperanza and her regulars presumably camped on the high ground—Catemaco once again hurled fiery pieces of itself into the air. Cleaving to their respective posts on the reubenite bridge and beside the makeshift tiller, Nora and Kevin dodged the flying stones. Sulfur poured down, clawing at their eyes, scourging their throats, scorching their lungs.

"Damage report!" screamed Nora.

"Another hole in the starboard boiler!" cried Kevin.

Surveying the western shore, she saw that the volcano was relentlessly destroying Lucido's empire. Piece by piece the Church of Earthly Affirmation came apart, seasoning the molten stew with trellises from Orgasiad's grove, balconies from Risogada's palace, and cul-de-sacs from Idorasag's labyrinth. Priests and priestesses met Dantesque fates. Acolytes burned in droves. Reubenite idols rose from the lava like condemned athletes playing water polo in Hell.

As the *Queen* steamed through the Uspanapa delta and into the harbor beyond, Coatzacoalcos shook with a million mingled screams. Protected by a network of arroyos and ravines, the city would evidently be spared the lava, but the hot ashes and deadly gases had inspired an entirely understandable panic. Wailing and howling, the plague families sought sanctuary in the bay. Some swam. Others launched boats: dinghies, skiffs, rafts, cockleshells, tree trunks. Briefly Nora entertained a fantasy of bearing Gerard into Coatzacoalcos and searching among the fleeing survivors for a doctor, but the vapors and the crazies argued overwhelmingly against it. The only sane plan was to quit this toxic place forever, running due north until they bumped into Texas. With any luck they'd make their way to Galveston, find some semblance of a hospital, and get the staff to remove Gerard's bullet.

"Steady as she goes!"

They navigated the bay, gaining the Gulf after forty minutes, and then Catemaco spewed out another blanketing cloud of cinders and dust.

"Quarter speed! Steady!"

Kevin pulled back on the throttle. The *Queen* slowed, sailing through the blizzard of ash while Nora strode up and down the convoluted bridge, as enraged as Oedipus and almost as blind.

They had steamed perhaps fifty kilometers into the Gulf when dusk descended, its gloom multiplied by the omnipresent charcoal. Nora peered into the murk, alert for the lights of oncoming vessels. After all the trouble she'd taken to save Gerard's magnum opus from the volcano, she was determined not to lose the sculpture to anything so mundane as a shipwreck.

For three hours they cruised across the broad, choppy, invisible sea. Gradually the air grew cleaner, the heavens clearer, until at last Nora saw stars. They dazzled her. Here on the open water, far from smog and city lights, the constellations displayed a vibrancy no suburban skyscape or metropolitan planetarium could offer. Her Greeks, she realized, had routinely enjoyed such unfiltered vistas. Standing beneath the twinkling canopy, she pictured herself as a kind of celestial archaeologist, rapturously recovering an ancient sky.

Where was the Big Dipper? There? Quite so. She fixed on the bowl, then followed an imaginary line through Draco the Dragon to the Little Dipper. At the tip of the handle . . . yes, there it was, the mariner's best friend, the constant polestar. In principle, at least, staying a northerly course should be no more difficult than getting from Coolidge Corner to Harvard Square. She saluted the star and blew it a kiss.

"Half ahead!"

Throughout the night, while Fiona kept watch over Gerard, Nora and Kevin spelled each other at the tiller, using their breaks to catch some sleep in the cerebellum. The view from the stern suggested a case of macular degeneration: good peripheral vision, a void at the center. Nora didn't like the arrangement—the lack of a forward lookout increased their chances of a head-on collision—but it was the best they could manage, given Fiona's refusal to leave her husband's side. Not surprisingly, Nora had trouble sleeping, her insomnia punctuated by images of the divine skull mashing the steamboat in its bony jaws.

Shortly after dawn, the *Queen* consumed her last stick of firewood. The dual burners sputtered out; the engine died. With a pathetic croaking sound, the great paddle wheel stopped, leaving them adrift on a sea that appeared to stretch endlessly toward every point of the compass. After a brief consultation, they decided that Kevin should try repairing the starboard boiler, whereupon they would cannibalize the boat for fuel.

Nora scanned the sky. The death's-head flashed its impacted pessimism. She heard it speak—a hallucination, no doubt, spawned by her exhaustion—and yet the skull's words seemed as real as any other event of the last twenty-four hours.

Korty's dead.

"I don't believe you."

Blood poisoning.

She lifted her right arm and pointed to the North Star. "Somewhere along the Texas coast there'll be a town with a competent surgeon."

Bury him at sea. He'd like that. It's poetic.

Nora glowered at El Cráneo. "You should've knocked that damn gun from Richter's hand."

Intervention is not our style.

"You never intervene?"

Never.

"Not even to protect the innocent?"

Not even to protect the innocent.

"Then how do You live with Yourself?"

Good question, English teacher. We wrestled with it for many centuries, until at last the answer became manifest. How does God live with Himself? Simple. He doesn't.

Barry's Pageant

GOD WAS RIGHT, as usual—although you didn't have to be God, a computer scientist, or even a high school graduate to predict that Gerard Korty wouldn't make it to Texas. Entering the right hemisphere for the first time since their flight from the volcano, Nora found exactly what she'd expected, his lifeless body, rigid and pale, as if the artist's parting flourish had been to carve a marble statue of himself. His eyes were open. His lips curved upward; apparently he'd expired peacefully. Had Fiona told him about Deus Absconditus shortly before he left for the House of Dust? Or do the dying simply, in their final moments, get the joke?

What shocked her was the second corpse. It lay beneath the Romeo and Juliet diorama, adrift in fear syrup and dead white cells, riddled with stage-four pocks. On Fiona's chest sat an object that Nora instantly recognized as the plaque containing the lovers' speeches, turned upside down. Somehow Fiona had fended off her fetch long enough to write an iodine message on the blank surface.

HE SAYS TO TILT
IT TOWARD MYSTERY
AND THE GOD BEYOND GOD

Nora flipped the plaque over and read her favorite moment from the balcony scene. ROMEO: *What shall I swear?* JULIET: *Do not swear at all; or if thou wilt, swear by thy gracious self, which is the god of my idolatry. And I'll believe thee.*

Determined to keep Kevin from coming upon the bodies unprepared, she left the Hall of Artistic Passion, exited the brain through the cerebellum portal, and started aft. She found him in the ruins of the engine room, black with ash, chopping apart two wooden chairs and feeding the pieces to the burners.

"We'll have steam before you know it." Pausing, he mopped his brow and propped the ax against the gunwale.

"How's our starboard boiler?"

"I sealed the leaks using the blowtorch on my Swiss Army knife." Kevin grinned and patted the head of his Orgasiad. "Actually, I plugged them with hunks of rope."

She studied Kevin's wide, mischievous countenance. He would retain his boyish looks and guileless charm long into adulthood. The girls would go nuts. "Kevin, I have something sad to tell you. Gerard died last night."

Her son frowned, took up the ax again, and began converting the poop-deck fragments into fuel. "That bullet hole looked pretty awful."

"And I have more bad news. Fiona."

"Plague?"

"Plague."

"Give me half an hour, Mother"—he gestured toward the sternwheel—"and I'll get these paddles turning."

While Kevin chopped wood, Nora performed a burial rite. It was a typical plague-era funeral, abbreviated to the point of irreverence. Searching through the casino, the cargo deck's one relatively intact room, she came upon a large segment of fake Persian carpet, a ragged swatch suggesting a low-budget Cormanesque remake of *The Thief of Bagdad*. She carried the segment outside and, working in Erasmus's shadow, rolled up the bodies as if making an immense burrito, then secured the package top and bottom with mooring line. A coarse arrangement, redeemed somewhat by her decision to pose the bodies with arms intertwined. Gerard and Fiona might be destined for oblivion, but at least they would arrive embracing.

Drawn by the smell of death, a dozen seagulls appeared and hovered above the bodies, their feathers dusted with volcanic ash: a flock of aquatic ravens. The largest gull perched on Erasmus's upended heel. It squawked and spread its wings, feathers rustling. With her good leg Nora nudged the wool coffin, sliding it along the deck until at last it tumbled over the side. The melancholy bundle splashed into the Gulf and floated west, borne by a fast current. Screeching and circling, the black flock pursued the bodies as they crossed the Tropic of Cancer.

Kevin was as good as his word. Ten minutes after Gerard and Fiona had drifted from view, he appeared at his mother's side and said that he was ready to open the throttle.

"I think I chopped enough fuel to get us all the way to Boston."

"Galveston will do, dear."

As her son returned to the stern, Nora ascended the ladder to the pilothouse, shuffled through the ashes toward the cerebellum, and stared down at the naked engine room.

"Sun on your right! Half ahead!"

"Aye-aye, Captain!"

She took up her position on the crown. Above the glassy horizon, the skull gloated. Nora glanced to port, searching for the carpet coffin and its entourage of gulls so that she might offer her friends a final salute, though by now only the skull could see the procession, negligible specks on a wine-dark sea.

As the hot dreary morning progressed, Kevin did an exemplary job of keeping the *Queen* on course, bisecting the arc of the sun. If their fuel held out, in three days they would reach Texas, making landfall somewhere on the shores of Matagorda Bay, locus of Anthony's eternal shame. Nora wondered how the captain and his companions were faring. It would be great to track him down one day, partly to chide him about declaring the *Queen* unfit for another Gulf crossing, but mostly because he was such a mensch.

Staring at the endless breakers, she pondered the vast amount of

Promethean behavior the Corpus Dei had occasioned since its advent. By secluding the thing in the Arctic on no authority beyond papal paranoia and the ravings of two disintegrating angels, Anthony had surely been guilty of hubris. Then there was Thomas Ockham, who'd presumed to intuit the reasons for God's demise, subsequently outlining his brave new philosophy in *Parables for a Post-Theistic Age.* Bolder still was Martin Candle, drafting a legal brief against the Almighty, taking Him to court for His sins. In Nora's view the Stone Gospel was equally defiant, purporting as it did to replace theism with a religion of little myths. If Prometheus had stolen fire from the gods and given it to humankind, then Gerard had contrived to steal the gods from humankind and give them to a consuming fire.

And what of Nora herself? Was it not arrogant of her to imagine that, aided only by her adolescent son and a battered sternwheeler, she could haul thirty tons of world-saving reubenite from Veracruz to Texas in the teeth of erupting volcanos, stormy seas, leaking boilers, and limited fuel?

"Steady as she goes!" she bellowed toward the engine room.

Of course it was arrogant. Hubris squared. Defiance defined. Promethean in the extreme.

"Full speed ahead!"

At noon Kevin appeared atop the brain wearing the sort of pained face he'd assumed after Nora had refused to buy him the jade Orgasiad. "Pipework's clogged," he said. "Ashes, probably, from the second storm."

"You'd better bank the fires."

"Yeah, except I'm scared to get near them. The starboard boiler's growling like there's a pissed-off grizzly inside."

"Do you think it's going to blow?"

As if they were embedded in a second-rate sitcom, Nora's question was answered by the boiler blowing. A roar swept across the *Natchez*

Queen, followed by the clatter of iron shards raining down on the afterdeck and bouncing off the paddle wheel.

"It seems a distinct possibility, Mother."

When satisfied that the last piece of boilerplate had settled, they descended the ladder, traversed the corpus callosum, and made their way to the stern. Inspecting the damage, Nora experienced a disquieting episode of déjà vu: twenty-four hours earlier, she'd recognized Gerard's wound as terminal, and now a similar fatalism possessed her. The starboard boiler was split open top to bottom, its pipes a mass of random amputations, and its portside twin sported a jagged hole in the center. You couldn't use either tank to make a cup of tea, much less to power a steamboat.

"Okay, it's bad, but it's not *that* bad," she insisted. "If we hunt around, we can probably dig up a couple of cisterns, and if we kludge them together... we don't have welding equipment, true enough, but—"

Kevin closed his eyes and said, "Mother, it's hopeless."

His voice sounded strained, otherworldly.

"Hopeless?" she said. "Since when are you such a pessimist?"

Kevin, silent, stomped on a burning chunk of afterdeck planking.

He said, "I'm not talking about the boilers."

A sharp wind, straight from God's gullet, sliced through Nora.

She winced. "Quincy's back?"

"He's back."

"No." It seemed as if her heart had burst, flooding her chest with blood. "You just imagined it."

"Blind but... back." Shivering, Kevin extended his right arm. "He climbed inside me."

"Some sort of heatstroke."

"He's crawling through my veins."

Nora reached out and clasped his hand. Each finger was an icicle.

"I need to lie down," he said.

"The casino," she said.

"Bring my gods."

Combing through the remains of the afterdeck, Nora located a Louisiana state flag, which she quickly converted into a sack for carrying the mahogany idols. She took Kevin's frigid hand and led him through the cerebellum portal. They hadn't got halfway down the corpus callosum when a convulsion seized the boy, pitching him against the Albert Einstein diorama. He clutched his stomach and retched, soon ejecting a gallon of fear syrup. The viscous tar splashed onto the first draft of "The Electrodynamics of Moving Bodies."

Nora embraced her trembling child so tightly that the syrup became a kind of glue, and together they hobbled into the casino. Staggering toward the fake Persian carpet, Kevin collapsed on the woolen arabesques. She placed a foam life jacket beneath his head, then tore the felt from the craps table and slid it over him as a blanket. He shook uncontrollably, bones rattling, ligaments vibrating, teeth chattering like the windup dancing harlequin who'd so often assisted in his magic act. His breathing grew hollow and phlegmy.

"You can beat him," said Nora, arranging his gods in a row beside the makeshift mattress. A jet of blackness shot from Kevin's mouth. She sopped up the puddle with the Louisiana flag. "You're stronger than he is."

Slowly, blessedly, the shivering stopped. Kevin closed his eyes and yawned, drifting toward sleep. "No I'm not."

"You're so much stronger."

As the derelict *Queen* bobbed about the Gulf, rudderless, aimless, prey to capricious currents, Nora sat in stupefied silence. Kevin slept fitfully, his froggish gasps alternating with staccato moans and random snatches of hymns to Soaragid and Orgasiad. In a bizarre way he sounded as if he were in labor. But what was he struggling to bring forth? A new self, fetchless and robust? Or his own corpse? For the third time since her arrival in Mexico, she prayed—to the holy skull, the divine entrails, the Somatocist pantheon, whoever might listen.

The boy awoke. He groaned and shivered, the tremors decreasing slightly as he stretched toward his Orgasiad and caressed her coils. An unexpected smile lit his face.

"I've solved it," he said weakly. A filament of fear rolled from his lower lip. "I know how Dad got the ship in the bottle."

"Terrific."

"I'll need two clear glass bottles." Unhanding the idol, he fell back on the carpet. "One with a detachable bottom."

"Would jars do?"

"I guess."

"What else?"

"Two ship models." He closed his eyes and moaned. "No bigger than the jars."

Nora left the casino and entered the shattered galley, soon locating two unbroken quart jars filled with strawberry preserves, lodged amid a dripping heap of glass bits, loose olives, and coagulated catsup. She emptied the jam into a saucepan and washed the jars in the Gulf, then picked through the piles of wreckage in search of wood scraps and cloth fragments. She gleaned a bushel. The chart room yielded a roll of cellophane tape, ideal for mending maps and making toy ships. Sobbing, she returned to the casino and, while Kevin slept, constructed the first model. The project went badly. Dry and brittle, the cellophane tape failed to keep the hull planks in place, and she resorted to an unsightly mixture of chewing gum and window putty. Tears streamed down her face, dampening the tiny sails. It took her nearly an hour to finish the replica, which looked neither functional nor handsome, unfit for ferrying a mouse across a bathtub, much less bearing Odysseus to Ithaca or Jason to Colchis.

Odysseus. Trojan War. Among the right-hemisphere dioramas, she now remembered, was an homage to *The Iliad.* She tossed her shoddy model behind a slot machine and rushed toward the Stone Gospel. Inside the Hall of Artistic Passion, she approached the two beautiful 1:43-scale triremes, battered only slightly by the brain's fall. With a butter knife she fractured the seam of glue that held the ships to the Aegean Sea, which Gerard had improvised from a shaving mirror.

She returned to find Kevin conscious—pale and drawn, but no longer leaking black syrup. He looked at her, blinking rapidly, trying to focus.

"He's gone," said Kevin.

Forever, she prayed. "Forever," she said, crouching before him.

He saw the triremes and grinned. "Good job, Mother. Now I need to rehearse."

She kissed his forehead, rose, and walked into the blazing light of the midday skull, softly singing the famous paean to Idorasag.

"Your fur is soft as soft can be. Your milk is sweet and thick and free..."

Quincy stood on the foredeck, blind, naked, white as an egg. He leaned against the inverted Erasmus, massaging the humanist's left foot. "Guess what, Mrs. Burkhart? I finally settled on a title for my joke book. *Corn on the Macabre.* Isn't that wonderful?"

"Get off my boat."

"If it's any comfort to you, not only was Kevin the first to contract abulia, he'll be the last to die of it." The leveler's lips arced in a toothless smile. "Evidently the Almighty holds him in high regard."

"Comfort? *Comfort?!*"

"God's will can be quixotic, I agree. He barred Moses from the Promised Land on a technicality. At first blush His decision to deprive your son of adulthood might appear equally capricious, but last night I came up with a theory. Want to hear it?"

"No."

"Maybe you'd like to hear a joke instead."

Kevin's voice, raspy but intelligible, wafted out of the casino. "Mother, I'm ready."

"A skeleton walks into a bar," Quincy narrated, "goes up to the bartender, and says, 'Hey, gimme a beer and a mop.'"

When Nora entered the casino, she found Kevin sitting up in bed, a jam jar positioned by one knee, a miniature trireme balanced on the other. She stretched out beside the blackjack table and waited to be amazed.

In the middle of Sinbad the Sailor's eleventh voyage—so began

Kevin's patter—a sea serpent chewed a hole in the bottom of Sinbad's vessel, the *Crescent Moon.* Water rushed into her hull; she started to founder. Spotting an empty wine bottle afloat in the Arabian Sea, Sinbad got an idea. He summoned the ship's magician, the marvelous al-Mizar, and commanded him to make the *Crescent Moon* as small as a pomegranate, her crew as tiny as locusts. Al-Mizar accomplished the reduction in a matter of minutes, but before he could transfer the ship into the wine bottle, he fell overboard and drowned. The situation appeared hopeless... until al-Mizar's fourteen-year-old apprentice, Haroun, stepped forward to attempt the feat.

"It was the boy's first public performance," said Kevin. He set the ship and the jam jar side by side, covering them with his T-shirt. "Haroun said the magic words, 'Azimuth bazimuth kazimuth,' but they didn't work." Kevin lifted the T-shirt. The ship and the jar still lay side by side. He covered the props. "He said the words again, 'Azimuth bazimuth kazimuth.'" Kevin lifted the T-shirt. Nothing had changed. He hid the props a third time. "Finally, drawing on all his powers, Haroun spoke the incantation in his loudest voice, 'Azimuth bazimuth kazimuth!'"

"Azimuth bazimuth kazimuth!" cried Nora.

Kevin yanked the shirt away. The trireme lay inside the jar, safe from ravenous dragons and menacing currents.

"Terrific!" She applauded wildly. "Absolutely terrific!"

"Do you know how I did it?"

She had a pretty good idea. Shaking her head, she said, "You simply must be magical."

"Don't be coy, Mother. Please. Not today."

"Well, I suppose you put a model ship in one of the jars ahead of time."

"Right. Good. Nobody's magical, Mother."

She picked up the glass-enclosed trireme and caressed Kevin's cheek. "When we get home, I'll ask Mr. Barducci if we can turn the basement into our very own theater."

"You think he'd let us do that?"

"Oh, yes. We'll build a rostrum, rig up a curtain..."

"And lights?"

"Of course lights." She couldn't tell who was humoring whom. "We'll get folding chairs at a flea market."

"There must be a dozen great tricks I never learned because I didn't have a real theater. You know, zombie coffins suspended over the audience's head, stuff like that. I can't wait."

"Me neither."

"I love you, Mother."

"I love you, Kevin—my dearest, sweetest Kevin. You're the best person God ever made."

He settled back on the carpet, holding his Idorasag tight against his breast. He closed his eyes. He slept.

"Ready to hear my theory?" said Quincy, shuffling into the casino. He groped toward the roulette table and climbed on top.

Nora forced herself into a sitting position, spine against a slot machine, legs crossed like the Delphic oracle perched in her tripod above the omphalos.

"Why will this boy never get home?" Quincy continued. "In your innermost soul, you know the answer. 'I hoarded that diesel fuel out of love for my child,' you protest, unaware that your species's depravity traces not to a love deficit but to a love surplus. 'A love surplus?' you say. 'Of one's own kind,' I reply. 'The family bonds that exclude the larger world, the community ties that shun the stranger.'" The fetch flashed her a gummy grin. "And so you see that love, Mrs. Burkhart, makes monsters of us all."

Defying his blindness, Quincy shot off the roulette table and landed squarely atop Kevin, chest against chest, limb pressing limb, so that they fleetingly became Siamese twins. Remorselessly the fetch continued his descent, melting irretrievably into his host.

"No!"

Nora rolled over and hurled herself across her son. He awoke and tried to scream, but the phoneme lodged in his throat. She could feel him petrify beneath her, the stage-two paralysis spreading outward from his sternum to claim his limbs and larynx. Prying back his jaw, she fused their lips and blew. Stage-three crimson domes erupted everywhere like a hundred miniature Catemacos. Again she exhaled into his lungs, and again, and again, until her tears slicked their mouths and broke the seal. For the second time in Kevin's life, abulia's penultimate phase visited him, the abscesses drying up to form craters connected by deepening grooves. She massaged him fiercely, kneading his fissured breast and abdomen, as if she might somehow squeeze out the *demonio*.

The death throes, when they came, were prosaic, a few shudders accompanied by a low rattle. Kevin's eyeballs froze in their sockets. His grooves stopped growing.

Like steam rising from a soggy pyre, the sated fetch left his host, floated toward the ceiling, and disintegrated.

She couldn't let her boy go, of course. For three unbroken hours she pounded on his chest, weeping and moaning as she tried to move his blood. Her mind was a jumble, images colliding chaotically, mahogany gods, black seagulls, dying Imdugud birds, Korty Madonnas. Cretaceous comets fell on writhing maggots. Crab monsters vomited out glory grease. She collapsed on the floor and hugged Kevin's pocked body like Gilgamesh cleaving to Enkidu. There was a kind of insanity, she realized, in refusing to give up a loved one for burial, a supreme blasphemy, a septic perversity: but on that infinitely sorrowful March afternoon, the flower woman could not do otherwise.

Darkness settled over the Gulf of Mexico. Nora slept sporadically, dreaming that she'd caught the plague: her pores exuded fear syrup like pressed olives oozing oil. At dawn she dragged herself out of the casino, stumbled to the foredeck, and scanned the Gulf for hazards. The sky was the color of lint. Her muscles ached from long hours of weeping. Never before, not even when mourning Eric, had she understood grief's odd athleticism, its utter physicality.

A ship deformed the horizon, bearing down on the *Queen*, and by midmorning it dominated the starboard seascape. As the massive oil tanker drew within two hundred yards, near enough for Nora to read the printing on the bow, the lookout apparently spotted the danger. Siren howling, the tanker slowed dramatically and turned forty-five degrees.

Shafts of sunlight lanced through the cloud cover. The skull emitted a dull glow, as if made of pearl. With ever increasing astonishment, Nora absorbed two unlikely facts: she'd nearly been run down by the *Exxon Bangor*, and Captain Marbles Rafferty himself was speeding toward her in the tanker's motorized jolly boat.

"Nora Burkhart?" he said, stepping onto the *Queen*'s foredeck. "Inanna? Is it really you?"

"It's me. Aren't you supposed to be in Afghanistan or someplace?"

"Turkey. Never made it." Sweat glistened on Rafferty's ebony face and arms. "Halfway across the Atlantic, I realized I was in love with one of my passengers, Naomi Singer. Eccentric, but a flagellant only by default. Family, boyfriend, all dead of the plague—she had nowhere to go but Rome. We shacked up near the Piazza della Rotonda."

"What're you doing on the Gulf?"

"After Naomi got sick, I remembered how enthused you were about some clinic in Coatzacoalcos."

"It doesn't exist anymore."

"Damn."

"Buried by molten lava."

"Christ."

"I don't think it would've helped. They bought my boy a brief remission . . . but now he's"—when you actually have to speak that word, she realized, when you must set the thing on your tongue and launch it into the air, the raw profane fact of it sucks you dry—"dead."

She slumped against the sailor. His arms swung upward and inward, clasping her not just to his chest but to his bosom. She sobbed.

"You were a good mother, Nora Burkhart."

"I loved him so much."

"Yes."

"Tell me he isn't gone. Tell me it's a dream."

"I'm sorry, Nora."

"He has a birthday in five weeks. Sixteen years old."

"I'm so sorry."

She had no idea how long their embrace lasted. For an indeterminate interval, pulque time obtained aboard the *Natchez Queen.*

"I have to ask you something," said Marbles. "That humongous sculpture you're hauling—is it by Gerard Korty?"

"How did you know?"

Marbles told how. Ever since the Vatican squelched Korty's reliquary design, he explained, people had been expecting the sculptor to return in triumph with the piece he'd always wanted—a big bronze brain—and plunk it down in the Cinecittà quarry.

"It's become a cult thing," said Marbles, "like UFO believers waiting for some great mother ship."

"Gerard won't be returning in triumph. Three days ago, a petty bureaucrat shot him dead."

"Such awful times we live in."

Marbles marched through the pituitary portal, drawn by the gleaming icons beyond. Nora joined him inside the gland, then guided him down the corpus callosum and into the Gallery of Decency, where he instantly gravitated toward the Good Samaritan. The diorama was now a wreck, but its message remained coherent.

"Gerard always pictured his brain supplanting the obelisk in Saint Peter's Square," said Nora. "Will his disciples go along with that?"

Marbles answered without hesitation. If Korty wanted his brain in Saint Peter's Square, then that's where his fans would put it. Besides, Cinecittà was at the moment underwater. An enraged mob—furious at God (what was left of Him) and Catholicism (what was left of it) for failing to stop the plague—had dynamited the Garibaldi Dam, flooded the *Ben-Hur* quarry, and destroyed the reliquary. The holy bones had washed away down the Tiber and into the Tyrrhenian Sea.

From the cerebellum Nora and Marbles moved to the left hemisphere.

"Are the rumors true?" asked Marbles, reveling in Gerard's exquisite, albeit disheveled, re-creation of Isaac Newton confecting rainbows. "Did Korty end up carving idols for the Lucido Clinic?"

Leading Marbles from Newton to Charles Darwin, and from there to Albert Einstein, Nora recounted Gerard's days in Mexico: his employment by Lucido's church, his disillusionment with Lucido, his obsession with bequeathing the future a Stone Gospel based on *Parables for a Post-Theistic Age*. She told Marbles how, after her fetch had shown her two incompatible versions of the next millennium—a desirable one derived from Ockham's vision and a depressing one centered around a neo-Luddite nature cult—she'd pledged herself to the brain's survival.

In the Hall of Artistic Passion, Nora changed the subject to Marbles's friend and colleague, Anthony Van Horne.

"I owe you a great debt. You pointed me to Anthony. He took me to Mexico, and then came Kevin's remission, seven whole weeks."

"I'd settle for *one* extra week with Naomi. No more clinic?"

"Incinerated."

Marbles arighted the jade figurine of Dante Alighieri, centerpiece of Gerard's homage to *The Divine Comedy*. He turned toward Nora, offering her one of his rare smiles. "Big job ahead, huh?"

"Big job," she agreed.

"How does this sound? We take the *Queen* in tow to Galveston, then travel along the coast till we find a gantry. We load the brain onto the *Bangor*'s weather deck, plot a course for Rome, and set sail the next day."

"My last delivery."

"Huh?"

"I used to drive a delivery truck." She began reassembling the Bach exhibit. "Kevin's fetch told me I loved my child too much."

"Ridiculous," said Marbles.

"I can't seem to shake the thought."

"If I've learned one thing from the plague, Nora, it's this: Never suppose a fetch knows how the world works. Death is a lousy philosopher, and that's the truth."

Like many an author with a best-seller under his belt, Anthony Van Horne nurtured a strong desire to do it all over again. Now, suddenly, he had the material, a sequel to *The Gospel According to Popeye* recounting his latest adventures with the Corpus Dei—including the lucky breaks and brushes with catastrophe that had marked his journey from Coatzacoalcos to Los Angeles, where they'd ended up living in an Inglewood boardinghouse run by an affable crook named Alice Railsback. He had no immediate incentive for producing such a chronicle, of course, North America and Europe currently being without publishing industries, but one sunny June morning he found himself starting a manuscript anyway, under the provisional title *The Valley of Illusion*.

When Anthony wasn't working on his book, he and Cassie spent their time dragging Stevie from one alleged wonder-worker to another. They visited homeopaths and acupuncturists, aromatherapists and iridologists, Yaqui sorcerers and Zuni adepts. But the boy remained a stage-four abulic, enwebbed in pocks and grooves, fighting a hopeless war with Dominic.

Then one day a miracle occurred.

At 4:00 P.M. on a hot July afternoon, Stevie wandered downstairs, entered the front parlor, and stumbled into his father's arms like an Augmentation Institute customer undergoing a thaw. His pocks were gone; his fissures had vanished. "Dominic's dead," he said. Anthony's muscles went slack. His orange-juice glass hit the hardwood floor and shattered. From the center of his soul burst a cry so jubilant that half of Alice Railsback's clientele came running into the room. Taking his son in hand, he fled the boardinghouse, jumped into Lucido's car, and raced down the deserted San Diego Freeway. He exited at Braddock Drive and pulled up outside the Culver City Coven and Spiritual Healing Institute, an unassuming stucco house where Cassie had gone to place their son's name on a waiting list. Stevie in tow, Anthony charged unannounced into the vestibule, prompting his wife to shout with joy and a startled witch to pull a gun on him.

As the subsequent month unfolded, it became clear—could it be?

was it possible?—that the plague was lifting. No more levelers. No more omnipresent pyres. Everyone in Los Angeles had a different explanation. Some said Jesus Christ had eradicated the epidemic through divine fiat, an overture to his imminent return. Others said benevolent extraterrestrials had bathed the Earth in an invisible cloud of anti-Nietzschean vapors. For Anthony and his wife, no fundamental mystery existed. Plagues went away, that was all. Contagions arrived slowly, they retreated by degrees, but eventually they did go.

Only after the skull itself vanished did the Western world start believing in its collective heart that redemption was at hand. The dissolution occurred in stages. First fissures appeared, thousands of them, crisscrossing the surface until the Cranium Dei came to resemble an abused Easter egg. Next the teeth worked themselves loose, incinerating as they contacted the troposphere, a scene that alternately evoked the contrived razzle-dazzle of a fireworks display and the more natural spectacle of a meteor shower. Finally, the individual fragments descended, the flaming debris hitting the Atlantic Ocean and drifting irrecoverably into the Mohns Trench. For several weeks following God's fall, the skies over North America and Europe seemed curiously empty, a void that most people eventually managed to fill through a newfound appreciation of stars, clouds, and red-tailed hawks.

Expert opinion held that at least twenty-five years would elapse before Western civilization regained its infrastructure. It took ten. The average inhabitant of the Third Millennium found this era of frenzied rebuilding uniquely fulfilling, for how often is a technologically advanced civilization privileged to start all over again, reimagining itself from the ground up, avoiding most of its old mistakes and making only a few new ones? Yes, memories of the plague threw a shadow over the enterprise—abulia with its intolerable losses and unremitting grief—but if ever a society knew a *Saturnia regna*, it was the decade stretching from 2007 to 2017 as experienced by the industrialized democracies of planet Earth. To the question "Was the plague worth it?" the sane majority would have instantly replied, "No." To the question "Did Jehovah make the right decision in abdicating?" this same sane majority would have answered unequivocally in the affirmative.

Fueling the uncommon optimism, powering the unprecedented élan, was the huge reubenite brain in Saint Peter's Square and its faithful guardian, Desiderius Erasmus. Whenever a pilgrim visited this strange combination of museum and cathedral, encyclopedia and shrine, he invariably emerged transformed. The brain did not teach its patrons how to bring Heaven to Earth, or even how to bring harmony to their households. Its visitors did not learn the meaning of life or the purpose, if any, of the universe. But they did acquire a taste for what Ockham called "the West's great gift to the world, the miraculous faculty of rational doubt"—an ability so numinous and strange that even a spiritual guerilla like Oliver Cromwell could occasionally be provoked, in the bowels of Christ, to consider that he might be mistaken. Each pilgrim absorbed something else as well: a little myth or two, or three, an experience that for most people proved as galvanizing as a prayer breakfast with Saint Augustine, a beer with Jesus, badminton with the Buddha, or a dinner party hosted jointly by Dorothy Parker and Voltaire.

In the opinion of many Gospel visitors, of course, the thing possessed supernatural powers. Gerard Korty, they noted, had decreed a tilt to the horizontal axis, so that the sculpture would point toward "the God beyond God." Cassie, the skeptic, rejected all such metaphysical explanations of the brain's efficacy. That kind of thinking, she felt, belied Korty's manifest intention to root humankind in the here and now. Anthony agreed. The given world was sufficient. To imagine otherwise was to be a mere tourist on this amazing planet when you could have become a citizen.

Among the businesses that boomed during the golden decade was merchant shipping, a circumstance that sent Anthony on forty separate round-trip voyages between New York City and various European ports as master of the freighters SS *Poseidon Lykes* and SS *Argo Hammer.* He reached his seventieth birthday with a bank balance of

$324,000—a sum sufficient to negate his principal incentive for finishing and publishing *The Valley of Illusion.* (On the night of his retirement party, he merrily burned the existing manuscript, ninety-eight pages, none worthy of a better fate.) Cassie, too, enjoyed employment throughout this era, teaching high school biology in Cedar Grove, New Jersey, the town where they'd settled after leaving LA. In the plague's early months, Cedar Grove had been among several Jersey communities transformed into battlefields when the Anglo-Saxon Christian Brotherhood tried to stop the pestilence by attacking the local Jews. Now it was a placid and predictable place, qualities from which Anthony and Cassie drew considerable serenity after lives lived uncomfortably close to the eschatological bone. Their house at 319 Willowcrest Drive was an agreeable split-level with a birdbath and—over the garage—a sun-drenched, vaguely bohemian loft that Cassie found ideal for writing her unproduceable plays.

The planet kept circling its sun. The whiskers that speckled the sink every morning after Anthony finished shaving turned pure white, as did the strands caught by Cassie's hairbrush each night as she sat before her vanity. Stevie Van Horne became Steve Van Horne, editor of the Cedar Grove High School yearbook, and then Dr. Stephen Van Horne, a dentist with a thriving practice in Montclair. Much to his parents' delight, he ended up settling just around the corner in a ranch house that he shared with his marriage partner, a professional jazz saxophonist named Phillip Lawson. One glorious morning in October the postal carrier misdelivered to Anthony a letter from the Clearview County Courthouse (father and son were always getting each other's mail) and so it was that, a full hour before the good news reached Stephen and Phillip, Barry Lawson–Van Horne's grandparents learned a marvelous fact: the adoption had become official. That night the four grown-ups plus three-year-old Barry celebrated by eating at the Octopus's Garden in Bayonne, a "nonseafood restaurant" run by Sam Follingsbee, Anthony's chief steward from the *Carpco Valparaíso.* Unlike the high supplied by hyperion-15, the evening's euphoria was rooted in reality. Barry was a wonder: an irrepressible little person with black eyes, dusky skin, and a nascent sense of irony—and the older he got, the more wondrous he grew. By the time he'd turned six, the boy could name all the sails in Steve Dad's collection of model square-riggers. That same year, he became transfixed by Phil Dad's piano, soon learning to peck out nursery songs and Tschaikovsky themes.

When Anthony first read that the Stone Gospel had reached Saint Peter's Square through the combined efforts of his old partner in mishap, Nora Burkhart, and his former first mate, Marbles Rafferty, he assumed that finding his friends would be easy. They were, after all, the heroes of the new millennium. But both Nora and Marbles spurned the prophet role, disappearing from Rome as abruptly as they'd arrived. Although Anthony's own experiment with arranged anonymity—his flight from the public eye following Matagorda Bay—had sprung from rather different motives, he believed that he understood his friends' decision. Celebrity could be as confining as notoriety.

An intermittent and disorganized seven-year search eventually brought him face-to-face with Marbles in San Juan, Puerto Rico, where the aging sailor and his common-law wife, a recovered abulic named Naomi Singer, were managing a seaside bar, operating a charter fleet of fishing boats, and generally having a ball. Seeing each other for the first time in two decades, both men wept. Marbles was sorry to report that he had no idea where Nora might be hiding. They'd parted company in Boston, Marbles obsessed with nursing his thected lover, Nora still benumbed by grief.

"Grief?"

"You didn't hear? Kevin had a relapse," said Marbles.

"He died?"

"He died."

Anthony shook his head and sighed. "She probably knew the Lucido method was worthless—her sculptor friend must have told her. When the end came, I expect she was prepared."

"Prepared? Sailor, that's the dumbest thing I ever heard you say."

One sweltering August afternoon, summoned by the brass knocker,

Anthony opened his front door, and there was Nora, standing on the porch, a battered suitcase in her hand, older, grayer, and thinner, but her large dark eyes and high cheekbones looking as formidable as ever. It developed that they'd missed each other in LA by a matter of weeks. She'd spent the last two decades running a ragtag Santa Monica theater troupe called Beggars on Horseback, acting and directing under her stage name, Inanna McBride, but she wanted to spend her final years with what remained of her family—her brother, Douglas, and his second wife, Perdita, whom she'd never met. The cheapest maglev route to Boston involved a three-hour layover in New York City, and when a computer terminal in Pennsylvania Station displayed both an "Anthony Van Horne" and a "Cassie Fowler" living at the same Cedar Grove address, she'd decided to extend her trip by a day.

"I heard about Kevin," said Anthony. They were sitting in his living room, drinking Dr. Zinger's lemon herb tea and eating bricks of vanilla ice cream pressed between chocolate-chip cookies. "I'm so sorry."

She coughed and said, "I think about him every day."

"Yes." He poured himself a second cup of lemon tea. "Well, friend, you proved me wrong. That wretched old steamer was good for one last trip." He brought the tea to his lips and sipped. "I used to be a coffee fiend, but the damn stuff gave me migraines."

"I meant to hunt you up sooner," she said, "but I knew it would only... you know, I'd start picturing"—a bright tear hovered in her eye—"the *Natchez Queen* and Esperanza's place"—again she coughed—"Kevin setting his gods on the dock."

"I understand."

"We buried him in Massachusetts, Marbles and I, same cemetery where I got gas for my truck."

"A reliable seaman, Marbles."

"On Kevin's birthday, I always watch *Attack of the Crab Monsters.*"

"Do you have any idea what a great person you are, Nora?"

"You're pretty terrific yourself."

"No, I mean restoring the West to itself."

"I'm sick," she said abruptly.

"Would you like to lie down?"

"I mean all the time. I'm sick, Anthony. When Catemaco blew, I sucked in a ton of dust. For years I was fine. Now the doctors say my lungs are full of holes. I'm dying, Captain, but I'm not afraid. I've had quite a life, wouldn't you say?"

A thousand regrets converged on Nora, some superficial, some profound, the difference mattering less with each passing day, as she sat in her brother's Naugahyde recliner and suffered. It was a mistake, she realized, to have allowed Douglas and Perdita to tell the world that the Gospel's mysterious paladin, last seen in Rome, had resurfaced in Boston, where she'd gone to die of emphysema. From Douglas's perspective, of course, the announcement's effect had been wholly benign, releasing a deluge of cards, letters, telegrams, e-mail, flowers, and presents: affirmations that he hoped might raise her spirits and ease her breathing. But Nora felt worthy of neither public adulation nor private gifts. She hadn't created the reubenite brain; she'd merely transported it. Every time Douglas read her an epistle of appreciation (yet another gushy account of how the brain had launched the correspondent's career in astronomy, music, medicine, poetry, or counseling), Nora felt more alienated from herself, as if the woman now expiring in Jamaica Plain and the woman who'd piloted the *Natchez Queen* down the boiling Uspanapa were two different people.

"No more testimonials," she told him. "I've heard enough."

"They're helping you to love yourself."

"I love myself more than I deserve. Read me something else."

After their fourth such conversation, Douglas got the message. Not only did he and Perdita start reading Nora her favorite plays, he began dragooning Nora's visitors into the troupe, assigning them parts and insisting on at least two run-throughs before they brought the show to her bedside. Nora passed her last days in a swoon compounded of Shakespeare and friendship, Ibsen and oxygen, Shaw and

Demerol. She especially liked Anthony's heartfelt interpretation of Ken Talley, the legless Vietnam veteran and schoolteacher at the center of Lanford Wilson's *Fifth of July*. The play's final moments never failed to touch her: Talley reading aloud from his painstaking transcription of a science-fiction story conceived and then tape-recorded by a student who everyone thought doltish because of his severe speech impediment.

"After they had explored all the suns in the universe, and all the planets of all the suns"—before finishing the last sentence of the boy's story, Anthony paused, resting his palm on Nora's brow—"they realized that there was no other life in the universe, and that they were alone. And they were very happy, because then they knew it was up to them to become all the things they had imagined they would find."

The performance she most wanted to hear, of course, Percy Bell as Orpheus—or Hamlet, Stanley Kowalski, Willy Loman, Ken Talley, anybody—would never happen. She'd learned his fate shortly after noticing in *Daily Variety* that "two mesmerizing young actresses, Vicky and Valerie Lotz," were slated to star in the movie version of "*Keeping Score*, based on the nonfiction best-seller about Joyce and Janice Haworth, the identical-twin tennis champions who became serial killers specializing in wife beaters." Nora's former costars received her graciously on the set, which had just begun shooting within the high stucco walls of Paramount Pictures.

"He's dead," said Vicky.

"Plague?" said Nora.

"Plague." A mist enveloped Valerie's eyes. "Everything we know about art came from him."

"After a while we got good enough to tackle Inanna herself," said Vicky.

The sisters wrapped Nora in their arms.

"O Gilgamesh, to where do you run?" said Vicky.

"When the gods created man, they allotted to him death," said Valerie, "but immortality they retained for themselves."

"Do you still tread the boards?" asked Vicky.

"If you get off early today," said Nora, swallowing hard, "come by

Saint Paul's Episcopal in Santa Monica, and you'll see me do Stella in *Streetcar.*"

"We'll try to make it," said Valerie.

"You bet," said Vicky.

She never saw them again.

While emphysema was the enemy battalion in Nora's life, mirrors were the single spies. She took great effort to avoid beholding the leathery gray bag that had once been her face. If death was indeed a doorway, she hoped that the afterlife might resemble the Sumerian House of Dust, a shadowland where looking glasses were as uncommon as clocks.

Slowly, spasmodically, she floated toward nothingness on a river of morphine. Often she thought, "This is it. I'm dead now." But then she was still on the planet, fighting for air. She alternately longed for a miracle and prayed for the end. Death would at least shut down her subconscious, source of those cruel little melodramas in which the Cranium Dei's victims returned as functioning people aglow with health.

The worst of Nora's recurrent dreams began with Kevin standing next to her on a windy shore beside a roaring sea. A wild stallion the color of wheat galloped into view and halted before Kevin.

"Watch my trick, Mother!" Deftly he vaulted onto the stallion's back.

As the horse's great head dissolved, Kevin melded with its shoulders, sinking into the tawny, muscled flesh as if into quicksand, until the boy's arms and trunk rose seamlessly from a four-legged body.

"Climb on up!"

Nora had no trouble mounting the centaur. Pressing her legs against her son's flanks, she embraced him from behind...and they were off, racing along the beach, foam splashing their faces. For a brief interval Kevin turned into Percy, bearing her on horseback toward the Chattahoochee River, and then he was himself again.

"Stop, Kevin."

"You're not having fun?"

"Please stop."

"Is the spray bothering you? I'll head inland."
"This is it."
"What do you mean?"
"It's the end."
"I don't understand."
"This is it, Kevin. It's over. Stop."

To their profound and lasting regret, Anthony and Cassie couldn't attend the funeral. Barry was appearing in his third-grade class's Annunciation pageant later that same day, and even if they left the service early and caught the 4:45 P.M. maglev out of Boston's South Station, they would still miss the play, monorail service between Manhattan and Cedar Grove being spotty after rush hour. Instead they sent roses.

As it turned out, Cassie had to forego the pageant too. The previous afternoon she'd contracted strep throat, and now she lay abed, consuming antibiotics. It was a raw December night, bitter by Stephen's standards, bracing by Anthony's. Barry's fathers wanted the old sailor to travel with them via hoverbus, but Anthony insisted on walking the two miles to Cedar Grove Elementary School. When he'd laid the Corpus Dei to rest in its Arctic tomb, the thermometer had stood at –80° centigrade.

He arrived inside the school auditorium with ten minutes to spare. Stephen and Phillip had saved him two seats, one for his rump, another for his overcoat. Phillip handed his father-in-law a playbill. Anxiously Anthony scanned the cast list, noting with relief that the typesetter hadn't dropped or mangled Barry's name.

Narrator . . . . LETITIA WELCH
Tony Vonhorn, a sea captain . . . . . . ERIC TOWERS
Yvonne, his conscience . . . . SUSAN MARZ-NIKOLIC
Raphael, an angel . . . . TOM MALENTA

Gabriel, an angel .... CYNTHIA KUSHNER
Bob, a night watchman........... BARRY LAWSON–VAN HORNE
Darryl, an octopus .... DENNIS CHANG

Anthony had seen Annunciation pageants before, some featuring adult casts, some juvenile, but never one with his own grandson in the key role of the watchman. Beholding himself on stage normally disconcerted Anthony, especially when the actor in question was a child. In the long run he found this weird mirroring, this alien reflection, even more troublesome than the fact that the various Annunciation scripts, while differing from company to company, only intermittently recorded what had actually transpired on that fateful night he met the angel in the Cloisters. At times he considered calling up *Newsweek* and setting the record straight, but none of the errors was significant enough to justify compromising his privacy. The average citizen of the new millennium believed that "Tony Vonhorn" had died about ten years ago, and Anthony was glad to leave that misapprehension intact.

While the houselights dimmed, Barry's teacher, plump and bubbly Mrs. Roeder, strode into the orchestra pit and mounted the conductor's podium. She thanked everyone for coming, noted that the playbill had failed to credit Oscar Merkyl, the gym teacher, as the show's technical director, and reminded the audience that the children themselves had written this particular treatment of the Annunciation.

A spotlight hit the far edge of the curtain, illuminating nervous little Letitia Welch. Her tones were liquid and high-pitched, the voice of a cartoon starfish. "Our story takes place in the Cloisters, an old-looking fake monastery in New York City that happens to be an art museum too. The year is a very long time ago, 1992, during the last millennium, and it's late at night. Tony Vonhorn, a sea captain, needs to take a shower."

Letitia beat a hasty retreat. The curtain rose on a cardboard facsimile of a fountain. Blue paper streamers, set rippling by an invisible fan, conveyed an impression of flowing water. Dressed in swimming trunks and carrying a bath towel, the sea captain, a handsome Asian boy, entered stage right, stepping into the fountain. The night watchman—Barry—strode onto the scene, shining his flashlight in the captain's face.

"Who's there?" demanded the watchman.

"I'm Tony Vonhorn, the sea captain. Who are you?"

"I'm Bob, the night watchman. You're not supposed to be here." He snapped his fingers. "Hey, wait a minute—aren't you the same Tony Vonhorn who smashed up that big oil tanker in Texas last year?"

"That's me all right."

"I heard you dumped ten million gallons of oil into the Gulf of Mexico and killed a lot of otters."

"It's true, Bob. Ever since then, it's been like the oil was stuck all over me. I thought maybe if I washed myself in a sacred fountain, I'd start feeling clean again. It should take me only about ten minutes."

"I have to make my rounds. Be sure to close the door behind you, Tony, and don't steal any of our valuable paintings."

"I promise, Bob."

As the watchman exited stage left, a chubby black girl in a bathing suit entered stage right.

"Who are you?" asked Tony.

"I'm Yvonne, your conscience. Not many people in the twentieth century have consciences, but you do, which is why you feel so guilty."

"The fountain isn't helping."

"Fossil fuels are yucky. They don't wash off." Yvonne joined Tony at the nexus of the spray. "If only God would die or something. It might wake people up."

Two children charged onto the stage, a cherubic boy and a willowy girl, each outfitted with a plastic halo and papier-mâché wings.

"Who are you?" asked Tony.

"The Angel Raphael," said the boy. "Fear not."

"The Angel Gabriel," said the girl. "Fear not. We're here to tell you God just died."

"That's exactly what my conscience was *hoping* would happen!" said Tony.

"Well, *we* don't think it's good news," said Raphael. "It makes us want to cry."

Curling their fists into tight balls, both angels rubbed their eyes and sobbed pitifully for ten seconds.

"Right now," said Gabriel, "God's very large body is floating in the Atlantic Ocean near Africa. We want you to sail your supertanker there and wrap a chain around God's big toe, so you can haul Him to a special tomb we made from an iceberg at the North Pole."

"We've written down the directions," said Raphael, handing the captain a 3×5 card. "Can we count on you?"

"I'd better talk it over with my conscience," said Tony.

"Return here tomorrow, midnight, and give us your answer," said Gabriel. "If you don't take the job, we'll probably beat you up."

The angels rushed away.

"Well, Tony, what are you going to do?" asked Yvonne.

"If I bury God, then nobody will know He died. I'd better tell the angels to find another sea captain."

"They'll probably beat you up."

"I can take it."

"You have made a very brave and wise decision. Now I shall tell you that, even if you stick God in the iceberg, an earthquake will shake Him loose in a few years. Then a Pennsylvania judge will put Him on trial for tuberculosis and Hitler, and His skull will go into orbit and cause a plague of demons."

"So when the angels come back tomorrow, I can say I'm going to tow God to the North Pole?"

"That's right, Tony. And they'll be thrilled—so thrilled that they'll probably take you in their arms, flap their wings, and— "

Yvonne stopped speaking, her attention claimed by a rubber octopus, a shimmering red beast suggesting a mud heap with tentacles, rising from the fountain. Its huge eyes, constructed from aluminum pie plates, glittered under the stage lights.

"Good grief!" wailed Yvonne.

"It's an octopus!" shouted Tony. "Look out, Yvonne! An octopus is trying to get you!"

Bellowing like an enraged bull, the octopus extended a suckered arm and curled it around Yvonne's neck.

"Help!"

The commotion brought Bob the watchman on the run. Sizing up the situation, he raised his flashlight high in the air and brought it down hard on the octopus's head. Stunned, the beast released its grip on Yvonne and slumped back into the fountain.

"Thank you," gasped Yvonne.

"Glad to be of service," said Bob. He turned to Tony while pointing at Yvonne with the flashlight. "Who's that?"

"My conscience," said Tony.

"Oh. You two haven't been stealing any paintings, have you?"

"No, sir," insisted Tony.

"No, sir," asserted Yvonne.

The watchman faced the audience, grinned spectacularly, and said, "It's not good to steal!"

The curtain descended. It took only forty-five seconds for all seven cast members, octopus included, to array themselves across the stage, bowing proudly amid a storm of cheers and applause.

"That was *sensational*," said Anthony. His grandson's battle with the cephalopod, he felt, had a certain mythic resonance: Saint George slaying the dragon, Beowulf getting the better of Grendel. He wished that Nora could've seen it.

"He remembered his lines!" cried Phillip, leaping out of his seat. "The kid's a natural!"

"I suppose you'd rather eat worms than take the bus home, right, Dad?" said Stephen.

"You know me," said Anthony, pulling on his overcoat. "Stubborn."

"Stubborn's the word," said Stephen.

"Tell Barry he was brilliant," said Anthony. "I'll come by later and read him a bedtime story."

"Good plan."

The sea captain left the auditorium and slipped into the solitude of a dimly illuminated hallway, the newly waxed floor shining like a frozen stream. A dozen brisk paces brought him to an exit marked with glowing red letters. He pushed it open.

Snowflakes sifted out of the dark, ungodded sky, settling on fence posts and pine boughs. Burdened with snow, the lowest branch of a dead birch snapped free of the trunk and fell into the drifts. An irreducible strangeness lit the world. To Anthony the universe had never seemed more exhilaratingly enigmatic.

A crystal spiraled into his open palm, round and spoked, like the wheel of some impossibly small and delicate ship. Briefly he considered joining Barry and his fathers on the bus, then decided against it. The snow was exquisite, the temperature had dropped just slightly, and he had only two nautical miles to go before he slept.

He shoved his hands into his overcoat pockets, hoisted his collar against the winter wind, and, like a landlubber setting an adventuresome foot on a dory's wobbly bottom, stepped off the back stoop of Cedar Grove Elementary School and entered the uncertain future.